FOWL PLAY

A SMALL TOWN SPORTS ROMANCE

TUFT SWALLOW SHARED WORLD

CASSANDRA MEDCALF

Print ISBN: 978-1-960445-05-6

Ebook ISBN: 978-1-960445-04-9

TOWN OF TUFT SWALLOW

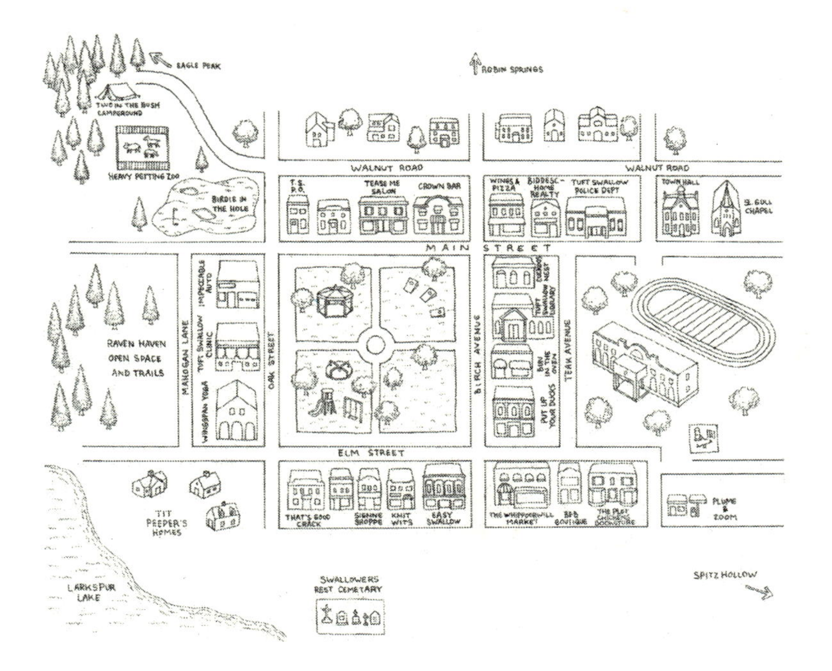

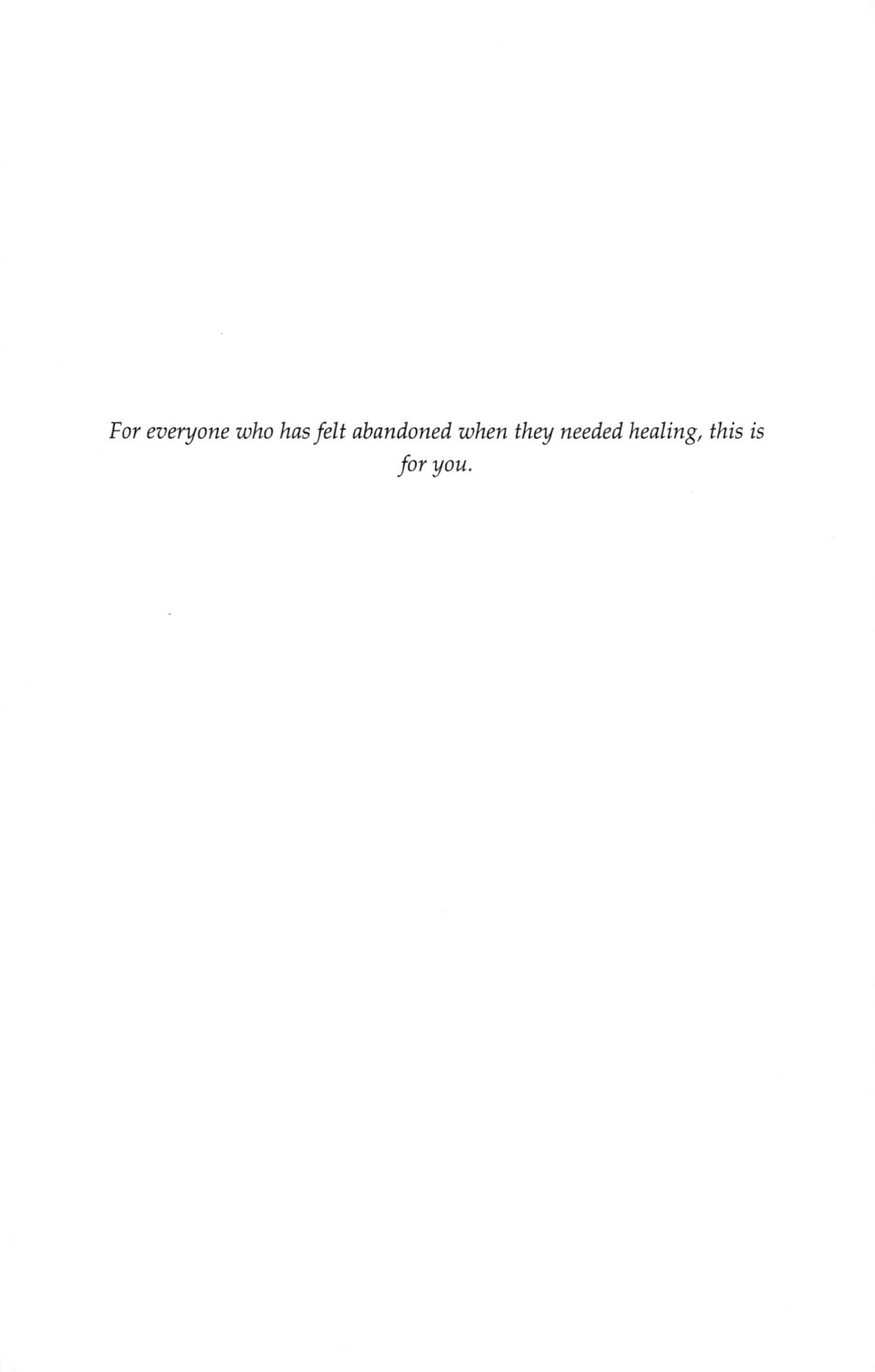

For everyone who has felt abandoned when they needed healing, this is for you.

QUICK NOTE

For the purpose of this book, "Shein" is pronounced like *shine*. It's a last name, not a clothing retailer.

I know that's a weird note to put in the front of this book, but my editor thought it should be changed and I'm too stubborn to take out the pun. So just, when you get there, that's how you're supposed to say it.

Also, since you're here, Content Warnings for this book include:

Bi erasure (it gets fixed)

Misogyny / homophobia (again, it gets fixed)

Family trauma

Problematic teachers and bosses

Bullying

Inappropriate doctor / patient relations

Some questionable gossip

Just, the *worst* ex ever

Some light dom / sub sprinkles, with a helping of switch sauce

Butt stuff, if you download the bonus epilogue and spicy scene from my website (hint, hint)

A concerning amount of alliteration and internal rhyme

Bird puns. Like, *so* many bird puns. I literally cannot prepare you for the sheer *audacity* we exercised in the execution of naming the shops and people in this small town.

Enjoy responsibly!

CHAPTER 1
KODI

"Shit, shit, SHIT!" My knee buckles. Papers scatter everywhere as I tumble to the floor. "Fuuuu–"

"Miss Gander! Language!"

I crane my neck to see Dr. Cratchet's white-tufted head bob its way toward me over the top of the fax machine. I groan. *Right. The patients probably heard all of that.* As I reach to massage the side of my leg where the spasm rages, I see the legs of his pleated pants and frumpy velcroed shoes land on the thin carpet in front of me.

"Really, Miss Gander. You've made an awful mess of things, haven't you?" Instead of bending down to help me clean up, the bulky toe of his orthopedic sneaker taps impatiently beside my ear. "Are you infirmed?"

"Spasm," I choke out, hissing through another twitch of angry muscle and connective tissue. The rubbing isn't helping. I need my meds. "Could you hand me my bag, please, Dr. Cratchet?"

He huffs disapprovingly before shuffling to the coat rack, where my purse hangs along with my blazer. He carries it pinched between two fingers as if afraid the feminine contents of my bag might somehow infect him with my affliction.

He knows better. Long before I was his clinic administrator, I'd been seeing Dr. Cratchet for my knee ever since I tore my ACL in high school. He's the one who prescribed me the muscle relaxers in the first place, after all. And the one who informed me I'd never play softball again.

I thank him for the bag and dry swallow a couple of pills, shifting into a slightly less awkward position and swiping a few of the papers that scattered when I fell. I shuffle them back into their folder after I wedge it out from underneath my pelvis.

Dr. Cratchet clears his throat. "Mrs. Wilkins is ready to check out, now. Will you be able to resume your duties in the next few minutes, or shall I tell her to await a call?"

Can you give me a frickin' second?

I hold my tongue. Sure, the Doc can be a little callous sometimes. But he *does* have a practice to run. And seeing as this is the only doctor's office in town, we have to stay on schedule. A few minutes behind in the morning could mean an hour or more by the end of the day, and that doesn't fly at the Tuft Swallow Clinic.

"I'll be at the desk in a sec, Dr. Cratchet, I promise."

He gives a noncommittal hum that could mean anything, before turning tail and exiting the office, leaving me sprawled on the floor between the front desk and the island in pain.

That's fine, no need to assist me… Gritting my teeth, I slowly stand up, carefully avoiding any shift in weight that might send my leg into another spasm. It's only a few steps between the fax machine and island where we keep all the printing supplies and the window that faces the waiting room, but each one elicits a grimace until I'm close enough to sink into my wheely chair.

I probably shouldn't be surprised that my knee is acting up. Last night was the town cornhole team's first practice with me as the new captain, and I may have gone a teensy bit overboard on the drills. Some might argue that half an hour of shuttle runs and burpees is overkill for a beer-league warm-up drill, but to those people I say two words: reigning champions.

The Mighty Swallows have been first in the league for over 50 years running, after all. Do you think I'm going to let *my* first year as captain be the one we lose that title?

Absolutely not. I already ruined one championship years ago. I'm not about to lose another.

But that doesn't change the fact that running last night was a bad idea. My leg throbs and twinges the entire walk back to the front desk, where I check out Mrs. Wilkins and divvy out paperwork to the patients in the waiting room. By mid-morning, the muscle relaxers are finally kicking in. So I feel confident getting up and walking back over to the counter to handle the insurance documents that need faxing and make a fresh pot of coffee.

Dr. Cratchet isn't the easiest boss to work for, but there are worse jobs in the small town of Tuft Swallow. All through high school, I expected to ride my way out on a College Sports scholarship–and almost did. But after tearing my ACL at the State Championships senior year, all the scouts withdrew their offers, and I ended up getting a bachelor's degree at TSCC in hospital administration.

Yep. From star pitcher to secretary.

At least I'm not living at home anymore. Clinic Administrator is a good career–or at least, good enough to afford the rent on one of the divided brownstone apartments on Walnut Street. I'm only a couple of blocks from the local restaurants and nature trails. Sure, I can't go jogging anymore, but it's nice that I've got my job, favorite café, and the town park right within walking distance.

As I wait for the coffee to finish brewing, I dig into my purse for my phone. Texting or social media on the job is strictly forbidden, so I keep it away from my desk to avoid the temptation. I scroll through my notifications, including a text from my best friend Lily.

LILY

OMG, Kodi, have you seen today's Pecker yet??

I hastily type a response, keeping an eye on the door just in case the Doc walks by and sees me on my phone.

ME

No! What's the goss?

LILY

Ok. So you know that two-story office/apartment colonial on Elm that's been for sale for months? Well, someone FINALLY moved in. A chiropractor! He got here a few days ago, and placed an order at the Signne Shoppe this week!

Uh-oh. Don't tell my boss.

Ugh. How's Doc Crotchety today?

The coffee pot dings. I grab my mug from the cabinet and fill it with the good stuff. Just black—no cream or sugar for me.

ME

Different day, same arrogance. I'm gonna check the mailbox, see if there's a Pecker in the pile.

I take a sip, tuck my phone back in my purse, and head to my desk for the maildrop key. After I file away the fax receipts in the cabinet, I swipe the jangling keyring off the desk and venture out to the waiting room to check the mail.

Around me, all of our waiting patients have their eyes glued to a copy of the local gossip rag, *The Nosy Pecker*. I spy the bold headline plastered across the front page.

That's Good Crack! New Doc Procures Punny Proof of Practice

Uh-oh.

"Miss Gander! What are you doing away from your desk?"

I flinch as I hear the squeaking leather of Dr. Cratchet's shoes shuffle across the lobby towards me. Slowly I turn to face him, wincing when I see our office copy of *The Nosy Pecker* crumpled in his gnarled fist.

"Just checking the mail, sir," I say cheerfully, attempting to stall the approaching meltdown I sense is on the way. From the anxious faces lifting from their papers around the waiting room, I know I'm not the only one gearing up for it.

"I've already procured today's mail, *Dakota*. And while I'm doing your job for you, perhaps I'll also check the calendar to see who's next on the appointment schedule, check them in, and send them back to the exam room." His face turns a delicate shade of mottled plum, and I swear his eyes begin to bulge slightly from behind his half-moon glasses.

"No need, Doctor, I can–"

"*Wonderful!* Glad to see I'm paying you to do more than just skulk around the corridor on the lookout for today's delivery of prattling babble!" Spittle flies from his mouth as his voice raises. His inexplicable accent becomes choppier with every word, and I swear the temperature in the room rises a few degrees from the steam pouring out his ears.

I approach cautiously, holding my arms out like I'm cornering an enraged bull at a rodeo. *Easy does it, Cratchet.*

"Mr. Landon?" I call out, not taking my eyes off the unstable doctor. "You can follow me back to exam room one, please."

The middle-aged man seated in the corner of the room hesitates briefly, and I shoot him a smile over my shoulder that I pray comes across more calming than desperate. "Right this way!"

He nods, rising, and I wait for him to reach my side before escorting him through the doorway toward the exam rooms.

"And leave that slanderous drivel behind!" The doctor roars behind us. Mr. Landon turns his wide eyes to me, his own *Pecker* still clutched in his shaking hands. He offers it to me.

"Thank you," I say, swiftly hiding it from view. "I'll take care of it for you."

"Is he alright?" The patient mutters. "I have a physical today, and if he's angry I'm not sure I want his fingers near my–"

"Everything will be just fine, Mr. Landon. Doctor Cratchet is a professional." *Mostly.*

I smile my most reassuring smile, the act easier once we pass the threshold to the back and we aren't in the same room as the boss. I direct Mr. Landon down the short hallway and leave him in the exam room, shutting the door behind me. As I return to my desk, I make a show of disposing his *Nosy Pecker* in the trash under my desk before calling out to the next patient to collect their intake paperwork.

The Doctor is still standing in the waiting room, his cheeks a less menacing shade of pink now, as his anger shifts toward embarrassment instead. The sound of my voice seems to rouse him from his thoughts, and he crumples what's left of the newsletter into a tight ball before shoving it into the bright red sharps disposal box behind the counter.

Well, there goes rescuing THAT *copy.*

Once he's safely behind the closed exam room door and I hear the familiar sound of latex gloves snapping, I know the coast is clear for a few minutes. I silently remove Mr. Landon's copy of the *Pecker* from the trash and fold it, before slipping it into my purse to read later.

After closing, when I'm far away from the furious eyes of Dr. Cratchet.

LILY AND HER *PECKER* ARE WAITING FOR ME AT OUR USUAL TABLE when I arrive at the Crowbar and Grill, along with a pitcher of domestic beer and a stack of plastic cups. *Must be Trivia Night.* She's a sucker for a deal, and every Monday there's a drink special she'll usually get roped into buying. Even if it's a bunch of crappy beer that neither of us would ever choose to drink voluntarily.

"Start reading. I'll pour you a beer."

She's already got a plastic cup in her hand before I can snatch the newsletter. "No, Lily, you know I hate that stuff."

"I can't drink the whole pitcher by myself!" She looks at me like I'm crazy. I shake my head and start to read, and she pours us each a cup.

Once again, the headline that I spotted in the waiting room this morning stares up at me.

That's Good Crack! New Doc Procures Punny Proof of Practice

Move over, sports fans! There's a new doc in town, and this one's set to make your spine tingle. On Tuesday, May 16th, Dr. Brian Gosling (no relation– I checked) closed on the charming Colonial at 324 Elm Street. According to the County Clerk, his new chiropractic practice was registered at that address under the name "That's Good Crack" this past week. Does this mean the Tuft Swallow Clinic finally has some competition?

"Oh my God. No wonder Dr. Cratchet was so angry this morning…" I stop reading to meet Lily's gaze. "I seriously thought he was going to rip Mr. Landon a new–"

"Have you gotten to the best part?" She interrupts me, bouncing in her seat. "Keep reading."

Our sources indicate that this young doctor is planning to start seeing patients soon. His website details that, in addition to traditional chiropractic, he specializes in Chinese Herbal Medicine, soft tissue manipulation…

"Chinese herbal medicine? Is that what you're so excited about?"

"*Ugh,* Kodi, you're hopeless. Right here!"

She points her finger down at the last line of the article.

We know you're all curious, and our sources haven't found any marriage licenses or domestic partnerships on file, meaning that a new bachelor is coming to town.

"You're kidding, right?" I roll my eyes and wave over a waitress. "Lily, didn't you *just* get out of a bad relationship?"

She nods wide-eyed. "Right? Perfect. Timing." She sips her beer and sticks out her tongue in disgust. "Okay, ew, this is disgusting. Kodi, why did you let me order a whole pitcher of this crap?"

"I didn't–"

"Hey ladies, what can I get for ya?" Charlene the waitress arrives, divvying out napkin-wrapped plasticware and depositing a bowl of roasted peanuts in their shells on our table. "The usual?"

Normally, Lily and I both get chicken Caesar salads, but my body is still recovering from practice the night before. If I'm going to be training this hard for the season, I need to keep my energy up, and that means protein.

"I'll actually have the bacon burger tonight." I scan the blackboard behind the bar for a look at the drink specials. None of them sound particularly delicious. "And can I get a gin and tonic with extra lime?"

"Absolutely, hon. And for you?"

Lily orders the usual along with a Cosmo. Charlene takes our orders back to the kitchen, the light green highlights in her short black hair glinting as she passes the neon bar signs. Once she's gone, Lily unloads the beer pitcher and still-full cups onto a nearby table.

"Why are you so desperate to start dating again, Lily? Don't you think that maybe you should take it slow?"

Personally, I've never understood my best friend's obsession with finding The One. Between sports, school, and work, there always seemed to be more important things than dating taking up the majority of my focus. Don't get me wrong, I like guys and all. I read the occasional kissing book to keep up with the lingo, even if I don't have the experience to back it up.

But when I lost my sports scholarship and any chance of leaving Tuft Swallow along with it, I sort of gave up on all the romantic notions I had for life after high school. Including finding Mr. Right.

After all, I'd grown up with the same cohort of potential suitors since I was three years old. If I had a future with any of the guys around here, wouldn't I have figured that out by now?

Why should a new doctor moving into town be any different? Not to mention, Dr. Cratchet would likely fire me on the spot if he ever found out I was interested in the owner of a competing practice.

I realize Lily is talking, and I haven't been listening to a word she's said. Our drinks arrive, and I poke my straw around to free the juice from my lime wedges and catch up with the conversation.

"...about the romance, you know? I'm twenty-four, for Pete's sake–plenty old enough to be starting a family. And now that I have a decent job at the salon, I feel like I'm ready to move on to the next phase of my life."

"Is twenty-four when we're supposed to move onto the next phase?" I sip my drink. My knee twinges, a reminder that it's been a full eight hours since I last took my muscle relaxers. *Ah, shit.* Now I'm drinking. *There goes taking any more medication tonight...*

Lily throws her hands in the air. "Kodi! Are you even listening?" Shoot, I wasn't. Again. "I thought you'd be more excited about this!"

I let out a sigh, rubbing at my knee. "Honestly? Yeah. We could use another clinic. We're always booked solid, and seeing as we've been getting more people moving to town recently, it would be good if we had another doctor around."

Even if it isn't a real *medical doctor.* I don't say that part out loud. "But with the way Dr. Cratchet was storming around the office today, the competition might make my life more difficult than it's worth."

"Ugh. How do you work for that guy? He's the worst." Our conversation pauses when our food arrives, and I take a giant bite out of my burger. *Heaven.* "Is your leg okay? You keep rubbing at it."

I didn't even notice when my hand started massaging the side of my leg while I chewed. I swallow.

"Oh. Yeah, just a flare up. Practice was tough last night."

"Yeeeaaah, about that. Um. I've been meaning to say something to you." A wrinkle forms above Lily's nose, and she sets down her fork.

I take a giant bite of bacon and beef. "Wha'?"

"Don't you think you're going a bit too hard with the whole 'team captain' thing? I mean, it's a beer league. It's supposed to be something fun we all do after work. Not training for the Olympics."

My bite turns to sand in my mouth. I wash it down with some gin and tonic. "Come on. It was the first practice of the year. Everyone's just out of shape. It'll get easier."

"That's the thing, Kodi, it's not supposed to *get easier*. It's never supposed to be hard in the first place. It's just cornhole."

I gape at her. "*Just* cornhole?? Lily, you know what town we live in, right? 'Cornhole Champions' is engraved on our welcome sign at the town border. It's what we're known for."

"We're known for more than just our cornhole team."

"Really?"

"I mean, I assume so." Lily munches on her salad thoughtfully. "But you seriously might want to back off a little. Not everyone was happy after practice last night."

"I didn't hear any complaints."

Which is mostly true. I heard some grumbling, a little moaning and groaning. But no actual verbal *complaints.*

A tiny knot of guilt twists uncomfortably in the pit of my stomach, souring my burger. I stare at the remaining half, no longer hungry. *Shit.* "Are people actually upset?"

The wrinkle above Lily's nose is back. "Upset is a strong word. I just noticed that the temperature after practice last night was a little… heated."

I contemplate that for a moment, thinking of the faces of the team as I packed up all the boards and bean bags the night before. But then, my old softball coach's face appears in my head, as clear as if he was sitting right there with me in the bar: contorted as he barks out drill after drill. Glowing, when we won the regional playoffs. Then heartbroken, as he helped carry me off the field after I twisted my knee and got rammed by the other team's catcher as I dove for home plate.

No, dammit. I'm tired of associating the word "champion" with my own failure to bring home the gold. This year, that's all going to change. I'm going to lead us to victory, and everyone will be ecstatic when it happens. I'll never have to see those looks of disappointment on everyone's faces ever again.

"They'll get over it. Once we claim champion status again this summer, no one will even remember how hard practice was the first few weeks."

Her face falls. "We're going to be practicing like that for weeks?"

"Yep. You're gonna be in the best shape of your life, girlfriend."

I toast her with my drink. She squints at the bite of salad on her fork.

"Hmm."

"All the better to win over that sexy new doctor in town…" I waggle my eyebrows.

Her lip curls up at that. "Well, I guess a little extra exercise couldn't hurt. And besides, if I get injured, that's just an excuse to make an appointment!"

"That's the spirit!"

And with that, we leave the topic of the Cornhole Championship behind, and Lily regales me with her plan to snare Tuft Swallow's newest bachelor.

CHAPTER 2
BRIAN

"Those boxes look awfully heavy. I bet you were the cock of the walk of your old town with arms like that!"

I freeze mid-squat on my way to lift another box out of the U-Tow and into my building. I turn and look out the back of the box truck, where an elderly woman dressed in a bright turquoise windbreaker, tailored sweatpants, white sneakers, and a pair of binoculars around her neck is leaning against the loading ramp.

"Uh, I don't believe we've met, Miz…" I extend a hand to her, waiting for her to provide her name.

"Mrs. Woodcock, dearie. And you must be Brian Gosling, the new town chiropractor! You wouldn't happen to be related to…" She looks at me appraisingly, meeting my handshake with a surprisingly firm grip for such cold fingers.

"Oh no, no relation." I chuckle nervously. *Who the frick is this woman? And how does she know who I am?* I follow her eyes out of the back of the truck and towards the front porch of my mixed-use office and residence, where a freshly-painted, plastic-wrapped wooden sign is leaning against the railing.

THAT'S GOOD CRACK
BRIAN GOSLING, D.C.

That was quick. I just put in the order at the Signne Shoppe two days ago when I had my refrigerator delivered. Although that does explain how Mrs. Woodcock knows my name and what I do for a living.

She starts to speak again. I load a stack of boxes onto a handcart and wheel them down the ramp, only half-listening to her ranting.

"...It's been an awfully long time since the old coot has had any competition, after all, but what with the yoga studio and boxing gym and all these other young folk moving into town, it's nice to see that there will be options for the more physically inclined! I'm sure you'll find we're quite the *active community* once you get to know us! Why, just the other day, Mr. Woodcock and I were out birdwatching..."

Thud. The handcart bangs against the wooden stairs as I pull the stack of boxes onto my porch and through the front door.

Mrs. Woodcock doesn't seem to mind the extra noise, even if it covers up some of the context of her story.

"...can be quite physically demanding, as I'm sure you know–" *Thunk.* "–as soon as he'd put his foot–" *Thunk.* "–did Mr. Woodcock–" *Thunk.* "–have the tits in his sights–"

Donk! "What now?"

I plonk the handcart down a little too forcefully in front of the door.

"Why, a delightful pair of tufted titmouse, of course! Right by your upstairs window. They're native to the area, you know. Are you a birder as well?"

I blink at the old woman. When did she start talking about birdwatching? "Uh, no. I'm afraid I'm not."

"Well, it's never too late to learn!" She holds up her binoculars and gives them a little wiggle. I give her a look that I hope comes across as more smile than grimace. Although, if being perceived as rude would get her off of my lawn...

"I'm sure. It's been a pleasure meeting you, Mrs. Woodcock, but I really ought to get these boxes inside."

"Oh of course, dear! We'll catch up soon. And if you ever need anything, don't be afraid to ask! We're just up the street at the lovely white colonial, there." She points at a giant home in the center of the residential block. I swear I see a pair of eyes peeking from behind a set of lilac curtains in the first-story window, but they're gone the second I try to look a little closer.

"Have a good evening, Mrs. Woodcock." *What an unfortunate name.*

I watch for a moment as the old woman walks right into the street, setting off a slight squeal as a car hits the brakes to avoid hitting the old woman. She waves at them as she crosses, and the driver shakes their head. I notice as she shuffles away that her windbreaker has "Tit Peeper" written across her shoulder blades in academic-style block letter patches.

I really hope that's referring to birdwatching.

Moving here from the city wasn't an easy choice. Tuft Swallow was a ways away from a few of the conveniences I'd come to expect. But I was tired of driving over an hour to meet up with my boyfriend, Zeke, twice a week for date nights. He participates in a recreational sports league in Spitz Hollow, the neighboring township, and it apparently gets pretty intense in the summer.

I suggested once that it would be nice if we lived closer to each other, and he didn't disagree. So I moved here to surprise him for our one-year anniversary. Now, instead of an hour and a half apart, there's only twenty minutes between his front door and mine—and no city traffic to keep us apart.

As if on cue, my phone buzzes. I stop rolling the handcart and reach into my pocket. Zeke's name flashes across the screen.

"Hey babe," I say, checking my watch. "What are you up to tonight?"

"I was hoping we could talk about something." His husky, British-accented voice rings out of the phone speaker. God, he's sexy. How I got lucky enough to snag the one British guy near me on the dating apps, I'll never know, but every time I pick up the phone I thank whatever power made it so. Supposedly he moved here from London for work a couple years ago.

Their loss.

"Sure. Why don't we meet up at my place?" *This is it.* He's going to be absolutely thrilled.

"Uh, babe, I'm not up for an hour-plus drive–"

"It won't take that long," I cut in. *Here goes.* "I got a new place."

There's a pause on his end of the line. It's long enough that I wonder if maybe the connection dropped, but then his response crackles through. "What?"

"That's right. I'm now the proud owner of a home/office building in the town of Tuft Swallow!" I grin, imagining his face as I look around the empty foyer of the first floor where my chiropractic business will be set up.

Truth be told, I've wanted my own space and practice for years. After chiropractic school, I worked for a big rehabilitation clinic and health club in the city. It was a decent enough job, but the boss had been so particular about how he'd wanted everything done. He was a stickler about how long we spent with each patient, too, which annoyed the hell out of me. Fifteen minutes just isn't enough to address people's chronic injuries or pain, and I always told myself that when I had my own practice, I'd actually schedule enough time with each patient to give them the care they need.

Now I can do that and have dinner with the man of my dreams every night if I want to.

"Tuft Swallow? Why on earth would you move to Tuft Swallow??"

That wasn't the reaction I was expecting.

I feel myself deflate a little. "Uh. To have my own practice? And it's closer to you. I thought you'd be happy?"

"Oh God, you didn't do it *for me,* did you?" A horrible, queasy feeling swirls in my stomach. I hear Zeke sigh, and I can just see him rubbing the bridge of his nose with his long fingers. His handsome, brown face scrunched in frustration. "Text me the address. You don't have my red jacket packed away in a box, do you? I need it back."

"Are you mad at me?" I flinch. I hate how pathetic I sound.

"No, no, that's not it. I just want it for this weekend. I'll pick it up when I come over."

"Okay. I'll send you the address now." I switch to speaker phone and text him the address of the new place as quickly as possible, wishing he'd say something to break the awkward silence. "Love you," I say once it's sent.

"Yeah, I got it. See you soon."

THE THIRTY-FOUR MINUTES IN BETWEEN HIM HANGING UP AND ringing the doorbell are absolutely unbearable. I fling the door open, and take in the sight of the perfectly-rumpled Zeke standing with his hands in his pockets on my front porch. He rocks that effortlessly tousled look, with big, mirrored sunglasses and his dark hair mussed and brushing over his forehead. He's still wearing his work clothes, just slightly wrinkled from sitting at his desk all day.

I reach out to hug him, and he hesitates before giving me the shortest of squeezes in return. I beckon him in, showing him upstairs to my actual apartment and offering him some lukewarm pizza that I had ordered earlier in the day. He declines, waving his hand nonchalantly.

"I already ate."

I look at the microwave clock, which I'd set while I waited for him to arrive. It's barely six o'clock. He ate before driving over here? Why wouldn't he want to have dinner together? I mean, sure, lukewarm pizza isn't the most appealing meal, but if he's already in my apartment…

"So. You wanted your jacket?"

I walk to the bedroom to get the red leather bomber jacket

from its hanger in the closet. He follows behind, fidgeting with his sunglasses, before tucking them in the collar of his shirt and taking in the surroundings of my new space. His eyes land on a box on the bed labeled **Zeke's things - Bedroom**.

"I think we should take a break."

I blink.

No, surely I didn't hear him correctly. The acoustics must be off in this house.

The house that I just purchased. To be closer to Zeke.

Zeke, who just said– "You want to break up?"

He removes a hand from his pocket and shoves his fingers through his hair, making it even more deliciously messy. But instead of the warm, fuzzy feeling I usually get in my stomach at seeing his finger-rumpled mane, there's only an empty gnawing there. It slowly spreads through my chest and down to my own fingertips. He buzzes his lips.

"Yeah, yeah, you're right, it's probably best to just have a clean break, eh? With you, focusing on building up your business in its new location and all, and me…well. You know."

I stare at him, my eyes somehow zeroed in and unfocused at the same time.

"No, babe, I don't know. What do you mean? What's wrong?"

"You really shouldn't call me that anymore, you know. Doesn't really go along with the whole 'breaking up' vibe we're going for here, does it?"

"We're not *going for a breaking up vibe,* ba–" I catch myself. "Zeke. For fuck's sake! I *moved to Tuft Swallow.*"

He snorts. "Yeah! That's a real case of counting your chickens before they've hatched, isn't it? But you're rather scrappy. I'm sure you'll do great around here. Loads of old folks with bad hips and the like, falling out of trees and such. Good for business!"

He snatches the jacket out of my limp hands and shoves it into the open box atop my comforter. My heart shatters. Then, when he casually props it under his arm and grins at me, so easy and aloof, the sight of the perfect dimple in his cheek melts the fragments that remain.

That devil-may-care attitude and cool British detachment sure are a real pain-in-the-ass when *I'm* the thing he's detaching himself from.

"Please tell me this is a joke," I say, shaking my head. "You're kidding, right?"

"Oh cheer up, mate—I'm sure they aren't *actually* falling out of trees. I'm just taking the piss."

"Not about the old people! About *us!"*

I'm shouting now. Oh fuck. This isn't a good look. No, no *no. Act cool, Brian. Cool like Zeke. Like the ironic, unflappable disaffected millennial you've convinced him you are.*

But my face won't listen to my brain. I can feel the vein in my forehead twitching, and my throat won't stop trying to swallow around the lump that's formed there. *Are those tears stinging the backs of my eyes?*

"Oh, God, man, you're not crying over this, are you? You know I'm absolute shite with tears." He shifts the box to his other side, and he's looking more and more like he's regretting his decision to come over.

Shit. *I'm* regretting his decision to come over. I was perfectly fine with how things stood an hour ago, when Zeke was still my boyfriend and I was still thinking he'd be happy when I surprised him with our sudden proximity.

"I thought–I thought we had something–" *don't say 'special,' don't sound clingy, "good*–here. We don't have to change. I mean, it can stay casual, you know? One night a week, a hookup here and there…"

Oh God just stop talking. You're making it worse.

"Yeah, I'm just not really feeling it, you know? Never been one to tie myself down, and what with the league starting back up. There are an awful lot of local hotties that toss bean in the summer and, well. I don't have to drive an hour to hook up with them, now do I?"

I don't answer, even though every fiber of my being is screaming at me to point out that he no longer has to drive an hour to hook up with *me,* either. I eliminated that pain point when I moved out to the suburbs, just twenty minutes away from him.

"Buck up, now, B–maybe we can pick things up again in the fall, eh? Get pissed or whatever it is people do for fun out here in the sticks. You're a great shag. I'm just feeling like I need a little time away, you know? For the league."

"For the league." The words sound hollow when I repeat them. Probably because I'm still in shock, trying to absorb what he's saying.

"Now you're getting it, B. You've always been crack wit. Hey! *Good Crack!* Like on your sign! I get it!" He laughs and pats me on the shoulder, not getting it at all.

Okay. Okay. No need to panic. Let's review. What has he said so far?

Not ready to tie myself down. We're moving too fast. Got it, that's understandable. I spooked him a bit. *You're a great shag.* So there's still chemistry here. He feels it, too. *Pick things up in the fall…* he just wants some time to enjoy the summer with his sports club. To "toss bean," whatever that means. *Must be some weird British sport like Cricket or Rugby.*

That's fine. This is fine. It's just a break. Doesn't mean it's *over.* Not like I packed up my entire life and my well-paying job at the health club for a relationship that the other person doesn't even care about.

He just doesn't care about it *right now.*

"Yeah, man, you're right. It's summer!" I force a smile and return the shoulder pat, adding in a hair tussle for good measure. It takes every ounce of my willpower to keep my fingers from lingering in that perfect, soft hair. "No sense in tying ourselves down when there's… bean to toss. Totally. We'll, uh, touch base come September. *Have a poke,* as they say!"

I stab a finger into his muscled arm as I say *poke.* And inwardly cringe as I realize how idiotic I sound.

He looks down at my finger, then coughs. "Right. Well then! Now that that's settled. I'll see you around, B."

He hoists the box of his belongings, containing all the reasons he might have to return, up on his shoulder and whistles as he exits the room. Then he dons his sunglasses and saunters through the kitchen and out to the second floor landing, flying down the wooden stairs to the driveway. I didn't show him that door. It's almost as if he scouted the place for exits when he came inside.

I hear his Mustang peel away, and then silence.

I rip open the pizza box and try to shove an entire slice in my mouth at once. Yeah, I know, eating my feelings is wrong. I went to fucking medical school, okay? But there are exceptions.

I'm not even done chewing before I'm grabbing my keys and heading to the gas station on the corner. I may have lost one man tonight, *temporarily,* but I've got two on speed dial for emergencies like this.

Ben and Jerry.

CHAPTER 3
KODI

Cracked Pipes? Waterworks at Tuft Swallow's Newest Business

Word on the street is that Tuft Swallow's Most Eligible's "bachelor" status is fresher than we'd previously reported! This little birdie (or rather, the bright yellow evening grosbeak perched outside his window) heard quite the kerfuffle last night when a tall, dark, and handsome man was seen leaving the second-floor entrance of Dr. Gosling's home with a moving box around 6:30pm. Now, we're not ones to speculate, but it is suspicious that a mere hour later, The Plume N' Zoom's entire stock of Chunky Monkey ice cream was sold out.

Could this have been a lover's quarrel? Perhaps any virile Tuft Swallow males who identify as "friends of Dorothy" should make an appointment sooner rather than later!

Happy Courting,
The Nosy Pecker

"Oh now, that's ridiculous." I scoff at the paper. Reporting a little town gossip here and there is one thing. But outing a new neighbor to the entire town is another.

This Pecker *is really getting out of hand.*

Lily sniffles beside me, mascara stains running down her cheeks in water black streaks.

"He's *gay?"* She blows her nose. "Why are all the good ones either gay or taken?"

I hand her another tissue and roll my eyes. "Really. You're just going to take the word of this gossip rag? This is all total speculation. Besides, he could be bi."

Lily gives me an exasperated look. "Please, Kodi. There's no such thing as a male bisexual."

A few encounters I witnessed at the football team parties back in high school could serve as evidence to the contrary.

I'm never one to assume someone's sexual orientation–likely because as a former star softball player, I grew used to people *wrongly* assuming mine. I open my mouth to correct her when the squeaking of Dr. Cratchet's orthopedics echoes down the hallway.

"Quick, put it away!" I hiss, reprimand forgotten, as I shove my own *Pecker* into my bra.

"Miss Gander! Socializing is for when you're off the clock!"

"I was just scheduling Lily here for a check up," I lie. "She has a bit of a cough, and it's really been bugging you hasn't it, Lily?"

She shoots me a quick glare before feigning a dainty *ahem-ahem.* "Oh, yes, it's persistent, too! Hopefully it's not *contagious."*

She directs another fake cough into my face.

"That's the third one you've had this month, Miss Cooley. Are you sure you've been taking your antibiotics as directed?"

I let their voices fade into the back room, mouthing a silent *thank you* to Lily as she covers for me once again. I keep telling her she needs to stop coming in to gossip while I'm at work. Every time we're caught, we have to pretend she's here for an appointment. If she keeps it up, we might have to have her tonsils taken out just to keep up the cover story.

I untuck the *Pecker* from my cleavage and continue to read up on Dr. Gosling. If the paper is to be believed, then the poor man was dumped by his boyfriend after moving to the neighborhood *for him.*

Ouch.

This only confirms why dating isn't worth the hassle, I tell myself, before googling the new doctor's practice on my work computer. One nice thing about working for Dr. Cratchet is that I never have to worry about him checking the browser history on the office equipment. Poor man can't even remember his own email password. I swear this place would collapse without me.

I page through the website, scanning paragraphs about the virtues of a holistic approach to wellness and Dr. Gosling's many certifications in chiropractic, soft tissue manipulation, and physical therapy. *Wait.* Physical therapy?

I rub at my knee, which has been throbbing continuously at around a three-out-of-ten on the pain scale since I started running cornhole practice. Last night we'd all met up at the local park again to do accuracy drills. Overall, I'd say the team enjoyed those more than running laps around the fitness trail. But I'd been forced to cut the training short at two and a half hours after a few of them complained that they needed to put their kids to bed.

Honestly. Haven't the people in this town ever heard of babysitters?

My knee twinges again.

Back when I'd first torn my ACL, I'd been rushed here to the clinic so Dr. Cratchet could handle first aid. He confirmed what my coach had feared: short of surgery, my knee was ca-put. I'd never play softball again.

I got the surgery, but PT afterwards had been a nightmare. After six weeks of little improvement, insurance stopped covering it, and Dr. Cratchet gave me an open script for muscle relaxers for when my knee would flare up.

Sleigh bells jangle through the quiet office, alerting me to someone entering the waiting room. I jump, quickly closing the browser window, only to look up and see the very man I was reading about waltzing through the door. My breath catches in my throat.

He's much more handsome in person than the photo on his website. Instead of scrubs, he's dressed in well-tailored jeans and a bright green polo shirt, which is the perfect color to highlight the green of his eyes. Unlike the clean-shaven face shown in his bio, his real-life jaw is scruffy with well-cultivated stubble. His brown hair has grown out a little, too, short-ish on the sides of his head and slightly messy on top.

I straighten in my chair. Regardless of how hot Dr. Gosling may be, it is a bad idea for him to be in this waiting room. My boss will freak if he sees him.

"Hello!" I chirp, jumping up from my wheely chair. *Stab.* And I crash right back down. "Ah!"

"Woah, are you okay?" Brian Gosling dashes over, darts his head through the window, and leans over the counter into the office, staring down at me clutching my leg in distress. "What kind of pain? Shooty? Stabby? Dull or sharp?"

"It's nothing," I grit out through clenched teeth. "Just an old injury that acts up sometimes, I'm fine."

"You don't look fine."

I look up to reassure him that I really don't need his help, but he's no longer in the window.

No. He's heading right through to the back hall and walking into the office, concern etched on his face. Before I can inform him that it's a *really* bad idea for him to be back here, he's kneeling beside me and holding his hands out next to my leg.

He's fast.

"May I?"

"You really–" I stop dead as I lock on to his gorgeous eyes with my own. *Wait, what color is that?* What at first appeared to be a vibrant green when he walked in the door is now almost blue-gray, as if the difference in lighting made them change color. And despite the confidence in his demeanor, they seem a little reserved. Almost sad.

They take my breath away.

"It's okay, I'm a doctor." The corner of his full lips tilt in a cocky little grin that gives me goosebumps.

What the hell is wrong with me?

"Uh, right. Like I said, it's an old injury. I'm used to it. I just need my pills."

His smile flips upside-down even more quickly than it appeared, matching his serious eyes. "How old are you?"

What does that have to do with anything? "Twenty-four."

"And how long have you been taking pain meds regularly?"

He's still holding his hands out, I realize, and I gesture my consent for him to examine my knee. His care and concern are surprising, but also refreshing. Even in my short stint in community college for hospital administration, professors were raising the alarm bells about opioid addiction and how it often started with over-dependence on prescription medications, especially in small towns like ours.

Not that Dr. Cratchet ever seems concerned about it. But the fact that *this* doctor is asking these kinds of questions makes him seem more trustworthy than the average stranger. I suck in a breath through my nose as he presses gently on various spots around my knee.

He smells good. Warm and clean, like fresh linens and sunshine and warm bread.

Despite the fact that I'm clearly affected by how close he is, his hands feel almost detached. They're warm, but not too warm. Firm and comforting, but completely devoid of any awkwardness or attraction.

Unlike his sad eyes, which burn into mine as he waits for my answer.

"They aren't pain meds. They're muscle relaxers. I only take them when I have flare-ups, which isn't super often. I'm very careful about that."

I'm telling the truth, and after studying me a moment, my answer seems to satisfy him. His expression softens, and he lowers his attention back to my knee, which peeks out from under the mid-length sundress I wore to work today.

"Hmm." His fingers zero in on a knot outside my lower thigh and press, *hard.* I groan.

Not in a sexy way.

In a *holy-shit-that-fucking-hurts-get-the-hell-off-of-me* way. He freezes and looks up at me. He meets my gaze.

And, noticeably, *doesn't move his fucking hand.*

"Ow! Stop, stop!" I hiss, all too aware of the fact that Dr. Cratchet is just across the hall with Lily, and will likely be coming out any second to see his brand-new arch nemesis kneeling in front of me with his hands up my skirt.

"You've got some angry tissue right here."

"Yeah, no shit, Sherlock!" I bat away his hands and scoot my chair back, immediately lowering my fingers to rub at the sore spot he found. "What the fu–I mean, *ugh!*" I remember in a rush that I'm still at work. No cursing on the job; Dr. Cratchet was just lecturing me about that. No matter how much pain I might be in, I need to act professionally.

Despite the fact that a literal stranger was just groping me when he's not even allowed to be here.

That's not fair. He asked permission. And you totally wouldn't mind him touching you in a less clinical setting…

I shake my head. I'm not sure what exactly has my ovaries standing at attention all of the sudden, but I need them to ease off, pronto. This is the same man who, according to the town rumor mill, just broke up with his *boyfriend* last night. I need to get my mind out of the gutter and back in the office. "What are you doing here, Dr. Gosling?"

The chiropractor straightens, slowly rising back to his feet. "You know who I am?"

"Duh. You're in the paper."

He looks like he doesn't quite know how to process that. I

sigh, grabbing my *Pecker* that had floated to the floor when I'd crashed into my chair earlier. I hand it to him. "Welcome to Tuft Swallow. We don't believe in privacy here."

His eyes widen as he scans the paper, and—*is that blush creeping up his cheeks?* Good Lord, he's way too adorable when he blushes.

"Where did you get this?" He practically whispers, pure terror building in his face as he scans the article.

My face scrunches in pity. "Oh, honey. They're everywhere. Those gossip rags get passed out like candy at a parade every morning."

He hands it back to me, and if looks could kill, that *Pecker* would catch fire right here and now. He raises a hand to his head and runs his fingers through his hair, holding them there and staring off into space for a moment as if his whole world just came crashing down around him.

Which I suppose now that I think about it, it has. He's just had a very private moment with his boyfriend announced to an entire town full of strangers.

I place my hand on his forearm in what I hope is a comforting gesture. "Listen, on behalf of this entire ridiculous town, I apologize. Truly, I do. I've lived here my whole life, so I understand just how devastating it can be to have your dirty laundry aired to everybody." I remember being the subject of a few issues of the *Pecker* myself. The very same day I lost my softball scholarship to UCLA, the whole town knew about it. For weeks I couldn't go anywhere without everyone asking me about my injury, how I was holding up, what my plans were now that I couldn't go to school for softball anymore.

I look up and meet the withered gaze of the man before me. Suddenly, it's like all the anger and sadness I felt back then hits me like a tidal wave. I *know* how he feels right now. Or at least, I have an idea.

This poor man. This is no way to start your life in a new town.

I slap my hands on the armrests of my chair, and the noise

makes him jump. I can't fix what the gossip-hungry townies did to Dr. Gosling, but I *can* show him that not everyone in Tuft Swallow is a rumor-spreading asshat. "Have you had lunch yet?"

"Lunch?"

"Yeah. Lunch. You know, after breakfast, before dinner?" I pull up a fresh tab in the browser on the desktop (thanking my lucky stars that I already closed out of the last tab I had open) and type in the name of the best diner in town. He snorts as I point to the screen.

"Easy Swallow? Really?"

"Trust me, it isn't the worst pun you'll find in this town. But the food is legit. My treat." I check the clock. 11:45. A little early, but no one's due for an appointment until one, and it's imperative that Dr. Cratchet doesn't see this man standing in his office. So I leave a sticky note on the computer screen informing him that I'm going out for my lunch break and move to stand and grab my purse.

That's when I remember that my knee is not at all interested in cooperating today. My shoulders tense in anticipation of the impending collapse…

But it never comes. *What?* I look down at my knee, supporting the left half of my body just as it should be.

Huh.

The chiropractor reaches out a hand. "Feeling better?"

I let him support my arm as I take a few careful steps toward the coat rack. It's sore, and a little wobbly, but it isn't buckling like it did before. "That's weird."

"It'll probably be a little tender for a while. Just be easy on it. And you should probably make an appointment at some point so we can actually diagnose what's going on there."

"What did you *do*?" I move us as fast as I can on my suddenly-not-throbbing leg across the waiting room, breathing a sigh of relief as the sleigh bells play us out without the boss spotting us. I continue to lean on Dr. Gosling as we proceed down the couple of steps to the sidewalk and down the street to the Easy Swallow.

"Just a little acupressure. Doesn't feel great in the moment, but you can't argue with the results." He smiles at me, and it's as if a switch has flipped. *This guy's the real deal.* Barely five minutes ago, he looked like he was about to have a breakdown, but now he's grinning at me and talking about my injury as if there's nowhere in the world he'd rather be.

"You really love what you do, don't you?" I stop in the middle of the sidewalk, looking him up and down with fresh eyes. My knee is feeling more and more sure with every step, even though I can definitely feel that I overworked it yesterday.

Something is nagging in the back of my mind, but I can't put my finger on what it is, except that it's decidedly *different.*

He cocks his head at me, and I realize I've been staring at him for too long. His hand returns to his hairline, a nervous tic. "I like helping people feel better. Chronic pain is… well, it's a pain!" His voice gets breathy when he says that, half-laugh, half-speaking voice. He reaches into his shirt pocket and pulls out a business card. "Here. You really should make an appointment. And I'm not just saying that because I'm new in town and I need the business, although…" He shrugs, and his lips tug up in that intoxicating smile again. I feel a weird little flip-flop in my stomach as our fingers brush when I take the card. "Well, I am trying to build the business. But that situation there?" He gestures to my knee. "You could use my help. Twenty-four is too young to lose your leg."

I nod, speechless.

I'm sorry, Kodi. You can keep up the exercises, but… you're probably going to be in some kind of pain for the rest of your life.

"Well, I've got more of these to hand out." He pats his shirt pocket, and for the first time I see the outline of the stack of business cards he has there.

"You don't want lunch?" It's a physical effort to drag myself back to the present and realize he's saying goodbye.

Another flash of that sadness in his eyes, which now shine a stormy gray in the bright midday sun. "No, that's okay. I'm not really hungry."

Disappointment tugs at my stomach. *That's weird. Maybe I just need some food.*

"Oh. Alright, well. Thanks for your help! It was nice meeting you, Dr. Gosling."

"Call me Brian. And you are…?" He leaves the word hanging, and I stick out my hand.

"Kodi Gander. Rain check on the Easy Swallow?"

An emotion passes across his face, too quickly for me to recognize what it is. But he shakes my hand.

"You have my number."

He lets go, but I can still feel the reassuring warmth of those fingers grasping my palm. At once clinical and caring. Unlike any handshake I've ever felt in my life.

I'm beginning to think there's more to this Dr. Gosling than they've been clucking about in *The Nosy Pecker.*

CHAPTER 4
KODI

"I'll send in a prescription for some antibiotics, but you should honestly think about getting your tonsils removed. It's not just for kids, you know!"

Dr. Cratchet chuckles as he leads Lily out of the exam room. I'm back in the office; I decided against greasy diner food when Dr. Gosling left to go distribute more of his business cards. I can feel the one he gave me poking against my hip in the pocket of my sundress as I follow them into the waiting room. The Doc announces he's grabbing lunch at the bakery across the street, and I wait for the door to shut behind him before I take it out to show Lily.

"The way that man hands out prescriptions for antibiotics... he didn't even make me do a swab. Isn't that supposed to be bad or something?" She shakes her head and looks at me expectantly. "What's that?"

"Guess who showed up to introduce himself while you were in the back?" I hand her the card, and she gasps enviously.

"No. Way. You met Dr. Hottie??"

"Don't call him that."

"It's better than Dr. Homo," she mumbles. I smack her.

"What is this, the 1960s? So he likes guys, Lily, get over it. Men do not exist only to be potential suitors for you."

"Potential suitors? Now who's stuck in the 1960s?" She studies the card in her hands. "Brian Gosling, DC. What does the DC stand for?"

"Doctor of Chiropractic. He's introducing himself to the neighborhood, and he didn't know about the *Pecker.* I feel so bad for him. I know they weren't mean about it this time, but the paper basically outed him to the whole town. That's really awful."

She tilts her head at me, and hums pensively. "Is this about the people who called you a lesbian in high school?"

I snatch the card back. "No, Lily, it's about how making assumptions about people's private life in general is a shitty thing to do. Why does everyone around here have to be such…muckrakers?"

Lily blinks. "You know, it's really a shame you lost your sports scholarship to UCLA. You totally would have fit in with all those west-coast smarty-pants with your fancy SAT words." She flops onto the couch in the middle of the waiting room and leans her arms against the back of it, facing me with her chin in her hands. "So what did Dr. Hottie have to say?"

I feel my face heat, and I duck back behind the desk. Suddenly, I don't want to tell her about Dr. Gosling coming to my rescue when I collapsed. The way his eyes changed color when he looked at me, or how his hands magically made it so I could walk again.

Luckily, I'm saved from answering when Dr. Cratchet returns, turkey sandwich and a bag of tasteless baked chips clutched in his gnarly hands. He glances between Lily and me, and sighs. "Fraternizing on your lunch break, Miss Gander?"

"Yes sir," I answer cheerfully. He can't get mad at me for talking to my friend when I'm literally off the clock.

"Don't think you're getting out of answering." Lily rises from her backwards kneel on the stiff couch and comes around to stand in front of it instead. "What did he want?"

"What did who want?" Dr. Cratchet asks, setting his lunch down. "Did someone come in while I was gone?"

I shoot Lily a *we're-going-to-have-a-conversation-about-this-later* look. I give myself half a second to try to put together a cover story to tell the man, but nothing comes to me in time. I brace myself.

"Dr. Gosling stopped by to introduce himself."

The Doc's mood sours palpably. Not that he's ever really happy, but he goes from a four to a seven on the grumpy meter almost instantly. "Well? What did he want?"

"Just to–" I pause. What *had* he wanted? Now that I think about it, we never actually got around to discussing why he'd come into the doctor's office, except to leave his business card. He and I both got distracted when he started touching me.

I mean, when I fell. And he helped me. You know, 'cause he's a doctor. *And that's what doctors do, Kodi: they help people when they fall while trying to do a perfectly simple thing like getting out of a chair.*

The significantly *less* helpful doctor that I work for huffs impatiently. "Miss Gander, do you always have such a short attention span?"

"Sorry! Um–he left his business card."

"That's all?" Both my boss and my best friend stare at me.

"Yep." I will my face to cool down. I have nothing to be embarrassed about here.

"Let me see it." He holds his hand out expectantly. I hesitate for a second, because part of me doesn't *want* to give Dr. Cratchet his card. Deep down, I know that my boss has no interest in fostering any kind of positive relationship with the chiropractor (even if their businesses really aren't in direct competition). I wonder why exactly that bothers me.

Reluctantly, I hand it to him.

I hope the Doc doesn't get *too* weird about there being a new chiropractor in town. After all, he didn't do anything to deserve my boss's hostility. He just moved here to set up his business.

"I like helping people feel better."

Brian's words echo through my head as my boss stares at me.

"How is that knee of yours doing, Miss Gander?"

Dr. Cratchet is tapping the business card against his fingers with a mischievous look on his face.

"Uh… fine right now, actually." Technically, it's the truth, even if I don't mention *why* it's fine.

"No it's not. In fact, I think you may need to see a specialist about it. Perhaps even this *Dr. Gosling*."

I feel the back of my neck prickle. There's no way that he knows what actually happened, right? Is my boss actually psychic?

I swallow. "Y-you do?"

"Yes. And you're going to report back to me exactly how much of a quack this guy really is. You, with your so-called chronic knee injury, are going to be my man on the inside."

"Don't you mean woman?" Lily asks unhelpfully.

"That's what I said. My woman on the inside."

I stare at him in disbelief. "You know my injury *is* chronic, right? You're the one who diagnosed me."

"Yes, yes, of course." He waves away my comment, returning the business card and retrieving his lunch from the coffee table. "More importantly, it's an excuse to make an appointment. Collect intel. Reconnaissance! The rotten spine fondler will never know what hit him."

I don't volunteer the fact that I was already planning to make an appointment after that magic he worked on my leg earlier. Instead, I find myself flummoxed by the depth of my boss's insecurity. "I'm sorry, are you saying you want me to *spy* on Dr. Gosling?"

"Of course!" A grin splits his face, and instead of making him seem more approachable, it has the opposite effect. He looks half-crazed, his yellowed teeth and graying eyebrows appearing crooked as his face adjusts to the unfamiliar stretch. "How else are we going to run him out of town?"

"Oh my God, Kodi, I think you're being given a *mission* right now," Lily whispers loudly, as if the man assigning it isn't standing well within earshot.

"A mission of utmost importance," he agrees solemnly, and I don't know what is more ridiculous. That my boss is asking me to *literally spy* on the new chiropractor in town, or the fact that my best friend seems excited by the idea.

"Uh, how is it so important?"

"Your very job is on the line!" Dr. Cratchet shouts, jumping at the volume of his own voice before leaning forward and cupping a hand against his mouth. He continues, more conspiratorially, "If you want this clinic to stay in business, it's imperative that we know our competition inside and out! You like this job, don't you Kodi? Like the comfortable lifestyle it affords you? Like helping the good people of Tuft Swallow when they are sick?"

"Yes, of course, sir, but–"

"Then it's settled! You are to book an appointment before the end of the week!"

"It's already Thursday, sir."

His eyes twinkle behind his glasses, and he winks creepily at me before swinging open the door to the back. "Then I suggest you make haste, Miss Gander. Time is of the essence."

MOM

Hi, honey. It's been a while since you've checked in. How are you? The ladies at Church were asking about you.

"YOUR BOSS IS KINDA NUTS, YOU KNOW THAT?"

I close out of my mom's text message without responding, instead turning back to Lily and our late lunch at the Crowbar and Grill. One of the nice things about Dr. Cratchet's ridiculous scheme was that he let me out early to ensure I had enough time to call and schedule my appointment with Dr. Gosling. One of the not-so-nice things (other than the questionable legality of spying on a rival business to force his only competition out of town) was the fact that it had only been two hours since Dr. Gosling had given me his card.

Now, I'm not one to play games or waffle about social etiquette when it comes to the customs between men and women (or, you know, any two people who might be sexually inclined). But like… aren't you supposed to wait at least a day before you call someone after they give you their number? That's not just a silly rule, that's like, an *institution.*

So little time has passed since the hot chiropractor gave me his card. I haven't even gotten my chicken club yet. Surely an hour and change is too short a time to wait before I call the most beautiful man I've literally ever seen.

Not that it matters that he's beautiful. He *just* broke up with someone.

"Hellooo? Earth to Kodi!"

"What?" I look up from the letters and numbers I've been staring at. Lily is raising an eyebrow at me.

"Well? What are you waiting for?"

"I'm not going to call him from a *bar,*" I scoff, dropping the card on the table. "That's a terrible first impression."

"Second impression, technically. Which reminds me…" She leans forward, and I lean back at the suddenly accusatory gleam in her eyes. "You've yet to spill the beans on how that first impression really went."

Shit! She's onto me. I fight the nervous pressure building in my chest and let out a little cough. "I told you. He came in, dropped off his business card, and…"

"And?" She taps her fingers on the table impatiently. "Oh, honey—there was no *'and'* when you told the story earlier in Crotchetty's waiting room. I *know* something is up. I haven't seen you this red since you forgot to bring sunscreen to basketball camp junior year."

That had been a wicked sunburn. Three days of aloe and cold

baths and I'd still had to go to the clinic for medicated lotion. I've got freckles I keep tabs on after recovering from that one.

But Lily's not interested in rehashing my medical history. "Kodi! You're stalling!"

"Alright, alright. He's hot, okay? You were right." I cross my arms, and the waitress arrives with my drink. *Not a moment too soon.* I down half of it in one long slurp through the teensy cocktail straw.

Is it warm in here?

Lily eyes me knowingly. "Uh-huh. What else?"

"Else?" I squeak.

Suddenly, she slams her hands on the table, sending the ice in my glass tinkling and the beads of condensation rushing into a puddle at the base of the glass. I flinch. *"Spill it, Gander."*

My shoulders drop. I should have known better than to come to a BFF Happy Hour half-cocked. Lily can sniff out sexual tension like a pervy bloodhound.

This is just the first time *I've* been on the receiving end of it.

"Okay. He came in to introduce himself to Dr. Cratchet. Apparently, he's going around to all the businesses in town to do that. It's really smart, actually." I take a breath, and Lily twirls her pointer finger in a *go on* gesture. "Well, I mean, you know what a rampage the Doc has been on since hearing about him coming to town. I had to get him out of there before you and he got out of the exam room."

"Ugh. Of course, I miss all the good stuff because I had to cover for you. Why can't I just get a job at the clinic? So we don't have to pretend I'm some kind of chronically coughing hypochondriac?"

I shrug. "Weren't you gonna finish your associates in bookkeeping? That could have gotten you in the door."

Lily sticks out her tongue. "Ew. I hate spreadsheets."

"Oh come on," I laugh. "They're not so bad. In fact–"

"Don't change the subject!" She points a finger at me and I put my hands up in defense. "You and I both know that if you get on the topic of spreadsheets or sports we're never getting the truth out of you about Dr. Hottie. Now *focus.*"

So much for that. "Well, I jumped up from my chair to get him out of there before you and the doc wrapped up, but then..." I gesture to my leg. Lily gasps.

"You collapsed?" I nod, my throat too tight to admit it out loud. I still hate that I can't trust my body to just *work* when I need it to. Lily knows that, probably better than anybody, as she'd been on the team with me in high school when I'd gotten hurt. "Oh, Kodi. I'm so sorry."

She reaches out a hand to grasp mine, and I'm reminded just how good a friend Lily actually is. Sure, she's a little bit of a scatterbrain and her hormones get the better of her sometimes, but she's been there through some of the hardest moments of my life. She was the one that signed up to go to TSCC with me when I lost my scholarship to UCLA, despite never wanting to actually go to college herself. She was the one who brought DVD boxsets of *Supernatural* and *Gilmore Girls* to my house to keep me entertained while I was on bedrest after my surgery (she had an incurable crush on Jared Padalecki at the time).

I squeeze her fingers, and it gives me the strength to go on with the rest of the story. Even if it does embarrass the hell out of me.

"One second, I'm jumping out of the chair. The next, I'm on the ground. And then, I swear, I *blink* and this guy is right there at my side. He was kneeling beside me, and asked me if he could look at my knee, and then he dug his fingers into a spot on my thigh–" Lily inhales sharply. I roll my eyes. "Not like *that,* Lily, it was...hard to describe. Like, it *hurt.* God, it was some of the worst pain I've ever felt, but then he's looking at me and his eyes are this blue gray green color that I couldn't pin down and then he helps me up, and..."

"And he kissed you?" Lily breathes.

"What?? No!" I snort. "No, I could actually stand and walk!"

Confusion blankets her face for a moment, and then her

eyebrows shoot up to her hairline. "Wait, *what?* He cured you? *With his hands??"* Her last words echo a little throughout the mostly empty bar, and the bartender looks over at us curiously. She waves him an apology, and the waitress, Ginger this time, appears with our sandwiches.

"I mean, I don't think he cured me." I take a hearty chomp out of my pickle spear. "But, let's just say I was definitely already planning on calling him. Just not, like… this afternoon."

Lily nods sagely. "It reeks of desperation."

"Right?"

She goes to take a bite of her sandwich, but pauses with it an inch from her lips. "Wait a minute. You talked about his eyes." She looks at me more seriously, and I wish I hadn't just finished my gin and tonic. Three drinks is too many to have this early in the day, even if I am working up the courage to call the sexiest man alive. "Does Kodi Gander, ice queen extraordinaire, have a *crush* on the hot new doctor?"

I swallow the bite I was chewing, narrowly avoiding choking as it slides down the wrong hole. I cough for a minute, tears forming in my eyes. Ginger comes over with a glass of water, and I gulp it down gratefully.

The whole time, Lily stares at me archly. I narrow my eyes at her.

"I just met the guy, Lily."

"And he's gay."

"We don't *know* that," I lie. Is the *Nosy Pecker* a gossipy asshole? Yes. Are they ever wrong about anything? Not that I can remember.

I think about how Dr. Gosling's hands felt on my legs. Completely devoid of sexuality or attraction. Purely clinical.

But he also had the most reassuring presence, and the way he looked at me, helped me up… I guess I could chalk it up to bedside manner, but does anyone have *that* good of a bedside manner?

My mind turns to Dr. Cratchet, and I snort. Yeah, no. I've

never met a doctor who's 'professionalism' gave me butterflies like Dr. Hottie's did. There's something more there. I can feel it.

"Leave it to you to finally fall for someone, and it's literally the least available, least straight guy in town. And also your boss's nemesis. What are you going to do?"

I sigh, and pick up the business card once more. "I'm gonna see if this guy can actually fix my knee." I move to take out my cell and dial the number, when Lily slaps my arm. "What the hell was that for?"

But I don't need her to answer. The second I look up, I see the reason for her alarm.

Dr. Hottie just walked in the bar.

CHAPTER 5
BRIAN

After hours of walking around Tuft Swallow, and fielding more than my fair share of side eyes from old people with binoculars around their necks and newspapers in their hands, I'm more than ready for a drink.

The Nosy Pecker. No wonder Zeke was so embarrassed for me when he learned I moved to Tuft Swallow. Between the pervy bird watchers and the town's knock-off *Lady Whistledown* spreading gossip about everybody, I'm more than ready to admit that moving here was a mistake. But now I've signed away my life for the next 30 years to a mortgage I can only afford if my practice takes off–*fast*. How the hell am I supposed to build a business here when people are more interested in my love life than my services?

I finally managed to grift a copy of the latest *Pecker* when I left Wingspan, the yoga studio. Since there had been a class in session when I'd arrived, I hadn't been able to introduce myself to the instructor. But in the waiting room there had been a stack of *Peckers* by the door, meaning my trip wasn't entirely in vain. Emblazoned on the front page, the headline made it sound like there was a plumbing leak at my new office building. Only, when I read the first paragraph, it became clear that the "Waterworks at

Tuft Swallow's Newest Business" was actually referring to my break-up with Zeke.

How the hell did they find out about that?

And that was when I realized it. All those nosy neighbors. The elderly townspeople I kept seeing at every shop and street corner. *Tit Peepers.*

They're everywhere. Wearing their ridiculous windbreakers and sporting their binoculars in random places about town: the barbershop, the cafe, the grocery store, all in broad daylight. These people aren't bird watchers. They're peeping toms.

I've moved to a neighborhood of spies.

I force myself to finish reading the article, then crumble my *Pecker* and dump it into one of the tidy, green-painted trash cans that are placed conveniently every few blocks along the sidewalk. Zeke calling a break on our relationship was painful enough already. But learning, on top of that, the whole town knows about it before they've even met me?

Like I said: I need a drink.

I walk into the nearly empty Crowbar and Grill (seriously. Crowbar? What is the deal with this town and its bird puns?). I'm hesitant to be out in public drinking this early on a weekday when I'm trying to establish a reputation as a responsible business owner, but I'm beginning to think my reputation is already ruined for this Godforsaken town.

I scan the tables, and lock eyes with the only thing that could possibly raise my spirits in this moment: the beautiful receptionist from the town clinic I stopped in earlier this morning. The one with the leg injury. She's the only sane person I've crossed paths with so far today, and she somehow was able to distract me a little from the mess that is my life.

She's sitting with a curvy redhead at a two-top near the bar. They also seem to be hitting in the sauce a little early.

I guess Thirsty Thursday is alive and well in Tuft Swallow.

Her eyes widen as she looks me up and down, and I feel a smile tug at my lips in reflex. She's cute, alright. Dirty blonde hair and a sprinkling of freckles dotting the bridge of her nose and her exposed shoulders. That sundress she's wearing fits close to her athletic body from the waist up, before flaring just above her hips and fluttering around her muscular legs. Surprisingly muscular, considering she's supposedly recovering from an injury. She must still exercise quite a bit.

But regardless of how pretty she may be, I know it would be a terrible idea to think of her as anything but a potential patient. And it isn't just because of my broken heart. As a chiropractor, I tend to get more handsy than most when first meeting someone. By design, I see each new person first through a doctor's eyes before letting myself get to know them better. It's safer that way. Part of why I started using dating apps to meet people outside of town is because... well, dating people that I meet at work can get a little messy.

Although, truth be told, dating for me always seems to get messy sooner or later.

That being said, seeing this woman–Kodi, I think her name was–makes different areas of my brain light up than just the doctor parts. Which is a little confusing so soon after Zeke called for a break.

She returns my grin, and her friend whips around to smile at me, too. She waves.

"Dr. Gosling! You should join us!"

Oh no. Hot receptionist notwithstanding, joining their table is a very bad idea. I'm already in a bad mood, and if drinking before the end of the workday was a bad idea, getting drinks in town with my first potential patient is a *horrendous* one.

"That's kind of you, but I'm just grabbing some takeout," I improvise. *And a beer while I wait.* Not that I'm hungry. I wonder if I could get an IPA to go...

"Nonsense! I was just leaving, and Kodi could use the company!"

The two women exchange what appears to be a remarkably nuanced conversation with only their eyebrows for a moment before the redhead hops out of her chair and gestures for me to take a seat.

Fuck. "I couldn't take your spot–"

"You *really* could," she purrs, her voice dropping an octave out of nowhere as she yanks my forearm and practically pushes me into the seat. Kodi covers her face with her hands and shakes her head across from me. "See you tomorrow at practice, girl!"

"Thanks, Lily." Only she doesn't sound particularly grateful.

Before I've fully adjusted to the view of the restaurant from my new seated perspective, Lily twirls away and prances out the door. Kodi pushes her bangs out of her face and draws a noisy sip through the cocktail straw of her drink, which sounds as though all of the liquid has already been drained.

"I'm so sorry about her," she mumbles on an exhale.

I shrug, letting out a breath of my own. "Honestly? That's probably the nicest anyone in this town has been to me so far. Other than you."

A look of surprise crosses her face, but before she can respond, a waitress walks up to our table to check on us.

"Everything tasting alri–where'd Lily go?"

The woman blinks at me, as if attempting to decipher how the short, curvy woman who had been occupying my seat transformed into a tall, scruffy-faced man while she'd been getting the check.

"She insisted I take her spot." I look between the scantily-clad waitress and my new lunch companion, and my stomach growls loudly.

"Sounds like maybe you need that sandwich more than she does." She slides the plate closer and shoots me a wink, adding, "although I hear you're more of a tossed salad kinda man."

My eyes widen, and she laughs, licking her lips. Then she refills our waters and walks away. My cheeks burn. *Oh God. Was that…? Did she just…?*

Across from me, Kodi slides down in her chair as if attempting to disappear. Once again, she covers her face with her hands. I recover from my surprise, and she finally takes a deep breath and reaches across the table toward me.

"On behalf of our entire town, I want to issue you the sincerest of apologies." She can barely keep eye contact, and her freckles almost disappear behind a fiery blush that ignites her face. "I swear she didn't mean anything, uh, discriminatory by that. Ginger is just very…vulgar."

She meets my eyes then, and I feel my shoulders relax a bit as I hold her gaze. Okay, so the waitress is just a pervert, and that wasn't some vicious dig at my relationship preferences. The ones that the whole town is likely speculating about at this very moment. "I get the impression that's fairly common around here?"

Kodi takes a big bite out of her sandwich and nods apologetically. "Yeah," she chews.

And then, the strangest sensation takes over my stomach. At first, I assume it's just the nausea that's been building inside me since Zeke left last night. Or maybe it's anxiety from being the object of everyone's whispers and stares all day. Regardless, it writhes and swirls in my stomach, traveling all the way up my chest and throat until I can't hold it back anymore. I cover my mouth, not knowing if I'm about to hiccup, burp, or hurl, only for the sensation to erupt from my mouth—

As a laugh.

This is ridiculous. All of it. The invasive bird watchers, the articles in the town paper, the promiscuous waitress, Zeke breaking up with me after I uprooted my entire life to move to this bonkers New England town. It is absolutely, positively ludicrous. It can't be real. Any minute now, I'm going to wake up alone in my apartment in Boston, and everything will be back to normal.

I pinch my arm in between laughs, wondering if this is all some funhouse dream or nightmare, but it definitely hurts.

Ginger returns with a beer, confused by my sudden outburst. I try to stop for long enough to thank her, but the closest I get is a cough and a weird half-nod when she sets the glass down on the table. She darts away after that, and Kodi looks at me with concern.

"Uh, Dr. Gosling? Are you–"

"Brian, please," I choke out, wiping tears from my eyes. I manage to slow my breathing and calm my shaking shoulders. The episode passes, taking some of the tension that's been coiled in my chest since last night along with it. I take a long gulp of my beer. "Sorry. I uh, don't know what came over me. It's been a long day."

Kodi looks at me with concern. "You seem a little tense."

"Ya think?" I eye the sandwich in front of me, at once starving and also completely lacking in appetite. As an awkward silence descends upon the table between us, a nugget of guilt forms in my gut. Even as my world is crumbling around me, I'm still a professional. The last thing I want to do is make a bad impression on one of the very few kind people I've met today. "I'm sorry, Kodi. That was rude of me."

"Oh, no, not at all," Kodi says, hastily swallowing. "Like I said, it's me who should be apologizing. You've had an awful introduction into town. And anyway, I was hoping to talk to you."

"Really?" She just met me. What could she possibly have to talk about?

She nods. "That… *thing* you did to my leg. What was that?"

"The fascia release?" She stares back at me blankly as if I said something in a foreign language. I start talking with my hands, grateful that we've switched to a topic that, one, isn't my love life and two, I'm actually knowledgeable in. So I let myself switch into doctor mode. "Whenever someone gets injured, their body makes adjustments to allow it to heal, right?"

Kodi nods, her deep brown eyes following my every movement as I demonstrate on my arm. "Let's say you break your wrist. There are a ton of ligaments and tiny muscles that all facilitate wrist movement, and all of them are affected by the inflammation and scar tissue that develop around the break. So what happens? Our bodies adjust to the new sensations. Suddenly, even after the bone heals, moving your wrist in a particular direction hurts, so you avoid moving it in that direction. When muscles and ligaments don't get to move and stretch over a period of time, lactic acid and inflammation and all sorts of crud can collect in pockets throughout all the connective tissue that covers your arm: skin, fascia, fat–all of that stuff."

Usually, I'll lose people when I explain how all of this works, but Kodi's attention is rapt. When I pause, she just nods at me, and gestures for me to continue.

"Uh, well. So, around your knee, which I assume you haven't been moving normally for some time, there's a lot of angry stuff built up in between all the parts that help you move freely. Which, in turn, makes it harder to move them. If you don't help your muscles and connective tissue let go of it all, eventually you'll lose mobility, or certain muscles will atrophy. Meaning–"

"Meaning they won't support your weight," she finishes for me. Then she leans back, crosses her arms, and stares at me with distant eyes, as if she's seeing me but not really looking at me. After a moment, her eyes refocus, and her dark, full brows furrow. "How is it that you managed to explain in thirty seconds something that none of my doctors or surgeons or physical therapists could figure out how to tell me?"

I chuckle dryly. "It's more common than you'd think. Doctors and surgeons, in particular, are often more worried about insurance and getting patients in and out the door than they are about actually helping people maintain a healthy lifestyle." *If I'm not careful, I'm going to end up on my soapbox.* "I guess, to be fair, there are plenty of doctors that *aren't* like that, and plenty of chiropractors that are just as guilty of that kind of behavior, too, but *I'm* not one of them. Bodies should move. They need to stretch and run and lift and do things, you know? And most of the time–not all the time, of course, but usually–young healthy people have all the tools they need to keep their bodies doing what they need to do. Even after injuries. It just takes a little work."

The entire time I talk, neither of us touch our food. I go to reach for my beer, when Kodi grabs my arm.

"I want to make an appointment." I raise an eyebrow at her, and she removes her hand. "Sorry. How soon can you see me?"

I've never seen so much intensity in someone's eyes as there is in Kodi's when she asks that question. My arm still burns where her fingers were, and for a breath, I'm paralyzed. Who exactly *is* this woman?

"Uh... let me check my schedule–"

"Can you see me today?"

I have to look away from her. The passion in her face is scary, and I don't trust myself not to look too much into it. I reach into my pocket for my phone and make a show of checking my calendar, even though I know damn well I don't have any appointments yet. "Don't you have to go back to work?"

"Dr. Cratchet will understand. I need it."

"Well, hold on," I say, realizing I need to temper her expectations. "Recovery from a long-term injury takes time. It doesn't happen overnight or with one appointment. I'll need to do an assessment, too, and that–"

Her hand is back on my arm, and my eyes lock onto the spot where her skin meets mine. Her touch is scorching. It cuts me off from finishing my sentence.

"Brian. I know it's not going to happen overnight. I've been in pain for years. I've done weeks of physical therapy. I've tried pilates, yoga–nothing has helped. But now I'm back on a team again, and I want–*need*–to be able to trust my leg again. When you touched me this morning, I thought you were trying to break me all over again, but then I could walk without pain for the first time since *high school.*"

A lump forms in my throat, and I swallow. People like this, like Kodi, are why I became a chiropractor in the first place. She's been failed by every part of the medical system when she's a young, healthy woman with decades of activity ahead of her. And she's looking at me like I have the power to make all of her dreams come true.

Which, I suppose, I do. Why make her wait a second longer?

All my frustrations and worries from last night and today fade away, just like they did when she fell in the clinic this morning. When that happened, my only thought had been to run to her and fix what was wrong. Immediately, I knew where the problem was and where to press to stop the spasm. For the second time today, my brain collapses into a singular focus. The world tunnels in around us, and it's just me and her and the place where our bodies are touching.

"Come over now. We'll get started."

"I'll get the check."

CHAPTER 6
KODI

One of my favorite things about Tuft Swallow is how walkable it is. As Brian and I head to his office from the Crowbar, I'm able to enjoy it even more than usual, because my knee isn't twingeing painfully with every other step.

Brian walks slowly enough to accommodate my shorter stride, and I get the impression he's used to adjusting his presence to make all of his patients feel more comfortable. It's something I've never witnessed any man do before. Dr. Cratchet doesn't have enough empathy or awareness of other people to even listen to them most of the time, never mind actually adjust his own body language or demeanor to accommodate them.

Of course, I've seen Lily change the way she acts around guys to make them feel stronger or smarter, just like I'd seen many of our friends from high school adjust their personalities to accommodate their boyfriends and later, husbands. But to see the way Brian alters his stride to match mine, or weave closer to me in anticipation of a young boy passing us on his bicycle or Mr. and Mrs. Johnson walking by on the sidewalk, is something else.

It reminds me of the way we used to all be mindful of each other during warm-ups in softball. Whether we were running laps or practicing outfield plays, we were all constantly aware of where each other were. It made us a good team, and practicing our awareness became just as important as drilling pitches or swings or anything else.

"Do you play any sports?" I ask him as we walk towards the corner of Main and Oak Street.

"Not sports, no. I've done martial arts my whole life, though."

"Really?" I imagine him in a white karate uniform with a black belt, and get stuck on wondering whether or not he has chest hair that would peek out of his gi. I quickly push away the thought before it can lead somewhere dangerous. "You know there's an MMA gym that just opened up a few months ago. You should join!"

"Here in town?" He looks surprised. "This, uh... doesn't seem like the kind of place to have an actual fighting gym."

"What, you don't think Mr. and Mrs. Woodcock can hold their own? Their son is the chief of police, you know. And he had to have gotten his muscles from somewhere."

Brian raises one eyebrow. And I gotta say, never in a million years would I have thought one eyebrow lift could be sexy enough to distract me from the thought of our jacked police chief, but somehow that one movement wipes thoughts of all other men from my brain.

Not that I was ever particularly interested in any of the ones in this town, but just about every girl I went to school with had their first sexual awakening when Officer Woodcock came into our homeroom to talk to us about *D.A.R.E.* I'm pretty sure no one in that class absorbed anything he said about marijuana or ketamine. There wasn't a dry eye among Tuft Swallow's eligible when he and his high school sweetheart Delilah got back together earlier this year.

Then I remember that Brian had a boyfriend. For all I know, he might be just as interested in meeting our muscled police chief as all the girls in Mrs. Sanderson's sixth grade class. And very much *un*-interested in me.

Why are you even thinking of him that way? You're seeing him for a chiro appointment, not a date. Oh, and to spy on him for your boss.

Not that I have any actual intentions to spy on Brian. What would that even entail? Snooping through his booking software? Sneaking a bug into his table?

I snort at the thought of me dodging lasers, Mission Impossible-style, and planting a tiny microphone on the underside of a paper-covered headrest. Brian shakes his head at me.

"Alright, apparently there's some sort of inside joke I'm missing about Chief Woodcock." He looks away for a moment, then shakes his head. "Other than the unfortunate name. And I thought 'Brian Gosling' was bad."

"No relation, I hear?"

"No. No relation. Which is good, because if I ever meet him..." A smirk spreads across his lips, and I swear I see his tongue dart out and lick them for a moment. Then we meet eyes, and both of us freeze in place as we realize what we've been talking about.

And then we both burst out laughing.

"Okay, okay," I gasp out, clutching a stitch in my side. We've stopped at the corner of Oak and Elm, and his practice is right there on the tree-shaded street neighboring the town square. His face is beet-red, but unlike earlier today when *The Nosy Pecker*'s rumors came up in conversation, he doesn't look angry or upset. Only good-naturedly embarrassed, as if he's been caught with his hand in the cookie jar. "Tell me, Dr. Gosling, since it's come up. Are you actually gay, or are the Tit Peepers full of it?"

His face becomes more serious as he wipes a happy tear from the corner of his eye. "You aren't just taking what the paper says at face value?"

I shake my head. "Of course not. Not about that. First of all, it isn't any of their business, and second..." I trail off, wary of spilling too much of my own history to the man mere hours after meeting him, but something about the way he tilts his head curiously as I answer him has me opening up.

"I played softball in high school; you might have already

guessed. That's how I hurt my knee in the first place." I take a breath, and he nods. "Well, kids are dumb and mean, and don't know how to handle girls in sports apparently, so. Freshman year, there was a pretty popular rumor that I was a lesbian. And I mean, there were a few girls on the team who were, and it wasn't a problem or anything, because like, live your life, right? But, *I* wasn't. I'm straight, I just wasn't interested in dating anyone in high school."

His face is unreadable as he studies me. "So what happened?"

I shrug. "Well, you know how high school is. The harder I denied the rumors, the more the bullies doubled-down. So I just ignored them. I didn't date any guys, though, so most people just assumed the rumors were true. Half of them still do, probably. And it's dumb. What do they know? What gives them the right to assume anything about anybody, you know? Just because I haven't met somebody yet that I want to–" I stop abruptly, realizing who I'm talking to. And realizing just how much I'm revealing about myself in the process. I clear my throat, and twist my hands uncomfortably. "Anyway. My sex life or preferences are none of their fucking business. Neither is yours. You don't have to tell me, either, of course, but it's just you were talking about Ryan Gosling, and–"

"I'm bi," he says simply. I blink.

Oh? I ignore the sleeping panther in my loins that raises its head at his declaration. *Simmer down, kitty.*

"Alright then!" I silently vow to give Lily a resounding told-you-so tonight at practice. "See? What do people know?"

"They know that my boyfriend dumped me last night." Brian starts walking toward his office again, but this time his small steps seem more defeated than considerate.

"They also know that you enjoy puns." I catch up to him, trying to cheer him up. "And you'd be surprised how far that gets you in Tuft Swallow. I bet you'll fit in better than you think right now. The Tit Peepers are annoying and crazy and inconsiderate at times, but they're not all bad."

"Just like the kids you went to high school with?"

I grimace. "Okay. Point taken."

We cross the street in silence, finally arriving at his front porch, where the *That's Good Crack!* sign hangs from the wooden railing. Over the years that the building has sat unoccupied, the gardens that used to bloom with daffodils in the spring and hydrangeas in the summer have wilted considerably. More browns than pinks and blues spring from the weedy beds and the grass could use a good mow. Half hidden among the sad shrubs is a scraggly, white goat munching at the weeds.

"Is that… what I think it is?"

"Winston!" I walk right up to the ruminant and scold our de facto town mascot for trespassing.

"Winston?" Brian looks at me incredulously. "Did you just call him Winston?"

"Yeah, he's the Mayor. I wonder if his dad's around…"

I sweep the block for any signs of the grumpy mountain man out and about on a late lunch break, but I don't see him anywhere. Then I turn back to the goat. "Winston, where's your Hot Daddy? Did he let you out of your pen again?"

"Okay, you're going to need to explain this to me."

I lift my head, uncertain of what exactly Brian needs explained. Winston *baas*. "Um… we have a town goat named Winston? He's the mayor, and he's eating your grass."

"Yeah, I got that!" He lifts his arms in frustration, then shakes his head as if he can't actually believe what he's saying. "Who the heck is his 'Hot Daddy'?"

"No one really knows his name, actually." I give Winston a pet, and shrug my shoulders. "He's harmless. I'm sure he'll move on soon enough.

"The goat, or his–" Brian shakes his head and rummages in his pockets for his keys. "Nevermind." As he walks up the porch stairs and unlocks the door, giving Winston a wide clearance, he mumbles something about Tuft Swallow and its ridiculous inhabitants. "Go on in. Just give me a second to wipe down the table."

A wall seems to have been erected between us in the few feet between the sidewalk and the threshold, but I have a feeling it has little to do with Winston or our earlier conversation. Just like how his hands had felt warmly neutral when he'd adjusted my knee in Dr. Cratchet's office this morning, Brian's demeanor has completely shifted. Instead of his joking or more pensive attitude, he now has an air of polite courtesy. The laughing, smiling, and–*dare I say flirty?*--man who had walked me down Oak Street was gone. In his place is a stoic professional.

He closes the door behind me as I follow him inside and passes through an archway to the right, through which I can see a drop table and a yoga ball, along with a few bookshelves piled with things I recall seeing back at my physical therapist's office: resistance bands, spiked mats and balls for pain relief, and rolls of kinesiology tape. He grabs a tub of alcohol wipes from one of the shelves and wipes down the facerest of the drop table before covering it over with a u-shaped pillowcase that he pulls from a tidy pile of folded linens in the corner. Then he turns around to face me and plops down onto the yoga ball like a chair.

"Would you walk for me, please?"

"Huh?" I blink. "Don't you want me to lie down on the table?"

"Nope."

He stares at me expectantly, and when I don't move, he makes a sweeping gesture with his hand, telling me to get on with it.

Warily, I walk through the archway, down the length of the small room and back as if it's a runway–only not nearly so graceful or sexy as that. I'm imminently aware of his unblinking eyes assessing me, which only increases my self-consciousness about the length of my dress and the gait of my walk. I try to remind myself of all the things I learned those years ago in physical therapy, to tuck my tailbone in and keep my toes pointed forward and rock heel-to-toe and—

"Relax. You don't need to be nervous. Nervous walkers are stiff walkers, and stiff walkers hurt themselves. Let yourself wiggle."

"Wiggle?" I snort, but try to relax my tailbone and shoulders. I feel my hips resume their natural sway, and I stop noticing where my toes are pointing so much.

"*Much* better. Women are meant to be a little wiggly."

"What do you mean by *that?*" I stop immediately, facing him and putting my hand on my hip. "That's sexist."

"No." He grins. "It's biology. Look at your posture right now."

I look down at myself, and see that I've posted my weight on one hip and thrust out the other as I scolded him. It is, I realize, a rather wiggly stance.

I straighten, evening out my pelvis and put both of my hands on my hips. "You made me do that on purpose."

"I swear I didn't. Now, turn around."

"Like, in a circle?"

"Yes. Slowly, please."

I twirl awkwardly, shifting my weight from one foot to the other on the foam mats that he's placed on the floor. My feet sink as I do so, exaggerating every movement of my hips and knees and making me feel silly. Injury or no, I know I'm more graceful than this. But between the squishy floor and feeling like I'm under a microscope I seem to have lost all my poise.

"Stay there."

I freeze, with my butt facing him. I hear the yoga ball squeak a little as he gets up and approaches behind me. For a long moment, neither he nor I move, and I wonder if he's maybe just so quiet that he was able to disappear without me knowing it.

"May I?" He says, and his mouth is so close that I can feel the warm air leave his lips and brush past the curve of my neck below my ear. I don't know what he's asking permission for, but my pulse begins to race, and suddenly it doesn't matter *what* he intends to do. I know I want it. I nod, and brace myself for him to shove his fingers into a pressure point again.

Instead, he just lightly places his hands on my hips, applying gentle pressure down on one side, and then the other. He moves the flat of his hand to the small of my back, crawling his knuckles up my vertebrae until he reaches my rib cage, then presses slightly on either side. "Does any of that hurt?"

"No," I breathe.

"Good. Relax." He brushes my shoulder as he says it, and I feel him step away as I exhale. "Face up on the table, please."

"Face…up?" Once again, any expectations I have of what a chiropractic appointment is supposed to be fly out the window. "You're not going to like. crack my back or press on my spine with my face in the pillow?"

His lips tilt in a half-smile, and that impeccable professionalism drops for a fraction of a second. His voice is husky when it leaves his lips. "Would you like me to push your face into the pillow?"

I blush, and that pesky panther that stirred earlier in my stomach lifts its head again. He laughs.

"Not today, Kodi. We're just going to focus on your knee for now. You've definitely been favoring it for a few years, huh?"

"Uh, yeah. Can you tell?" I lower myself onto the drop table and lay face-up, like he said. My skirt flutters around my thighs, and I curse myself for not wearing cropped pants and a button-down like I do every other day for work. *Why did tomorrow have to be laundry day?*

Despite his little joke about shoving my face into the table (which, of course, I can't stop thinking about), Brian seems totally absorbed in his work, and unphased by the length of my skirt. Not that it's super short or anything. It hits mid-calf when I'm standing. But of course, it rides up when I'm seated or *lying prone on my back in front of Dr. Hottie.*

He reaches for my ankle and gives it a quarter turn to either side. I feel a slight twinge in my bad knee. "Oof."

"That hurts?"

"Just, uh, a little twinge. Not like, bad." I say eloquently. *Jesus, Kodi, he's a doctor. Would you act like this in front of your boss?*

Oh shit. My boss. I'm supposed to be gathering intel or something while I'm here for him. Or at least, trying to come up with some kind of lie that I can tell him in place of intel so he doesn't fire me for using my afternoon off to flirt with the competition.

"Okay. I was worried about that. This isn't going to be pleasant."

"What isn't going to-*ohJesusMaryJosephHChristthesonofFUUUU-UUCK!*" Every thought other than *GAH* leaves my head in a rush as Dr. Gosling pushes the pad of his thumb one inch from the spot he'd fingered earlier that morning. My whole torso heaves upright involuntarily as I reach to push the cause of the pain away as quickly as possible.

He doesn't move. "Relax. You're tensing."

"No *fuck* I'm tensing! That fucking hurts!"

"Lay back down. Five more seconds."

"Aaaaggghhhh..." Slowly, I curl my spine back onto the table, my leg twitching in Brian's hold the entire time. While not as blindingly painful as the first five seconds were, the last few stretch uncomfortably onward all the same. Then he releases the pressure, and I breathe a sigh of relief.

"Good. Now one more."

"Wha–"

Gooooooooood dammit!

I clench my mouth shut on another stream of curses as he presses his thumb into my thigh again, half an inch closer to my knee this time. I'm breathing heavily like I'm about to go into labor, every muscle clenching in reaction to the white-hot knife piercing my patella. Through the slits between my squinted eyelids, I see Brian lift his other hand and poke my nose.

"Boop," he says, a cheesy, toothy grin splitting his face as he once again releases his hold on my leg.

"Are you fucking *enjoying* this right now??"

"It's my favorite thing." He palpates the muscles around my knee gently, just stretching it with the palms of his hands this time instead of jabbing into my very soul with his thumb of death. It actually feels nice after the torture he just doled out. "Gotta get through the hurt before you can feel better."

"You're just taking out your anger towards the town on my poor leg," I argue. I glare at him, and he pushes the pad of his thumb into another spot on my thigh. I prepare myself to see stars again, but this particular nerve bundle doesn't seem to be as bad as the others. It doesn't feel *good,* but it's not sending me into a sailor-mouth spelling bee, either. "So that's all the crap that's stuck in my fascia, then?"

"Among other things. It's a place where your muscle's been tensing to compensate for the weakness of your ligament. You know how your mom used to tell you not to make ugly faces, cause they'll get stuck that way?"

I wince as he moves his thumb to another tender spot. "Yeah."

"Well, she wasn't right about your face, but your muscles will definitely get locked up if they tense for too long. And the best way to get them to let go is–" he moves his finger to a spot an inch above and to the right of my kneecap on the inside of my thigh and presses.

I let out a wordless cry.

"Oh yeah. They're angry alright." He wiggles his finger a little, and the way my muscles throb in response is strangely soothing after the white-hot stab of pain. Only red-hot.

He moves his fingers again and I place my hand on his shoulder.

"Can you just give me a minute?" I pant, and he scoots away on his yoga ball to give me space to breathe.

"Sure. I gotta move to the other side anyway."

"The other side?" I squeak. He nods cheerfully.

"Yep. That side may be the one with the injury, but this leg is the one that's been compensating for it all these years. Ready?"

I'm not.

CHAPTER 7
BRIAN

After half an hour of soft tissue work, Kodi is standing again and walking stiltedly around the office. Despite her careful steps, it's clear that her legs are in a totally different state than they were when she came in. Her bad knee is actually carrying weight now, and the leg isn't bowing inward like it was before. Her hips are sitting level over her ankles, and the arches of her feet appear to be distributing the weight of her steps into her toes instead of sinking towards the floor like they were earlier.

"How do you feel?"

"I think I feel good?" Her voice is slightly nervous, and she tugs down at her skirt a little, bending stiffly at the waist as she does like a child pretending to be a little teapot.

"You look like you're walking better."

"Yeah?" She takes a few more steps, this time more surely, with her hips swaying more naturally as she makes the small circuit around the office. "Alright. Cool!" Every step brings with it a little more confidence as her feet squish into the foam-padded floor of my office. I smile. "So, what do I owe you?"

"Right! Uh," I pause for a moment, looking around the office as I try to remember where I put my card reader for taking payments. Then I remember that I could just put her information into my payment and booking software, but my laptop isn't on the desk where it should be.

Shit. This is the kind of thing that the health center took care of for me when I worked there. Obviously, I knew that when I started working for myself I'd need to handle all the administrative duties in addition to seeing patients. So I *did* invest in the software I needed to make that happen.

Doesn't mean that I actually figured out how all of it works yet.

"Um. Can I send you an invoice later?" *Once I figure out how invoices work?*

"Sure. How much is it, just so I know what to budget for?"

"Uh. Well, it's a first appointment, so..." How much had I decided those should cost? First appointments are a lot more paperwork than follow-ups, so normally we would charge extra at the center for those, but I had floated around the idea of offering a discount to new patients to get them in the door while I was setting up the practice... "Um. Fifty?"

She tilts her head at me, looking amused. "You sure about that?"

Oh shit. I'm used to being in the city, where the prices are probably a lot higher than they are here. What even is the median income in Tuft Swallow? "Sorry. Forty?"

"I'm not trying to bargain with you," she says, laughing a little. "You're worth every penny. I'm just wondering why you sounded unsure. Don't you have a price list?"

"Well, yes, but..." I rub my neck. "What with the grand opening and all, I was going to have introductory rates." *I think. Yeah. That sounds like a good idea.*

"For a medical practice?" Kodi squints at me, making me shuffle uncomfortably. "You mean like, free consultations? Or actual discounts on adjustments? Just charge me full-price. I feel like you gave me my freebie this morning at the clinic."

"Oh. Sure, uh, just let me run and get my computer really

quick. I left it upstairs." I dart out of the office and up to my apartment as quickly as I can, sweating a little by the time I make it back to the room and plug in my ancient laptop into the wall outlet behind my skinny desk. It takes forever to boot up, and I can feel Kodi growing anxious behind me as I load up my software.

As soon as I open it, it informs me it needs to run updates before I can actually use it. I groan.

"I'm sorry, like I said, I wasn't expecting patients until next week, and I don't really have myself set up for taking payments just yet. Why don't we chalk this up to a free consultation and I'll just charge you normal price next week?"

"No."

I stare at her. Is she actually denying free medical care right now?

What kind of Reaganomics pipe dream is this?

"What?"

Kodi walks over and plops herself onto the yoga ball, scooting under the desk and helping herself to my booking software. "Ooooh, I see what the problem is. You use the self-hosted version of Medi-Cal? Oof, and on Windows 10? No wonder it's running updates. You need to get the cloud-based version. Otherwise you'll never be able to get into this when you need to."

"The what-hosted?" I watch in disbelief as Kodi somehow bypasses the update lightbox and accesses the settings and preferences of my booking software. Her hands fly across the keyboard, and suddenly she's so deep in menus I've lost track of where she is. "How are you doing that?"

"What, opening preferences?" She looks over her shoulder at me. "How long have you been using Medi-Cal?"

"Uh... I just got it a few weeks ago."

"And you still haven't figured out how to change your preferences?" Kodi stares at me expectantly. I shrug.

"Hey, I'm a doctor, not an IT guy. I just got this because it's what Google said I needed to book my own appointments and take credit cards."

"Oh boy." She lets out a breath. "So you've never actually used this before?"

I gulp. I do not like the look on her face. "...No?"

She closes her eyes and puts her hands on her lap. When she opens them, she's looking at me like she would a toddler to whom she's explaining how blocks work for the first time. "Okay. Let me give you some advice. You've got a small practice here, right? It's just you?"

"Uh, yeah." The easy feeling I'd had while working on Kodi during our appointment disappears as I feel her unveiling my weakness as a practitioner: the business part.

I went to chiropractic school. Not business school. I was taught how to chart out medical history and diagnoses, but no one explained to us how to organize a calendar or a payment schedule. I figured it couldn't be that hard (after all, people do it every day in small businesses all across America), but the look on Kodi's face has me feeling like that was a dumb assumption.

"This is not the version of the software that you want to be using. In fact, you could probably get away with the browser version for now. It's a monthly fee, but for now it'll be less expensive than the yearly service and hosting contract on this version. The web version is also way simpler, and I'm getting the impression that you aren't exactly tech-savvy." She uses finger quotes around 'tech-savvy'. I wince. "No offense."

"None taken," I say reflexively. Even if it does sting a little to have her call it out. But hey–when the lady's right, she's right.

She tilts her head again, only this time she has a different kind of gleam in her eye. The corner of her lip tilts up. "Would you be open to a trade?"

"A trade?" I wrinkle my nose. "What trade?"

"Look, I don't want to be rude, but this stuff has a bit of a learning curve. Because it's medicine, and not just a normal small business, there's a lot more reporting and archiving that you need to do in order to be compliant with HIPAA and the state. It can be really easy to lose track if you don't know what you're doing."

"And you don't think I know what I'm doing," I say. It isn't a question.

She pauses. "Not yet, no."

"I see."

"But *I,*" she continues, holding up a finger triumphantly, "just so happen to know what *I'm* doing. And know what you need to do."

"How?"

"How do I know?"

"Yeah." I cross my arms. "I'm not just going to let anybody into my business records and filing systems. How do I know that you know what you're doing?"

She gestures to the laptop and herself sitting at my desk. "You just let me open your booking software and adjust your preferences."

"Well..." I fidget uncomfortably, before snapping to my senses. Realizing that I've let her walk all over me, I straighten my back and narrow my eyes.

Then I scoop her up from her perch on the yoga ball and deposit her back onto the drop table. She lets out a little squeak when I lift her, and I can't help but smile a little at her surprise at my strength. *Not so high and mighty now, are you?* I rearrange my face back into a reprimanding look before I set her down and point my finger in her face. "Stop it."

She seems to have recovered from being swept off of the yoga ball except for a pink tinge coloring her cheekbones. "I have a degree in hospital administration, okay? We did a whole semester on private practice and the different booking systems."

She sits up straighter, and puts her hands back onto her hips.

I'm realizing she does that a lot.

She continues, "you need my help to get you set up before you start taking patients. I'm not comfortable letting you give me adjustments for free, but I *am* okay with bartering professional skills if we're both benefiting from it. And you, sir," she pokes my chest to emphasize *you*, "would seriously benefit."

"As would you," I point out.

"As would I." She nods in agreement and sticks out her hand. "So do we have a deal?"

I look into her warm brown eyes, taking in her serious expression. Her strong brows are drawn down in a confident stare, and her pink lips are resolute. Even in a graduating class full of smart women, I don't think I've ever met someone like Kodi Gander. She's straightforward, intelligent, and aggressive in a way I'm totally unaccustomed to. This is a woman who knows what she wants, and is prepared to advocate for herself to get it. It's kinda hot.

What? No! Not hot. Impressive.

I must still be off-kilter from the emotional roller coaster of the last few days. I grasp her hand, and we shake on it.

"You have yourself a deal."

CHAPTER 8
KODI

"I'm sorry. *What* did you promise Dr. Hottie?"

Phloot-phloot! I give two short blasts on the whistle, indicating that the next row of players run to the cones on the other side of the park and back.

"I'm going to help him get the business side of his practice up and running, and he's going to fix my knee. Get those knees up, Callie!"

"Sir, yes, sir!" Callie jokes, and she slaps her knees with her hands as she switches to a high-step on the way back to the lineup. I let out a small chuckle before blowing the whistle again.

Phloot-phloot!

The next row of cornhole players take off across the field, and Lily takes her place in the front of the row.

"So you're giving yourself guaranteed time with him every week?" She nudges my ribs. I toot the whistle in her ear in response, and smack her on the ass as she takes off. One of the guys, a young police officer by the name of Brad Pecker (yet *another* Pecker I have to worry about), elbows the guy next to him and they snicker to each other.

"Something funny, Brad?" I holler at him, and the pale, skinny cop visibly shrinks under my glare. The last thing I need is the next generation of cornholers spreading more rumors about me being a lesbian.

Again, not that there's anything wrong with being a lesbian. I'm just tired of people making fun of me for something that one, isn't something anyone should be made fun of for, and two, isn't fucking *true.*

Seriously. I have plenty of actual flaws that people could pick on me for. So how does it make sense that they instead choose to make up stories about me sleeping with my best friend? *As if anyone could believe* Lily *is anything other than straight.* I watch her as she purposely slows her running pace to a crawl so she can check out the ass of Nick, the former MMA fighter and *hopeless* cornhole player, carrying a cooler of Gatorade up the side of the field.

"Alright team, huddle up!" I call, and a few relieved sighs and groans reach my ears as everyone gathers around me in a circle. "First match of the season is this weekend against our old nemesis, Spitz Hollow. And remember what we say?"

"Spitters are quitters!" I hear them chant back at me. I grin.

We're a town full of punny perverts. So sue us.

"Tonight we're gonna drill knock-ins. I don't want us to leave any woodys on the table on Saturday, you hear me? It's a bag-in-the-hole or nothing. So as you can see, I've set up four sets, so all of you can double up against each other. Each set has two bags on each board, and your goal is to clear the board of bags: you're trying to knock your opponents' off, then get yours in, understand?"

"Yes, Jesus, Kodi we know how Cornhole works. We've literally won every championship for the past seventy years."

I glare at the boy who's giving me attitude. Logan Gilgax just turned twenty-one in May, making him barely eligible for the Tuft Swallow Beer League. He was the one sniggering with Officer Pecker earlier.

"Fifty-four, Logan. Or did you fail math in addition to English at TSCC?" I sneer at him. He hocks a loogie on the ground. *Gross.*

"The goal today isn't just to score cornholes. It's to practice navigating and moving the bags around the board. But if you're so high and mighty, why don't you demonstrate with me?"

"I get it, Kodi, you don't have to call me out." He rolls his eyes and jerks his thumb at me, as if to say *"Women,"* to the guys standing behind him. I cross my arms. Alright, he wants to play ball?

Let's play ball.

"No, I think we could all benefit from your obvious mastery and expertise, *Logan*." I smirk at him. "Grab a set. Let's show everyone what we're trying to do."

His eyes dart around his cadre of cronies, before he squares his shoulders and sneers at me. "Fine. You're on."

I grab two blue bags from the bucket by my feet and toss them to him. He catches one, fumbling the other as he tries to pin it against his chest, only for it to fall to the ground at his feet. I chuckle. *Oh, this oughta be good.*

We square off across from each other beside our plywood practice boards. I give him a mocking curtsey as I square up on the field. "Ladies first."

I step forward on my newly-adjusted knee, confident as it accepts my weight. I wind up my red beanbag and toss it in a soaring arc across the field of play. It lands right onto the board where it slides perfectly up the side of the hole, knocking the blue enemy bag I'd placed there out of the way and taking its place, its corner dangling right over the goal opening. Logan's confidence wavers for a fraction of a second, and I can see his Adam's apple bob all the way from across the field as he swallows nervously.

"Lucky shot," he grumbles. I grin.

"Show me what you got, kid."

He steps forward and chucks the bag straight at the board, where it smacks into the front edge and skips. It sails over the hole and back edge, then tumbles into the grass behind it. A few of the guys chuckle behind him, and I grab my last red bag and ready my tossing hand.

"And the sinker," I call, spinning in a little pirouette before planting my foot forward and sending my second bag sailing high into the air, landing squarely on the hanging corner of my previous bag and sinking them both into the hole. Just like I knew it would. "That's two cornholes! Your go."

Logan glares at me as he tries a higher throw like I did, winding up his arm like a major league pitcher, sending the blue bag so high that we all squint as we follow its ascent into the bright summer sunset. It arches in the air before starting its parabolic descent, crashing into my pre-placed red beanbag on the plywood next to me, knocking my third bag into the hole along with his blue one.

"Ha! I got two, too!"

"No. You canceled out your own point. Looks like you need to practice more, buddy. Otherwise you're gonna leave us all with bluebags."

"Ha! Logan's got bluebags," Brad shouts as if it's the funniest thing anyone's ever said. I resist the urge to roll my eyes.

"Partner up, everybody! We're doing this until everybody's sunk ten of their bags in a row! If you knock in an enemy bag, count restarts at zero!"

"Oh come on, Kodi, we've already been out here for an hour. That could take another two!"

"Yeah, happy hour ends in twenty minutes!"

A few more dissenting grumbles sound around me, and I shrug.

"Well then, I guess you better start tossing, team." I shoot them all a grin and replace the bags Logan and I displaced during our demonstration. "On your marks, get set–" *Phloot-phloot!*

"How are you not sore after that? I thought you'd be in just as much pain as the rest of us."

Lily is wincing above her Dirty Shirley as she rubs her shoulder. Callie gives her a pitying glance for a moment, then chomps down on a french fry.

I sip my iced tea, trying to hold in my absolute glee. She's right: I *should* be in pain right now. Granted, I didn't do the running drills with the rest of the team since Brian had told me to take it easy after the appointment, but I was tossing with the rest of them for most of the night. Not to mention scurrying back and forth across the park to offer pointers and help people with their form.

"I don't know. Maybe I just have a new guardian angel looking out for me." I smile to myself, and Lily narrows her eyes.

"More like a guardian *chiropractor*."

"Oh? Did you go see the new doctor in town?" Callie leans forward. "Is it really true what they're saying about him in the *Pecker?* Poor guy."

I shake my head. "He's not gay. He's bi. But he didn't say much else."

"I didn't mean that, although it is awful that they felt the need to blast that out to the whole town before he even had a chance to get settled. I meant his boyfriend. Did he really break up with him as soon as he moved to town?"

A weight sinks in my stomach. In all the talk about him and Dr. Cratchet and the booking software and everything else going through my head today, I had totally forgotten about the actual content of that morning's *Nosy Pecker.* I take a glance around the bar, and inventory all the patrons. There are a fair number of cornholers, except for the few who went home to their families or have to get up early for work. But Brian is nowhere to be seen. I wonder if he's sitting at home by himself, lonely. Thinking about his ex.

That's no way to start a life in a new town.

"I-uh, didn't ask for the details."

Callie nods, sipping her Cosmo. "It's impolite to pry."

Lily snorts. "Some good *that* is in a town like this. It's pry or be pried around here." I'm about to point out that's not really a thing, but then she smacks her hands down on the table, shaking loose a fry from Callie's basket. "Oh my God. You said he's *bi.*"

"Yes."

"Well?" Lily's eyes are wide as she leans toward me expectantly. I lean back a little, slightly frightened of her crazed look.

"Uh… well, what?"

"Are you gonna hit that or what??" Lily squeals, and half the bar turns their heads to our small table. I laugh nervously, trying not to draw anymore attention to us.

Out of the side of my mouth I mumble, "Lily, that is not the point."

"Speak for yourself. Piping hot sex is *always* the point."

"Did I hear–"

"Oh my God, shut UP, Logan!" Lily doesn't even have to turn around to smack the kid across the arm when he inserts himself into the conversation. He gives a surprised "Oof!" and walks away as quickly as he'd arrived.

"You really should give the poor guy a call back, Lily," Callie says pityingly. "He's been trying to get your attention ever since practices started."

"Oh please, he's practically still in diapers. Not to mention he's friends with all the cops. Not sure if I'm eager to let such a whiny baby give me a pat-down." As they banter back and forth about Logan's obsession with my best friend, the town mechanic walks past us to get his usual evening beer. His broad shoulders brush against the back of Lily's chair as he squeezes by, and all conversation ceases for a moment. Lily sighs after his retreating form. "I tell you what though, I'd let *him* pat me down any day. Diaper or no."

"Hey!" I call to him, breaking the town protocol that Winston's Hot Daddy is to be admired from afar, but never spoken to. He stiffens, tilting his head only slightly towards me to indicate that he heard. "Winston was at the new chiropractor's office building earlier! Did you find him okay?"

The mechanic stares at me with his piercing blue eyes, and I freeze under his gaze. Then, he gives an almost imperceptible nod, before turning back to the bar and perching himself on his usual stool. He orders his beer, then digs around in his bag and pulls out a set of knitting needles attached to a scarf-in-progress.

I let out a breath in a *whoosh,* grateful that the old goat is okay, and Lily and Callie stare at me.

"You're fearless, you know that?" Callie breaks the silence. I blink.

"What do you mean?"

"The whole town is intimidated by that man, but you call him out with zero hesitation. Between that, working for Dr. Cratchet, and the way you boss everyone around at practice, it's just kind of amazing to watch. You're unstoppable, Kodi."

"Total Gryffindor." Lily agrees.

"Oh please," I roll my eyes. "I have my fears just the same as everybody else." *And someday, I will conquer them.*

I rub my knee under the table, once again amazed at how much it doesn't seem to be bothering me for once. After years of thinking that I'd never be able to live up to my childhood dreams, I've actually got reason to hope again.

"Fears like losing half of the cornhole team because they're fed up with training for the Olympics?"

I scowl at Lily. She sees my glare, and raises me an eyebrow. "What? You're going overboard. I'm telling you because I love you, Kodi, but I haven't been this sore since..." she pauses for a moment, thinking. "Honestly, I don't think I've *ever* been this sore. I need another drink."

She downs the rest of her Dirty Shirley and gets up to head to the bar, letting her hips brush past Winston's Hot Daddy as she passes.

"Do you think I'm going at it too hard?" I turn to Callie.

Her deer-in-the-headlights look worries me a little. "Um. I'm fine with it. I like the extra workout!" It doesn't go unnoticed that she didn't really give me an answer. She fiddles with her straw.

"But I think I might schedule myself an appointment with that new chiropractor, too. What's his address again?"

I fish his business card out of my purse and hand it to her. While she's copying his contact info into her phone, I go over the past few practices in my head. The muttering, the groaning, and the seemingly endless complaints whenever I announce the next drill.

Am I going at this team captain thing too hard?

"And it looks like Gander's out for the count at the bottom of the sixth! The score is 9-9 going into the final inning."

The memory surfaces out of nowhere, the announcer's voice as clear as if he were broadcasting in the bar right beside our table. I down the rest of my iced tea, feeling a twinge in the side of my leg for the first time since yesterday morning.

For the past six years, everyone's been convinced that I'm *so* fragile. That I'm no longer the champion I used to be. *Poor Kodi, losing everything at eighteen. Kodi Gander–could have been one of the greats.*

No. I'm not going too hard. I'm training us up to be the best dang Cornhole team in the county. We've got a title to defend, after all. And now that I'm on the mend, nothing's going to be able to stop me.

And if anyone's too weak to see it through…well. It's best they quit now before they *really* get hurt.

CHAPTER 9
BRIAN

Saturday Scrimmage Soured by Sore Sackers?

It's a hard day in Tuft Swallow for this year's cornhole team, as it looks as though four of the twenty teammates are out for the count for the first match of the year. Word on the tweet is, new team captain Kodi Gander has got herself a case of the try-hards, according to our sources who wished to remain anonymous in case she decides to take it out on them again at next week's practice.

Of course, we all remember that devastating States Championship game where our dear Kodi lost her shot at the title, her Division I scholarship, and the use of her leg in one fell swoop. Here's hoping that a taste of victory against our bitter rivals, Spitz Hollow, will be just the thing to drum up a little team spirit.

See you all at the Eagle View Football Stadium!

Happy Game Day,

The Nosy Pecker

As I wait for my breakfast sandwich at the bakery around the corner from my new place, I allow myself to peruse the local gossip rag. Yesterday was slightly more successful than my first day exploring the town. I managed to acquaint myself with the owner of the boxing gym and the yoga studio, even making plans to meet up for coffee to discuss free consults for their members.

I'd been nervous that everyone in town would be wary around me after Thursday's scathing article. But overall, the sentiment among Tuft Swallow's working class is surprisingly non-judgmental. If anything, both Nick and Caleb–the retired MMA fighter and yoga instructor, respectfully–seem more excited about having another doctor in town to send their injured clients to than worried about my sexuality.

Despite that, there's still an emptiness in my stomach that even my favorite breakfast foods can't seem to fix. Zeke's absence weighs heavy in the new place, and it's been pushing me outside to socialize more than I ever thought I'd be comfortable with. Especially in a town that seems so embroiled in stirring up the latest scandal. Today's paper didn't have a single word about me or my floundering love life, though. So maybe things are looking up.

Shame about Kodi, though. While she'd told me she played softball in high school, I had no idea she'd lost a scholarship due to her injury. That had to have been devastating. The woman has guts to keep competing after something like that.

At the various tables scattered about the bakery, Tuft Swallowers of all ages are reading their own *Pecker*s and yammering about the upcoming match. I notice even the elderly Tit Peepers are sporting colorful jerseys under their bright turquoise windbreakers. It seems like this kind of thing is a big deal in this town. And here I thought the welcome sign boasting their "Cornhole Champions since 1969" status was just some homophobic graffiti.

As I pick at my ham, egg, and cheese croissant and sip on my black coffee, I consider my plans for the day. As bad as my first impression of this place was, it would be a good idea to meet a few more of my neighbors on my own terms. Attempt to fill the Zeke-shaped void, make a friend or two. Maybe I should check out this cornhole game that everybody's so excited about.

WHEN I ARRIVE AT THE HIGH SCHOOL STADIUM AT TWO O'CLOCK FOR the game, it's packed. They've taken over the football field, with bleachers set up on either side of a rubber track and townspeople of all ages filling up the stands. Along the 30-, 40-, and 50-yard lines are pairs of plywood bean-bag toss sets like people would have at backyard cookouts, only these are much more ornate. They're high-gloss works of art emblazoned with what I assume are the team colors and logos of the opposing towns: Spitz Hollow and, of course, Tuft Swallow.

I feel like I've heard of Spitz Hollow from somewhere outside of the talk of the day's match, but I can't remember where. But when you look at a map, all the towns around here have bird names: Robin Springs, Eagle's Peak, Tuft Swallow...I'm sure I'm just getting them confused with each other.

Out on the field, I see a few familiar faces dressed in what I now recognize as the signature turquoise and orange of The Mighty Swallows . It's the same shade of turquoise as the Tit Peeper's windbreakers, and matches the game boards on the home-team side of the field. Both Nick and Caleb recognize me and give me a wave. I return a little two-finger salute, and then my eyes land on Kodi.

Like the others, she's toting a turquoise short-sleeved jersey with bright orange-and-white letters across the front, as well as a white silhouette of a swallow in flight above her breast. Her orange shorts are... quite a bit shorter than I would have expected for a family-friendly sporting event, honestly. All the women on the team are sporting bottoms that could pass for Hooters uniforms.

However, none of them pull them off quite like Kodi does.

That confident, determined personality that I glimpsed only briefly in our exchanges earlier in the week is out in top form. She's blasting on a whistle that she wears around her neck, looking more like a bonafide college sports coach than just a mere beer league captain. Her hair is pulled back into a glossy ponytail that shows off the highlights in her dirty blonde locks. Her bright eyes glisten with an almost manic energy that seems to have some of her teammates on edge.

I try to catch her eye and give her a thumbs-up for luck, but she's distracted by the rival team entering the field.

AC/DC's *Thunderstruck* starts to play from the tinny loudspeakers that sit above the press box, and I can't help but laugh. It's like something out of *Varsity Blues*: the Spitz Hollow players in their matching red-and-white jerseys and eye black smeared across their cheekbones marching onto the field to their own personal soundtrack. Although this sporting event has some unique additions.

Tuft Swallowers young and old are milling about the sidelines, high fiving over coolers and sharing tupperwares of jello salad. Children run in and around the legs of older fans, waving colorful flags and noisemakers, as their parents chat with each other and pass out beers. On the track in front of the 50-yard line, a group of young girls ranging from ages four to ten wave pom-poms and try in vain to follow the choreography of a woman dressed in a flamboyant afghan with long, brown pigtail braids.

Even the town goat–*Wilson? William?*–is tied up next to the recycling bins, dressed in a knitted turquoise-and-orange scarf and yarn baubles hanging from his curly horns. He's munching on discarded soda cans while an absolute lumberjack of a man I can only assume is his "Hot Daddy" scowls at him from a makeshift concession stand, where he's manning a grill lined with hamburger patties and veggie dogs. On one side of his station a Girl Scout troop is selling raffle tickets and boxes of cookies. On the other side, a table of old ladies with crochet hooks and knitting needles are handing out hats and scrunchies in the town colors and collecting names for their crafting club, the *Dirty Hookers*. Their banner *(Sign Up to Become a Hooker Today!)* is particularly eye-catching.

And that's about where I draw the line on getting to know my neighbors a little better. This little dose of hometown spirit is more than enough for me to handle. But as I turn to leave the stadium, something catches my eye on the field that makes my throat go dry.

No, not something. Some-*one.*

At that very moment, Zeke marches onto the field, and I know in an instant that I won't be going back home. Without my conscious direction or permission, my feet walk me past the Girl Scouts and Hookers and Winston's Hot Daddy over to the chain-link fence that separates the crowd from the players.

My only thought is that it's been almost a whole week since I've heard from him, and I've missed him so much in the last few days. Every night, I've returned to an empty apartment, eaten a microwaved Lean Cuisine alone, and curled up in a cold bed, wishing I could just scrounge up the courage to send him a text or call to hear his voice.

Before I'm even aware of it, I'm weaving my fingers through the holes of the chest-high chain link fence that is the only thing separating me from my ex, and I'm shouting his name.

"Zeke! Zeke! Over here!"

As he looks over, confusion, followed by embarrassment, flashes across his face, and my brain catches back up with my body. Humiliation floods my veins, and he gives a cheeky little wave before nodding to his teammates and laughing. The sound cuts right through the music and the chatter, hitting me like a punch in the gut.

Oh God. He's making fun of me.

I snatch my hands from the chain link as if it's burned me, stepping back from the edge of the track and accidentally bumping into an elderly couple in line for burgers, sporting matching turquoise windbreakers. I wince. A couple of Tit Peepers are the *last* people I want to be bumping into right now.

A pair of gnarled fingers taps my arm.

"Why, Dr. Gosling! What a pleasure to see you out and about in the community. Do you *toss bean,* as the kids say?"

The old woman's words bring me back to my last conversation with Zeke.

"There are an awful lot of local hotties that toss bean in the summer and, well. I don't have to drive an hour to hook up with them, now do I?"

Oh God. Oh my *God*. Zeke isn't in some weird-but-sexy British sports league for the summer. "Tossing bean" isn't a cheeky British euphemism for playing cricket or rugby or polo or something delightfully masculine yet homoerotic like that.

It's literally *bean* bag *toss*. Cornhole.

He plays *cornhole*.

He dumped me for a backyard picnic game made for drunks. So he would be free to hook up with gaggles of attractive tech bros and laugh at me in front of them.

"Dr. Gosling? Are you alright?"

I stumble forward, out of the old woman's grasp, shaking my arms out in an attempt to get my bearings again.

"Fine, yes–sorry, Mrs…?"

"Woodcock, dearie. We met just the other day, don't you remember? This is my husband, Harold. Honey, this is Brian Gosling, the new chiropractor."

"The one with the boyfriend?"

I feel heat rise to my cheeks and at the same time, bile rises in my throat.

"That's none of your business," I say through gritted teeth.

The old man is unperturbed, and surprisingly kind when he says, "Ah, don't sweat it, Brian. A young fella like you will find someone else in no time. We have no shortage of attractive young men who've moved to town, after all!"

I blink at the pair of them, wishing more than anything that I could disappear on the spot.

"Oh *hiiiiii,* Dr. Gosling! Kodi! Did you see? Dr. Gosling is here!" A voice that I just barely recognize as the flirty chirp of a redhead's from the Crowbar and Grill a few nights before calls from across the field. I look up at the same moment Kodi does, and we lock eyes. She tilts her head in confusion, and I look away, embarrassed.

Giving the redhead a wave of acknowledgement, Kodi jogs over to the patch of the fence where I'm standing, and I can't help myself from looking at her injured leg to see how it's holding up. I wouldn't have recommended she be jogging so soon after Thursday's intense adjustment, but she makes it over to the edge of the field without any apparent signs of distress. Then she goes up onto tip-toes and leans her elbows over the top of the four-foot barrier.

"Brian! What are you doing here?"

I'm far too conscious of the curious eyes of Mr. and Mrs. Woodcock following my every movement, and Zeke and the Spitz Hollow team stretching and pregaming within earshot. I can't escape now without it looking suspicious. I take a couple of steps back towards her and try to adopt a relaxed posture. It's harder than I want it to be.

"Oh, you know. Just checking out the society event of the season," I joke weakly.

"You read about it in the *Pecker*?" She gives me a knowing look.

My eyes dart to her knee again. "Yeah."

Her eyes narrow at me, and she pushes herself off the fence. "Oh, I see how it is. Now that you know my whole sob story, you're gonna be awkward around me, huh?"

"What? No!" I raise my voice without meaning to, and I glance around quickly to make sure I didn't garner any more unwelcome attention before lowering my volume to a hiss. "No, that's not why–I'm just–"

"Just staring at my leg like I'm about to collapse all over again?"

She puts her fists on her hips, and I stifle a chuckle at the defiant posture that I'm coming to recognize. *This woman is something else.*

"No." I sigh, leaning in closer to the fence. "I'm trying to avoid staring at my ex on the other side of the field." I glance over her shoulder and tilt my head ever so slightly at the lithe, sweaty form of Zeke, who's hacky-sacking a bean bag back and forth with a circle of painfully attractive teammates. *Okay, maybe cornhole is more sexy and homoerotic than I gave it credit for.* Kodi follows my gaze, and her eyes widen.

"*That's* your ex? Number 17?"

I grit my teeth. "Yep. In the flesh."

"Oof."

"Yeah," I cough out a humorless laugh. "Oof."

A contemplative look crosses her face for a moment, and then her lip curls in a Grinch-like smirk. "Well you know what you have to do now, right?"

She's got that gleam in her amber eyes again. The same one that she had when she suggested we barter her administrative skills for adjustments. I feel the muscles in my cheek tug upwards while I wonder what solution she could possibly be Macgyvering, and she flashes her teeth deviously.

"What's that?"

"You have to beat his ass in cornhole."

CHAPTER 10
KODI

The look on Brian's face when I suggest he show up his ex by wiping the field with his skinny ass is one of surprise and disbelief. And then he wheezes out a dry laugh. I guess not everyone was born with the same competitive spirit that I was.

I shrug at his disappointing response and cross my arms. *Damn. We could actually use a guy like him on the team.* Not one to back down from a fight, I lean into the fence a little, lowering my voice. "Trust me. Guys like that? They're never going to pay any attention to you unless you prove to them that you're worth their respect. And the best way to earn a guy's respect is by beating him at sports."

"Is that so?" His eyes, which were trained on his ex as he stretched his hamstrings, flicker to me. His lips quirk up in a smirk, and I can't tell if he's intrigued or amused. "Or are you just trying to get me to replace one of the Tuft Swallow players that quit the team this week?"

My cheeks heat. *Damn Nosy Pecker.* He laughs, and I splutter in response, "No! I know what I'm talking about, okay?"

"You do, huh?" His face is still alight with laughter, and I reach my arm over the fence to smack his shoulder. "Ow!"

"Serves you right!" I humph. "That's payback for Thursday."

"You mean when I fixed your leg?"

"I mean when you had me writhing on the table in agony!"

The curious faces of Mr. and Mrs. Woodcock peek out from the concession stand. *I may have said that a little too loud.* Brian's and my little spat has started to garner the attention of more than a handful of Tuft Swallowers, and even a few of the cornholers from Spitz Hollow are looking at us curiously.

Brian leans forward into the fence, lowering his voice as he angles his lips close to my ear.

"You didn't seem that upset about it after the fact." The timbre of his teasing voice makes my stomach flip-flop.

"Why you–"

"Hey, Bri-Bri! Long time no see!"

I look over my shoulder to see number 17, Zeke Chopra, trot over to our section of fence. When I turn back, Brian's gone pale.

"H-hey, Zeke! Yeah, well, you know. Busy with the new business and all." The easy smirk that he was sporting while he and I argued is long gone, and in its place is a nervous kind of hope—and it's absolutely heartbreaking to witness. His voice loses its low, sexy quality and instead sounds choked and tinny.

He's still got it bad for this jerk.

Zeke Chopra has a bit of a reputation around Tuft Swallow. Back when I was in high school, the rivalry between Tuft Swallow and Spitz Hollow in the county cornhole league was stiff, but good-natured. Who doesn't love a little competition between neighbors, right?

But a few years ago, one of those weird cryptocurrency startups opened up in our rival town, and ever since then, new recruits from all over the country and abroad started to play for the cornhole team. Rich, entitled tech bros that all think they're better than the old-school neighborly folks about town. And each year, that friendly rivalry we'd all known and loved got just a little bit meaner.

While we haven't been able to prove it yet, we all know that Zeke's one of the worst offenders for playing dirty. In his first season on the team, one of our boards collapsed during the championship, causing two of our sacks to slide off during the final round. Last year, we found bean leaks in half of our bags when we were cleaning up from the playoffs.

Spitz Hollow might be able to claim it's all circumstantial. But I have my eye on him this year. And seeing as I'm captain, you better believe I'm not going to be letting him get away with any of his unsavory cheating under *my* watch.

Seeing Brian's one-eighty at Zeke's appearance makes the hairs on the back of my neck stand up. I already don't trust this guy. And this year, he's sporting a jersey with inverted colors from the rest of his team, indicating that he's been made *captain*.

My rival.

Even if Brian and I weren't connected at all, I'd be inclined to advise him to stay away from him.

"I see you're not sporting the hometown colors. Glad to know the Swallower's *garish* taste hasn't rubbed off on you yet."

Brian laughs at the douchebag's insult, and a fire ignites in my belly.

Oh, hell *no.*

I get that maybe the two of them have a history, and the poor guy's still a bit smitten by Mr. Tall, Dark, and Douchey. But laughing at one of his digs at the home team? Within earshot of the unofficial ringleaders of the Tit Peepers?

I scan the crowd behind him to see if anyone heard Zeke's nasty comment, and I spot one or two skeptical looks. Brian barely survived the first couple *Peckers* about him when he moved to town. He might not be able to handle the kind of ire he'll receive if *The Nosy Pecker* gets wind of his divided loyalties.

And if he leaves town? I might never get my knee back into shape.

Desperate, I do the only thing I can think of that might be

interesting enough to the town rumor mill to get them off the scent trail of Brian and Zeke's dating history.

"Babe, I didn't know you and Zeke knew each other." The second I say the words, a little more loudly than I'd normally speak, I feel every single Tit Peeper's eyes laser-focus on me. Mrs. Dougherty even drops her knitting needles to grab her binoculars. Brian raises his head, confusion lining his handsome features. Before he can respond, I weave my fingers through the thick-gauge wire between us and stretch to land a kiss on his cheek. "How do you two know each other?"

Brian locks eyes with me, and I arrange my face into the most loving, happy-go-lucky smile I can muster. My gaze bores into his as I concentrate every brain cell on telegraphing my intentions to him. *The bleachers have eyes. Follow my lead.*

For an agonizing second, his face is a blank slate. I double-down, resting my palm on his–*oh shit, is he flexing right now?* My fingers squeeze appreciatively around his triceps, and for a moment I forget that this is just an act. I lean into his side over the fence and feel the warmth radiating off of him, before refocusing and forcing out an airy laugh. "I didn't realize you were so close with *the competition."*

Understanding lights in Brian's eyes, and he squares his shoulders, inadvertently bringing me closer to his side. As I gasp a little in surprise, I inhale his scent: that comforting blend of clean laundry, subtle-spicy deodorant, and a warm base note reminiscent of baking bread. Head spinning, I adjust my feet so I'm not leaning on him too heavily or awkwardly with the fence between us. Then I school my expression so that I'm looking expectantly at him.

"Oh! Yeah, uh, *babe.* Zeke and I…" He trails off for a moment, and I worry that he's going to ruin the improvisation. Zeke's eyes ping-pong between the two of us, gaze burning when it lands on my fingers grazing his muscles. On the field, Lily is watching us with hawk-like eyes, clutching at Callie's arm so hard I can see the indentations from her nails all the way from the sidelines. The rest of the team has also caught on that something interesting is happening, and have angled their warm-ups in a way that lets me know they're eavesdropping on their captain's conversation. I squeeze Brian's arm again, and he snaps his attention back to me.

He shrugs, the picture of apathy, and I mentally high-five him for his Oscar-worthy performance. "Eh, it isn't really anything you need to be concerned about."

And then he does the absolute last thing I ever would have expected.

He pulls back the arm I've been hanging onto, which has me turning into him, until my chest is pressing into his over the top of the fence. Then he sweeps his arms under my shoulders and lifts me onto my tip-toes, bringing my lips up to his in a dizzying, breathtaking kiss.

In that moment, his scent, which had only been a pleasant backing track to my senses, overwhelms me. I breathe him in as his soft, warm lips slant against mine, moving and interlocking in a dance that has me mesmerized. *What the–?*

I hear myself moan softly against him, and feel his arms tighten around me as his body reacts to the sound. Behind us, somebody whistles.

He breaks us apart then, and I blink until the world comes back into focus. When it does, the first thing I see is Brian's crystal eyes, wide in what I assume is a mirror version of my own expression.

Not sure why he seems so surprised when *he* was the one who kissed *me.*

"For good luck," he breathes, and then sets me back down onto my (now unsteady) legs. Then, more loudly, he repeats, "Good luck, babe!"

I try to say *thanks* back to him, but there's blood rushing in my ears, and I'm unable to hear whether or not I actually managed to form a coherent word. I take one step back, and then another, and he beams at me with smiling eyes so blue, they put the cloudless summer sky above us to shame.

As the starting horn blares from the loudspeakers, I snap out of my… whatever it is I'm feeling, and gear up to destroy Zeke Chopra right in the bags.

I smile back at Brian, and his eyes sparkle with something resembling mischief as he calls after me.

"Break a leg!"

CHAPTER 11
BRIAN

As I walk uncomfortably towards the bleachers to take a seat and watch the match, I can feel every rheumy eye of Tuft Swallow's geriatric population on me.

Not exactly the best circumstances in which to hide a chubby.

I'm still shaking from my body's reaction to Kodi's and my fake kiss. Or, what I had intended to be a fake kiss. I may have gotten a little carried away when she moaned into my mouth. *I guess I'll add "impressive actress" to the growing list of that woman's surprise skills.*

Do I find the receptionist attractive? Of course. I have eyes, after all. Even a man who was 100% gay could admit that Kodi Gander is a beautiful woman.

Between her wavy, dirty-blonde hair with natural gold highlights, her toned body, and her strong brows, innocent freckles, and dark pink lips— lips that I now know are also incredibly soft…

Fuck, Gosling, you better find a place to sit down STAT.

I park myself in the row immediately to my right, which thankfully has an open spot right next to the aisle. I'm not prepared to scooch myself past a row of bleachers full of families with a noticeable bulge behind my zipper.

But *fuck.* Who would have thought I'd react so strongly to something as silly as a pretend kiss to make my boyfriend jealous?

Ex. Ex-boyfriend.

Eyes shift away from me as I take my seat and the game begins. I'd been so caught up in seeing Zeke again, I'd lost sight of how dangerous it would be for me and my business if the townspeople found out I'd dated public enemy number one. My head is swimming with Kodi's quick thinking. Not to mention the fact that she would take it upon herself to try to save me from the incredibly awkward situation of seeing my ex play for the rival cornhole team. Her solution is mind-boggling. And nerve-wracking.

With one sentence and a kiss on the cheek, she probably has that *Nosy Pecker* so turned around in trying to keep up with my cyclone of a love life—*or what they think is my love life*—that they may not even write about it next week.

She straight-up Bonnie Raitt'd the Tit Peepers. People are talking? Let's give them something to talk about.

I need to talk to *her* about it. There's no way we can keep up the act of the two of us being in a relationship until I get settled in Tuft Swallow. How long exactly is she planning to keep up the ruse? Through cornhole season? Through the summer?

Suddenly, the music over the loudspeakers cuts off, and a voice broadcasts over the field. To my surprise, it sounds as though a professional radio DJ is announcing the game, his voice eerily similar to the color commentator that calls for the Sox games I used to listen to on the ride to work. As he announces the players on all the teams, the respective fans in the bleachers roar their appreciation, with a few rounds of cheers going on a little longer than others. It becomes apparent there are hometown favorites on either side. To my surprise, Zeke garners the loudest applause from the visitor's side, but I try to limit my reaction. I can still feel a fair amount of attention on me from Mr. and Mrs. Woodcock, and I'm not eager to give them any more honest fodder for tomorrow's *Pecker.*

I clap along when the announcer calls the names of the few people I've met in the week since I arrived into town, including Caleb, Nick, and Lily, who's been gawking at her best friend ever since she stumbled back onto the field. When he calls out Kodi's name, I actually let out a vocal cheer.

Until I understand her intentions with this whole fake relationship, I suppose I need to play along, right?

I'm not the only one to change my response for Kodi's name, though. A small but enthusiastic chorus of *boo*s rings out from underneath the home bleachers.

What's that about?

On the field, Kodi, who has been running from player to player, whispering into ears and clapping shoulders, freezes for a moment: her furrowed forehead tilting toward the bleachers. I'm not sure if she can see me, but I give her a thumbs up.

The moment passes as quickly as it came, though, and the announcer barrels on to explain the rules. As I've never played cornhole outside of a couple of Fourth of July barbeques over the years, I pay attention.

"For today's match between the Mighty Swallows and Spitz Hollow, we'll be playing doubles as laid out by the American Cornhole Association. Any player who steps beyond the foul line at the opponent's side of the league-regulation boards gets two warnings before they earn their team a penalty. Three penalties results in an automatic forfeit of the match–so make sure to stay in your lanes, baggers!"

Interesting. Of course, I know that there has to be regulations around distance and such with any game or sport, but I wasn't aware that Cornhole had an official association tied to it. Are there people in other towns this serious about yard games?

"For today's match, hanging chads are only worth one point."

"Aw, come on!" One of the Spitz Hollow players shouts. "Two-point chads!"

Immediately, the visitor's side bleachers erupt in a rhythmic chant of "Two-point chads! Two-point chads!" Two middle-aged men dressed in black and white striped polos and black shorts, who I assume to be referees, march onto the field and mutter to each other. One of them waves to the press box from center field, and I straighten in surprise as the distinctive crackle of a headset mic buzzes through the loudspeakers over the noise of the crowd.

"League regulations. One-point woodies, one-point chads, three point cornholes."

They have mics for the referees. Like in the NFL.

Dazed, I look around me at the rest of the townspeople, checking to see if anyone else is as surprised by this extravagance as I am. But I'm met with un-ironic rapt attention and concern at the unruly behavior of the opposing team and cheering section. A few parents even tsk and shake their heads.

The commotion eventually dies down, and the announcer continues explaining the rules, the most important of which is that each pair of teams are to play to a score of 21, which is to be kept by the referees. Three teams from each town face off at once, and the in-progress scores are to be kept by the refs on their respective sides of the field.

For this match, there will be three rounds of six total games, with a final tiebreaker played between the two team captains in a singles round, if needed.

Four teams square off at the 40- and 50-yard lines, the air horn sounds, and the games begin.

CHAPTER 12
KODI

Lily is at my side the second the first round is underway.

"What the hell was that? Do you have something you want to tell me about Dr. Hottie?"

I'm not about to let my hormones distract me. There's only one thing that demands my focus in this moment, and it's filled with beans. "Not now, Lily, the game's started!"

Within minutes of the air horn sounding, yellow flags are already on the field announcing fouls from Spitz Hollow. Lily's sputtering at me, but I don't have the time or the attention to spare for her right now. There will be plenty of opportunity to catch her up on the gossip after we get through this match.

The Spitz Hollow boys are already out for blood on the court. I grit my teeth as all the bros on the red-and-white team clink their IPAs with each other and do shotguns while their half-drunk teammates toss at the 40-yard lines.

As I scan the field to observe my own teammates, I have to admit that I'm pleased with the progress they've made. Delilah's aim has been unreliable since she started tossing for us at the beginning of the season, but she's already bagged two woodies so far this round. Her partner, Jonah, has even managed to sink a cornhole since the beginning of the match, too. They've proven to be a decent addition to the starting lineup.

Geneva, our youngest player, is acting as our switch for this match. And even though she isn't the sharpest crayon in the box, she makes up for it in enthusiasm. She's paired up with Brad because his usual partner, Logan, never showed today. Part of me wonders if he's the source that the *Pecker* mentioned in their article this morning, and if he's the reason for the chorus of "boo's" I heard when the announcer called my name earlier.

It's fine. They're already up 6-4 against their pair of Spitzers, who seem to have pregamed a little too hard before toss-off. They've already got two fouls between them on the scoreboard.

Spitz Hollow's unruliness is nothing new, of course, but as I observe the matches, I can't help but feel like there's more animosity in the air than usual. It's then that I notice Zeke is also pacing back and forth between the courts, and he's shouting out the occasional neg to my players. I glare at him, and as if he can sense it, he looks up and meets my eyes from across the field.

He licks his lips, then gives me a sneer.

Alright, douchebag, I see how it is. While I'd love to pummel these corn nuts into the ground with a 6-0 shutout, I find myself itching for a chance to show this guy just how much better than him I really am.

At cornhole, that is. Better at cornhole.

My lips tingle, and I break eye contact with the rival captain. Once again, that weird flip-flopping sensation I felt in my stomach earlier is back, and I convince myself that I'm just feeling the first-match-of-the-season nerves.

Five minutes later, Geneva and Brad have won their match against Tweedledrunk and Tweedledrunker, and the scoreboard flashes 1-0 for the home team. I pump my fist in the air, jogging over to the two players to give them a pat on the back. Just after I do, the ref blows his whistle on the other side of the field, and calls Jonah and Delilah's match for Spitz Hollow, in a devastating

22-20 loss when the other team knocked in a hanging chad with a spectacular air-bag.

Fuck. 1-1.

Lily and Callie step up to their boards, along with Mr. Landon and Ginger. The waitress has got her turquoise jersey tied in a knot just under her bra, and her shorts (which were already pretty short to begin with) rolled down at the waist so low that everyone can see her blinding white G-string poking out against her spray tan. The three teams face off at the courts set up around the 30-yard lines, and a few of the Spitz Hollow guys whistle. A couple volunteers run on the field to reset the center boards.

We get our first foul during round two, when Ginger and her partner topple over the line. She got distracted, wagging her ass at a couple of Spitz Hollow guys so vigorously that she tripped over Mr. Landon's feet and landed right on top of the poor guy. He stumbles a bit in his next throw as his gaze wanders to his teammate, and I race over there to remind him to play with the head on his shoulders, not the one in his pants.

He blushes. Ginger rolls her eyes at me, but I'm not about to feel bad for stepping in. She's free to flirt and shake what her mama gave her as much as she wants *off* of the field, but she's not about to cost us the match because she wants to show off her bits. There are children watching, for Pete's sake.

The three matches are tight. Unfortunately, Lily is distracted and she misses knocking in a few easy hanging chads at the end of her round, forking over what should have been an easy win. They end up beating us squarely for the round, sending the overall score tumbling to 1-3, visitors.

As our best players face off on the reset 40-yard line, I start biting my nails. A bad habit of mine. D'Shawn and Piper should easily dominate this round, but Tammy and Finn haven't been playing together long enough for me to be able to predict how they'll do in a real game.

I shift my weight. I'm feeling my leg start to ache a bit from standing on the hard turf for too long, and I start to pace at the sideline to keep myself occupied. For the first time since they announced me over the loudspeakers, I turn to face the crowd.

As if they were drawn there by a magnet, my eyes find Brian's, and the nerves in my stomach kick into overdrive. The flip-flops are back, and the urge to bite my nails disappears along with the dull throbbing in my knee. A shy smile lights across his lips, and he gives me a little wave and a thumbs-up, before mouthing something to me I can't quite catch.

"What?" I mouth back.

He moves his lips again, but I still can't make out the words. I put my hands palms-up to my sides and shrug, as if to say *sorry, I can't understand you,* and to my surprise, he cups his hands around his mouth and shouts.

"You got this, Kodi!"

My heart stutters in my chest, and I know that heads are turning in his direction. Is this part of the act? Or did he know I was getting nervous?

I catch my breath, and both refs blow their whistles. While I was distracted, both of our teams won the third round, bringing the total score to a dead heat.

Three-to-three. A tiebreaker to win the match.

Brian and I lock eyes again, and to my utter surprise, he starts to chant.

"Ko-di, Ko-di, Ko-di!"

The rest of the home crowd joins in, and my stomach leaps into my throat. My heart is pounding against my ribcage, and a swarm of butterflies erupts in the space below my diaphragm. Lily and Callie run up to me, hard seltzers in their hands, to pat me on the back and join in the cheers. Lily hands me a seltzer, too, and suddenly the whole team is surrounding me. Brad is shouting for us all to do a group chug as we go into sudden death.

"Ko-di! Ko-di! Ko-di!"

I grab the proffered can, crack it open, and thrust it into the sky. "Let's GOOOOO!"

The rest of the team raises their cans (except for Geneva, who raises her Gatorade) and we let out our barbaric yawps, stomping our feet. We all toss our heads back, down our drinks, and slam-dunk the cans into the giant recycling bin that one of the community volunteers stole from Winston. Then the team joins in on the crowd's chant as they surround me, hyping up for the singles showdown.

My ears ring with the cheers, and the field around me blurs until I can almost imagine that I'm back on the pitcher's mound, dominating the diamond, throwing out after out as the stadium goes wild.

When I blink my vision clear and head to the 50-yard line for the tie-breaker match, feeling the buzz of the alcohol and the crowd, I raise my chin to face down my opponent.

The horn blares, and I ready my bag to throw.

CHAPTER 13
BRIAN

One thing you have to know about Tuft Swallow: this town goes *hard* for cornhole.

I'm still chanting along with fans and neighbors lining every row of bleachers, and it's almost like I'm back in high school at the Homecoming football game. But even back then, I never experienced the thrill of an entire community of fans single-mindedly cheering on their star player for a bottom-of-the-ninth tiebreaking match-up.

It's electric. Beside me, the dad of a family of five reaches into the cooler at his feet and hands out bottled waters to his children. Then he nudges me and holds up a beer.

"One for the team?" he shouts, and I can only barely hear him over the roar of the crowd.

"Yeah, thanks," I shout back, and we cheer along with his wife as Kodi and Zeke square off at the 50-yard line.

Oh fuck.

Despite all my outward enthusiasm for Kodi, when I see Zeke step onto the field beside the turquoise and orange board with that cocky smirk on his face that I know all too well, my guts twist. I take in his stance, his body, the way the sunlight flashes a halo of highlights against his soft, black hair, and a singular thought fills my brain.

You're rooting for the wrong team.

The euphoric high that's been building since Kodi's and my kiss comes crashing down all at once. Suddenly, I don't even recognize myself. Who is this man, screaming his head off in a high school football stadium and drinking beer next to a couple of strangers with three small children? What am I turning into?

Is this my life now? Rooting for some former high school softball player I barely even know to out-perform the man I love at a community cornhole game? For what purpose? To keep some gossip rag from airing out my dirty laundry? To get revenge? To save face?

It's like someone came up behind me and poured a cooler full of ice water down my back. I'm frozen by how bizarre it all feels, like I've stepped into some kind of alternate 1950s universe where neighbors actually care about each other and nothing matters more than beating the town rivals.

Kodi's a nice girl and all, but do I really want her to win against *my* Zeke? Do I want to see him run off to his teammates for comfort, watch him spiral further and further away from me and what our relationship could be?

I hold my breath as I stare at the gorgeous man who, only a few short days ago, was important enough to warrant me leaving my life in the city to take the next step together. The same man who then stomped on my heart along with whatever plans I had for us. He's tossing his bright-red beanbag up in the air and catching it repeatedly, an easy grin teasing that sexy dimple in the middle of his clean-shaven cheek, and my chest aches to see it.

I still want him. I want him so badly.

And I can't have him.

I have to get out of here. I don't care that I should stay to keep up this ridiculous ruse that Kodi started, to show Zeke that I can move on, just like him. To playact at that aloof carelessness that he seems to value so highly. To convince this town that I'm not still pining after their biggest rival.

I'm not a liar. I've never been one to deceive or keep secrets. I wear my heart on my sleeve; I always have.

That's why it hurts so much that my affection meant so little to him. When it had meant so, *so* much to me. It still does.

The noise, the crowd, the tension in the air… it's suffocating. I can't stay here a second longer.

I rise from my seat, beer can still clutched in my hand, and push my way through the cheering crowd down to the space between the bleachers and the sidelines. But as I reach a break in the bodies milling around me, I hear someone calling my name.

"Brian! *Brian!*"

It's Lily, Kodi's curvy redhead friend, along with another woman with pink hair and tattoos–her teammate in the second round. I shake my head, avoiding eye contact. My heart is broken, my introverted soul exhausted, and my capacity for people today completely spent. I need to get off this roller coaster, and fast.

A hand clasps around my upper arm, and I wince when I turn around to see that she's caught up with me anyway. "Where are you going?"

"I need to leave," I shout back to her, too drained to come up with an excuse. "I can't do this anymore."

"Look here, bucko." Her fingers dig into the skin under my t-shirt, pinching a little. I turn back around to face her, surprised by the venom in her voice. Pink Hair's eyes widen with mine when she hears Lily's brazen tone. "I don't know what's going on between you and Kodi, or you and number 17, but whatever it is that's got your knickers in a twist needs to take a backseat. Your girl *needs* you."

"*My* girl?" I yank my arm out of her grasp, turning to face her completely as I lean over the fence and into her face. I have to shout to hear myself over the raucous crowd. "Are you kidding me? Kodi doesn't need me. She's got this whole town cheering her name. She's in her element right now. And I'm–" my chest squeezes as I gesture to the field and take in Zeke bagging a cornhole and the crowd erupting into a roaring swell of cheers and boos, "I'm very much not, okay?"

"Dr. Gosling, wait," Pink Hair calls out, and the imploring look in her eyes makes me hesitate. "You don't understand. This is Kodi's first big match like this since her injury. I know that she seems, like, unstoppable all the time, but this is a big day for her, okay? Please. Don't leave her. Not now."

"What makes you think I'm so important to her?" I throw my hands up in the air, getting really annoyed at these people's insistence that I stay and watch my ex rub his physical prowess in my face for a moment longer. *Kodi and I hardly even know each other.* These women are Kodi's best friends; do they actually believe for a second that there's something going on between us? When we only met three days ago?

"She gave you her first real kiss, for starters."

What now?

All the blood rushes from my head as I stare at the redhead in disbelief.

She can't be serious. No way.

Did I just steal some poor woman's first kiss? And a patient's, at that??

She's not some teenager. This is a woman in her twenties. I can't possibly…

Shit, shit, *shit.* I've really stepped in it this time. I'm pretty sure I've broken about a thousand and a half rules, spoken *and* unspoken, with this one.

Lily crosses her arms. "Yeah, doc. So you better stick around to make sure you either give my girl a victory smooch or a shoulder to cry on, because I'm sure as heck not gonna be the one to break the news that her boyfriend ran away during her moment of glory."

Fuck.

I look to the field, just in time to see Kodi toss a perfect throw. Her bag arcs in a glorious sweep across the 27-foot regulation court and knocks two hanging chads clinging to the edge of the plywood circle right into the goal.

The refs blow their whistles, and the hometown side of the stadium erupts in a cacophony that makes my eardrums ring. Barely audible against the roar, the ref's voice crackles over the loudspeakers:

"An amazing *three* cornholes, nine points to number 12: Kodi Gander! Mighty Swallows win the round and the match!"

"Come on!" Lily yells at me, and tugs my arm until I'm practically toppling over the fence. Pink Hair lends me a hand and they forcibly pull me over the barrier. I lose track of Zeke in the tumble of limbs and faces.

Somehow I land on my feet, and they tug me to the team huddle around Kodi, where she's got her hands lifted in a victory stance as a couple of teammates spray her with beer. She squints against the spray, a wide, open-mouthed smile splitting her face as she squeals for the players to stop drowning her. When she's safe to open her eyes, the sparkling brown orbs find me in the huddle, and the euphoria on her face has my lungs pushing all the breath from my body.

Her clothes are soaked, ponytail dripping with amber liquid, and her cheeks are dotted with splotches of red between her freckles.

She's *radiant*.

My brain short-circuits, and my legs take over. The next moment I'm at her side, lifting her into the air and spinning her around like a real boyfriend would. She arches her back and swings her arms into the air as we pirouette together, before I come to a stop and she slowly slides down my chest, wet jersey rippling up between us and revealing her smooth, white skin beneath my fingers. Her lips are only a breath away from mine.

In a fraction of a second that lasts an eternity, her brows lift in a question as our gazes lock.

I'm not sure if it's the adrenaline or the exhaustion, or even the energy of the crowd, but my awareness tunnels in around us until all I can take in is Kodi and me.

Her sparkling gold-flecked eyes, flushed cheeks. The damp wisps of dirty blonde hair framing her heart-shaped face. My fingers splay across the exposed skin at her waist, and her lips open on a breath. I take them in mine, teasing at that space between us with my tongue until she lets me in. And I give her the victory kiss that she deserves.

That every girlfriend–fake or not–*deserves* from her boyfriend for her first kiss.

Or her second, at least.

We stay locked in each other's arms for a second, two, three—until my heart restarts and I release her gently back to the ground. She blinks rapidly as we separate, and Lily, Pink Hair, and the rest of the team swarm her in celebration.

I back away, allowing the team a chance to maul their victorious captain. Then I look over to the visitor's side of the field.

Zeke is standing stock-still, beanbag still in his hand, taking me in with an unreadable expression on his face. When I catch him staring, his lip curls in his signature cocky grin, but it doesn't reach his pitch-black eyes.

He tosses the bag high above his head, and before it can reach its full descent, snatches it from the air. Then he waggles his eyebrows at me, gives me a wink, and turns around to join back up with his team of losers.

The butterflies that always flutter in my stomach when that man winks at me go at it in full force, and I swallow around the sudden lump that forms in my throat.

And then I return to the kettle of Mighty Swallows to fulfill my role as the captain's fake boyfriend, exhausted.

CHAPTER 14
KODI

I'm gonna be honest, I don't remember much about what happened after the game. I *do* remember Lily leading the charge of the entire team hoisting me on their shoulders and the two rounds of complimentary tequila shots at the Crowbar for the reigning champions. I remember the subsequent margarita that I ordered after that, as well as the first couple of nachos I snatched from the giant table-long plate that Callie ordered us.

What I don't remember is the two rounds of margaritas after that, the supposed impromptu karaoke competition, or the fact that Lily and Callie had to apparently carry me back to my apartment sometime early in the morning. *Ugh. I need a bacon sandwich and a coffee, stat.*

My phone buzzes on the nightstand beside me; thankfully I remembered to plug it in before I crashed into bed. A quick glance shows me it's Mom–*again*–but I'm too hungover to even think about texting her back right now.

As I stumble out of bed, head pounding, and make my way to my bathroom with heavy footfalls, I feel every one of those drinks I don't remember.

I flush and splash my face with water, pull my sticky hair into a scrunchy at the base of my neck, and stumble back into the hallway of my one-bedroom apartment. It only takes a few steps to make it to the open space that serves as my living room, kitchenette, and breakfast nook.

That's when I see large feet hanging off the arm of the couch directly in front of me.

"The fuck!?"

I'm not exactly eloquent when I have a hangover.

"What? Who's there?" A shirtless man shoots up from his reclined position on my couch, before immediately regretting it. He rubs his lower back and groans, shaking his head. "How're you feeling, Kodi?"

"What the fuck are you doing in my apartment? What–did you–?"

And then I remember more of what happened after the game yesterday. And before. The kiss. Both of them. Lily's painful matchmaking all throughout the night. And all the curious glances from the team and the bartenders and the crowd and...

And Zeke Chopra.

Brian spins to put his feet on the floor, then walks over to me and puts a large, warm hand on my shoulder. I avert my eyes from his bare chest. He smells like he did that first time we met, only with a greater emphasis on the warm bakery smell that must just be *him*. It's so weirdly comforting. And not at all what I'm used to boys smelling like.

"Where do you keep your coffee? I'll make us a pot. We need to talk."

"I STILL DON'T UNDERSTAND WHAT YOU'RE DOING HERE. WE DIDN'T–um," I lift my arms hesitantly and make a weak, lewd imitation of intercourse with my thumbs and pointer fingers. "Did we?"

Brian looks at me slack-jawed for a moment before he chuckles. "No. I don't do–" he imitates my gesture– "with anyone without explicit consent. And you were a little... beyond consenting last night."

"Oh *God,"* I moan, collapsing on a stool at the kitchen island. "What did I do?"

"After your fourth margarita? Basically pass out," he answers, handing me a mug of coffee, and then cracks two eggs into a frying pan he's already heated on the tiny kitchenette stove. He still isn't wearing a shirt, but he's tied one of the frilly aprons that my mom bought for me as a housewarming present over his sculpted chest. He's already placed a rack of bacon in the oven, and had two bagels toasting with cream cheese softening beside the pan on the warming stovetop. "Lily insisted I carry you back to your place. You weren't really walking that well."

He pauses, taking a sip of his coffee, and then gives me a concerned look. "You really should be taking it easy with your knee."

I take a sip of my own coffee, hiding from his too-observant eyes behind my mug. Even with the pink ruffles framing his pectorals, his attention is withering. My knee has been killing me all morning, almost as bad as if I'd never had an adjustment at all. "I haven't been doing anything out of the ordinary."

"Is that so? No shuttle runs or four-hour long practices of pacing up and down an uneven park field? No dancing on bar tops?" He cocks an amused eyebrow. I furrow mine.

I danced on top of the bar?

"My practices are not *four hours long."*

"A few of your teammates at the Crowbar last night said otherwise."

"Okay, *Doctor.* If we're going to shame each other for our sins, wanna tell me why you were gathering intel on me all night long only to spend the night on my couch and make me breakfast, then?"

After kissing me like your life depended on it–TWICE–yesterday?

His expression grows more serious. He focuses on flipping the eggs. "You got sick in the bar parking lot. I didn't have anyone's number, and I wanted to make sure you were okay."

"Oh." I don't know what else to say. Except… "Um. Thank you."

"You are, right? Okay?" And once again, his piercing blue eyes are boring into me under those concerned eyebrows of his.

"Yeah. I mean. My knee is killing me, and I'm hungover, but yeah."

He shakes his head, a grin tilting up the corner of his mouth. The toaster dings. He grabs the everything bagel from the spring-loaded slot and smears a healthy serving of cream cheese on one side. He butters the other, then spatulas the two eggs on top. "You want the bacon on the sandwich or on the side?"

My mouth waters. *Um, if this is what waking up with a man is like, I'm beginning to understand what Lily likes about it so much.* "Both."

"You got it." He opens the oven to check on the heavenly-smelling strips, then dons an oven mitt and takes them out. As he moves about the kitchen, he hums a little to himself and moves his hips and shoulders a bit–almost like he's dancing.

No, not almost. He's totally dancing. It's subtle, slight enough movements that someone who wasn't used to watching people move or train wouldn't really notice, certainly not with the sound of the vent hood blasting and no music playing in the background. But I do.

"What's the song?" I ask, as he tongs two chewy-looking strips from their pool of grease on top of the eggs. He straightens, surprised, and then gives a quiet, embarrassed laugh.

"Pennies from Heaven," he says, then starts whistling in earnest as he finishes the sandwich and pops another bagel in the toaster. He hands me my breakfast on the part of the melody that would be "sunshine and ravioli," and I mouth the call-and-response *(macaroni!)* when he whistles it. His eyes twinkle at me, and then flicker down to the plate. "Eat up. Then we can talk."

I let out a breath, defeated. "Okay."

I take a bite and immediately make a very indecent noise. *This is fucking delicious.*

Luckily, Brian is already over at the stove again, frying up eggs for his own sandwich and chomping on a piece of bacon. By the time he finishes up constructing his plate, I'm already licking my fingers clean and hopping around the island for another piece. "That was really good."

"I heard."

Heat rushes up my neck as I realize that he *didn't* miss my moan when I'd taken that first bite. I smile shyly as I chew my bacon strip, shrugging my shoulders. "Good, then. Consider it a compliment."

"I always do when someone makes a sound like that. Speaking of…"

I shake my head, waving another piece of bacon at him while I work through my mortification. "No, you finish your breakfast first, too. I'll make more coffee. Did you want milk, or sugar or anything?"

"Nope," he says, popping the "p" and taking a giant bite. "Shuit yershelf. Yer jush duh-layeeng the inev'ible."

"Didn't your mom ever teach you not to speak with your mouth full?"

"Nope." He shoots me a toothy grin, complete with bits of half-chewed food stuffing his cheeks, and I shake my head.

"You're ridiculous." Even more so with that apron hanging from his neck. "Where's your shirt?" He nods his head toward the back of the couch, where the t-shirt he was wearing yesterday looks like it's air-drying. I tilt my head. "Why is it wet?"

He winces. "Remember when I said you got sick in the parking lot?"

I freeze. "Oh my God. I'm so sorry."

He waves a hand. "Don't worry about it. I think the apron is cuter, anyway. Really brings out my eyes, don't you think?"

He bats his eyelashes at me. Despite my mortification, my stomach flutters and my lips curl up in a grin.

"Pink really is your color."

CHAPTER 15
BRIAN

Finally, with both mugs refilled and breakfast digesting, we take seats on opposite ends of Kodi's couch. She takes a deep breath, and then starts launching into something she's clearly been rehearsing in her head while making the coffee.

"Okay. About yesterday. I'm sorry I–"

"Was that really your first kiss?" I blurt the thing that's been weighing on my mind for the past twenty hours, and her apology flies out the window. She gapes at me like a fish for a moment, before exclaiming:

"What? What makes you think that was my first kiss?"

I narrow my eyes, putting a pin in the fact that her response wasn't an outright denial. "Lily."

There's the briefest flash of murder in her eyes, but then she blinks, schooling her features. "Look, that's neither here nor there. The reason I kissed you is because this town takes their cornhole league *very* seriously. If the Nosey Pecker figured out that your ex was *Zeke Chopra* of all people, you might never actually get your practice up and running. I mean, outside of cornhole season, it's probably fine, but at the game? And the first game of the season, at that? I had to save you."

I didn't hear half of what she said. I'm still stuck on, "*You* kissed *me?*"

She looks at me like I'm stupid. "Yeah. At the fence?"

"Pretty sure *I* kissed *you*."

"No!" She clears her throat. "I kissed you on the cheek, and pretended to be your girlfriend, and then you yes-anded me."

"I *what* you?"

"Yes and. Like, in improv?" I stare at her blankly. She leaps at the change in subject. "You know, like when you're improvising with someone, and they come into the scene like, *'The sky is on fire!'* The number one rule is you don't deny it, you play along and add something to the scene. So instead of 'No it isn't!' you'd say like, 'Oh my God, *yes! And* the newscaster is saying it's because a dragon is attacking the capitol!'"

I blink at her. "You do improv?"

"I had to take a couple electives in college, okay? It was either that or badminton, and I was still recovering from surgery at the time." She takes a frustrated sip of her coffee. I mirror her, hiding a grin as I imagine her limping around with a boot on her foot with Wayne Brady and Colin Mochrie on *Who's Line is it Anyway?*

"So what you're saying is, I *yes-and*-ed you by kissing you back."

"Right! But I kissed you first."

"On the cheek," I point out. She rolls her eyes.

"Yeah, and?"

I can't resist. "I thought it was *'yes, and'*?"

She scowls out me, and I'm pretty sure she'd be telling me to go fuck myself if I hadn't carried her home last night after she threw up on my shirt. It's hard to stay angry at a man in a frilly pink apron after he takes care of your drunk ass and makes you breakfast in the morning. It's just a fact. One I take full advantage of as I tease her.

"I still did it first," she mumbles. I take another sip of my coffee.

Yesterday should have been one of the worst days of my life.

Going to an obnoxious cornhole match, seeing Zeke among all his attractive teammates, and getting dragged into some deceptive conspiracy in order to fool the entire town into thinking I'm dating their star athlete? It all sounds like a recipe for disaster and heartbreak.

And yet, everything about Kodi is so unexpected, I find it hard to stay focused on any of the things I should be feeling. Who is this woman? And how is it that I seem to forget all my grief when I'm around her?

I come back to the conversation we really ought to be having.

"So you're saying that trying to get Zeke back is a bad idea. And you thought you could save me by...what, distracting me from him?"

She opens her mouth to speak, but hesitates for a second. Tapping her fingertips on her mug, she takes a breath before hedging her answer.

"I'm not trying to distract you," she begins carefully. "And whether or not you get back together with Zeke is...your business. However, I know firsthand just how frustrating it is to get back on your feet while the whole town is invested in your story."

She speaks slowly, measuring each word as she says it, as if she's trying to impart only the most necessary information. I cradle my mug as I wait for her to continue.

"Why–sorry. No." She takes a long pause, and I wonder what she stopped herself from saying. "You still love Zeke, don't you?"

"Yes." I don't even hesitate. It might be naive of me, it might be hopeless, even. But what can I say? Of course I still love him. Even if his loss doesn't seem to hurt as much this morning.

She takes a sip of her coffee and nods slowly while she thinks over what she wants to say. "Okay. Do you... Is he the type of guy to take you back, do you think?"

It takes all of my self control not to ask her what she *isn't* saying. That's the third time she's stopped herself from asking one thing, only to turn her words around to ask something different.

I fill in the blanks. "You think that little of him, huh?"

"I didn't say that."

"I know you didn't 'say' that. But you almost did." I hold eye contact with her, and blush rises from her slender, tan neck up to the base of her ears. My throat goes a little dry, and I take another sip of coffee. She blinks, breaking off the staring match. Then she gets up off the couch and starts to pace. When she speaks again, she doesn't look at me.

"I don't like him, no. He's got a bit of a reputation around here, okay? He's snobby and British and a cheater and whenever I've been around him he's given off bad juju, okay? But I can see that your experience with him is different, so…I'm trying to account for that."

Well, jeez, don't hold back. "Why do I get the feeling you're judging me right now?"

"I'm not judging you."

She says it quickly, like a reflex. I raise my eyebrows. She huffs out a breath and sits back down beside me. "How well do you know Zeke?"

"I mean, we dated for a year."

I brush off the question. She slowly nods, but doesn't respond. Which of course, gives me a second to overanalyze the situation.

When I start to think about it a little bit more, I remember my surprise at the way he acted around his teammates, how I was blindsided by his reaction to my moving here.

I down the rest of my coffee, then jolt back up to get a refill. "Besides, that's not what we're talking about here. What I want to know is what your little plan was yesterday when you decided to recruit me as your improv buddy."

She rises to follow me. "I was trying to protect you."

Clunk. I lose my grip on the coffee pot while taking it off the burner. Thankfully, it doesn't spill, just rattles on the stand before clicking back into place. "From Zeke?"

"From the Tit Peepers!"

"Oh please, I think I can handle a couple of old Tits." I roll my eyes, succeeding this time at topping off my mug. "What are they going to do, gossip me to death?"

"Or turn the whole town against you!" She fiddles with her hands as she stands across the island from me, looking strangely nervous instead of angry. *What is her end game here?* Every time I think I have Kodi Gander figured out, she goes and throws me a curveball.

"And how does kissing me at the local high school remedy that?"

"The only thing that those old fogies like better than a scandal is a *sex* scandal. They're gonna talk about anything and everything they can get their claws on; they always have. But their absolute *favorite* kind of rumors are the ones that end in wedding bells. They did it with Chief Woodcock and his wife Delilah. They did it with Tina and Nick, too! Actually, come to think of it, this year they've been playing matchmaker with just about every new person who's come to town..."

"So you want them to play matchmaker with *us?* You and me?" I gape at her. "Why?"

She puts her face in her hands and rubs her eyes, this conversation clearly exhausting her. When she finally does speak up again, her face is red from holding back her frustration. "What I'm saying is, they're gonna talk about something regardless. So let's give them something to talk *about.* While you get your business up and running, and while we wrap up cornhole season. Once we beat Spitz Hollow in the playoffs and you've got a regular clientele, once you're accepted by the town for who you actually *are,* then we can stop pretending and you can get your boyfriend back."

A full minute passes before I realize my jaw is still on the ground. I shake myself back to reality, only to find myself gaping at her a second time. Then finally, I utter, "*What?*"

"Plus, it'll make Zeke jealous!" She slams her hands on the island, and I jump. Leaning into me conspiratorially, she whispers, "did you *see* the way he was looking at you during that first round? After you smooched me senseless?"

Her face is inches from mine. I can feel the wispy hairs that have sprung out of her ponytail tickling my forehead. I swallow. "Um…"

Why *can't* I remember how Zeke was looking at me during the first half of the match? What had I been paying attention to then?

Kodi blinks and leans back to her side of the island, grabbing her mug to refill. She clears her throat. "All I'm saying is, if he did still have feelings for you, he was ignoring them. Until we showed him that you were unavailable. Then he couldn't take his eyes off you."

Is that true? I stand for a moment in silence while she makes her way around the kitchen to the coffee pot. For some reason my brain is fuzzy. Not only can't I remember how Zeke was looking at me during the game, I'm finding that the only memories I *can* cling to are the ones that involved Kodi.

But then I remember the very end, in the team huddle, when Zeke and I caught eyes. That wink he gave me. The one that he knows gives me butterflies…

"Oh my God, you're right," I breathe.

"Yeah, I fucking know." Kodi's washing up the dishes from breakfast and placing them on the drying rack. Her tone is very matter-of-fact. "I'm probably the smartest woman you've ever dated."

I snort. "Seeing as I haven't dated a girl since high school, you're probably right about that."

A plate clunks extra loudly into the drying rack, and I look over at the scheming blonde. She blushes, adjusting the dishes before grabbing another dirty one with soapy hands.

"Well, you didn't seem rusty to me."

Once again, she throws me for a loop with the unexpected compliment.

But something still isn't adding up. I can see what I gain from pretending to date the captain of Tuft Swallow's Cornhole League.

I evade the Tit Peepers from finding out about and broadcasting my *actual* personal life, make nice with the neighbors as the new boyfriend of a hometown hero, and make my ex realize he's made a mistake. Three birds with one stone.

But what about her?

I cross my arms, waiting for her to finish up the dishes. When she dries off her hands and turns around to face me, I tilt my head. "Why are you doing this?"

"The sink will smell if I don't take care of the dishes right away."

"No, I mean, why would you agree to help me like this? What are you getting out of it? You don't need a boyfriend to distract you from cornhole season. You also apparently hate Zeke, so you don't have any interest in making *him* happy. You've offered to help me with my booking and billing software, and now you want to help me win him back. Why? What are you getting out of it?"

She fills a cup of water and opens the cabinet to grab a couple of ibuprofen, then gestures for me to follow her to the couch. She takes a seat, then swallows her pills, biding her time. I sit across from her, waiting, seeing the cogs turn inside her skull.

When she looks up at me, her eyes are fierce.

"You're my secret weapon, of course."

CHAPTER 16
KODI

Why? *Why?*

Oh God. The longer he stares at me, the more the cacophony of thoughts in my brain pounds at the inside of my skull. *I'm too hungover for this question.*

There are so many things I could say to answer that question, and none of them are the least bit appropriate. *Hmm, let's see. One, I feel guilty about my boss wanting me to dig up dirt on you in order to run you out of town, and I really would prefer if you never find out that's why I called you in the first place. Two, Zeke Chopra is a fucking douchecanoe and I like to watch him suffer. Three, I have a grudge a mile long against the Tit Peepers for never giving me a scosche of privacy about anything in my life, and I think it would be fun to mess with them. Four…*

I'm terrified that if he leaves town, my knee will never ever be back to normal.

Even now, my leg is aching after only one weekend of activity. I need another adjustment, and quite honestly? I want this man on speed dial so I can always call him when I need him. It might cost me my job if I ever admit it, but I need Brian Gosling more than I've ever needed any doctor in my life. He's given me *hope*. I can't let him leave town now, or in the next few weeks, once he realizes how ridiculous Tuft Swallow and our gossip columns and our town goats and our bird puns on every business front on Main Street are and makes the sensible decision to split.

I at least need him to get me through cornhole season. I might not get another chance to bring home a championship once he leaves.

And he's bound to leave, I realize. I hate to admit it, as I've been stuck here since my parents moved us here when I was eight, but this town is *not* a place where people with a shot at success elsewhere stay. If my softball scholarship had actually panned out, I would have been on the first bus outta here as soon as I got my diploma. I mean, I suppose there are a few people that fell in love here and started a family, of course, but Brian's way too smart to do that.

Besides, he's already got someone he loves. So luckily for me, there's no risk here of him falling for me.

But I can't tell *him* any of that. He probably already thinks I'm crazy after I spontaneously kissed him out of nowhere. He basically said as much.

So this is where my A+ in those two semesters of improv are going to pay off.

"You're my secret weapon, of course."

I can see on his face that I've thrown him for a loop with that. Good. That gives me a moment to figure out what the fuck that means.

"Your secret weapon?" He asks, jaw agape. I do my best to look at him like *he's* the weird one, here.

"Well, yeah. My ace in the hole." And that's when it clicks: *the hole.* As in, cornhole.

Brian and I dating is the perfect distraction for Zeke, which will throw him off his game, which will win us the championship. Done! Easy. Perfect explanation. I'm a genius!

It's not at all because I want to kiss him again, like I've been thinking about doing since I first saw his washboard abs peek over the edge of my couch. It has nothing to do with the tantalizing-yet-tasteful tuft of chest hair peeking out from behind the pink frilly apron he's wearing. No. Of course not. That's silly. I'm Kodi Gander: I'm literally the least sexually interested girl in town. So what if I'm apparently a little hormonal this week? It'll pass. It always has whenever I've had fleeting crushes in the past (to Lily's annoyance). This will be an easy way to get them out of my system and keep the gossipers entertained while my knee gets better and I can put together a new life plan as a healthy, decorated champion.

Who knows? Maybe I can even find a softball league that'll take a 24-year old rookie. Anything is possible.

Brian's staring at me expectantly, and I realize that I haven't been paying attention to his response while I formulated my grand plan. *Oops. Noobie mistake.* I'm better at improv than this.

I roll my eyes to save face. I take a guess that he's probably still confused. "Nothing will distract Zeke Chopra more than his rival cornhole captain dating his ex. With you and me in league together, I've got this championship in the bag."

He blinks. A few seconds pass, and I wonder if maybe I should have been paying more attention to his question after all.

Then he says, "Jesus Christ. You all are really fucking serious about cornhole, aren't you?"

I stifle my sigh of relief with a laugh. "It's on our town sign!" He shakes his head, and another thought crosses my mind. "Although, if you want to sweeten my side of the deal a little…"

He raises his eyebrows at me and leans in. I catch a whiff of his scent, mixed with the smell of bacon from the amazing breakfast sandwiches he made us this morning. My hangover must really be hitting me hard, because suddenly I want nothing more than to curl up against his chest and take a nap. My eyelids droop, and I can feel his arms calling to me.

"Yes…?"

I jerk a little, shoving my eyes back open and refocusing on Brian's face. "You could join the team. Give those hungry Tit Peepers something to spy on so they don't think we're keeping anything from them. Imagine how much flirting we could do in a two-hour practice."

Brian laughs in earnest now, tilting his head back as tears spring to his eyes. I straighten, frowning at him. What's so funny about the idea of him joining the team?

He looks at me and catches his breath. "You can't be serious. I've never even played. I'm probably awful."

I shrug. "So? More for the rumor mill to chew on."

He narrows his eyes. "I'm not sure I'm ready to go full Tuft Swallower just yet. I've got a business to get off the ground, after all."

"It's great networking," I sing. "Plus, you'd be the first to know if someone gets injured at practice. Put those magic fingers to work, win over a client."

"What, you're gonna run them into the ground so I can build a clientele?" He snorts and gives me a mischievous look, his eyes dancing. "Who knew you were such a hustler?"

"There's a lot you don't know about me yet, Brian Gosling."

"Well, I guess I'm about to learn."

I pump my fist in the air. "So that means you're in? We're doing this?"

He shakes his head, that airy laugh of his once more ringing through my living room. My stomach flip-flops as the full weight of this plan begins to sink in. *Oh my God. I'm going to fake-date my new chiropractor to get back at all my enemies...*wait 'til Lily hears about this!

He locks eyes with me, and the flip-flopping intensifies. He sticks out his hand.

"Let Operation Win Back Zeke commence."

I wince, but shake his hand.

"We're gonna need to work on that title."

"Miss Gander!"

My phone leaps from my hand and I jump about a foot off of my chair when Dr. Cratchet comes barreling around the corner. *Shit!* I'm going to be in so much trouble when he sees–

"I've heard the good news! It was all over this morning's bird report."

"Bird report, sir?" I attempt to covertly shove my phone down between my thigh and the office chair cushion, but he waves off the action with a smile plastered across his wrinkled face.

"Honestly, Miss Gander, you've already been caught. I assume you're texting your new *beau?*" He winks at me.

I wasn't. I was texting Lily. Or rather, Lily was texting me. Repeatedly. In all caps. The angry buzzes vibrate at regular intervals under my butt as she continues to berate me for not calling to give her every detail about my weekend. My excuse of nursing the hangover from hell apparently isn't enough for her.

"My new beau, sir?"

Dr. Cratchet throws up his hands and gives an exasperated sigh before pulling over a chair and sitting across from me. The office is empty; it's only 8:16 and the coffee pot is still hissing and spitting its inky lifeblood into the glass carafe. His first appointment isn't until ten today, so he's supposed to be filling out prior auths and updating charts.

Instead, he leans forward and places a cold and clammy hand on my knee. *Ew.*

"Kodi. May I call you Kodi?" He doesn't wait for me to answer. "I must commend you. I'll admit, I wasn't sure you had it in you, but I'm nothing if not able to come clean when I've misjudged someone. And *you,* my dear, are more cunning and devious than I ever would have guessed. Tell me. How much am I paying you?"

"Twenty-two dollars an hour, sir."

"Twenty-tuh–" He splutters, his signature grouchy scowl returning for a fraction of a second as he shakes his head. Then he plasters the fake smile back onto his face, albeit with a few cracks.

What was that he was saying about being able to come clean about his own misjudgements?

Through clenched teeth, he continues, "Well, I was *going* to say you deserve a raise for going above and beyond, on a weekend, no less, but… that is neither here nor there."

I'm about to interrupt and say that I'd very much like to explore that idea further, but he continues, pulling a wrinkly *Pecker* out of his front trouser pocket.

"*Gosling spotted fleeing the Gander's nest after late-night post-game celebration!*" He reads, smacking the *Pecker* with the back of his hand. "Why, Miss Gander. To think you are so devoted to the Tuft Swallow Clinic that you would go so far as to *seduce* the competition into such a scandalous scenario! With absolutely no regard for your own reputation or dignity in the process. I have never been prouder of a peon, my dear. And I use that term with the utmost respect: it's so difficult to find devoted peons these days."

Uh…what? "Th-thank you?"

"You keep texting that beau of yours now. Keep him on the hook. Whatever it takes! I assume you have a very public and tragic break-up planned once he's fully invested? Shatter his very manhood for all to see? Perhaps even at the championship game itself! Oh, you've always been an ambitious one!"

"Sure, sir. About that raise–"

"To *raise* such stakes! And all for loyalty to your superior and hometown team. Outstanding. Feel free to text as much as you need for the rest of the day–*the week*, even! As long as it takes to see our little plan through, eh? Provided you don't shirk your office duties in the meantime. I am still paying you, after all."

"Right, and speaking of pay–"

"Chop, chop, Miss Gander! Don't waste the day!"

He hums as he strolls away with a spring in his step, any and all talk of that supposed raise evaporating in his wake.

One of these days…

The coffee pot dings and I fill the mug Lily bought me specifically for the office. It's plastered with an image of Garfield and his catchphrase "I hate Mondays," but more importantly, it's enormous. Armed with caffeine and my boss's blessing, I unlock my phone and catch myself up on Lily's texts.

LILY

HE SPENT THE NIGHT??

Kodi, I need DETAILS. Stat.

Are his arms as big as they look in his button-up shirts?

OMG WHAT ABOUT HIS 🍆???

Kodi. I've been more than patient. You're so overdue on this that no extra credit will ever dig you out of this hole.

NONE, I'm telling you.

KODI

KODI GANDER YOU TEXT ME BACK THIS INSTANT

KODI YOU CAN'T DO THIS TO ME

THIS IS YOUR FIRST BOYFRIEND, FAKE OR NOT, AND YOU WILL NOT CUT ME OUT OF THE JUICY DETAILS!!!

Oh my God, did he actually wear your apron? Are you into that?

...Girl we might need to talk.

I mean, obviously, we need to talk.

But like, your apron? Seriously? Is this some feminist kink thing I haven't heard about yet? Are you a dominatrix???

...Was he naked underneath the apron?

Okay, that might actually be a little hot 💦🥵 Have you been holding out reverse patriarchy BDSM fantasies on me? You know I'll try anything once.

Like, with a guy.

OMG, could you imagine Logan in a frilly apron? ☠️

Oh right, I just remembered you're at work. But seriously. Text me as soon as you get this!!

WITH DETAILS

Or I swear I'm getting tonsillitis for real this time.

I'm surprised my asscheek didn't go numb from all the notifications.

ME

Easy there, tiger. Nothing happened. Except the apron, that did actually happen. How do you know about that?

LILY

OMG way to finally get back to me

Um, girl, your frilly pink apron is literally ALL the Pecker can talk about 👙 Don't you have your copy yet?

Oh God. No, Doc took it this morning. He's thrilled for me by the way. Thinks I'm out to break Brian's heart

Brian, huh? First name basis now? 😏

I mean, we DID kiss, so I'd hope so? Speaking of, why did you tell him that was my first kiss??

Because it WAS

No it wasn't

Oh please, girl. Seven minutes in heaven with Cooper Swan at Rowena's thirteenth birthday party does NOT count 🙄

Just because I'm a virgin doesn't mean I'm clueless. So we kissed. No biggie.

OMG, Kodi. You're killing me here. Literally, knife in my heart, twisted eleven times and currently pouring margarita mix in the wound 🔪❣️🍋
TELL ME ABOUT THE KISS

What's there to tell? The man has lips.

Really soft, commanding, lingering lips. Lips that I've been trying to *avoid* thinking about because it makes me sweat in awkward places. Not sure what exactly *that's* all about.

LILY

You're impossible, you know that? You're lucky I stick around

ME

I know

We agree to meet for drinks after work to share details. As I get around to copying files, faxing insurance documents, and taking calls, my knee starts to twinge again. Probably all the getting up and down.

I glance at my phone. Should I text Brian? Make another appointment? I should probably get to work on his booking and payment systems, too. Honestly, we have a lot still to iron out about our fake relationship. Maybe we could get dinner tomorrow, and–

Dinner? Seriously?

…Maybe just a text.

• • •

ME

Hey Brian. I've got a question about my knee when you have a sec.

HE'S NOT NEARLY AS QUICK TO RESPOND AS LILY. BY THE TIME SHE comes to pick me up for happy hour at the Crowbar, he still hasn't texted me back. Which makes me wonder if he's having second thoughts about the whole fake relationship after this morning's 'bird report' after all. By the time Callie walks in and orders a round of cocktails at the bar, I've caught Lily up on everything from the weekend. We talk in hushed tones just in case any Tit Peepers have their hearing aids turned up.

Lily finishes her cosmo in one long gulp when I finish. "So you're actually *fake* dating? Seriously? I'm sorry, did someone walk in here and replace my best friend with Mary Kate or Ashley Olsen? Have I stumbled on set for their comeback blockbuster, The Chiropractor Trap?"

I roll my eyes. "Come on, Lily, it's a good idea! And I'm pretty sure *The Parent Trap* was Lindsay Lohan."

"It's a terrible idea!!" She ignores my correction. "Look, I know you're all proud of your spreadsheets and your improvisational skills, *nerd,* but this is too much even for you, Kodi. You don't even like regular dating! What makes you think you're going to enjoy doing the hard part with none of the good stuff?"

I don't give her words a second of consideration as Callie comes back to the table, bearing drinks and nachos, waving off her concern. "Hey, as far as I'm concerned, fixing my leg IS the good stuff."

"Ooo, where's he fixing to put your legs? Catch me up, I'm behind. Wait–is THAT where he puts them?" Callie gestures excitedly behind her head, cosmos still in hand, and ends up spilling half of one down the back of her shirt. "Ah shit, this is a new bra..."

The word "bra" seems to attract the attention of the guys at the table behind us. None other than Brad and Logan, as a matter of fact. Logan perks up when he sees Lily with an empty martini glass beside her.

"Is it just me, or do we seem to keep running into each other?"

"SHOVE IT, GILGAX, IT'S GIRLS NIGHT." Lily grabs some napkins and starts dabbing at the back of Callie's shirt. "Ugh, come on, let's use the hand dryer in the bathroom. Kodi, watch our drinks, and keep the boy scouts out of our nachos."

I snort at her calling Brad and Logan *boy scouts*. I still haven't forgiven Logan for being the suspected informant to this weekend's article listing me as Tuft Swallow's resident drill sergeant. I glare at him, and the two of them shrink back to their table. As I wipe off Callie's chair with more napkins, a smooth baritone breathes into the hollow of my neck.

"Is this seat taken?"

"Brian!" I jump, then arrange my face into a smile. Despite my racing heart, it doesn't take all that much effort. My lips lift automatically as I take him in. His jaw is stubbled with the same scruff that lined his face yesterday morning, only he's swapped the pink apron for a cobalt blue polo that has his eyes looking bluer than ever. "What are you doing here?"

"What, I can't surprise my girl at happy hour?" He leans in and kisses the air beside my jawline, so close that I can feel his lips tickle the fine hairs on my cheek. "I figured you and Lily would be here."

His proximity is distracting. I'm pretty sure nobody would doubt we're actually an item with him standing so close.

What should I do now? Hug him? Kiss him–again?

That seems overkill. I opt for a teasing smirk.

"Not even a week of dating and you already have my schedule memorized? Impressive."

"Nah, she posted your first round on Instagram." He grins at me as he takes a seat. *So. He's following my friends on Instagram now?* Is that a thing that boyfriends usually do? Or is he just researching his role? "Cosmos, huh? You didn't strike me as a Carrie."

"Carrie?" I wrinkle my nose. "What does a horror movie have to do with Cosmos?"

"You're kidding right?" He stares at me. "Sex and the City? Carrie Bradshaw? Come on, like, every Buzzfeed quiz of the early 2010s was based around which of the main characters was your personality type."

I sip my pink drink. "Sorry. Before my time."

"Oh my God, how old *are* you? This little stint between us isn't going to land me in jail, is it?"

He looks me up and down, and I slap his arm. I swear it's made of fucking *steel*. My palm stings from the impact. "I'm twenty-four."

His eyebrows shoot up towards his hairline, but he seems to recover from his surprise quickly. "We span the Gen Z/Millennial divide, then. Fuck. Does this mean I'm going to have to get on TikTok now?"

"That's more Lily's thing than mine. Apparently it's all thirst traps and smutty book recommendations? I just have Facebook."

A smile curves at the corner of his lips, and that weird tug in my stomach starts up again. His eyes sparkle as he says, "An old soul. Can I add you on Farmville? We're not *really* fake official here until we water each other's crops everyday."

"Shh! Not so loud," I hiss into his ear, terrified someone might overhear him using the word *fake*. Brian laughs, slipping an arm over my shoulder as if it's second nature.

The girls return, and their eyes dart between the two of us. I immediately scoot back in my chair; Brian and I ended up much closer to each other than I realized. He straightens, too, and sticks out a hand to Callie. "I don't believe we've met officially. Brian Gosling."

"Hi there." She giggles a little. "Callie Stavropoulos. I've heard so much about you."

"She loves a man who wears pink," Lily adds. Brian blushes, and it's maybe the most adorable thing I've ever seen.

Logan pops over Lily's shoulder. "I thought you said it was girl's night?"

"I swear to God, Logan, if you don't stop cutting into my conversations–"

Brian leans into me again, and I tune out their bickering as he mutters in my ear. "Is it really girl's night? I can head out. I just got your text and thought we could figure out a time to barter this week."

The giddiness I'd been feeling from the alcohol fades a little when he brings up business. "Oh, right. Why don't we meet up after work tomorrow, before practice? Lily has Monday's off at the salon, which is why we usually meet up, but Tuesdays she works late. Does that work for you?"

"Your knee will be good until then?" His face is scrunched with concern, and I swear my heart melts. But I keep it professional.

"I've survived six years with pain way worse than this. I can last another day."

He nods, concern not completely gone from his face, then rises from his chair. The air around me chills without his proximity. He taps Callie and Lily on the shoulder, cutting short their argument with the boys. "I'll leave you to your night, ladies, sorry for interrupting."

"Oh, it's no trouble!" Lily bats her eyelashes at him and levels me a knowing look. Callie just grins and catches my eye when he bends down to wrap his arm around my shoulder in a half hug.

"See you tomorrow, *babe.*" Once again, he pushes his lips so close to my face that anyone in the bar would think it made contact.

Anyone but me.

"Bye, hon. I'll catch you later." I also kiss the air next to his scruff, but he tilts his head as he backs up, and my lips catch the corner of his mouth. His scruffy mustache tickles my upper lip, and I open my mouth in surprise.

His gaze meets mine, and in the space of a breath he asks me an unspoken question. *Do we…?*

I give my head the most imperceptible nudge downward to indicate *yes*. Time seems to stop as we close the space between my open mouth and his, casually. Naturally.

My heart totally isn't about to beat out of my chest or anything.

Our lips only touch for a short moment. Compared to the kiss after we won the season opening game, it's barely a blip on anyone's radar. Brad and Logan aren't even paying attention to us anymore, and the girls have gone back to arguing with them over something inconsequential.

It's all inconsequential.

Despite the contact lasting only half a second, it's long enough to render everything other than me and Brian completely and utterly meaningless. In the space of a breath, my world collapses to the softness of Brian's lips and the warmth of the crook of his arm around my shoulders. I close my eyes and breathe in his smell–the one that I already feel like I could pick out of a lineup of every man I've ever known in a heartbeat. And that's saying something, given how fast my heart is beating now.

I'm sweating again. In between my legs, particularly, it feels like there's a swamp under construction as the warmth of his mouth on mine spreads in a tingling wave down my shoulders and all the way to my toes.

He pulls away, retrieving his arm. My mouth stays open, eyes still closed, until he clears his throat and I come back to myself.

He gives me a tight smile, says, "I'll text you," and walks out of the bar.

It isn't until Lily calls my name that I turn away from his retreating form and try to get back to girl's night, dread building in my chest.

Because that kiss? That didn't feel fake.

At least, not for me.

CHAPTER 17
BRIAN

I toss and turn all night.

My reasons for going to the bar to see Kodi had been twofold. First, we had to schedule a follow-up appointment. Her knee had been looking rough since the game on Saturday, and despite her winning performance, it was important that she rebuild the strength she needs to combat the bad form she developed over the years.

But the second reason was entirely selfish.

After a whole day organizing my office and trading in my software for the version Kodi told me I needed, my brain wasn't able to stay focused on work. It kept floating back to thoughts of Zeke, and Kodi, and how complicated my social life had become.

Would it be hard to fake-date Kodi? Not really. My romantic relationships have always moved fast in the past, so all I needed to do was mimic that honeymoon phase without the feelings. Considering my whole body has felt numb since Zeke broke up with me, it shouldn't be hard to turn off the feelings part when acting my role in her scheme.

Shouldn't.

And yet, what started as an act when I cornered her at Girls' Night: leaning into the slender curve between her ear and neck to whisper hello, pecking her on the cheek when we said goodbye, etc. Somewhere in there, things started to feel…

Well, they started to *feel.*

Sick of pretending to sleep, I threw off the covers and decided to start tackling my to-do list for the day a little earlier than normal. By 7:00 am I'm already on my second French press of coffee, and I sit at the kitchen table checking my laptop calendar and trying to figure out how to sync the damn thing to Medi-Cal.

"Come on, I know you're supposed to integrate. The website said it was supposed to be seamless!"

I open a help article in another tab, and no sooner have I scrolled down to the "features and integrations" section that a chatbot pops up over the text, asking if it can assist me. I groan.

"Go away, goddammit, I'm trying to–"

I click the barely-visible "x" in the corner, only for another pop-up to replace it half a second later.

Enjoying Medi-Cal? Please Leave Us a Review!

This time, I can't even see an x anywhere on the screen.

"UGH!"

I scoot my chair back furiously and punch the plunger down to get more coffee. By the time I pour it into my mug and take a sip, I realize I let it steep too long. It's bitter.

And my session has timed out on the software.

"Son of a–"

A series of melodic chimes alerts me to a phone call from an unrecognized number. I pick it up. "This is Brian Gosling."

I do everything I can to keep the frustration out of my voice, but I'm pretty sure a little gets through, because the man on the other end starts laughing.

"Rough morning there, Doc?"

"Who is this?" I growl.

"Sorry to call you so early, but I've got an eight AM class and I wanted to make sure we chatted before I got into it. It's Nick, from the gym."

It takes a second for my brain to make the connection. *Gym... Nick... Oh!* The owner of the MMA gym where I left my business card last week. I pull open my notes app on my laptop so I can write down anything important from our conversation.

"Nick! Hi! Thanks for calling!"

"Yeah, I wanted to touch base about coffee. When did you want to meet?"

"Good... question..." I try to pull up my calendar again, only to get blue-balled by Medi-Cal once more. *Who am I kidding? I don't have anything going on.* "Are you free later today?"

"That depends... you up for a workout?"

Two hours later, I've got sweat soaking the sides of my t-shirt, shin guards, and leaking into my asscrack as Nick doesn't give me an inch of wiggle room. We're squared off in the practice ring at his fighting gym downtown, and I'm breathing harder than I have in months. I'm no slouch when it comes to martial arts–I've been practicing one form or another for most of my life–but I am nowhere near fit enough to hold my own against a retired pro fighter.

He swings at me with a right cross and I dodge out of the way, only to get yoinked right in the jaw with his uppercut follow-up. My teeth clench around the mouthguard he insisted I wear, and I'm suddenly grateful for his foresight. I also see a star or two from inside my head guard.

"Time! Time!" I pant, giving the universal sign for a break by forming a "T" with my arms. He nods, and I rush to the edge of the mats for my water bottle.

"You ain't half-bad there, Gosling," Nick appraises. He's not even out of breath.

"Ha, you say that." I gulp half the bottle and gasp. "But you're kicking my ass."

"I mean, you're like, 30% bad." He grins at me. I cough out another laugh. "Better than my white belts."

I like this guy. Pretty sure we could be friends.

He assesses me for a second, seems to realize I'm done for the day, and reaches for a towel. We both grab a seat on the bench by the painted wall mural–for some reason, the entire gym has a rubber-ducky theme–and take off our gear. I stretch my ankles and wrists.

"I gotta say, man—I wasn't expecting to find a spot like this in a little town like Tuft Swallow. What brought you here?"

"Grew up here. Always thought it would be the right kinda place to start a family."

"Even after your career, though?" I tilt my head at him. "I mean, with your record, you could easily get a brand deal or something in the works."

"Nah, man. Money's just money. But this place has got something that money can't buy." He smiles, and I can tell his mind's gone elsewhere.

"Oh yeah? What's that?"

"Her."

He points to a photo hanging on the wall by the equipment, of him with his beefy arms wrapped around a pretty woman in front of a local pizza place I've only seen in passing. He's glowing in the picture. I glance back at him to see that he's wearing the same face now.

"Must be a special gal."

"Well, you get it. You've already found someone here, and you just got to town a couple weeks ago, didn't you?"

I force a smile and choke out a laugh. *Right.* Everyone thinks Kodi and I are already head-over-heels for each other after that article in the *Pecker*. I didn't think I realized how far that rumor had spread already.

"Regardless, if you're already in love, you're probably here to stay. Which means you're gonna need to grow that practice of yours."

"Yes!" I beam in earnest now. "I'd love to run a special for your members, if you'd be alright with it. I was thinking I could do a free consult and maintenance plan for fighters, as well as a discount on their first adjustment. I'm sure that could help some of your guys with injuries."

"No doubt. I could use a better plan myself, since I don't have a manager paying for regular PT anymore. How about we set up an appointment for me, and then once I know you're not a quack–no offense–we can finalize a deal?"

My old boss would have absolutely taken offense to Nick's brazen statement. But I've seen firsthand the types of greedy jack-offs that manage to graduate and start a practice. Hell, half the reason I left the clinic in the city was because I was tired of not being able to provide the level of care I wanted to. I'm more than okay with Nick wanting to see what I can do before he promotes me. In fact, it proves to me that he genuinely cares about his clients and their health.

And I respect that.

"Absolutely. You free tomorrow?"

KODI

Hey Brian! Should I head over after work, or...?

The rest of the afternoon goes by in a blur, as Nick and I grab lunch at his girlfriend's pizza place to get to know each other better after our workout. I'd almost forgotten that I'd told Kodi I'd text her for a follow-up appointment.

"That your girl?" Nick asks, tilting his head. "She's not mad at me for stealing you away for the day, is she? I know she can get pretty intense."

"Can she?" I send her a quick text back to say that after work is fine. It's already coming up on 4:00, so I figure we'll get back to my place around the same time.

Of course, I'll need a shower before we get down to business, but I don't need to text that to her.

"You haven't seen her at cornhole practice," he grumbles. I

grab another slice from the lukewarm pie on the table between us and give him a questioning look. He's playing with the paper wrapper of his straw and chewing on his lip a little.

"Uh-oh," I mutter around my bite, then swallow. "I'm sensing there's a story here."

"I mean, I don't know her all that well. Her whole softball ordeal happened a little after I'd left town. And I suck at cornhole, so I'm not really one to judge, but…"

"But?"

"Let's just say, she really wants this championship."

I put down my pizza, suddenly full. "What all *did* happen with her and the softball team? I mean, I read the piece in the paper last weekend, and I know she got injured, but she's smart enough to know that a little community cornhole isn't the same as States, right?"

Nick shrugs his shoulders a bit, avoiding my eyes. "I wonder sometimes…I know a lot of the guys aren't thrilled about her coaching style."

"Coach?" I snort. "I mean, she's just captain. She doesn't like, drill you guys, does she?"

He shuffles his shoulders in his seat. I swallow as a lump forms in my throat. *Who exactly is this woman I'm dating?*

Nick looks at his watch and throws a couple twenties down on the table. "I've got class here in a bit that I gotta get ready for. Thanks for the fight. Let's do it again soon."

I reach to shake his hand, and Nick turns it into a half-hug as he pats me on the back with his other hand, hard enough that I wonder if I'll have a bruise there tomorrow. "Yeah–I'll see you tomorrow for your appointment, man!"

"Looking forward to it!"

He hops behind the counter to give his girlfriend a more intimate goodbye before heading out of the restaurant, and I wave at her before heading out myself to get ready for Kodi's adjustment.

Half an hour later, I'm just hopping out of the shower. Then I hear a voice from downstairs.

"Brian? You home? The door was open..."

"Yeah, just a second!" I holler down the stairs, clutching the towel to my waist. "Sorry, I was at the gym with Nick and got a workout in. Go ahead and make yourself at home!"

But instead of heading back to the office, I see Kodi swing herself around the bannister of the stairwell, bookbag in hand. "I found my old notes on record-keeping and thought I'd bring them over–"

And then she lifts her gaze and spots me, dripping wet, with nothing but a towel covering my junk.

CHAPTER 18
KODI

Oh my God.

Call me crazy, but when I texted Brian an hour before coming over for our predetermined appointment time, I expected him to greet me at the door.

Clothed.

So when I hear his voice upstairs, telling me to make myself at home, I don't think twice about coming up to deliver some of my stuff from college that might help him navigate his record keeping. I didn't think he'd be showering at 5:00 pm.

That is, until I see him dripping wet, naked at the top of the stairs.

"Um, I–I'm so sorry!" I squeak, before turning around and bounding back down the couple of stairs to the ground floor. Unfortunately, my brain realizes the awkwardness of the situation a little more quickly than my legs, which are still frozen in place after halting their ascent.

And I don't know if you've ever had your brain scream *run* while your legs are in a hormone-induced state of shock, but in case you haven't, allow me to fill you in. Literally, every part of my body is on a different wavelength, and I'm pretty sure my nervous system short-circuits. Here's a snapshot of what that looks like from the top-down.

Eyes: OH boy, y'all we got a code red right here.

Brain: *MAYDAY. MAYDAY! Get. Away. From. Naked. Manchest.*

Throat: Incoming! There's a blockage here but our girl needs words!

Heart: *dum-Badum-Badum-Badum*

Stomach: Guys, I'm feeling bubbly and gassy and nauseous all at once here, can I get some confirmation from thyroid as to what's going on?

Ovaries: Um, I might have an update for you, stomach.

Legs: Ovaries, I'm getting the signal you want to move forward, right?

Brain: *Legs, abort! About face! ASAP!*

Ovaries: No, no, no, Brain, we've kissed this guy, this kinda seems like my territory–

Me: *ABORT! ABORT!*

By the time I wrestle control of my limbs back under central command, all of me has already gotten tangled. So instead of gracefully returning from whence I came, I just kind of…crumble. Tumbling backwards like a marionette down the stairs.

"Kodi!" Brian scrambles toward me, and my ovaries speak up again.

Oh, he-LLO there, handsome…

"No!" I scream. Not sure to whom–or what, exactly–but it's out of my mouth before I can accurately pinpoint the subject. Regardless, Brian's already kneeling at my side, wet hair dripping onto my white work blouse as he checks me over.

With his bare, muscly, just-slightly-hairy chest glistening at me.

"Are you okay?"

I blink at him. Keeping my eyes SQUARELY. On. His. Face.

And his waist for a second.

Dammit!

I catch my breath, before breathing a sigh of relief. The towel is still there.

Sigh.

"I'm fine!" I scramble back from him, but his strong, damp arms hold me in place in his lap. So I squirm.

Enthusiastically.

He lets go, and I end up flopping back frantically, dragging his towel with me as it gets tangled in my scrambling limbs.

Fuck on a cracker!

He reaches for the towel, and I squeak out a noise that's somewhere between a scream and a gasp for air. I cover my eyes with my hands.

But not before catching a glimpse of curly, dark hair and an enthusiastic blur of flesh that will be burned into my memory forever.

Ovaries: Vagina, you can take it from here, yes?

Oh, FUCK no.

"Uh. I–um. Don't–don't move, okay? I'm going to get dressed. Stay right there. You may have twisted something."

I'm still covering my eyes with my hands like a baby playing peek-a-boo as I hear him dart back up the stairs. "Kay," I mutter, mortified.

Don't peek, don't peek, DON'T PEEK.

I maybe peek.

TEN MINUTES LATER, HE'S GOT ME ON THE TABLE FACE UP WITH HIS hands holding up my leg. Everyone's got their clothes on, and the room is dead silent.

Given the absolute mental puree that is my brain right now, I have no intention to break that silence.

From how hot I feel under the collar of my polyester blouse, I'm guessing my face is a shade of red somewhere between firetruck and black cherry. Other than a slight pink tinge to his cheeks when he first ran back down the stairs and gingerly lifted me off the floor, he's been entirely in doctor-mode since we entered his office.

That's what I'm going to call it: doctor mode. The way his hands are touching me have that perfectly asexual quality about them again, clinical and warm and setting my limbs perfectly at ease, despite the flashes of hair and muscle and… *flesh* that keep playing on a looping slideshow in my brain. He was a perfect gentleman as he got me to my feet and accompanied me to the table, hands politely poised beneath my elbows to make sure I didn't take another spill.

Meanwhile, I was short-circuiting.

My virginal ass is never going to get over the fact that I saw Brian's penis.

"Can I ask you a question?" I blurt out a few minutes later as he massages the tissue around my knee.

"Sure."

"Your hands…" I start.

He pauses. "Yes?"

"They always feel so…blank," I finish lamely. He sets my leg down and tilts his head at me, a ghost of a smile teasing the corner of his mouth. His still-damp hair falls in little clumps against his forehead. I swallow.

"Explain what you mean."

"Well, like. You know how when someone touches you, like a friend or someone who might be…more than a friend, or even just someone of the opposite gender, there's like, a vibe there?"

He doesn't answer aloud, but he nods at me.

"Your hands…don't have that."

"Ah," he says, grasping my leg again. This time, he firmly grabs each ankle and presses them softly into the cushion of the table, before twisting each one a little to each side. "Healy hands."

"Healy hands?"

"Yeah, that's what my professor used to call them. Chiropractors, massage therapists–basically anyone certified who needs to touch patients physically for their job, need to be able to turn off the less clinical parts of their brain when they're working on a patient. For legal reasons, obviously, but also for patient comfort." He smiles at me, and my stomach does a little flip. "I'm happy to hear you say that about me, though. Not everyone who does what I do quite masters it."

"So you're the healy-hands master?" I joke, finally beginning to relax now that we're having a genuine conversation.

I mean, I know we're fake dating, and we need to be comfortable with a little PDA in public. I suppose I would have probably seen him without a shirt on at some point in the summer, too, seeing as he goes to the gym and such. That's not that big a deal; the guys at practice take their shirts off all the time.

But I got more than a glimpse of Brian's chest earlier. In his *home.* And I wasn't expecting us getting into *that* territory until…

No, not until. Never.

Right?

"I don't know if I'd go *that* far," he says. I blink. *What were we talking about?* "Face down."

"You know," I say, turning and grunting a bit as I take it slow, "It's a good thing you've got those healy hands. Otherwise I'd feel a little vulnerable lying here with my face in the cradle."

"After what you just saw when you walked in the door, I don't think *you're* the one who has any right to feel vulnerable."

His thumbs press on either side of my spine, and the rest of his fingers wrap around the squishy sides of my midsection under my ribs. For a moment, something changes, and the way his fingers graze my side suddenly doesn't feel the same.

Where before, his touch was warm and comforting, it's now sending a cool zing down my back. I shiver, and he pulls his hands away. He hesitates for a second, then moves his hands lower to my tailbone.

The feeling passes.

"Everything alright back there?" My voice comes out muffled by the headrest.

"Yeah," he says, voice suddenly quiet. He pauses. "Your hip's just a little out."

He pokes and prods me for another half an hour, and I moan and groan as he adjusts the more tender spots around my knee. Finally, he helps me into a seated position.

"I'm sorry for barging in when you were–"

"I'm sorry you had to see me–"

We both freeze, having started talking at the same time. Then we laugh awkwardly.

"Can we just forget that ever happened?" His face is so shy as he asks the question, and I breathe a sigh of relief.

"Yes! Absolutely." I reach out to shake his hand. "Now. What do you say we get to work on that software?"

CHAPTER 19
KODI

Friday morning, I head to the office early to get a jumpstart on some paperwork. We've got an earlier practice tonight to make sure the team can get plenty of rest before our first real match of the season against *Spring Chickens,* the adult living community in the next township over.

Most of the team doesn't think we need to practice at *all,* seeing as we'll be playing a bunch of senior citizens. But retirees have plenty of time to practice–they could be tossing bean six hours a day if they wanted to–a fact that everyone but me seems to forget. I swear, sometimes it feels like I'm the only person who takes this cornhole league seriously.

Regardless, with all the extra practices and 'reconnaissance' on Brian (as Dr. Cratchet calls it), I've fallen dangerously behind on faxing insurance claims and prior authorizations. We've started to get phone calls.

I promised the boss I'd come in at seven today to take care of them, and when I walk in the door I'm surprised to see the old man himself seated at the office computer.

"I didn't expect to see you here this early, sir." I hang my purse on the hook and set down my travel mug beside the coffee pot. Then I start brewing a batch for the two of us.

"I'm just checking on my investments." He doesn't even look away from the screen. "It's never too early to save for retirement, you know, Miss Gander. Have you begun your portfolio yet? There are some promising companies close to home that might surprise you!"

"Can't say I've given it much thought, sir."

"It's never too early to invest! A penny saved is a penny earned, you know. I always keep a close eye on my portfolio." His mustache twitches, and he spins around in my office chair. "Speaking of, how is our little intelligence mission going?"

My neck prickles uncomfortably at his steady gaze on my back. I technically never agreed to spy on Brian. However, I have been taking advantage of the time off Dr. Cratchet has given me in order to get my knee fixed.

The problem was, I wasn't expecting to like Brian as much as I do. As a friend. As a professional. Despite his lack of business skills, there's no denying he's incredibly intelligent and talented at what he does. And it's not just me that's going to benefit from him moving to this town: now that he's got an in at Nick's gym, he's bound to get a ton of regular patients.

I pretend to be preoccupied with filling the carafe and measuring the coffee grounds. When the doctor clears his throat impatiently, I feign ignorance. "What was that, sir?"

"Your reconnaissance assignment! On *the spine cracker.*" He's standing behind me now. He leans in as he whispers the words, infusing them with a conspiratorial air. I flinch, still facing the sink away from him.

"Well, sir, I believe it's going well. I had another appointment." *The one we're not going to talk about.* My face heats at the memory. Despite agreeing with Brian to forget that I ever saw his penis, I just can't seem to think of anything else.

When I'm washing dishes in the evening: *penis.*

Out for drinks with Lily and Callie at the Crowbar: *penis.*

Planning out the weekend line-up for our cornhole match: *sexy V of muscles pointing directly into a patch of curly hair with a big ol'—*

"Another one?" Doctor Cratchet puffs a dismissive breath from his hairy nostrils, disturbing his walrus mustache. "Seems a little odd to be *supporting* his business. I thought we settled that incongruity with the *romantic relationship* idea. Gain access to his practice without paying his bills, yes?"

"I'm not paying him," I say, realizing a split second after I do that it was completely inappropriate to do so.

Not to mention, it puts me at risk of revealing the true nature of Brian's and my bargain: he gives me free adjustments and I help him set up the business side of things. Shoring up his practice so that it has a chance at becoming a mainstay in the community.

Doctor Cratchet can't know about that. *At all.*

"Oh-ho-*ho!*" He slides out of my office chair, a spring in his squeaky step. "Are you trading *unsavory favors,* Miss Gander? A little *tit* for *tat* as they say?"

He practically giggles with glee as he approaches me, putting a hand on my shoulder. "Your loyalty knows no bounds. To think, a formerly upstanding woman such as yourself would turn on her own values for her duty to her place of employment. Fealty over honor!"

His gnarly fingers dig into my deltoid in an iron grip. "Uh, sir, I'm not–"

"No, no, Kodi. No need to defend yourself. I knew the day I hired you, you would be an inscrutable asset to this team. Inscrutable, because I could not, at that time, comprehend the extent to which you'd debase yourself for this firm and its values. You're earning that twenty-one dollars an hour!"

"Twenty-two, sir."

"Ah, and enterprising, too!" His eyes twinkle at me behind his glasses. I swallow. "Fine, fine, you're right. You deserve it. Twenty-*two.* I'll recommend the increase to the board." His grip finally loosens and he pats me on the back. "Now you make sure you save that extra dollar into something that will earn you dividends! I recommend that new crypto company in Spitz Hollow–

you didn't hear it from me, but they are making waves!" He says the last bit over his shoulder as he makes his way towards his office, leaving me to my sanctuary in the rear lobby / office / breakroom that is my domain. "Be a dear and bring me a cup when the coffee is done brewing. You know how I like it."

"Yes, sir."

Once I hear his door click closed behind him, I run to the desk and crouch over my keyboard to close out of whatever browser the doctor had open. *What is it with doctors and insecure computer protocol?* For someone who's supposedly investing in tech, he doesn't seem particularly invested in understanding it.

But before I close out of the window, I see the number at the top of Dr. Cratchet's stock portfolio. The one displaying his total assets. My knees buckle.

Not that that's anything new, but this time it isn't pain that does it.

That's a lotta zeroes!

Intrigued, I scroll down to the little exclamation mark highlighting a new notification.

Highest Return Q2 Investment: Spitz-Shein Inc.

A couple more clicks, and I'm now looking at a graph comparing his individual investments and returns. The bookkeeper in me is intrigued, and my fingers are itching to comb through all the data.

Maybe there's something to this investing thing.

The coffee pot dings, bringing me back to reality and alerting me to the fact that I've been nosing around my boss's private financial records for the past five minutes instead of getting started on paperwork. I finally close out of the browser, but not before I see that "Spitz-Shein Inc." has returned 800% on Dr. Cratchet's significant early investment.

I make a mental note to do a little more research on them later.

By the time I bring the boss his coffee and settle down with my own cup at the computer (now displaying the documents I actually should be focusing on), I hear the metallic clatter of the mail-drop cover, along with the *thunk* of today's post falling into the box.

Always right as I sit down...

The *Pecker* is right on top of the pile as always.

Muscle-Men Mingle, Marketing MMA Mark-Down

That's right, sports fans! You heard it here first: Tuft Swallow's newest tenant is teaming up with Hometown Hero Nicholas "Odd Duck" D'Onofrio to offer a discount to members of the MMA gym Put Up Your Ducks! So if you've taken one too many hits, take a gander at this Gosling's offer of a free health consultation and fitness plan for any fighter at That's Good Crack!

It might not be as steamy as the other rumors swirling around Tuft Swallow's newest Doc, but our sources did manage to capture a picture from the business negotiation. Seems like Pizza Queen Tina Falcone and Captain Kodi Gander are some lucky ladies, indeed!

Below the story is a picture of Brian and Nick, decked out in protective gear and squaring up in the practice ring at Nick's gym. They're both wearing sleeveless shirts, and while the photo itself is fairly tame, the way the sweat pouring down their arms is making both men's muscles shine in the fluorescent lights is... downright sinful.

I lick my lips and wipe my mouth of the slight dribble of drool as the sight reminds me of another time I saw moisture drip down Brian's–

Nope!

Nooooope.

Not gonna go there!

I slam the paper face-down on the island in the middle of the break room, and flip through the rest of the various junkmail and weekly periodicals. The actual newspaper is also in the bundle, which I gather up with a few promotional pamphlets and deposit them into the file holder on my boss's closed door.

Is it hot in here? I pick up the rest of the mail and fan myself with it as I walk back to my desk.

I really didn't need any more reminders today of how attractive my fake boyfriend is. I certainly don't need those thoughts distracting me *yet again* from getting important work done.

At this rate, I don't even *need* to help Brian with his business. I'm already giving him an edge by shirking my duties here. By the time I piss off all the patients at the clinic, they'll be clawing down his door to get some actual help. Then he won't need me at all anymore.

I try not to read into the twinge of disappointment that curls in my chest at that thought.

PHLOOT-PHLOOT! "AGAIN!"

"I swear to God, Kodi, I'm going to rip that whistle right out of your mouth–"

Phloot-phloot! "What's that, Lily?" I toot again on the whistle, gesturing for the next line of players to run to the end of the field.

"Why–are–we–doing this–again?" D'Shawn, one of our better tossers and a teacher at Tuft Swallow Middle, pants as he jogs back to the starting line.

"Endurance!" I shout back. He clutches a stitch in his side.

"Maybe we could take five, Kodi? Even I'm a little out of breath." Finn, the Middle School gym teacher, does seem to be losing steam.

The sun is already sinking below the treeline at the park, and we only have about a half an hour of daylight left. We still haven't gotten through all the drills I wanted to before this weekend's match.

I frown at Finn. "Really? I thought this would be easy for you guys."

He gives me an incredulous look. I shrug. *Phloot-phloot!*

A series of groans echoes through the field as the next row starts their sprint (or, really, a pathetic jog) down to the cones at the other end. I clap my hands together and admit defeat.

"Alright, everyone, hydrate! Then back to the field for practice games. Go!"

No one makes eye contact as they pass me to get to their water bottles and gear at the end of the field. A few of them mutter to each other, but the second I hear more talking than drinking, I blow on the whistle again to get everyone back on the field.

An hour later, we wrap up, and the team hobbles off to their cars. Except for Lily and Callie, who make their way over to me.

"Kodi," Callie whines. "You have a problem."

"Tell me about it. We're never gonna win at this rate."

Lily rolls her eyes. "Yeah, because half the team is going to quit."

"What?" I snort. "Yeah right, Lily. This town eats, sleeps, and breathes cornhole. Nobody's going to quit the team and risk losing the championship."

A look passes between Callie and Lily. One that I don't quite understand. Lily nods to her as if answering an unspoken question, and Callie starts gathering up the practice boards on the field. Then Lily lifts her eyes to me and takes a deep breath.

"Are you…okay?"

I stare at her. "Never better. Why?"

"You seem…" She trails off, shuffling her feet a little as she searches for the right words. "Like you did back in high school."

I cross my arms. "What's that supposed to mean?"

Softball was my life in high school. By junior year, Coach had me staying after school an extra two hours a day practicing my pitch. Training me to make sure I was in tip-top shape for when the college scouts would come around. I wasn't just Tuft Swallow's star player, I was one of the best in New England. After the spring season that year, I had offers from six different Division I schools.

But I could always be better. Coach made sure I knew that.

"You're getting obsessed. Like nothing's good enough. Like you were back then."

I tilt my head at her, still not understanding. "We can always get better, Lily."

"Yeah, but like, why? Why do we have to? Why can't we just have fun?"

I shake my head. Of course she would feel that way.

Lily had already been headed for community college after high school. Whereas I studied and practiced hard, aiming to go out of state on a full ride when I graduated, she was content to stay in tiny town. And there's nothing wrong with that. It just means that she doesn't have the same ambition that I do.

"Not everything's about having fun," I mutter.

Now it's her turn to cross her arms. "Excuse me?"

"You know what, it's fine. I get it. You and I just look at this kinda thing differently, okay? We always have. You've never had the whole team's success on your shoulders. It's never been up to you to bring home the gold. You *get* to have fun. You get to party on the bus home from regionals, and you get to hook up with the wrestling team after pep rallies. Meanwhile, there are other people working to make sure we get where we're supposed to go."

A beat. Then, *"What?"* Lily throws her hands up in the air, looking at me like I just grew another head. "Kodi, what the fuck are you even talking about?"

"Nevermind. Just drop it, okay?"

"No! I won't *just drop it*. Who the hell told you that school sports and cornhole aren't supposed to be *fun*?"

A few evening joggers look at us curiously, as well as a couple of seniors in turquoise windbreakers who happen to be sitting on a bench nearby. I shiver. The air has gotten damp since the sun set, and a gusty breeze makes it feel like there might be a thunderstorm rolling in.

"Kodi," Lily begins, more quietly, as if she too has noticed the other people around. "This doesn't have to be life-or-death. It's a beer league. Sure, we want to win. But it's not supposed to be *work.*"

I shake my head. Coach always said that some people just aren't cut out for the competition. That's why I had to work extra hard. To make up for their shortcomings.

I had to practice. I had to get closer and closer to pitching perfect games, so it didn't matter how good the rest of the team was. As long as I could make sure the other guys didn't score, we were fine. *I* was fine.

And once my knee is back up to snuff, I'll be fine again. I won't have to worry about the rest of the team. But until then, everyone else needs to step up their game.

Callie walks back up to us, and I snap out of my memories long enough to realize she packed up all the equipment while we were talking. She hands me the keys to my Subaru. "They're all in the trunk."

"Oh. Wow Callie, thanks."

She and Lily share a look again. And, again, I feel like there's something I'm not getting.

"Kodi, do you want to get a drink and talk about this a little more? Somewhere you feel comfortable?"

Comfortable? Why wouldn't I be comfortable on the field?

"Not really." I fiddle with my keys, finding the car fob and picking my bag up off the ground. "Actually, I kinda just want to go home and rest. Someone's gotta make sure everything's ready to go for the game tomorrow."

"The match, you mean," Callie says.

"What?" I look up at her, and she meets my gaze with wide, innocent eyes.

"It's a match, technically. Cause it's a bunch of single matchups? A game would be if it's a team sport, like football or soccer."

"Or softball," Lily adds pointedly.

I shake my head. "Right. Match. Well," I hike my bag on my shoulder and give the girls a wave. "Regardless, I'll see you tomorrow at the senior center."

"Take it easy, Kodi."

Not really sure what that even means, I head to my car and drive home alone.

CHAPTER 20
BRIAN

Mighty Swallows Stick it to Chickens in a Total Shut-Out!

Three cheers for The Mighty Swallows! Our team took home the W at their first away match of the season against the Spring Chickens Assisted Living Center in a 6-0 shut-out! Though crowd morale was bubbling, team spirits seemed settled at a simmer for the Saturday, subduing the usually jubilant post-match celebrations.

Attendees also noticed that one Brian Gosling, Captain Gander's recent catch, wasn't present. Perhaps that contributed to her sour mood during the match?

The special Sunday edition of the *Pecker* catches my eye as I pick up my bacon breakfast sandwich and red-eye at Bun in the Oven. The little cafe is quickly becoming one of my favorite local establishments: the coffee's good, the bacon is the perfect combination of chewy meat and crispy fat, and the bagels are fresh-baked.

Maybe there's something to living in a small town with its charms.

And loathe as I am to admit it, even the *Nosy Pecker* with its insufferable gossip has its perks. For example, I'm able to keep up on town news: who's engaged, what local businesses are having a sale, and what my supposed girlfriend is up to.

Kodi's been suspiciously distant since her appointment on Tuesday. And as much as I understand her discomfort being around me after everything she saw (and I mean *everything*), I'm starting to feel a little offended. Sure, I'm not the most manscaped individual. But I mean, my equipment's not *lacking*. I'd never gotten any complaints.

But my bruised ego isn't the only issue. I need more one-on-one help with Medi-Cal, and that's hard to schedule when she doesn't return my texts. I was able to read through her notes and figure out how to set up a catalog of session and appointment types and bill for them appropriately, but my record keeping is still all over the place. I have no idea if I'm following HIPAA guidelines with my password management system. And while I've been trying to remember everything she pointed out during the brief tutoring session we had after her appointment last week, I keep getting distracted by everything else that pops up when I think of her.

It's not just that she saw me naked.

She made me lose my healy hands.

It was just a second, I know. She likely didn't even notice. But as I was following the line of her spine along to her hips my mind wandered, and before I knew it…

I wasn't touching her like a doctor anymore. I was touching her like a man.

And that's not okay.

I finish my sandwich and leave my folded *Pecker* on the table, heading out to get my to-do list sorted for the day. Of course, half the shops in town are closed on Sundays, so I need to drive to the outskirts of the city to pick up the few office supplies I realized I didn't have this week: including a decent WiFi router for my office.

In fact, I should probably password-protect *that* too, right?

Damn cyber security. I didn't go into health care to fight internet hackers.

By the time I arrive at the nearest Most Buy in Spitz Hollow, my brain is all sorts of twisted about Kodi. I've started to spiral: going from feeling conflicted, to feeling frustrated, to being angry about her not keeping up her end of the deal. At this point, I've adjusted her knee–what, three times? And all she's given me is a couple kisses and some old notes. Good kisses, granted.

Really good kisses.

But that doesn't mean I should let her take advantage of me. This is supposed to be a fake relationship we *both* benefit from, after all. And a scribble-filled binder from Tuft Swallow Community College and a case of blue balls are hardly benefits.

I'm fuming when I enter the store, storming over to the connectivity section where the routers and modems live. I'm staring at the selection for what feels like hours before I finally hear someone clear their throat behind me.

"Lost?"

"Actually, yeah I–" the rest of my sentence evaporates. Because standing before me, looking extra tasty in his Lucky-brand jeans and rumpled white button-down over a vintage Atari t-shirt, is Zeke.

"Hey B. Long time, and all that." He grins, and the one dimple in his left cheek that was always my fucking Achilles heel dents in like a dream. I swallow.

"Hey Zeke," I choke. "Y-yeah, been a minute. How ya been?"

"Alright I reckon. Won a toss yesterday, so feeling a little knackered after spending all night at the pub, but duty calls, you know?"

My throat feels like sandpaper."Yeah. What are you shopping for?"

"Flash drives. Never can have enough of the bloody things. You?"

"WiFi router."

"Ahhh, hence the thousand-meter stare." He chuckles, and I can feel my face heat. He always did think it was cute how terrible I was with anything and everything computer-related. He was my personal IT guy, back when…

Well, I guess not anymore.

He leans down and plucks a white box with blue and black lettering, the font color literally being the only thing to discern it from the twenty other identical boxes on the shelf. "You want to go with this one. Fast, good range, compatible with anything, and quick set-up." He leans in close and places it in my basket, then murmurs next to my ear, "It's the one I got my mum when she needed me to set up her flat."

His proximity sends little pulses down my spine, but I do my best to keep my smile polite as I thank him.

He raises an eyebrow. "I could help you set it up, you know, if you need–"

"Oh, no thanks. Kodi can help me, I'm sure."

I'm not sure. But I can't let him follow me back to town. The trees have eyes. With binoculars.

His dark eyes flash. "Ah yes, the Captain. How's that going, then? Between you two?"

"Good," I lie. He snickers.

"Right, right. I hear they won their match yesterday too."

"Yep."

He grins. "You saw it in the paper?"

"Yeah, I–" I start to answer, then catch myself. *He's laying a trap. Testing you.* I wasn't at the match yesterday. And he knows that. His smile widens, baring his electric white teeth. "I mean, Kodi called me right after to tell me, of course."

"Shame you couldn't be there for her."

"Oh, I–"

"I understand. You're a busy man. Hopefully she can keep you on the hook. I'm sure someone like her wouldn't want to let a catch like you swim away." He winks at me as he says that, and I swear my ribs turn to putty.

What is he implying? That she isn't good enough for me? That *I'm* not good enough for *him?*

Then he takes a deep breath and shifts his basket of flash drives to his other hand. "Well, B, it was great catching up. Maybe I'll see you around?"

"Yeah, uh. See you around, Z."

He turns the corner of the aisle, and I lazily swing one foot in front of the other down row after row of printing paper until I'm certain he's left the store. Then I collapse into one of the display office chairs and put my face in my hands.

Oh God. He knows. He has to know that I'm not actually dating Kodi.

Otherwise, why would he ask those questions? And that grin when he realized I didn't go to her game?

Fuck. He's going to try to use that to fuck with her, I'm sure. With me.

Wait. I straighten in the surprisingly comfortable ergonomic leather seat. *Why would he be interested in sabotaging my relationship with Kodi? Unless...*

Does he want me back?

Unbidden, my brain plays back our entire interaction on repeat, slowing down in the moment he leaned in close to my ear. Offered to help me install my router. Winked at me.

Fucking hell. He wants *me.*

Leaning back, I let the leather wings of the backrest cradle my shoulders as I let that information sink in. This stupid plan of Kodi's is actually working. It's helping me win Zeke back.

Which means, I need to double down. Keep up the act until Zeke gets jealous enough to come crawling back.

But Kodi's right. If the *Nosy Pecker* got wind I was seeing the rival team captain, everyone in town would know about it instantly. And all of them would boycott me for sleeping with the enemy.

Literally.

I lean my head back on the padded neck cushion and file

through the implications of all of this. If this is going to work, my feelings for Zeke are going to need to stay under wraps until after the championship game. The easiest way to cover up those feelings is to get closer to Kodi.

I need to start going to these cornhole matches. I need to show vocal support for my girl, do the things that will make Zeke more jealous. But he isn't going to believe it if it's just a weak act.

I need to spend more time with her, learn more about her, be better about being seen with her in public. Otherwise, people will believe *The Nosy Pecker* and think we're on the outs.

If I know anything about Zeke, it's that he's fickle. He won't want to make something official until he's sure he can't get it any other way. And convincing him, and all of Tuft Swallow, that Kodi Gander is my girlfriend, truly is the best way to make him take a stand.

He always wants what he can't have.

Which means I have to make myself undeniably unavailable.

It isn't easy, but I pull myself from my thoughts and the indecently comfortable chair and take my purchases up to the front to check out.

"Anything else I can help you with today?"

"I'm goo–" I start to say, and then pause. "Actually, can I get one of those office chairs, too?"

THE NEXT DAY AS I'M SITTING AT MY DESK IN MY FANCY NEW executive lounger and messing with Medi-Cal, *again*. Rain pounds against the windows of the foyer, and the taps and splats are loud enough to battle the sound of Louis Prima playing in my office. After about twenty-five minutes of battling with preferences menus, I finally cave in and realize I need help.

Kodi's help.

"You have reached Kodi Gander. Please leave a message."

Fuck, I think to myself as I hear the voicemail tone beep. "Hey,

Kodi, it's Brian. Wondering if we could do another barter soon? I'm messing with Medi-Cal and it's just kicking my ass right now. Hope your knee is doing okay. And congrats on the win this weekend! Anyway, call me back when you get this?"

When I hang up, I already have a text from her waiting for me.

KODI

Hey, sorry I missed your call. Doc's on a rampage. Call you back during lunch?

ME

Sure.

Once that's sent, I remember my realization the day before about needing to make more of an effort as Kodi's fake boyfriend.

ME

Actually, why don't I take you out for lunch? I know a good pizza place.

I don't hear back right away, but that seems to be par for the course when Kodi is at work. Dr. Cratchet, who I already have a pretty low opinion of after seeing the kinds of prescriptions he'd written for Kodi's knee pain, seems to be just the worst kind of boss. Micromanage-y, weirdly inappropriate… I'm not entirely sure why she even puts up with him. Surely with her skills she could find a decent office job just about anywhere?

My phone buzzes, but this time, it isn't Kodi.

NICK

Brian. Emergency at the gym. Can you get here and help out one of the fighters? He twisted something real bad.

I jump out of my chair at the message from Nick. After seeing him last week, he'd made it absolutely clear he wanted to work with me to see to his fighters' health. This is my chance to prove it to the rest of the guys there.

ME

Put ice on it. I'll be right there.

"FUCK, FUCK, *FUCK!*" D'SHAWN GROANS AS I PALPATE THE MUSCLE around his hip. "Goddamnit, Doc, that hurts like a bitch!"

"Yeah he doesn't fuck around." Nick pats D'Shawn on the shoulder, and he flinches. I'm not sure if his reaction is to Nick, or the fact that I just found another bunch of angry fascia across his iliotibial band.

"Well it's no wonder you twisted it," I say. "Your IT band is crazy tight, man. It was only a matter of time before something got out of alignment. You need to stretch more."

"I stretch!"

"Not these muscles." I stick my thumb into the proximal end of his sartorius, which happens to be located in an unfortunate spot under the ridge of his pelvis. It doesn't exactly look pretty when seen by outside observers.

"Jesus Christ, dude, he's gonna crush your nutsack."

Nick glares at the guy who muttered, putting a stop to a chorus of chuckles behind me. "Brian's a pro. He knows what needs crushing."

"We hear you fight, too," One of the fighters, a young blonde guy who I'm pretty sure I've seen in uniform once or twice around town. "When are we going to get to face you in the ring?"

"Pretty sure he's coming to class on Wednesday." Nick catches my eye and smiles. I nod.

"Yep. That's the plan."

D'Shawn's breathing has finally smoothed out a bit, now that I've tackled the worst of it. He gingerly stretches out his leg and swings it back and forth.

"How's it feel?"

I watch him get up off the folding table I brought with me to the gym and slowly walk around in a circle on the mats.

"Uh…" He takes a few steps before committing to an answer. "Good? Yeah. Yeah! I feel pretty good!"

His stride grows more confident and his steps more sure as he realizes his leg can hold his weight. I grin at him.

"Well, take it easy for the next few days. No running. Let me show you some exercises you should do a few times a day to loosen up that IT band, too, otherwise you're gonna be right back where you started in a week."

"Yeah, you got it, Doc!"

"And everyone else, clear out! The 1:00 class gets here in five." Nick claps his hands, and the fighters bow themselves off the mat and head to the changing rooms.

"Wait, what time is it?" I snap my head around to look at the clock. *Dammit!* I've been here way longer than I thought. Kodi's lunch break is practically over, and I totally left her hanging. "Ah, fuck. One sec, D'Shawn, I gotta check my phone…"

"Uh-oh. Miss a date?" Nick winks at me as a knowing look crosses his features.

"Your lady ain't gonna be too happy about that," D'Shawn drawls.

I wave at them to hush as I check my voicemail.

"Hey Brian, this is Kodi. I just got off for lunch, wondering where you are. I tried texting, but didn't get an answer… I guess we can try for dinner or something later? Let me know. Bye."

"Damn," I grumble, sending out a quick apology text and shoving my phone in my pocket. "I was supposed to take Kodi to lunch."

"Oh shit, that's right. Your girl is *Kodi.*" D'Shawn shakes his head at me, and I wonder a little at his expression. "Oh Captain, my Captain."

"Yeah." I let out a nervous chuckle. "Uh, you two have history or something?"

"No, no, just wondering how on earth someone got the ice queen to thaw long enough to get her number."

Ice Queen?

"We talkin' about Coach Kodi?" The blonde fighter from earlier comes out of the changing area dressed in his cop uniform, next to another blonde guy who seems to be a couple years younger. I see **B. Pecker** embroidered above the officer's pocket.

Oh yeah, Pecker. What was his first name? Bill? Bob?

"Watch what you say, Brad, we got her boyfriend right here," Nick chimes in from where he's setting up some heavy bags.

Brad. That's it.

The other blonde speaks up. "Tell us, man. Is she as intense in the sack as she is at practice? You like 'em in control?"

Brad punches him in the arm, and the kid winces. "Not cool, man. Be respectful."

"Uh…sorry guys, I'm a little confused here. What's Kodi like at practice?"

"Brutal."

"Tough as nails."

"An absolute bitch."

They all answer at the same time, and Brad punches the rude kid in the arm again.

"Hey!"

"Seriously, Logan, knock it off," D'Shawn scolds him. "I get she embarrassed you at practice, but *you* were at least asking for it. Now the rest of us have to put up with her bad attitude."

"Bad attitude? Really?" I look back and forth between the three guys. "She's never seemed that way around me."

"Maybe you got something special then, man, cause she's never been anything but pure righteous determination 'round us."

I shake my head. None of the guys (except Logan) are saying anything particularly damning, but it's clear in their stances and expressions that they don't have the highest opinion of my fake girlfriend.

Are practices really that bad?

"Huh. I'm sorry, guys. Maybe I'll talk to her about it."

"No!" All four of them–even Nick–shout at me in unison. I flinch.

"Okay, okay, sorry for suggesting it!" I laugh nervously at their visceral reactions. "You all act like you're afraid of her or something."

A few glances are shared between them. I blink.

"You're not, right? Afraid of her?"

There's a pause, and then Officer Brad says, "she is a little scary, dude."

"I can't believe this. You all are literally fighters. You were just knocking the shit out of each other in here an hour ago. You're telling me Kodi, *my Kodi,* at five-foot-four with a bad knee, *scares* you?"

"You haven't seen her at practice."

I chuckle in earnest then, shaking my head. "This is too much. How bad can she be?"

Again, silence rings across the gym. This time, no one offers any answers for me. I run my fingers through my hair.

"Alright. I guess I'll need to see for myself then."

CHAPTER 21
KODI

By the time 5:00 rolls around, I am a walking corpse. My back is sore from leaning forward in my cheap-ass office chair reading through patient paperwork all day. Usually, I don't mind picking up the slack around the clinic, but today, the fact that Dr. Cratchet is too much of a cheapskate to allow the board to hire nurses to handle all of this crap weighs a lot heavier than usual. Especially when all I want to do is go home, take a hot bath, and work out some of the tension in my shoulders.

Maybe some other tension, too…

I clock out and grab my bag, blowing out a breath as I comb through my text messages.

LILY

Hey girl. Are we still down for cosmos at the Crowbar tonight?

Right. Girls' night.

To be honest, after the weird guilt-trip Lily tried to send me on after practice and her frosty attitude at the game last weekend, I'm not so sure I'm ready to be all buddy-buddy over drinks with her and Callie.

She seems convinced that I don't know the difference between softball and cornhole, which couldn't be more wrong. I know that nothing will ever be the same as softball. That ship sailed a long time ago.

Or, at least, I assumed it did. Now with Brian in the mix, and my knee feeling almost healthy half the time, maybe I'd still have a chance to play…somewhere.

Speaking of Brian, there's an apology text from him explaining that he'd had to deal with an emergency at the fighting gym, asking for a raincheck on our pizza date.

That's what he called it. A date.

A whole new wave of anxiety runs through me at that. I mean, sure, we're pretending to be dating; that was kind of the whole point of our arrangement. But that's only in front of other people. When it's just the two of us, like on our text chain, it's supposed to be like it's always been. Friendly, but professional.

Except when he's jumping on my prone body as he steps out of the shower–

NOPE! No. *Nō.* Bad Kodi. *Bad Kodi!*

A long time ago in my high school biochem class, there was a lecture about memory, and how the more you try to remember something that happened to you in real life, the more your brain replaces the real memory with your last recalling of the memory.

At this point, I've replayed that scene so often in my brain that it no longer feels real, like the innocent mistake that it was.

Now, I remember it as some Cinemax fantasy version of what actually happened. With Brian's dripping chest, his hair falling in thick pieces across his forehead and dripping onto my shirt, making my nipples pop against the white fabric of my blouse as he slowly lowers his head to mine–

BAD Kodi! BAD!

Okay, self, refocus on the actual task at hand before my ovaries turn on and hotwire my nervous system. Again.

Brian wants to raincheck. Cool. That's good. That gives me more time to cool off a bit. More time to forget the memory–both actual AND fantasy–of seeing his penis. And abs. And muscly arms. And toned thighs…

ME

No worries. Some other time than

Cool. Casual. Not even gonna correct that typo I made.

*then.

Old habits die hard.

By the time I close the door to the clinic and lock it behind me, Lily's sent another text, saying she and Callie snagged our usual table at the bar. By the time I get to my car, she sends me a picture of my go-to drink order, a gin and tonic with extra lime.

LILY

Order up, sugartits!

Goddammit.

TEN MINUTES LATER, I'M WALKING INTO THE BAR, HAVING LEFT MY Subaru on Oak Street outside of the clinic. There's no point in driving the block and a half to the bar, only to drive the rest of the two blocks back to my place. The only reason I even took the damn car to work in the first place was because it was pouring this morning, and I didn't want to fight with an umbrella and wet shoes all day.

Luckily, the puddles have mostly dried up in the hot afternoon sun, and I'm totally dry as I push open the door to the Crowbar to drink with my gal pals.

"Kodi!" Callie's already tipsy as she waves at me with her cosmo. "Over here!"

Lily greets me with a cautious smile, as if she wasn't quite sure I'd actually show up. I avoid holding eye contact with her for more than a second or so when I plaster a smile on my face in return.

"Thanks for the G&T." I take the remaining seat and cheers with them.

"Don't mention it," Lily responds politely.

An awkward thirty seconds follow.

"Soooo..." Callie finally breaks the silence, stirring the remaining ounce of her fluorescent pink drink with her cherry on its stick. "How are things with Brian?"

"Ooo, yes. We need deets." Lily leans in, eagerly jumping on the change in subject.

"What deets? You know the deal with us."

"Deal?" Callie blinks. Lily gives her a look and twirls her finger, waiting for Callie to catch on. "OH! You mean the Chiropractor Trap."

"You're calling it that now, too?" I roll my eyes. "Jesus, you two, that's not even remotely a fake-relationship trope."

"Shhhhh keep your voice down!" Lily hisses. "No one's supposed to know!"

"It's so exciting," Callie giggles, "nothing like this *ever* happened in the other places I lived."

"Not that you know of," Lily says.

"Good point." Callie pops one of the cherries in her mouth as she considers that.

"Nothing's happened. I haven't even seen him since Wednesday."

"What? Why?"

I squeeze the three tiny lime wedges into my glass, then stir the pale green pulp deeper into the bubbles. Lily taps her fingers on the table. "Hello, Kodi? Why not?"

This is exactly the reason I didn't want to go to girls' night. I knew these two would grill me about *something.* And it's really only a matter of time before I end up caving and spilling everything. Lily's persistent like that. They should hire her at Guantanamo.

"Our last appointment was a little… awkward. I don't know. I just think maybe we should keep things professional unless we're out in public or something."

"Well, when's the next time you're going out in public?" Callie asks, tilting her head. I take a breath to answer, then pause, and Lily jumps on my hesitation.

"Before you answer that, back up a hair. I want to hear more about that awkward appointment. What, exactly, was awkward about it? Did he smell bad? Was he wearing a sweater vest?"

"Oooo, that would be awkward," Callie agrees.

"It's more what he *wasn't* wearing," I mutter, and then realize my mistake.

"WHAT?" Lily shrieks. The whole bar turns to look at her, and she yells at Charlene, "Um, we need another round here! This just got juicy."

She leans in toward me, and I swear my face catches fire. I'm mortified. I didn't even mean to say that out loud, and now the whole bar is listening in to our conversation.

"Uhhh, no, I didn't mean–"

"I hear there's juice? That means gin." Charlene plops another gin and tonic down in front of me, as well as two more cosmos for the girls. *That was fast.* Then she even leans down and puts her elbows on the table. "Is this about the new hot chiropractor? You're seeing him, right?"

Is it possible to spontaneously combust from embarrassment?

"Uh, yeah, but you know. It's still early. We just–"

"He's totally swept her off her feet! Did you see them kissing at the match? My God. Talk about swoon-worthy." Now Callie's fanning herself, and I swear the elderly happy hour regulars are about to fall off their chairs from leaning in our direction. I'm beginning to hear the buzz of their hearing aids getting turned up.

"Guys, chill out, okay, it's private stuff–"

"What's private stuff?"

A whoosh of cool air rushes past my face as the group around the table collectively straightens, opening up my peripheral vision to reveal Brian.

Once again popping up behind me at the Crowbar on girls' night and pulling up a chair.

"What did I miss?"

As I'm washing my hands in the bathroom, Lily crashes into the swinging door like a wrecking ball.

"Spill. Quick. Before someone thinks you're pooping."

"Lil, seriously, nothing–"

"Cut the shit, Gander, and tell your best friend what you saw. You can mime it if you want. Was it this general area...?" She moves her hands in circles around her pelvis.

I wince. *Don't think about Brian's penis, don't think about Brian's penis...*

"Why does Kodi have penis face?" Callie asks, also barreling into the bathroom.

"Can a woman shit in piece? Jesus!" I cover my face with my still wet hands, then push my hair back. "Did you say *penis face?"*

"Oh my God you saw his *penis??"* Lily's voice raises three octaves in the last four syllables of her sentence.

"Oh God I'm gonna puke," I mutter, darting back into the stall.

"Do you want me to tell Brian you're sick?" Callie offers from behind the metal Hiney Hider. I shove down the toilet seat lid and sit down, burying my face in my hands.

"Yes."

"No." I can see Lily's feet part in her defiant hands-on-hips stance under the stall door. "She's faking it."

"I'm not," I lie.

"You're just trying to get out of telling us, your *best friends,* that you saw your first penis and can't stop thinking about it."

Maybe if I just don't say anything, the two of them will go away. *Should I fake puking noises?* I bet I'll actually make myself sick if I pretend I'm barfing.

This isn't exactly the cleanest bathroom in town after all, and I'd have to breathe pretty deep to make it sound convincing.

"Yeah, I'm gonna tell Brian you dropped your phone in the toilet." I hear Callie's footsteps retreat. A second passes, and then there's a thunk as Lily leans her shoulder against the stall.

"Kodi?" She asks, this time in a quieter tone. One I haven't heard her use in a long time, actually.

"Yeah?"

"Why don't you trust me anymore?"

I'm not sure if it's the way she says it, or the words themselves that take me completely off-guard. But I don't respond right away.

I do *trust her.*

Don't I?

"I–"

"Don't lie to me again," she whispers. "Ever since you graduated and started working at the clinic, moved out of your parents' place…you stopped telling me about your life. Your feelings.

"I tell you everything. I try to be your friend. But sometimes, it feels like you won't let me."

"Lily…"

"I *know* something's going on with you being team captain. I *know* it's gotta be bringing up memories for you, and how Coach Blevins abused you and put all that pressure on you–"

"What?" I slam open the stall door, and Lily jumps back. "What do you mean abused me?"

"He was awful to you, Kodi. He convinced you that you only had worth if you pitched a perfect game. He made you practice for hours–*hours*–after we'd all left and gone home. Your dad used to tell me to make sure you ate lunch everyday because you'd skip dinner and head straight to bed when you got home at night."

"Dad did what?"

"We all just want to be there for you, Kodi. I frickin' love you. You're my best friend, but you won't let me be yours."

I stare at her, gobsmacked, for a long moment. Long enough that Callie comes back in, looking like she has something to say, but I hardly even notice.

I won't let *her?*

"Hey Kodi, Brian says he hopes you feel better and he'll touch base with you tomorrow. And good luck with your phone. Also, Charlene says she doesn't have rice but has some panko in the back if you want to try to dry it out." I finally snap out of my stare and wave to Callie in recognition.

"Right, thanks."

Callie looks between the two of us, and hisses out a breath. "I, uh, I'll settle up at the bar and let you two wrap up in here. See you tomorrow at practice?"

I nod dumbly, and Lily thanks her.

Then it's just me and Lily again. She scuffs her toe against the tile floor.

"I used to think that maybe you really *were* gay, like everyone said, and maybe that was why you didn't want to talk to me about guy stuff. That maybe if I just gave you enough time, just let you process and come out in your own way, you'd realize that you could talk to me about it. When that didn't work, I made that whole big deal about Brian being bi to try to get you to admit it out of anger, but then I saw the way you two looked at each other at the match and I realized that it wasn't that at all. You like guys just fine, Kodi. In fact, you like one in particular so much, that you're manufacturing a fake relationship with him just so you have an excuse to spend time with him."

That wakes me up. "That's not what I'm doing!"

"Oh, please. It's absolutely what you're doing." She rolls her eyes, and the look is so quintessentially Lily that it brings an involuntary smile to my face. I cough out a half-laugh, and Lily's lips tilt up in a shy grin. "Hey. There you are. So what's actually going on with you? Can we like, talk about it for real? Like actual friends? For once?"

As I look into her eyes, it's like I'm seeing her for the first time again. All of a sudden, we're back on the playground in first grade and Lily's busting some kid's balls for stealing our kickball when I threw it out of bounds. Back when we'd hide out in the jungle gym for hours and talk about everything, and nothing at all. Then later, in high school, when we'd hike to the lake and she'd wax poetic about her future wedding while I talked about my dreams of going to the Olympics.

She's right here. She's been here the whole time.

I'm feeling so many things that I don't understand right now, and you know what?

I could really use a friend to talk to about it.

"Yeah, actually," I sniff. *When did I start crying?* "I'd like that."

TWO HOURS AND THREE PINTS OF BEN AND JERRY'S LATER, I'VE caught up Lily on the entirety of mine and Brian's fake relationship. We're in my Subaru at the Plume n' Zoom, totally wearing out the battery listening to the same driving mix CD that's been in the car stereo since I bought it in 2018 on repeat.

"Oh my gosh, so he literally was trying to save you from hurting your knee again, and the towel just flew off??"

A couple flecks of chocolate ice cream and marshmallow fluff fly out and hit my cheek as she talks around a mouthful of Phish Food. I laugh at myself and wipe it away.

"No, no, that's the most ridiculous part, it didn't fly off until he was already beside me and I was panicking so hard that I was like, kicking him off of me, and the corner of it caught under my hip and then, *shwoop!*" I mime an avalanche with my hands. "There goes the towel. Full view of the goods."

"Was it nice?" She waggles her eyebrows.

"Oh man, Lily, I don't know!" I groan, shoving a spoonful of The Late Dough in my mouth. "I don' havv a-nee-fing to com'pair it 'oo."

"Okay, okay, I'm gonna start spreading my hands apart, and you stop me when I get to the right size, okay?" She holds her hands in front of her like she's praying, and then slowly separates them.

One inches. Two. Three. Four…

"Oh my God, Kodi, was he like, hard when this was happening, or–"

I shake my head. Her face pales.

"Jesus." She looks down at her hands, now almost half a foot apart. "And this is *flaccid??"*

"I mean, that I remember? I was also in full panic mode, like, literally convulsing and trying not to look, but as far as I remember…"

Not that I can trust my memory of that moment anymore. Pretty sure there wasn't Usher's *Love in this Club* playing in the background or any candles burning in wall sconces, despite me picturing them in my mind now whenever I bring it up.

She shakes her head, and we both chew another few spoonfuls in quiet reflection.

"Well," she finally says, smacking her lips. "You know what you gotta do, right?"

"What?"

Her eyes flash, and my stomach drops. "You gotta sleep with him."

"No way." I dig another heaping spoon of ice cream out of the carton. "Not gonna happen."

"You're never gonna stop thinking about it if you don't."

"I've lasted this long without sex," I argue. "Clearly it's not that big a deal, or I would have imploded by now or something."

"Yeah, but you didn't *want* sex before. *Now* you want it. Bad."

I chew for a minute, letting out a sigh through my nose. "No, Lily. He still likes his ex. It's not gonna happen."

"He only still likes his ex because he doesn't realize you're interested yet. Trust me, Kodi. The way he looked at you?" She whistles. "He's gonna fall for you hard. If he hasn't already."

I chew on the ends of my plastic spoon. "I don't know, Lily…

that's not what this is about. We have a deal. I don't want to fuck that up just because I'm… *horny*."

She gives me a hard look, as if she's about to disagree. But then a moment passes, and her eyes soften. She pops in another spoonful of *The Late Dough* and then gesticulates with her spoon.

"Well then, just fuck him to get it out of your system! I mean, come on. Once you ride his giant dick and realize the sex is just fine and he's totally mediocre at it, you'll buy yourself a vibrator and it'll be back to Operation: Win Back Zeke."

"Or I could just use the vibrator I have."

"Text him tonight. Tell him you'll meet him tomorrow after practice for a late-night nerd session. Then seduce him."

I chuckle, the picture of *me* attempting to seduce anybody too ridiculous to ignore. "I'm gonna be exhausted after practice."

"Not if you end it on time for once," she says pointedly. I sigh. She doesn't relent. "Which brings me to–"

"Can we not talk about that tonight?" I place my pint on the dashboard and meet her eyes. She raises her eyebrow at me, giving me a look that says, *are we really going back to not talking again?* "Not because I'm hiding it from you, I swear. I just… I…"

I don't know how to process what you said earlier.

I don't think I was abused by Coach Blevins.

Was I?

"I can't open that can of worms right now. There's too much going on," I finish lamely.

Lily narrows her eyes and assesses me for a second, but whatever she sees seems to satisfy her. She nods once, and puts the lid back onto her carton. "Okay. We'll table it for now. But you're seeing him tomorrow."

"Okay."

"And you're gonna tell me all about it."

"You got it."

"As soon as he pulls out."

"Lily!" I smack her with my spoon. She winks at me and opens the passenger door, tossing the unfinished pint in the front seat.

"I'm walking home. I'll text you in the morning."

"The Doc doesn't like tex–"

"I know, I know, I won't file a missing persons report if I don't hear back until after lunch."

She leans down into the wedge of space in the open door and catches my eye. We share a smile.

"Thanks, Lily. And…I'm sorry."

There's so much more in those two little words than their syllables can contain. My throat catches as I try to say more, try to figure out how I can explain how my whole life felt like it ended at eighteen, and I didn't think anyone could understand what I was going through. How I'd been so isolated from the late night practices, and the scholarship rescindment letters, and the antidepressants, that I couldn't even bring myself to get out of bed until she'd shown up at my bedroom door with DVDs and Doritos. And then when I *did* finally get my act together, I was terrified that if I confessed to anybody the thoughts that had been running through my mind on any given day…

She waves it all away with a flick of her wrist.

"I know. And you're welcome."

CHAPTER 22
BRIAN

KODI

Hey, sorry I bailed on you at the bar. I wasn't feeling well.

ME

Your phone works!

Haha, yeah, that old rice trick works wonders!

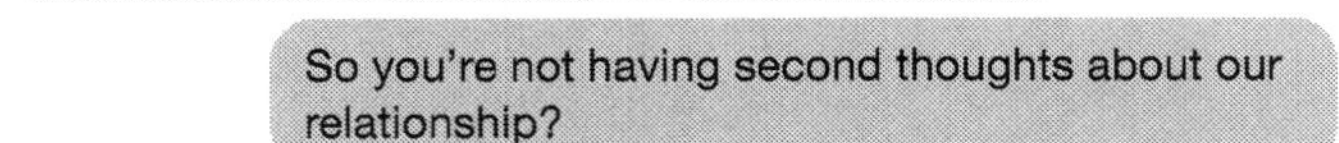

No! Course not. I still owe you a few Medi-Cal lessons, don't I?

Yes! Tomorrow?

In between work and practice okay?

I breathe a sigh of relief, then close out of the messaging app and return to the task at hand. It's about 8:30 am and I'm pushing a mostly empty grocery cart in the cereal aisle, chewing over how I'm going to handle seeing Kodi tonight.

So far, our appointments have been mostly professional, not delving too deeply into each other's personal lives. But yesterday at the gym, the things I learned about my supposed girlfriend make it a little bit harder to stand to the side while she beats around my other patients.

After all, I'm just now starting to make some real connections in town. Nick has been an incredible asset to my business, singing my praises to all the athletes in town, and his little emergency phone call yesterday gave me an opportunity to show everyone down there what I'm capable of. D'Shawn's already made a follow-up appointment, and Brad asked me for a few of my business cards to hand out to some of the guys from the force who need help recovering from past injuries on the job.

So finding out that Kodi's antagonizing my future customers by busting their balls three times a week at cornhole, of all things? Not exactly good for building a strong professional reputation.

And isn't that the main reason why we're doing this? So I can get *That's Good Crack* established and thriving?

Well, not the *main* reason, I suppose.

Even as my interactions with the guys make me want to treat Kodi with caution, I know that I don't stand a chance of winning back Zeke if she and I don't get closer.

Zeke. Whereas in the first few days after our breakup, I agonized over him, I now can't seem to think about him or our flirty exchange in the router aisle without Kodi's face popping up in my mind.

The constant hijacking of my thoughts has been confusing at the best of times, and frustrating at the worst. It's been going on for a while now, too. I can't even jerk off anymore without her light brown eyes and freckled nose creeping into my me-time at the worst possible moment. Because of that, I haven't gotten a real release in over a week.

It doesn't make sense. Sure, we had those few intense kisses at the match, and then later at the bar. Honestly, I still haven't really unpacked that night–our first public outing together since agreeing to the whole relationship ruse. I thought I'd been doing a decent job improvising, and she was totally playing along. It was innocent. Fun. Until a quick peck on the cheek turned into something altogether…

Sinful.

And then she saw me naked...

I'm still contemplating the whole mess when an older, fashionable woman with a blonde Blanche Devereaux haircut approaches me.

"Excuse me, are you Brian?"

I slip my phone into my pocket and meet her eyes, surprised that she actually asks me. So far, everyone in town has been rather shameless about already knowing who I am from the *Pecker*. "Yes?"

"It's so nice to meet you," she says, sticking out her hand. "I'm Linda Gander, Kodi's mom."

"Oh!" *Shit.* "Uh, hello, Mrs.–"

"Oh please, call me Linda. We're practically the same age, after all." She looks me up and down with a face that's entirely unreadable and fluffs her hair.

Fuck. I can't help it; I panic. I'm not sure if she's trying to say that *she* isn't that old, or that *I'm* not that young. And to her, I probably seem like some kind of predator.

Which is a little rude. Granted, I'm 34. Which *does* present a bit of an age gap with her daughter, I suppose. And yeah, I've got a few gray hairs in my beard that I earned back in my residency that make me look even older in the right light. But Kodi and I aren't actually dating. And even if we were, Kodi seems much older than 24.

Oh God. That's the kind of thing that groomers say, isn't it? *Does Mrs. Gander think I'm grooming her daughter?*

Too many seconds pass before I remember that it's my turn to say something, and that all of this isn't worth overthinking anyway because I'm not *really* dating a 24 year-old. I force out an awkward laugh and attempt to be charming.

"Linda. There's no way you could be Kodi's mother. You don't look a day over 35!"

Fuck. Is 35 considered young? Am I old? Did I just insult my fake girlfriend's mother in Tuft Swallow's only grocery store? God, why do I have to be so awful with parents? I need to come back here if I want to eat. I can't avoid the grocery store if I accidentally make an enemy of Kodi's mother.

A beat, and then Linda laughs, revealing a mouthful of sparkling white teeth. "Oh, you're a charmer! I can see what Kodi sees in you! I'm teasing, by the way. You seem like a very nice young man. And you're a doctor!"

"Of Chiropractic, yes." God, this is uncomfortable. What on earth am I supposed to say to the mother of the woman in whose kitchen I've been photographed wearing a frilly pink apron? "It's nice to meet you."

Oh.

Lies. That's what I'm supposed to say. Well, that makes it a little easier, I suppose.

"Do you golf? You and Marty should schedule a tea time. I'm sure he'd love to get to know the man who charmed our daughter so…quickly."

I swallow.

If I'd known that Kodi's parents lived in town, I'd have been a lot more careful about our public exploits. I wouldn't have made out with her in front of the whole town, for one. And maybe not spent the night at her apartment when she got drunk after the game.

But really, it's not the fact that her parents live in town that's the problem. It's the fact that that town is Tuft Swallow, and Tuft

Swallow is home to the Pervy Publishing Society of Elderly Espionage, and our entirely chaste sleepover was spread across the morning news in black-and-white.

Where it was likely *read* by her parents.

"I've never played, actually."

"He'll let you borrow his spare clubs. I insist! What's your number? He'll call you."

I'm trapped. If I don't give her my number, she'll think I have unsavory intentions for her daughter. If I do, then her husband is going to make me play golf and give me the third degree about the unsavory intentions they'll *still* believe I have for their daughter. It's a catch-22.

I scrabble in my pocket for a business card and hand it to her. "Here. It's my office number."

"Fabulous! Well, I have milk in my cart. Marty will talk to you soon! *So* nice running into you."

She takes the card from my hand like she's selecting a weapon for battle. Then she flashes me that ten thousand watt smile again before click-clacking her sensible heels past me and down the aisle.

I pick up the rest of the ingredients for dinner in record time.

BY THE TIME KODI MAKES IT TO MY OFFICE AFTER WORK, THE CHICKEN parm I whipped up for the two of us is baking in the oven. She rings the doorbell and I run from the upstairs kitchen down to the front door to let her in.

"Hey! Sorry I'm late. Three different moms brought in their toddlers with chicken pox half an hour before closing. Then the Doc had me cancel his early morning appointments so he could sleep in." She rolls her eyes, shifting the weight of the backpack on her shoulders.

Moms. Oh God. Should I tell her about running into her mom at the grocery store earlier?

"Anyway, ready to dive into Medi-Cal? I managed to find more of my notes from scho–oof!" She shifts her weight to take off the backpack and her knee buckles a little. I just manage to catch her before she stumbles onto her good leg.

Her hair wafts across my face as she falls into my arms, and I get a whiff of the scent of her shampoo. *Strawberries.* My arms tighten around her instinctively, and suddenly her smell is everywhere.

And…it's nice. Really nice.

I lean in closer to her, the instinct to kiss her so close to the surface that I almost forget why she's here.

But then her backpack clatters to the floor, and I remember. I place her gently upright on the floor, and clear my throat, backing away a respectable distance.

That was just a reflex. I don't actually *want* to kiss her. It's just become something we do now, for the sake of the act.

"Why don't we do an adjustment first? Then we can talk software," I suggest. *And maybe breach the topic of golf with your dad.*

Why am I so nervous all of the sudden?

She nods, wincing as she straightens her knee. "To the table?"

I nod, swallowing. "Face up this time."

I take her backpack and she hobbles to my office. As she goes, I observe her gait, shifting my thoughts into doctor-mode. One of the most important things I learned in school for chiropractic was how to set aside personal feelings when working with a patient. Call it bedside manner, call it professionalism; when working with a patient's body, it's crucial to see it as just that: a body. A system of muscles and bones and connective tissue. As a chiropractor, it's my job to observe it clinically so I can fix the issues without awkward emotions getting in the way.

Even in the wide-leg trousers she's wearing, I can see that her hips are off-kilter. The fact that she can't support weight on her left leg is causing all sorts of other problems up the chain of her musculoskeletal system. I'm amazed that her boss let it get this bad. Isn't he a doctor, too?

He should know better than to let a healthy, dynamic twenty-four year-old woman with an ass like that walk crooked for the rest of her life. It's appalling.

"You coming, or what?" She hollers from the office. I set her backpack down by the stairs and follow her. "You know, lying face up and staring at the ceiling, I'm realizing you should have some glow-in-the-dark stars or something up there to look at. Ooo, maybe a crossword? Or a fireman-of-the-month calendar?"

I snort and place my hands on her ankles, checking the alignment of her legs. "No way. If I'm putting a pinup calendar in my office it's gonna be where *I* can see it. Did you know your hips are an inch off? Have you felt any pain around your pelvis or lower back?"

"I mean, my back usually gets sore by the end of the day. Dr. Cratchet isn't exactly known for investing in ergonomic office chairs."

I hum in acknowledgement. "Remind me to check your neck and shoulders later."

"Oh, you're not going to crack my neck, are you?" She shivers on the table, and for a second I think it's because I move my hand to her thigh. I wonder if I've somehow messed up again. *Am I slipping with my healy hands?* Then she looks at me fearfully and I realize it's the thought of having her neck adjusted that's making her shiver.

Unlike last time.

I give myself a little shake internally. No. We're not going to think about last time. We agreed to forget that last appointment ever happened. I shift gears, falling back into doctor-mode once again.

"Does it make you uncomfortable?" A lot of people don't like getting their neck adjusted. I understand; there are plenty of quacks out there who have seriously hurt people. But damn, there's nothing better than just the right *crack* to get your head back on straight. "I won't do it if you really don't want me to. But I assure you it's safe."

Her eyes are wary as she considers me.

And then I push my thumb into the distal end of her sartorius muscle.

"Motherfuu–" She can't even finish the word as all the air bleeds from her lungs.

"Yep. There it is." I hold steady pressure while I wait for the muscle to unclench. I knew from observing her walk in here that she'd have a knot. *"That's* from planting your weight wrong when you toss your beanbags."

"Wh–what?" She pants, face still contorted in pain. "How the fuck do you know I do that?"

I lean into her, and speak softly into her ear. "Because I've seen you play." I feel her breath hitch, and I lean back. She pants like a Lamaze instructor in her second trimester as I hold pressure—not uncommon considering how tightly her muscle is wound. Her brow smooths at the exact moment I feel the fascia release. "Have you ever tried yoga?"

"What's yoga got to do with anything?" She grunts as I move my fingers out to the vastus lateralis.

"Stretching is good for you. Stretchy muscles are happy muscles. Yours aren't very stretchy."

"You don't say?" She mutters another string of curse words as I work my way up the outer thigh along her iliotibial band, the same place I'd worked with D'Shawn. Especially when people have had ACL or MCL injuries, they lose a ton of flexibility from overcorrecting during rehabilitation. They think they need to protect their joints more, which makes them move more stiffly–first on purpose, and then unconsciously. Eventually, they lose mobility altogether.

I don't want that to happen to Kodi.

"You need to reestablish range of motion in your joints. You're young. You should be wiggly. You were stiff as a board when you walked in here."

"Isn't that what muscle relaxers are supposed to help with?"

I frown at her. She gives me a shit-eating grin that turns into a grimace when I find another bundle of fascial tissue just to the side of her butt cheek. She jerks up from the table. I laugh at her toes curling, and I'll admit it: I *may* enjoy the sight of her thigh muscles spasming under me a little *too* much.

I pull my hand away, the sight of her writhing beneath me making my mind drift into dangerous territory. I pray that the heat I feel rising up my neck isn't visible to her, and will myself back into Doctor-mode.

I take a deep breath, find another spot near her hip, and press. She tenses.

"Yoga would help better."

Her jaw slowly unclenches, and she gives me a questioning look. "You mean help more?"

I remove my hands, and I swear the woman wilts from relief. "No. *More* is not better. *Better* is better."

She clasps her hands over her stomach as I walk around to the other side of the table to check out her right leg. She tilts her head a little, contemplating. It's interesting to see how much she's relaxed since she first laid down on the table. I wonder if it's just the adjustments that's helped her feel better, or if there was something else on her mind that had her so tense.

"I don't know if I agree with that."

"Agree with what?" Her hip is still tilted a bit, likely from her compensating while she's been walking. I motion for her to turn on the table. "Face down."

"That more isn't better." She shifts gingerly, and I gesture for her to take her time. I've done a lot of work on her muscles, and she shouldn't be moving too fast. She slows down, talking as she rolls. "I mean, practice makes perfect, doesn't it?"

"Ah, but what if you're practicing the wrong thing?"

She doesn't respond as she places her head in the facerest, but I imagine she's chewing on a comeback. Her back and shoulders are quite tight. I release a few knots in her lumbar spine and tell her to take some deep breaths, then straighten her vertebrae back into shape as she exhales. Her cartilage pops and crackles in harmony with her grunts as I do. When I tell her to sit up (slowly), she sniffs at the air.

"Is something… burning?"

The chicken parm!

"Fuck!" I jump back from the table and sprint up the stairs, shouting over my shoulder, "Stay there!"

CHAPTER 23
KODI

Brian is gone for five minutes before I start to get antsy. The burning smell has already begun to fade away, assuring me that nothing's on fire. Crisis averted, but without sign of my chiropractor, I decide I'd rather earn my keep than wait around for more torture. His texts earlier mentioned that he was pretty stressed about Medi-Cal, and I'd rather get to work on it than waste the precious time I have before practice.

Slowly, I raise myself from the drop table, feeling weakness in my lower back that wasn't there before. It's like I just ran a marathon. All of my muscles are bone-tired, especially in my thighs, which feel like leaden jello. Not wanting to walk or stand more than I have to, I perch onto the fancy-ass office chair that's tucked under the slim desk against the far wall, and open up the laptop sitting there.

Oh shit, this thing is comfy. Leave it to a chiropractor to have a seat with proper back support, I suppose. I scoot further back and relax into the lounger as the home screen pops right up.

His computer isn't even password-protected. As soon as the welcome screen clears, I have access to every single icon and document on the man's laptop. *Really?*

I'm not just going to have to share my notes with the guy; he needs a whole lesson on HIPAA compliance in the digital age.

"Um, excuse me!" A hand swats me off the keyboard, and I roll back from Brian's desk. "You can't just barge onto my computer like that! There are other patient records on there!"

"Yeah, it's almost like you shouldn't leave your office with your laptop logged in and a patient in the room." I roll my eyes. "We'll fix *that* later. Regardless, I'm going to be messing around on your laptop anyway. Did you take care of the fire upstairs?"

"There was no *fire,*" he mutters. I start to turn back to the screen and he swats me again. "Dinner just got a little burnt."

"You made dinner?" I wasn't expecting that. *A man cooking me dinner?*

My stomach does that thing again, and I can hear Lily's voice in my mind. *"He's gonna fall for you hard. If he hasn't already."*

"Of course I made dinner. I didn't know how long you were planning on staying, and you don't know how terrible I am with computers, so I figured the least I could do is feed you while we go through it all." He reaches over and unplugs the laptop from its power cable, closing the screen. My shoulders fall back into the seat a bit at his logical explanation, and I try to ignore the twinge of disappointment in my gut. "How do you feel? Is your knee still hurting?"

"Other than the bruises you punched into my legs, and feeling like I weigh about a thousand pounds, I feel good. I think." I reach my arm across my chest to stretch my shoulder, which I'm noticing feels tight now that I'm sitting. I switch arms to stretch the other side. "My neck is a little stiff, but I'm okay with that."

"You sure you don't want me to adjust it?"

No way. I shake my head.

"Stand for me." He watches me like a hawk as I straighten my legs, and I feel his gaze like a physical thing. I make a concerted effort to distribute my weight evenly across both feet like they told me to do years ago in PT. But as I try to tuck my tailbone, the muscles in the front of my hips tug awkwardly. He shakes his head. "Face down."

"I thought dinner was ready?"

"Dinner can wait. Face down."

After twenty more minutes of poking and prodding and cracking (and a fair amount of grunts and cursing on my part), he lets me get back on my feet.

This time when I stand, I don't feel quite as fatigued as before. My shoulders, in particular, are much looser. Brian even smiles as I walk around the room and get my legs under me again.

He grabs his laptop and we go upstairs, but as I bend to grab my backpack by the landing, he stops me. He puts his laptop on the floor and halts me.

"Wait, set that back down."

I look over my shoulder at him. "Why?"

"So you can pick it up again the right way."

I resist rolling my eyes. He shoos me away and demonstrates. "Like this."

As I watch, he steps over his laptop, bends at both knees in a narrow lunge, and hinges at the hips to grab it from the floor. Then he pulls it into his chest, waiting until his hips are back over his ankles before straightening his legs. He's acting like his laptop is a 40-pound kettlebell. I blink at him.

"You seriously think I'm going to do that every time I need to pick something up off the floor?"

He raises a solitary eyebrow. "If you want your knee to get better? You should think about it."

I stare at him, waiting for a punchline. A chuckle. Something to indicate he's joking. But he doesn't budge. Just locks eyes with me in some kind of stand-off.

I sigh. *Fine.* I'll try it his way. But I'm not going to look as dumb as he did. I'm going to do this gracefully if I'm going to do it at all. "So… how do you start–?"

"Bend both knees like you're going into a lunge: not super wide, try to keep your hips centered between your legs." I do.

"Good! Now once you have one knee on the ground, pull your backpack towards your center… that's it. Then lift it with your arms, stand back up…perfect! So much better."

"I feel like an idiot," I mutter. I look *exactly* as dumb as he did when he demonstrated it. Probably dumber. My backpack is clutched to my chest instead of hanging off one shoulder like I usually have it. He puts a hand on my arm.

"You're very much *not* an idiot." The look on his face is unbearably kind. Something resembling pity crosses his eyes, and I feel foolish. Embarrassed. But for some reason, his sympathy doesn't carry the same sting as the pitying looks I got back when I was first recovering from surgery all those years ago. There's something else there in the lines at the corners of his eyes, something akin to experience.

He takes a deep breath. "I know how frustrating it can be to do things the right way. To go slow. To ask for help. To trust other people when they tell you you've been doing something wrong. Getting better isn't a battle of will. It's a matter of dedication, knowhow, and time."

I feel my face heat.

He's saying I've been doing it wrong, I realize. *I* don't go slow. *I* don't ask for help. *I'm* stubborn.

While I did listen to the doctors and physical therapists for a while after my surgery years ago, nothing they said to do got me back to normal. So I went about it my own way instead, the way Coach taught me. Working myself to exhaustion. Pushing through the pain. Assuming that maybe this was just my life now: some people deal with mental illness or diabetes, I deal with chronic pain.

Thinking about Coach has me remembering everything Lily said last night, too. *Is everything he taught me… wrong?*

Brian's hand moves to my shoulder, and I realize he's been rubbing up and down my arm as he talks. His hand feels…*different.* The same warmth, and comfort, but this time there's an intimacy there that isn't usually present in his touch.

It's nice.

But as soon as I notice it, he removes it, and I snap back to the present and we lock eyes. The look on his face is unreadable. He clears his throat.

"It's hard, Kodi. Managing a chronic injury is one of the hardest things you can do. But it doesn't have to stay painful, and you don't have to do it alone."

He locks eyes with me for a long moment. Or maybe it's only a few seconds. I can't be sure. All I know is that it feels like he's not just seeing my face, or my pain, but seeing *me.* All the darkness that's left over from my injury. My fear that maybe I'll never get better. The raw, freshly exposed kernel of *hope* that maybe, with his help, I *could.*

That, combined with Lily's words from last night...it's too much. This isn't just a few stretches every morning or before I go to bed. They're asking me to dig deep into everything I've ever believed and tear out the foundation.

That's far too much for me to handle right now, and *way* too much for Brian to see. Not when I've been thinking about his body the way I have, and confusing our arrangement with actual attraction.

The stuff he's talking about? This isn't fake boyfriend/girlfriend stuff. This isn't doctor/patient stuff. These are feelings; this is...*real.*

I mean, maybe if there were a chance of something actually happening between us. Something more than just a ruse to get his ex back and his business established. If this were real, if our relationship wasn't just an act we were putting on for the town so I could get treatment and he could make Zeke jealous, then maybe things would be different. Maybe I could let myself be vulnerable around him.

But it isn't real, I remind myself. No matter what Lily said, no matter what tingles I get in my stomach whenever I think about him leaping to save me with only a towel on or the incredible way his lips feel against mine, Brian's just a friend. Not even–just my *chiropractor.* Our "relationship" is an ongoing improvisation–a scene. A limited-run production until the end of the summer, when he can go back to the *real* love of his life and I can fix my knee and win our town the championship I should have brought home six years ago.

I shake my head, bringing myself back to reality, and to the point of all of this. Of everything Brian and I agreed to, and the role I agreed to play. This isn't about getting butterflies when Brian touches me, or overcoming some trauma that Lily's convinced I need to face.

It's just recovering from my injuries. It's just yes-and. Take what he says, build on it, and carry on the scene. It doesn't need to be anything more intimate than that.

It can't be.

All his talk about doing things the right way, asking for help, taking it slow… it reminds me of the real reason Brian and I are fake-dating. His business needs to thrive, so he can stick around and I can get better. He says I don't have to recover alone and he's right: for now, I need him.

But eventually, he'll go back to Zeke, I'll go back to being single, and I'll be healthier for it.

He's looking at me with a gentle, expectant smile on his face, and the thought of those perfect lips looking at me with disappointment for getting caught up in our little act, or pity for me for catching feelings when I'm supposed to be focusing on my recovery…it's too much to bear. I know those looks too well. I never want to see them from him.

"Yeah, sure. I know." The tiniest wrinkle forms in his forehead as I pull away. "Let's get to work on Medi-Cal. I have to leave for practice in an hour."

CHAPTER 24
KODI

"Again!" *Phloot-phloot!*

"Seriously?" Ginger groans. "My shift starts in twenty minutes, Kodi, what the hell?"

"Yeah, the sun set half an hour ago!"

"We're not leaving this park until everyone sinks three in a row!" I shout back. Beside me, Lily runs up and crouches like she's tying her shoe.

"Uh, Kodi?" She mutters. "Don't you think you're going a bit too hard here? We just won a match."

Phloot-phloot!

I watch the team gather the bean bags at each of their practice fields for another round. I'm still waiting on Piper and Mr. Landon to land their three bags. Once they get them in, we can *all* go home.

Seriously. Don't they realize *I* also don't like staying out til 9:00 on a weeknight? I've got work in the morning, too. I had a long day of paperwork and bartering, and *I'm* still committed to practice.

But everyone's aim could use a little work. We used to do these kinds of drills all the time back in high school.

"More is not better. Better is better."

Brian's words ring in my head, but I shake them away. These *are* good exercises, and practice breeds results.

"Lily, you were on the JV basketball team. Didn't Coach Kyle run layup drills exactly like this all the time?"

"Yeah, well, first of all, it helps when you can see the fucking basket," she hisses, wheezing in between words. "It's dark out. We can hardly make out the difference between the red and blue bags anymore. Seriously, Kodi, it's a *Tuesday night.* Call the damn practice."

Sigh. *Phloot-phloot!* "Alright, everybody, good enough. Thanks for your hard work out there, today, and you two–" I gesture to Piper and Mr. Landon, "Take a set home with you to run drills before the weekend. I'll see you all Friday."

"Finally," D'Shawn says, rubbing his back. "I need my heating pad after all that running."

"You can say that again," Delilah and Jonah say in unison. Then, "Jinx!"

"If I had class tomorrow, I'd be showing a movie." Finn says. D'Shawn gives a tired chuckle.

"How exactly does that work in gym class?"

Their voices fade, and I can just barely make out Finn saying something about "the miracle of life". As Callie runs up to gather cones with Lily and me, I hear a few extra grumbles from the other players heading to their cars. Ginger in particular shoots me a nasty glare as she tightens her ponytail on her way out of the park. Lily narrows her eyes at her in return, but I shrug it off. A little animosity towards the captain is totally normal. They'll all adjust their tune once we win the championship.

I'm a little bit slower gathering up all the bags and cones this time, trying to inconspicuously bend and lift the way Brian advised me to. It makes me feel ridiculous, hugging each cone to my chest before straightening my legs. It does put less stress on my joints, but it slows down the process.

I try not to think too much about Brian and our awkward dinner while I walk from cone to cone. Even though I'm sure I'm doing the right thing by checking my feelings around him, I can't deny that I'd been entertaining the fantasy that I could have tried to have something more with the attractive Doctor after my talk with Lily the other night.

There goes any chance of sleeping with him to get these…feelings out of my system.

I know in my heart that getting too emotionally involved with Brian would be a bad idea. It would completely fuck up the plan we've made, and I'm not about to sacrifice my shot at fixing my knee by letting things between him and me get tangled.

Lily might think I'm in love with the guy, but that's silly. "Love" isn't getting tummy tingles or spending hours trying to hash out what a person's eye color is. Those feelings, those distractions–they're just hormones. Lust.

And while I may not totally trust Lily to tell the difference, I *do* believe she's got the right idea about one thing: I need to get these distractions out of my system.

I just need to figure out how.

Lily and Callie have already moved on to the remaining practice boards while I'm still gathering my final cones.

"Long day," Callie sighs, breaking the silence.

"Yeah," Lily agrees. "Woulda been nice to get home before midnight."

"It's not even ten yet." I roll my eyes. "Why is everyone such a wimp all of the sudden?"

"Why are you such a hardass all of the sudden?" Lily snaps back. Callie gasps.

I rear my head in surprise. That was a little harsh, even for Lily's normally brash attitude. "Is something wrong, Lil?"

She shakes her head. "It's just that…" She looks at Callie, whose eyes widen. Then she seems to change her mind. "Nevermind."

"What?" I ask. I look between the two of them. They're hiding something.

"Kodi, you know that *we* have a blast at practice, right?" Callie smiles at me, but I can feel a "but" coming. I narrow my eyes.

"Uh-huh…?"

"A few folks are tossing around the idea of quitting the team."

I stare at Lily, who refuses to meet my eyes, despite the fact that she just dropped a bombshell in the middle of the park.

"*What*?" I shout. Jumping at my own volume and glancing around to make sure I didn't cause a fuss, I compose myself. "And you didn't think to tell me this last night??"

"I've been trying to tell you for weeks!" Lily throws her hands up in the air. "Why do you think I keep telling you to take it easy?"

"Who wants to quit?" I ask angrily, changing the subject.

"No one in particular just yet," Callie tries to reassure me. "It's more of a vague collective concept right now."

"Why?"

"Why do you think, Kodi? We're exhausted!" Lily grabs the stack of cones from me and throws them in my trunk. "You're too hard on everyone."

"Any winning team–"

"Enough with that!" She slams the hatch closed. "We're *already* a winning team! We don't need to drill *fucking cornhole*, Kodi. It's a stupid lawn game!"

"It's our town's pastime!"

"Which is kinda weird, right?" Callie chimes in nervously. I think she's trying to lighten the mood, but Lily and I are currently staring daggers at each other, and she hasn't been in town long enough to realize just how heated the two of us can get when we start arguing. "I mean, I'd never even heard of competitive cornhole before I moved here–"

"You need to let it fucking go, Kodi."

I freeze. Callie's eyes dart nervously between me and Lily, as if she realizes that this fight goes back way beyond when she lived in Tuft Swallow.

"This is about making up for States, isn't it? That's why you're out here like Coach, drilling us for perfection. Doing to us what he did to you. Because this is your chance to change the outcome."

I feel the muscles in my jaw twitch. *Dammit.* When she says it like that, it just sounds stupid.

And I'm not. Stupid.

"I said I wasn't ready to talk about that yet, Lily."

"Well, that's too fucking bad, girl. Because it isn't just your problem anymore. You're making it everyone's problem. And I love you, but I'm not willing to let you torture me just because you haven't dealt with your trauma."

"What *trauma?*" I'm shouting at her now, sick of this same line she keeps shoving in my face. Telling me I was *abused,* for Pete's sake. I wasn't abused. I worked hard. I *trained.* Just like I always have.

And then Brian trying to feed me all that crap about how hard it is to recover. I *know* how hard it is to recover. I'm not *afraid* of hard work. I never have been.

As the team pitcher back in high school, I worked harder than everyone to drill plays and throws with Coach. To him, no game was good enough but the perfect game. And he was right: for me to get a scholarship? To attract the pros? I needed us to win. And that's all on the pitcher–knowing how to judge each batter and sink each pitch to strike out every last one.

So I'd stay late. Drill until dark. Night after night. It's just what I had to do.

"Your obsession with perfection. With needing to be the best. Pitching the perfect game." She uses air quotes around "perfect". "But you can't do that in softball anymore, so now you've decided to do it with cornhole."

"Don't be stupid, Lily. There's no such thing as a perfect game in cornhole."

"No, but three sinks in a row every turn would be pretty close, wouldn't it?" She shoots back.

"Okay, guys, why don't you take a breather. I have a feeling this is getting into some testy territory."

Both of us look up at Callie, and I see the confused and slightly worried look on her face. I shake my head.

"It's nothing," I say. "Just a stupid thing from high school."

"It wasn't stupid to you," Lily says. "You didn't lock yourself in your bedroom for three months straight because you thought a perfect game was stupid, Kodi. Coach had you–"

"Enough."

I don't raise my voice this time. I don't even make an angry face. Because suddenly, all of that anger and fight I was feeling has leaked out of me. Now? Now I'm just tired. Callie's right. This isn't going anywhere. Even if…

No. Not here. You're not going to solve anything by cracking open those old wounds.

I just want to go home, to my bed, where I can be alone without Brian's or Callie's or Lily's worried eyes on me anymore.

"Thanks for helping me pack up, and warning me about the team. I'll–I'll think about what you said."

And then I elbow past them, climb into the driver's seat, and peel away, avoiding their faces in the rearview.

CHAPTER 25
BRIAN

I watch Kodi storm off to her car from my vantage point behind the maple trees, gobsmacked.

What the hell, Kodi?

Lily and Callie, her two friends, are also staring at her retreating form, looking like they're at a total loss for what to do.

"Should I know something about that?"

I approach them, abandoning the copse of trees, and they jump at the sound of my voice. Lily's curly red ponytail swings as she turns her head to me and plasters on a smile. "Brian! Hi! What are you doing here?"

"I came out to watch practice, see what all the fuss is about." I don't tell her that I wanted to see for myself why the guys at the gym had been complaining. Now that I have, I don't blame them for feeling a little cold toward Captain Kodi. I'm even a little frightened by what I just saw. "What's wrong with Kodi?"

"Don't worry about her, she's just had a hard day–"

"Oh I know all about her day. She was just at my place before practice," I interrupt. Lily's face falls, but Callie smiles.

"Oh! Did you two have a date?"

I grimace. *Not quite.* "I made her dinner. What's this about her obsession with the perfect game?"

"Oh, that?" Lily laughs nervously. "That's nothing. Just some silly little thing from high school..."

She trails off, and then the pieces start to come together.

Her obsession with perfection. Her injury.

As someone who's done martial arts for most of their life, I've seen fighters with an obsession with winning. Usually, it's that kind of all-or-nothing attitude that leads to injuries. One of the main reasons I decided to go to chiropractic school was so I could help people actually recover from those defeats.

But often, in cases like that, it's just as much a mental game as it is physical. Kodi didn't just lose a game or a scholarship when she tore her ACL. She lost her sense of self.

It's hard to believe that someone as confident and smart as her would succumb to those kinds of feelings, but maybe that's part of her coping mechanism. She fell back on other talents, which was enough to make her *seem* okay to everyone around her, but now that she's back in competition mode she's reverting back to bad habits.

Something tells me Dr. Cratchet never exactly gave Kodi the kind of support and instruction she needed to learn any of that after her surgery. It seems like nobody in Tuft Swallow did.

Instead, she took on her recovery alone. Worked herself to exhaustion, got hurt, and was left out to dry when she wasn't a champion anymore.

No *wonder* she shut down so fast before dinner. When I tried to let her know I understood. No one in her life has ever understood, and she still hasn't healed.

Not just physically. Emotionally.

"How can I help?"

Callie and Lily stare blankly at me, taken aback by my comment, which I realize now probably seems a little out of left field. But then the redhead gets a gleam in her eye and looks me up and down appraisingly.

Uh-oh. I don't like that look.

"I think I know something that might help her *open up* a little."

She crosses her arms, taps her finger to her chin, and her lips curl up into a smile that I can only describe as 'Grinch-like.' Callie looks between the two of us, and a lightbulb goes off above her head. Meanwhile, my stomach is sinking further and further into my knees with every tap of her pointer finger.

I have a feeling I'm going to regret this.

CHAPTER 26
KODI

Since practice on Tuesday, I've been ignoring just about everyone in my life and focusing on work. This is our bye week, so there's no game on Saturday, and I send out a group text on Thursday night telling the team to take the night off on Friday.

Do I want to skip practice? Of course not. But I can't risk losing half the team because they all think I'm too much of a hardass. I figure giving them the weekend to get drunk and calm down will pacify them long enough until their collective hatred of Spitz Hollow gets them riled up about practice again.

We face them again next weekend, and I need to make it clear to everyone that I do *not* intend to let up on practices until they prove to me that they're ready to beat them handily this time.

I don't want to leave Zeke's defeat up to a tiebreaker.

After I send out the text, the stress and tension in my neck calls out for my attention. I'm about to take my favorite waterproof toy into the bath for a little "me time," when I hear a knock at the door of my apartment.

I glance at the microwave clock. It's almost 8:00. *Who the heck would be coming over at this hour?*

I'm in my stretchy leggings and scissor-cropped *Mighty Swal-*

lows tee-shirt, but I figure it's presentable enough considering I didn't expect company. But when I open the door, I immediately regret not throwing on something slightly more modest.

Shit.

"Hi, Brian! Uh… what are you doing here?"

"Surprising you." He's holding one bag of Chinese take-out and another from the Plume N' Zoom. "Can I come in?"

"Uh…sure." I open the door and he breezes up to me, kissing me on the cheek as he crosses the threshold. "What–?"

"We've got an audience," he mutters into my ear, and the feeling of his breath on my neck sends a shiver down my spine.

Then his words register, and I peer over his shoulder at the sidewalk.

Sure enough, across the street at the bus stop, a couple of Tit Peepers are pretending to read a bird guide together on a bench. I don't buy the act for a second.

"Come on in, sweetie. Smells great!" I practically shout for the peanut gallery's benefit before closing the door. Once we're inside, I cross my arms. "Okay, what are you doing here for real?"

"I can't buy my *sweetie* some dinner?" He smiles innocently, holding up the bags.

"Well, seeing as we didn't have any plans…"

"Since when do we need to plan?" He sets down the bags on my kitchen island, and I walk over and lean against the counter in front of him. "We've been pretty good at improvising so far."

He takes a step forward and places a hand on my exposed waist. I freeze.

Those aren't healy hands.

His fingertips aren't that assuring, comforting kind of warm they usually are.

No. This time, they're hot. And little sparks shoot through me where they make contact with my bare skin.

I jump back. "What are you doing?"

"I realized it's been a minute since we had a little PDA. Why is that?"

My heart races. *What?* Since when is Brian actually interested in pursuing anything except Operation: Win Zeke Back?

"What are you talking about? You just kissed me in the doorway. That'll probably be front page news tomorrow. PDA quota for the week, met." My voice falters a little in that last sentence. And my throat is dry.

Then I remember my vibrator waiting for me on the bathroom sink, and my stomach drops. *Crap!* Brian can't see that.

"Um, give me a second, I need to change." I start to dart past him back towards the hallway to my bedroom, but he catches me by the arm.

"You look fine. Seriously, I see way more skin at the gym every week."

"Not my skin!" I squeak. He laughs.

"Kodi, let's just relax tonight for a change." He slowly turns us so we're facing each other, and gives me just enough space to breathe without my nose being overwhelmed by his spicy cologne. *Fuck, he smells good.* "We haven't had a chance to hang out without some kind of motive since…well, ever, really. And you could use a break."

His hands rest easily on my hips, and my body starts to relax into his hold without me realizing. *What was I going to do? There was something I needed to take care of…*

I can't seem to remember with his blue-green eyes boring into mine.

"I brought shrimp lo mein," he says.

My one weakness. "I love shrimp lo mein."

"And Doritos."

"Cool Ranch?"

"Is there any other kind?" His eyes twinkle.

My resolve crumbles a little more. But I have to stay strong. "Almost perfect, there, Brian. Except we don't have–"

He pulls a carton of *Phish Food* out of the Plume N' Zoom bag. "Dessert?"

I almost cry on the spot. "How did you know…?"

"A little birdie told me." He leans in, touching his forehead to mine, and I breathe in those magic, artificial scents that fragrance companies engineer with erotic names like "amber" and "black oak."

They smell so good on a real man...

"Wait." I snap my head up, realizing what "little birdie" happens to know all of my favorite foods. "Did Lily put you up to this?"

"Wh-what?" He scoffs. "Why would you...can't a guy just get his fake girlfriend dinner and come over for a little Netflix and chill?"

"Netflix and chill?" I narrow my eyes. *There's no way this was his idea.* "You know what that means, right?"

He glares at me. "I'm not *that* old, Kodi."

"So you came over to *seduce* me with lo mein and *Phish Food?* And you expect me to believe Lily's not somehow involved?"

He blinks. Then sighs.

"Fine. Yes. Lily suggested I take you on a date. But you weren't returning my texts, so we compromised."

"So you *planned* this?" I finally back away from him, and immediately I feel cold without his arms around me. I ignore it and collapse onto the couch. "Great. Just great. Now my best friend is conspiring with my fake boyfriend. Why? Does she think getting me pity laid will somehow loosen me up and make me less of a hardass at practice?"

I feel absolutely betrayed. Would I love to let Brian continue touching me? Sure. But not if it isn't his idea. Not if he's being *coerced* by my alleged best friend.

Silence from the kitchen confirms it. I pop up and spin on the couch, pointing an accusatory finger at Brian as I lean against the backrest. "Oh my God. That's *exactly* what you're doing!"

"I wasn't going to *seduce* you," he groans. "I was going to help you relax. Stuff you full of comfort food and give you a foot rub while we watch something mindless that you like. I don't know, *Bridgerton* or whatever."

"You think I watch *Bridgerton*?" I snort. "Yeah, right. That's Lily's bag, not mine."

"Well something else then!" He rips the takeout containers out of the bag angrily. "God, you're infuriating! Just take the free dinner!"

"I don't want your *blood takeout*."

"Blood takeout?" Now he's snorting at me. "Kodi, your friends can see you're stressed and they're worried about you. I literally am certified in muscular manipulation and soft tissue work. I've got every one of your favorite foods here and you've literally got Netflix *up on the television*. Now take your lo mein, put your feet up, and let me pamper you, dammit!"

I cross my arms again, huffing.

Why does that have to sound so goddamn perfect?

"Fine." I grumble. "But I'm eating dessert first."

"Your terms are acceptable." He hands me the carton and a spoon, and then takes the remote off the coffee table. "But I'm picking the show."

CHAPTER 27
BRIAN

Just to spite her, I scroll through her Netflix suggestions and cue up episode one of Bridgerton. I can practically hear her eyes roll behind me, but I know firsthand just how much an addictive, sexy show can help distract someone from their own problems. I may have binged a few episodes myself when Zeke first broke up with me.

Don't judge me. Rege Jean Page is hot as fuck, and he's totally got that unaffected don't-hate-the-player-hate-the-game thing that I find so unbearably attractive *down.*

But as I settle into the couch with Kodi, grab her legs, pull her feet onto my lap, and dive into the shrimp lo mein, a comfortable silence falls over us as we both get whisked away by Julie Andrews' narration.

"Oh my God," Kodi mutters twenty minutes into the episode, now munching on Doritos. "Is Lady Whistledown like London's version of *The Nosy Pecker?*"

I almost spray my mouthful of noodles over the coffee table at her observation. "Uh, more like the other way around, I'm pretty sure."

"Excuse you," Kodi snorts. "Tuft Swallow has existed way longer than whatever book series *this* is based off of."

I shake my head. "Sure, babe. Whatever you say."

"Don't call me *babe*." She tries to pull her feet away from me, and I snatch them back over my lap before she can.

"Nuh-uh-uh, Miss Independent. Once I eat my fill of this, you are getting the foot rub of a lifetime. No ifs, ands, or butts about it."

She scowls at me. I scowl back.

"Fine."

Her sour attitude softens when I begin the foot rub in earnest. The episode plays on, and aside from a few appreciative moans at my massage skills, we enjoy the rest of it in silence.

Until I start digging into the arch of her foot, and her noises get a little more suggestive.

"Oooo, that feels…really good," she says in a low, relaxed tone, that I would almost describe as sultry if I didn't know better. I chuckle at her, rubbing little circles under the ball of her foot. She moans again, and this time the sound coming from her throat elicits a different reaction in me.

Woah, there. Down boy.

I shift a little, and she cranes her neck up from the arm rest. "You okay? Are my legs too heavy?"

"No! No," I assure her, scooting her feet a few inches toward my knees to prevent her from feeling the bulge starting to form in my pants. "You're fine. How are you liking the show?"

"It's…not bad," she admits. "It's really pretty to look at."

"Relaxing, right?"

"Mm-hmm." Her agreement comes out as a hum of pleasure, and my pants get tighter around my stiffening dick.

Okay, if she keeps making noises like that with her legs on my lap, we may have a problem.

I move my hands up to her ankles, kneading her soft, smooth skin with my fingers, and I feel her relax further into the couch. Her foot tilts and leans back into the crease of my lap, and I hold back a groan.

Fuck. That was hardly a brush. *Why am I reacting so strongly to her?*

I literally touch bodies everyday for work. What is it about Kodi that makes it so hard for me to keep professional distance?

I switch to rubbing her other foot, holding it a safe distance away from my hardening dick. Kodi didn't exactly react kindly to the idea of us sleeping together earlier. The last thing I want is to undo all of her relaxation when she realizes I'm getting the most inconvenient boner of all time.

She's going to think I have some kind of foot fetish.

Which I *don't,* to be clear. This has nothing to do with me rubbing her feet, and everything to do with those indecent noises she's making.

"Mmmm, there. Ugh, Brian, you *are* good at this."

A lump forms in my throat. *Jesus, don't say my name like that.*

This was a bad idea.

"Um, can I use your bathroom?" I toss out the question like a hail-Mary, desperate to get out from under her legs for a second so I can clear my head.

"Oh, sure." She retracts her legs, and I try to adjust myself as subtly as I can while I get up. Luckily, her eyes are still fixed on the TV. "It's just down the hall."

"Thanks."

The last bit of daylight that was streaming through the windows when I arrived has faded into dusk, darkening the apartment aside from the glow of the television. I stumble off to the bathroom and flick on the light, closing the door behind me before leaning into the sink.

That was close.

I turn the faucet and splash some cold water on my face, then dry it off with the hand towel hanging on the rack, giving myself a minute to calm down. For a single person in her twenties, Kodi has a surprisingly clean and well-organized bathroom. Matching linens are stacked on a shelf above the toilet, and the sink is neatly lined with scented hand soap, her toothpaste, toothbrush, and—

I freeze. Whatever relaxing my dick had accomplished in the minute it took for me to wash my face is completely undone when I see what's sitting on the edge of her counter.

Is that…?

Fuck.

Fuck fuck fuck.

I back up a step, bumping into the closed door behind me and collapsing against it. So far, I like to think I've been doing a good job of being professional with Kodi. Sure, there have been moments like tonight where my attraction gets the better of me, but I've always been able to stay calm and keep my distance. She's my patient, after all, and even with all this fake-girlfriend nonsense, we've limited the touching and kisses to a minimum. Retained a safe, friendly wall up so as to not blur the line between us.

Because in none of the scenarios we've negotiated have we ever discussed actually…*having* a relationship.

A real one.

A kiss or two is nothing. Child's play. Easy to turn on and off. But I've been under the impression that anything more than that, anything that would be inappropriate to do in an environment where some Tit Peeper could see it and get their *Pecker* in a twist, was off the table. Especially when the whole reason she agreed to pretend to be my girlfriend in the first place was so I could win my ex back.

And part of how I've kept that a distinct impossibility is by refusing to think of what anything *more* with Kodi might look like.

Feel like.

But the second I see her waterproof, hot pink, magic wand vibrator on her bathroom counter, all the thoughts I've been keeping at bay since we first kissed at the cornhole game flood directly into my bloodstream, bypassing my brain and heading directly to my cock.

Fuuuuuuck.

The sounds of Kodi's moans of pleasure from her foot rub

replay in my head, this time replaced by visions of my hands grasping even further up her legs, holding that toy of hers right to the spots that drive her crazy…

"Gahh–" I gasp out, my dick pressing insistently against my zipper. I adjust myself again, which does nothing to relieve the pressure there. *Think of anything else, anything–do NOT think about sleeping with your fake girlfriend.*

"Brian?"

Kodi's voice rings out from behind the door, and I jump. She sounds like she's shouting from the couch.

"Yeah?"

"Mind if I start episode two?"

"No, go ahead, sorry–I'll be right out!"

"Everybody poops, man. It's okay."

Heat rushes to my face. *Great.* Well, that's *one* way to kill a boner.

I take another minute to calm down enough so I can pee, then wash my hands and get ready to head back into the living room. But as I'm drying my hands (again), I realize I don't hear the sound of the TV anymore.

"Fuck. Brian?" Kodi calls again, and I stiffen.

Her voice is closer. Much closer. A second later, there's a knock on the door.

"Brian?" She sounds panicked. And that's when I realize exactly what's happened.

She knows I've seen the vibrator.

A slow, evil smile spreads across my face, and I catch my own scheming expression in the mirror. *Oh, wait.*

Before, *I* was the one who was nervous. I saw her hot pink sex toy in the bathroom, and it was my little secret. A secret that drove me absolutely crazy, because it made me think about Kodi getting off, but something for me and me alone.

Now, she *knows* that I know about her evening activities in the bathtub. And if the tone of her voice is any indication, that's driving *her* even more crazy. It wouldn't make sense for me to hide it anymore, it's out in the open. She's just as horny as I am.

Suddenly, I'm tempted to tease her about it. See how she *yes-and*s her way out of this one.

This could be fun.

I pick up the wand and turn to face the door, twirling it between my fingers. "Yes, Kodi?"

"Um. You didn't happen to–uh, you didn't see, um…"

I turn the door handle open with my free hand and study the vibrant toy with the other. "See what?" I ask innocently.

Even in the darkness of the hallway, I can see the bright red of Kodi's face spreading straight down her neck.

"This?" I take a moment to examine the toy curiously, feeling the heat radiating from the woman before me. "I was admiring it, actually. I've never seen one like this before. Does it have multiple settings?"

Her eyes go wide, and she silently pleads with me to stop touching her vibrator. I realize it's cruel to tease her, especially when I was just fighting a boner in here a minute ago, but I can't let this opportunity go. Not only am I saving *myself* embarrassment, but seeing Kodi worked up like this…

Oh fuck.

It's too much fun.

I should stop.

I don't want to.

What if I…

I press the button on the handle, and the heavy silicone ball at the top of the wand begins to buzz excitedly.

A noise escapes Kodi's throat, and I think she might be about to scream.

I click the button again, and the buzzing increases.

"I didn't realize my massage skills had competition."

"I didn't–you didn't tell me you were coming over–"

"Were you playing with this when I got here?" I ask, suddenly flush with the picture of her doing that very thing, pleasuring herself in the bath, the hot water steaming up the mirror above the sink…

"No!" She shouts, coming to her senses, reaching to snatch the toy out of my hands. "Give it back!"

Instinctively, I raise the arm holding the wand above my hand, and she presses herself against me, pushing me into the sink and stretching to steal it out of my grasp. "Brian, give me my–the–"

"Your *vibrator*?" I click the button again, and this time it pulses. Her face gets impossibly redder, and she presses harder against me, now scrambling with her legs as if she can climb the eight inches' worth of height difference between us and take away my fun. Her body rubs against mine, and I feel the pressure of her midsection grind against my pelvis, reawakening the erection I'd only just managed to calm down.

"Oh!" Kodi gasps, reeling back onto her heels, but I wrap my arm around her waist instinctively to keep her from falling. My cock pushes harder into the curve of her lower stomach, and I clench my teeth together, now just as embarrassed as she is.

We lock eyes, breathing heavily after our brief struggle, the only other sound mingling with our panting the mechanical buzz of the vibrator above our heads.

And then I crash my lips to hers.

CHAPTER 28
KODI

Fuck.

That feeling.

It's that feeling again.

My stomach is a witch's cauldron of flip-flops and bubbles and butterflies as Brian's mouth devours mine, his tongue bypassing my open lips and claiming me wholly. His body, hard with muscle–*and other things*–rams against me, pinning me against his ridiculously strong arm like a vice.

Fuck.

His scent, that intoxicating cologne he's wearing, invades my senses, turning me to putty in his hands. My body, already warm with embarrassment, flushes again as blood rushes to all the places it normally ignores, particularly the ones in contact with his. My core pulses with it all: the close contact, the smell of him, the tight band of his forearm digging into the small of my back. I'm losing track of where I end and he begins, and the unrelenting passion of his kiss is blurring that line even further.

Fuck.

Before I realize what's happening, my legs are widening and one of his is between them, and I'm slowly grinding into him to feed the insatiable ache that's exploded between my thighs. *How can I need him closer?* He's already so close, so tight against me that I'm having trouble breathing. His tongue swirls in my mouth, his lips clashing with mine as we both drink each other in like spring water in the desert. My head starts to spin, my world collapsing to two tiny pinpricks at the center of my vision until I remember I can breathe through my nose. I inhale like I've been drowning, so hard that my lips start pulling him in. Then I'm biting his lower lip as it sucks between my teeth, and we abruptly break apart on a gasp.

Fuck.

I can't stop. *I can't stop.* I dive back in for more, straining my calf muscles on tip-toe, claiming his lips like he claimed mine, and once again I'm tasting his tongue. Heat rushes to my core with every slant of his lips. My ears are buzzing, the noise filling my head until I realize it's not coming from my head–it's the vibrator, still racing away in Brian's hand.

Fuck!

The realization snaps me out of my sex-crazed trance, and I jump back out of his grip. He lets me go, removing his arm from my waist to rub at his mouth, which is turning purple and swollen from my bite.

"*Fuck,* Kodi," he rumbles, his sometimes-green, sometimes-blue eyes sapphire with lust.

I swallow, still panting for breath. I cross my arms around my exposed waist, suddenly so cold in the absence of his scorching hot body.

"*Fuck* is right," I mutter, and his eyes flash.

His grip on the wand twitches, and the buzzing stops. The ensuing silence is deafening.

"Do we…talk about it?" His words sound thoughtful, calm, measured–but his gaze is anything but. There's fire in the way he's looking at me, and when I lower my eyes to take in the rest of him, I see the line of his erection pressing desperately against its denim prison.

My throat goes dry. I'll be honest, I have never understood the impulse to suck a dick before, but in this moment, I want nothing more than to sink to my knees and release his cock. Touch it. Lick it. Devour it.

It doesn't make sense. It isn't logical. It's madness. Pure, fucking instinct.

Words can't explain this. I certainly can't.

"No," I breathe. A question furrows his brow, and I shake my head. "I don't want to talk about it."

"What *do* you want?"

I stand as still as I can, my chest still spasming with short breaths, willing my heartbeat to slow even a couple beats per second. What do I want?

What do I want?

"I...I don't know," I confess. "I've never–I haven't..."

Recognition lights his features.

"Fuck," he hisses again, and eases himself into a half-seat on the edge of the bathroom sink. He runs his fingers through his short hair, and my stomach sinks.

The butterflies turn back into caterpillars, and suddenly I feel like I might throw up.

"I'm too much work." My voice is a broken, croaking thing. I wipe my face with my hands and find tears clinging to my eyelashes. "Aren't I?"

Of course he wouldn't be interested in fooling around with me. Not when I'm completely inexperienced. Not when I come loaded with the baggage of being a patient and Zeke's rival. It's too much–too heavy for something casual. Something temporary, fake.

Which is all this is. All this can ever be.

"What? No! No, that's not it at all." Hands grab onto my shoulders, and then his finger is tilting up my chin until my eyes meet his. "Kodi. Don't ever let me hear you say that again."

"What?" He's so close, my focus needs to dart from his left eye to his right and back again, the fire in them smoldering, but still there. Like embers, shining back from the cobalt depths.

"Never. Say. You're. Too. Much. Work. Again," he repeats slowly, never releasing me from his gaze. Then he pulls me close to him again, but instead of kissing me, he cradles my head against his chest and rocks slowly from side to side. "You're not too much work. And even if you were, Kodi, I…"

I curl into his hold, not breathing, waiting to hear what he's going to say.

"I'm not afraid of work."

He holds me like that, until the tears stop flowing, until my breathing calms. With a sniff, I pull away, and he tilts my chin up once again. Then he places a small, gentle kiss–just a press–to my lips, and wipes my cheek with his thumb.

"I think we need to revisit the terms of our fake relationship."

I nod slowly, taking in his words.

"Yeah. Yeah, I think you're right."

This is where he's going to finally say it. Tell me that this act isn't worth it, that he's never been interested in me as anything more than a patient and a business partner, and that we never should have tried this ridiculous plan.

"I think…I think I may want more than just kisses in public."

My pulse races again. *He wants what?*

This can't be. I couldn't have possibly heard him correctly. Here I was thinking he was about to break things off completely, confess that this whole ordeal is getting too complicated to continue, and now he's saying he wants more?

"Really?"

His eyes won't let me go. "Yeah."

I swallow. Those kisses…I'm afraid to admit just how much I enjoy the act. Even when no one is watching. *Is he telling me that he enjoys it just as much?*

I want to know. Want to tease him, to test it. Continue our improvisation, and see just how long he'll keep saying *yes.*

Here goes nothing. "I think I might want more than just foot massages."

The corner of his lips twitch upwards, and he tilts his head. "Is that so?"

"Yeah."

"They're not good enough for you?"

I shake my head, my heart pounding against my ribs. "Not even a little bit."

His arms slide lower, and I settle into their new location encircling my waist. I raise my arms to his neck, clasping my hands behind his head.

"Then what, pray tell, would be?"

How far can I go? I think for a moment, looking around the bathroom. My eyes land on the vibrator.

"Oh?" He follows my eyes, and his eyebrows raise. Then he meets my gaze.

My face heats.

"Would you like me to use that on you, Kodi?"

Despite the way my heart leaps into my throat, I don't answer right away. I think about it for a solid tenth of a second.

"Yes."

"Where?" He growls.

The butterflies in my stomach once again emerge from their cocoons. "Not my feet."

"Where, Kodi? Tell me *where*." He leans down, touching his forehead to mine, the pain in his voice palpable as he says the next few words through clenched teeth. "You make the calls here, you understand me? This is your first time, you are calling the shots. I am not doing a goddamn thing unless you expressly ask for it."

"But how do I know what I want?" I ask, shivering in his hold. *How do I know what* you *want?*

He pulls me in tighter. "You listen to your body. When it feels good, you tell me. When it feels bad, you tell me. And when it feels like everything in you will explode if I don't focus all of my attention, and desire, and fucking *everything* into that *one. Spot.*" He takes in a shuddering breath, and I swear I can feel it directly in my core. "You scream my name until you fucking fall apart."

Fuck.

"Okay?"

He opens his eyes, staring directly into my soul. My body is shaking with anticipation, every nerve alive and alert in his presence as I answer, "Okay."

His voice is like liquid smoke when he confirms with me one last time.

"Okay?"

"Okay."

Then he pulls me closer and presses a kiss to my forehead, his hot, hard body enveloping mine.

"Tell me what to do."

CHAPTER 29
BRIAN

Kodi's eyes dart back and forth between mine, and I'm gripping her body like it's a buoy in a hurricane. This woman is *everything*.

The smell of her shampoo has been teasing my nose ever since she tackled me against the sink. My cock is *aching* against my zipper, and it is taking every ounce of self control I possess to keep from ripping my clothes off and fucking her like a teenager after prom night.

It's her *first time.*

Her first kiss. Her first time. So many *fucking* firsts with this girl, and she's trusting me with all of them. Why? Why me? Why in this fake, ridiculous relationship?

There's nothing fake about this.

Fuck.

The feelings that have been nagging at the back of my mind since I first kissed her at the game–*no*. Even before that. Since the first time I saw her in the office at the clinic, and pressed my fingers to her perfect legs. The feelings that didn't make any sense, because I didn't think I could think those kinds of things about anyone other than…

No. Don't even mention his name.

Tonight isn't about him. It isn't even about me.

This is all about her.

And I am going to make sure it's everything she could ever dream of.

"Tell me what to do."

She draws in a deep breath, and I instantly feel her retreat.

"No, no, no," I say, squeezing her a little in my hold. "Don't let yourself get embarrassed. You said you wanted more. Tell me about that."

She looks at the vibrator again, and I let one of my arms fall from her waist so I can pick it back up. I hold it in between us.

"You want me to use this?"

She hesitates for a second, then nods.

"Use your words."

"Yes."

"Where?"

She breathes in again, and I can tell there's something she wants to say on the tip of her tongue. She's just afraid to say it.

I'm tired of her censoring herself around me. I want her to open up to me, in more ways than one. My voice is hoarse when I try a different tactic.

"Where do you put it when you play with yourself?" I ask, leaning into the shell of her ear. Maybe she's too nervous to spell it out. Maybe she just needs a little help.

As she considers my question, I realize that we're still standing. In the bathroom.

Which is possibly the least sexy room in the house. And likely contributing to her nerves a little. It's hard to be comfortable in a bathroom.

"Hold that thought." I put a finger against her lips. Her eyes widen in surprise, and my dick twitches again at the perfect, sexy innocence in them.

Fuck. I'm going to hell.

But damn if I won't enjoy myself on the way down.

"Would you be more comfortable in the bedroom?" She nods against my finger, which is still pressed against her lips. I smile, and lower my hand down to her hip. "Okay, then. That's a good start. Why don't we head there?"

"It's a little messy," she whispers.

The degree to which I don't care is impossible to put into words. So I just shake my head. "That's fine. I'm not going to be looking at the mess."

"Where will you be looking?" She asks earnestly, and my heart clenches.

This woman.

"Kodi. Do you have any idea just how gorgeous you are? If I'm able to tear my eyes away from you long enough to take off my own shirt, I'll be lucky."

Her eyes dart down to my chest and back when I mention my shirt. I grin.

"Would you like me to take my shirt off now?"

"Yes please." She doesn't hesitate for a second this time.

I chuckle. "Okay. I can do that."

I set down the vibrator I'm still holding for some reason, and let go of Kodi's beautiful curves to remove my shirt. I feel her gaze travel up and down my body as I do, and when I toss my shirt onto the ground, her eyes freeze on the tent still straining in my jeans.

"What about…those?" She asks, pointing at them.

"You want me buck-ass naked while you're still fully clothed? Is this becoming a pattern?" I cock my head at her. She blushes. Again.

Fuck. She's killing me.

"You haven't seen me yet." She crosses her arms over her chest. I wait for her to continue.

Oh, but I want to, baby girl.

I'm not about to force her into anything she doesn't want to do. Even though I want nothing more in this moment than to see every perfect inch of her—if she wants to take her time getting comfortable with my body before she lets me see hers, that's okay. She's right. She's seen me naked already.

Not on purpose, but…

I undo my belt buckle. Her back straightens.

"Can–can I?" She asks, placing her fingers gingerly on my waistband.

Fuuuck. "Yeah."

She undoes the button, pulling the fabric towards her to relieve the pressure on the zipper while she slowly tugs down. *Jesus.* I clench my teeth and hiss out a breath as she slides the fabric down my legs, sinking to her knees, only to return her fingers to my waist to repeat the same step with my boxer briefs.

I grab her wrist. "I'm going to warn you. I'm really fucking hard right now."

"I can see that," she deadpans, and her sassy tone is such a 180 from the nervous, innocent one she was just using that I want to spank her.

My cock jumps at the thought. She jerks in surprise, and I laugh out loud.

"What was *that*?"

"That?" I say, still laughing. "That was me thinking about spanking you for your smart mouth."

Her cheeks turn scarlet. And then I realize where her head is.

Fuck.

"I'll show you how smart my mouth is," she snarls, then rips my boxer briefs down to my ankles and shoves my cock into her mouth.

The soft, wet heat of her tongue wraps around me, and I stumble forward, catching myself on her shoulders. She doesn't tease me, doesn't take her time working me up, just goes from dick out to wholly inside her mouth in one excruciating move.

She's not even trying to be sexy. She's just going all-in like she does with everything else.

Then her lips close around the base of my shaft and I almost fucking lose it right then and there.

"Christ," I grunt, and I feel–*feel*–the giggle bubble up her throat.

She feels so good. So eager. So fucking—

My balls tighten, and it takes every single ounce of self-control I have to keep myself from erupting right down her pretty little throat. She pops off my dick with a *smack*.

"Huh," she says, pursing her lips. I catch my balance, head spinning with the hot and cold. My eyes flutter open and take in her curious expression. "That's…not what I was expecting."

"What?" I demand, suddenly self-conscious. "Was it bad?"

"No." My shoulders relax, and she rises to her feet. "But it was saltier than I thought it would be."

I hold back a smirk. "Yeah, that checks out."

"Are all dicks salty?"

I raise my eyebrows. "Oh, you assume I'm some kind of expert?"

She shrugs, and peers up at me through her eyelashes, smiling. "I mean, you've got more experience than I do. Zeke's a pretty big dick."

Fair.

Oddly enough, the sound of his name doesn't even phase me. I'm still reeling from the feeling of Kodi's hot mouth. I place a hand on her cheek.

"Yeah, they're pretty salty."

"Are women salty, too?"

I consider the question. "No…not in the same way."

"What do women taste like?"

I take a step forward, and she steps back. The fear that was hiding in her face earlier, the nervousness at her lack of experience, is gone now. It's as if the act of tasting my cock has given her courage. Her eyes are now filled with curiosity and something else…something I've seen before in her eyes, I realize.

A challenge.

Just like that, the Kodi I met weeks ago, the one who jumped headfirst into fake relationships and business arrangements, who yes-anded her way into my life, is back. But this isn't Cornhole

Kodi, or let's-solve-each-other's-problems Kodi; this is some kind of Kodi 2.0.

Sex Kitten Kodi.

Whereas the woman who opened her front door and let me in tonight was running from something, this one is running towards it. She's staring at me with a hunger in her eyes, and I'm all too eager to feed her sexual appetite.

"Unique." I take another step forward, and another, pushing her back. She meets me step for step, and we march ourselves right into her bedroom until I pin her against the foot of her bed. She puts her hands on my chest, digging her nails into the muscle there. I hiss. "Do you want to know what *you* taste like, Kodi?"

Her eyes flash, and a swallow travels down the line of her slender throat.

"Tell me what to do," I remind her.

"Take off my pants."

Finally. "And then?"

"Tell me how I taste."

CHAPTER 30
KODI

Three things happen in quick succession.

First, Brian bends down, grabs me by the thighs, and literally *throws* me onto the bed.

Next, he reaches up with his impossibly long arms, digs his fingers into the waistband of my leggings, rips them down my legs and tosses them onto the floor.

And then, he lowers his shoulders under my ankles and dives forward onto the bed, thrusting my legs up in the air and his face directly into my exposed pussy. It isn't measured. It isn't gentle. It is fast and hungry and *hot as fuck.*

I squeal. "Brian!"

And then I feel a cool rush of air slide past my lower lips as Brian breathes in my scent, opens his mouth, and licks a long line up my slit.

Sensation erupts across my center, goosebumps prickle up and down my entire body, and my back arches clear off the comforter. *"Brian!"*

"Heaven. Sweet and tangy like tequila with a lick of salt."

"What?" I breathe, barely holding onto sanity as my brain still catches up to the fact that my pants are off.

"That's what you taste like."

He secures his arms tightly around my thighs, holding me open while he looks up at me from under the mound of my pussy. I shake my head, breathing in short pants. "That's not–a real thing."

"No?" He tilts his head, and smirks. "Guess I'm going to have to go in for another taste."

And he does.

Jolts of electricity shoot from his tongue through my center and out to my fingertips as he opens my pussy with his hands and licks in short strokes around my clit. The fire that's been building in my belly since our kisses stokes anew, these new kisses in my most intimate places driving it harder and hotter than before. The tingling feeling rises up my abdomen, to my chest, and I feel like the rest of my body needs…more. More contact, more air, more…*something.*

"Brian–*Brian,*" I gasp. "Stop, I need–"

He pulls back immediately, forehead wrinkled in concern. "What? What do you need?"

"I need my shirt off."

The worry leaves his face in an instant, and he raises to his knees. A grin stretches across his face. "Yes. Yes you do."

I reach for him, and he grabs my hands and pulls me into his chest, switching his grip to my waist as I press against him. He slides his fingertips under the hem of my shirt and pushes it up my rib cage, grazing the sides of my breasts through the fabric of my bra. Tingling follows his touch, and suddenly there is nothing I need more in this moment than to feel his fingers on my skin.

He reaches around to undo the clasp, and I sigh when the elastic springs apart at his deft fingers. I shrug out of both garments, throwing them off the side of the bed among other discarded clothes, and feel his big, strong hands spread across my shoulder blades as he takes me in, seeing my fully naked form for the first time.

I return the favor, taking in every inch of him that I can see, in earnest this time. His toned fighter's body is glistening with the slightest sheen of perspiration, highlighting the definition of his pecs and the muscles feathering his ribs. As my gaze travels lower, I appreciate the light smattering of hair that thickens into a line below his belly button, pointing directly to his thick, impressive erection springing forward between us.

I don't need to think about it when I wrap my fingers around the smooth, curved shaft and feel the skin slide with every movement of my hand, gripping the firm flesh with purpose. It's instinctual. The most natural thing in the world.

"Fuck, Kodi, that feels so good." His voice is strained and desperate. His eyes fly open, and I see him struggle with his self control for a moment as I squeeze him again and again. It's addicting. I want to stroke him up and down, watching him tilt his head back in ecstasy until—

He grabs my wrist. "We should talk safety. Birth control."

Right. That makes sense. Luckily: "I'm on the pill."

He sighs in relief. "And I'm clean—I test regularly. I don't have condoms with me, though. I never expected…"

My hand loosens a bit as I realize what he's saying. *Oh.*

As much as I want this, my fervor cools a bit at his admission. While I trust that he's clean, and have no reason to assume I'm not, I can't help but think I should listen to the hesitation in my gut.

I'm not sure if I'm ready for that yet.

Do I want him inside me? Absolutely. It's like a switch has flipped inside my virgin brain, and my hormones have taken over. His cock filling me over and over is literally all I can think about right now, and I don't even know what it'll feel like.

But this is still my first time. And even with birth control and STD tests, diving into my first time without a condom just feels risky to me.

"I don't…I don't know if I'm ready for that," I admit, heart sinking. Brian swallows, and nods, taking the hand wrapped around his hard length and removing it, holding it in both of his.

He looks me in the eyes as he says, "that's okay, Kodi. We don't need to do that tonight."

"But I want–" I pause. He waits patiently for me to gather my thoughts, rubbing little circles against my wrist with his thumb. "I don't want to stop."

"I didn't say we had to *stop*." He grins at me, and slowly leans forward, coaxing me back until I'm lying on the bed. He splays one hand across my stomach, reaching the other slowly up my rib cage towards my breast, dragging his fingers along the sensitive skin. I gasp. "I said we don't need to do *that.*"

He cups his hand around my breast, giving it a gentle squeeze, before walking his fingers toward the center of the mound and giving my nipple a playful *flick.*

I gasp again, jerking as lightning surges straight from my nipple to my core.

"There is still plenty we can do without sticking my cock in your sweet pussy, baby girl."

His words light a fire in me, and I grasp his biceps, tugging at him until he rises over me. I crane my neck up and taste his lips again, running my tongue across the seam of his mouth until it opens for me. I need the fireworks that erupt inside me everytime I taste this man's tongue.

He posts his elbows on either side of my head, and we stay like that, chest-to-chest, mouth-to-mouth, bare skin to bare skin, as we explore each other with our mouths. Fire spreads inside my chest as the kisses turn hungrier, deeper. I break away for air, and his kisses travel lower, trailing down my jaw until they reach a sensitive spot on my neck that makes me croon.

"Ahh!" I weave my fingers through the short hair on the sides of his head, until they find purchase in the longer strands at his scalp and tug.

He groans. "*Yes,* baby girl. That's it. Put my mouth where you want me."

Fuck. Something about the way he's saying "baby girl" in that husky, horny voice of his is driving me positively *feral*. My arms move of their own accord, dragging him to my breasts again, where he takes one of my rock-hard nipples into his mouth and sucks greedily.

I *keen.* His name dropping from my lips in a voice I've never fucking heard before. The feeling of his lips, his *tongue,* grazing and sucking along the sensitive flesh of my breasts: positively *decadent.*

I owe Lily the biggest apology in the world. If *this* is what sex is like, then I completely understand her obsession with it. It's tingly, it's fiery, it's amazing, it's–

"Oh, God!" I cry as Brian's tongue laps in a frenzied whirl around my nipple, sending sparks coursing through my body and wetness dripping between my legs. It's like my stomach is full of Pop Rocks. My legs twitch of their own accord, and stars erupt behind my eyelids when I close them on a wordless whimper.

"You like that, baby girl?" He breathes against my sensitive skin, and I nod frantically.

"Yes! Oh my God, yes."

"Are you ready for more?"

I look down in disbelief as he shifts a bit, leaning on one side and reaching his other hand down between my legs.

He groans. *"Christ,* Kodi, you're fucking dripping for me."

He runs a finger up and down the same path his tongue warmed up earlier, and I can feel how right he is. I'm slick with arousal down there, his finger easily slipping between my folds and rubbing at my entrance with little resistance. When the tip of his finger pokes gently inside me, I clench around him, unused to the intrusion.

But it feels so good.

Like too much and not enough all at once.

What would his cock feel like?

I can feel it grazing against my leg, a teensy bead of moisture dripping onto my hip where the tip of it rests between our bodies. I want to feel him with my fingers again, give back some of the incredible pleasure he's giving me, but then he slides another finger inside me and my mind goes blank.

"Oooooh, fuck," I moan, amazed at how full I feel with just two fingers inside me. He's stretching the walls of my pussy in a delicious way, and I find my hips bucking up against his hand to seek out more of this new sensation.

"Wait a minute. Stay right here." He pulls his hand away, and I feel cold and empty in his absence.

"What–"

"I almost forgot," he calls over his shoulder, darting to the bathroom and confusing the hell out of me, until I see him appear at the doorway again with my vibrator in his hand.

He returns to his perch between my legs, and flicks on the wand with a buzz.

I tense in anticipation.

"Have you ever had something inside you while you rub this against your clit?"

I shake my head. It sounds amazing, though, and I know without a doubt that I want it.

He grins, his teeth flashing in the dim light of my bedroom. "Let's fix that."

The first touch of the vibrating head of the magic wand to my clit is deliciously familiar. *Yes.* This is the high I crave when I need to relax, to give myself a release. I feel the familiar tensing build low in my abdomen, and I tilt my hips up, sinking into the slow spiral of pleasure.

Then Brian's hand slips under the toy, swirling in my wet folds before pressing once more inside me.

And everything changes.

I jerk my hips upwards again, and the pressure within me intensifies. But Brian doesn't just fill me with his fingers, he swirls them in circles within me, pressing cyclically against my inner walls which clench in time with the vibrations against my clit.

"Fuck," I moan, grinding deeper against his hand and the wand, the feeling altogether more intense and somehow emptier

than before. Without his fingers, I'd been fast approaching an explosive, but shallow climax: one I knew would leave me quaking and satisfied. But now…

Oh God.

Now, an aching, pulsing need arises deep, deep within me–so deep I'm not sure if it's in my vagina or my ovaries or my fucking spine. Brian's fingers are relentless as they curl in regular pulses against some spot inside me that's making me see stars.

At the same time, my clit is going crazy, bolts of pleasure radiating from that little nub out to my thighs and up to my breasts, making my whole body quake with my impending orgasm. But somehow, he's got every zing of sensation anchored at his fingertips, and every wave crests higher and troughs deeper than any build up I've ever had before.

"Fuck, you are stunning," he rasps above me, and I meet his eyes. That fire I saw earlier is raging there now, irises glinting like emeralds with his arousal. My mouth opens on a wordless cry as he holds my gaze, urging me towards oblivion with every twitch of his hand, until finally the crests and zings and bolts all coalesce into an all-consuming, explosive climax, and I shatter around him.

"Fuck! Brian! Brian!" I scream his name, just like he told me to, again and again until I'm hoarse from cumming. Amazingly, my body doesn't become oversensitive right away, and I'm able to ride the peak of pleasure for what feels like forever, grinding against his hand and the delicious buzz of my magic wand in a continuous ride of bliss.

At last, when it feels like I'll faint from the tensing of my muscles, I collapse against the bed. Only the involuntary tremors that rack my thighs betray my body's absolute exhaustion, and I sigh against my pillow as Brian slowly pulls his hand and the toy away.

"That was…" My voice is little more than a broken whisper, my larynx completely shot from the endless screaming. Brian leans into me and presses a kiss to my forehead, and I wrap my tired limbs around him like a sloth, craving contact with his warm, beautiful body.

He lets me cling to him, leaning his forehead into the crook of my neck. "You are something else, Kodi Gander."

"Me?" I huff a voiceless laugh. "I didn't do anything. *You*. You're the real hero here."

"Was it good for your first time?"

I nod, my eyes closing of their own accord. "So good. So unbelievably good. Holy fuck. I had no idea it could be like that."

I feel his cheeks stretch into a smile, and it's so wonderful. I want him to lay beside me all night.

He pulls away, and I open my eyes. "Where are you going?"

"Cleaning up," he answers, and I wince as his erection–still painfully hard–bounces as he climbs off the bed. I roll to the edge, reaching towards him.

"Wait–don't you want to come, too?"

He hesitates a moment, then shakes his head. "No. I'm fine. Tonight was about you."

"But that's not fair."

"Fair?" Brian raises an eyebrow incredulously. "You want to know what's not fair?" He swings back onto the bed, leaning over me and raking his eyes up and down my body. "The fact that someone as achingly beautiful and strong as you has kept yourself from experiencing the bliss of falling apart like that for your entire life. You should be this hoarse from screaming in ecstasy every morning when you wake up and every night before you go to bed. The fact that I'm the only person who's seen you in the throes of pleasure and heard you scream their name while you do it–*goddammit,* Kodi. It's *so* un-fucking-fair."

I gape at him, stunned into silence.

What…what do I say to something like that?

"I'm the luckiest goddamn man alive tonight, Kodi. Don't you think for a second that I've somehow gotten the short end of the stick here."

He leaves the room, and I hear the rush of the faucet as he

cleans off the toy in the bathroom. A moment later, Brian's back with his boxers on, climbing in beside my still naked body and pulling me into his chest. He holds me, and I wrap my hands around his strong forearms, squeezing until my fingers can't anymore, anchoring him to me.

His words play on a loop in my head, and tears threaten to fall from my eyes.

He said I'm strong.

He said I'm *beautiful*.

Slowly, my body relaxes into the reassuring warmth of his arms, and we don't say another word as the two of us drift off to sleep.

CHAPTER 31
BRIAN

Waking up in Kodi's bed, breathing in her smell all around me, has me sporting the *worst* case of morning wood I've ever had.

Or maybe it's just *her,* still snuggled beside me, relaxed and breathing softly with her dirty blonde hair splayed across the pillow. The sunlight peeking through the blinds of her first-story window scatters beams of light cascading across her freckled, naked skin, and I want nothing more than to trace them with my fingers as I sink myself inside of her.

Damn.

I like her.

Of course, I've enjoyed Kodi's company since our first meeting at the town clinic. She's smart, funny, and has a competitive spirit that, while a bit intimidating, I can't help but respect. She's strong, too, battling with so much more than I could have ever gleaned from our limited interactions.

Seeing the way she was at practice was eye-opening, too. After overhearing her fight with Lily about her softball coach, I can only imagine how badly he fucked up her sense of self-worth. And then to get injured and lose all her scholarships on top of that?

How is she even still standing?

I run my hand lightly up and down the curve of her hip, grazing down her thigh and settling on her knee. No poking and prodding the muscles this morning. Just appreciating her body for what it is *now,* here, in my arms, and all the things it's capable of.

Like how it fell apart last night.

God, the image of her spasming in ecstasy, calling out my name until she could barely speak, is one I won't soon forget. Even without getting off myself, that was some of the hottest sex I'd ever had. This woman is electric.

Lying here beside her, it's hard not to compare last night with mine and Zeke's sexual encounters. We tended to go about things a little more quickly: starting the night with a text, maybe a drink, a healthy squirt of lube and then we'd be out of each other's hair in half an hour or less.

Occasionally I'd spend the night, but I learned quickly that Zeke liked to run to the gym first thing in the morning, and I was never that comfortable alone in his apartment with his spoiled, overweight bulldog. I'm good with pets, but Killer was a rescue that Zeke had never really trained to be comfortable around strangers.

Odd that even after a year of dating, Killer still seemed to think of me as a stranger. Maybe I should have pegged that as a red flag.

Kodi stirs, turning in my arms to face me. She slowly opens her sleepy eyes and crinkles her nose in a shy smile. "Hi."

"Hi." I grin at her.

We stare stupidly at each other for a moment (the kind of thing that Zeke would never have tolerated), and then Kodi stretches, letting out an adorable little squeak as she does. Her back arches into me, and her pelvis grazes my raging hard-on.

"Oh!" She snaps back into her more relaxed pose, eyes wide. "Hello there, Little Brian."

I snort. "Little Brian? No. You're not going to call my penis that."

"Why not?" She runs her fingers through her hair. "It has a nice ring to it. It's cute."

"You think my dick is *cute?*" I give her my most judgemental look. "Word to the wise there, sunshine. 'Cute' is not considered a compliment when someone's using it to refer to a man's package."

"Who said it was a compliment?"

She shoots me a shit-eating grin. I smack her on the boob.

"Ow," she fake-cries, cheeks twitching as she fights a smile. "Rude!"

"You like it," I argue, relaxing my fingers into the soft mound of flesh and squeezing tenderly until her nipple starts to stiffen. "And you know what? I think you like my cock too."

"You do, huh?"

"I do."

She opens her mouth to say something smart, but it turns into a gasp as I flick her swollen nipple. She bites her lip.

"Oh yeah. You *totally* like it."

"I like your *fingers,"* she argues. "Jury's still out on your penis."

I stop rubbing her, pulling my hands back. "Fine then. No more hands or fingers for you until you get back with your verdict."

She lets out an offended little scoff, and I roll upright and slowly get off the bed. But before I fully rise, she grabs my wrist and yanks me back down.

She leans over me, Spiderman-style, her head upside-down with her lips above mine and her tits hanging over my forehead. My eyes dart from her mischievous eyes to her jiggling breasts, and I smile at my delicious predicament.

There are worse views to wake up to.

I reach my arms up and grab her ribcage, lowering her chest down to my mouth as I take one of her nipples in an indulgent pull. She gasps again, and pounds her arms helplessly against my abdomen as I hold her right where I want her.

"Gah! What are you–*Brian!*" Her fingers rake down to my hips, slapping fruitlessly. I suck harder, swirling her areola with my tongue. "St–stop it–"

I shake my head like the brat I am, not letting go of her perfect breast. Then she wraps her hands around my cock through my boxers.

I release her with a *pop.* "Woah there, easy, baby girl!" I wince at the pressure building in my balls. "I'm still wound up from last night. I don't want me blowing my load in your hair to be your first experience with that, okay?"

She lets go, and I twist to sit across from her. She nods, hair falling in her face. As she pushes the strands behind her ears, she rubs her arm absentmindedly.

"When…when should that happen?"

I blink. "What?"

"My first experience, with…" her eyes lower to my tented boxers.

I shift into a cross-legged position, tucking myself up into my waistband so it's a little less intimidating. The head of my dick pokes out, drawing her eyes immediately.

I tilt her chin with a finger until her eyes rise to meet mine. "We should talk about that."

Her shoulders slump, and she looks away. "Do you not want to?"

"What? No!" I rear back, shaking my head. "Fuck, Kodi, what the fuck would make you think that?"

She shrugs. I rub my hand over my face.

"I need you to understand something, okay?" I thought I'd made it perfectly clear last night, but apparently Kodi struggles a lot more with her self-confidence than I thought. "I *want* to sleep with you. I think you are *very* attractive, I absolutely enjoyed last night, and I one hundred percent want to get my dick involved in our sexual activities if you're amenable."

Her cheeks glow pink. "Okay."

"But I gathered from last night that I should probably buy a box of condoms before that happens."

She lets out a breath. "Yeah. I'm just not comfortable–"

I hold up a hand. "I get it. And you're right: safe sex is good sex. I'm bi, remember? Condoms are my best friend."

She smiles, then her eyes widen slightly. "Wait. Um. How does that work with two guys?"

I blink at her dubiously. "You're kidding, right?"

"Is it, like," she lowers her voice to a whisper. "Butt stuff?"

I try not to laugh at her, but I don't do the best job of keeping the chuckle out of my voice. "Yes, Kodi. Among other things."

She straightens, taking a second to think. Then she says, "is that actually…good? Like, pleasurable?"

This time, I can't hold in my laugh anymore. "Why else would anyone do it?"

She shivers. "I just can't even imagine what that would feel like."

I tilt my head at her. "Well, if you're ever interested in finding out, I have quite a bit of experience. Just let me know."

The pink on her cheeks turns magenta, slowly enveloping the rest of her face. "Um…noted."

I nod. "Cool. Now that *that's* settled, how about some breakfast?"

EVEN THOUGH KODI HAS TO BE AT WORK BEFORE NINE AND I'M STILL wearing my clothes from yesterday, I decide it's high time we're seen in public once again. Although truth be told, part of my desire to take her out for breakfast is simply not being ready to leave her company just yet. Last night was special; she gave me a *real* piece of herself, fake relationship or not. And I'm not about to just step out on her with a wave and a peck on the cheek before she heads to work.

After she showers, she reminds me that I still haven't been to the famous diner she wanted to take me to back when we first met.

"They're by far the best breakfast in town," she says as she brushes out her long hair. The highlights glow bronze as they dry in the light from her bedroom window.

"I don't know, I'm pretty partial to the bacon sandwiches at *Bun in the Oven.*"

"Trust me. You haven't lived until you've had the *Swallow's* Eggs Benedict." She puts the finishing touches on her work outfit (black slacks, a purple blouse, and some black ankle boots), slips an elastic around her wrist, and gathers up her bag.

"Damn. You get ready faster than I do in the mornings," I observe, and she smirks.

"Why? How long does it take you to do *your* makeup?"

"Har, har. Come on, Gander, time's a'wasting."

She scurries in front of me to the front door, and I smack her on the ass. She squeals. "Hey!"

"Well, if you don't want a spanking, don't be rude."

With a playful scowl in my direction, she opens the door and we walk down the couple of blocks to *Easy Swallow.*

It's like stepping back in time. Red vinyl booths line the windowed front wall, where a surprising number of locals have already settled themselves. Another row of hungry customers sit at the diner counter, behind which I can see the rows of coffee pots and the big kitchen window, where paper tickets are clothes-pinned to a string of orders. I recognize one of the line cooks from the gym, and I give him a wave, but he's too busy flipping eggs and hashbrowns to look up and see me.

"Two for breakfast?" The waitress asks, and Kodi smiles at her.

"Yep!"

"Coffee?"

"You got it," she says as we follow the pink-haired woman over to a booth in the rear of the restaurant. *Yet another woman with pink hair in this town.* Old photographs and framed issues of the local paper hang across the walls, giving me a glimpse into the history of my new home.

Once settled, we're each handed a plastic-coated menu. Kodi waves hers away.

"I'll take the Eggs Benny, with a side of hashbrowns and double bacon."

"Hungry this morning, are we?" The waitress raises her eyebrows. I cough at her.

"Make that two." I hand her back my own menu, and she looks at us appraisingly.

"Alright. Two Bennies and a chonky squealer on a bed, coming up for the happy couple." She shouts the order back to the window, and a chorus of answering grunts echoes back.

Kodi raises her eyes to mine, and she wiggles her torso in a little dance. *She's literally dancing for bacon.* I reach out a hand to her, and she grasps it.

"You seem happy." I grin. I can't help it. She's adorable.

"Just excited for breakfast. I love this place. Small towns have their downsides, don't get me wrong, but you don't find spots like this in bigger cities, you know?"

"I do," I agree, lowering my eyes as the waitress returns with two mugs of steaming coffee and a couple red plastic cups of ice water. She tosses two straws down, as well as a carousel of creamers, and gives us an obvious once-over. As she does, I take in her name-tag, which reads "Eve".

"Hey, you're the new doctor, aren't you? The one who cracks backs?"

At her words, a few heads turn in our direction. I nod, wishing I had the foresight to stuff a few extra business cards in my wallet.

"That's me. Brian Gosling." I hold out my hand.

"Like the actor??"

Kodi hides her mouth with her hand, stifling a giggle. I shake my head.

"That's *Ryan* Gosling."

"Oh my God. I just loved him in *La La Land.*" She visibly

swoons, holding a hand to her heart and getting a faraway look in her eyes. "And the chemistry he had with Emma Stone? Ugh. I wish a man would look at me like that, you know?"

Kodi's eyes flash up to me from her coffee, and I feel my pulse race a bit. "Yeah, haha, I know what you mean."

"Is he your brother? Do you think you could tell him my Insta?" She hands me a card with an entire laundry list of social media handles on it. I blink down at it, shocked into silence for a moment.

"Umm..."

"He's not related," Kodi answers for me, and I shoot her a grateful look. "But if you know anyone who needs help with their chronic back or neck pain, or even could just use a little straightening out, he's the man to see!"

She reaches into her bag and pulls out one of my business cards. My mouth drops open.

"Oh, you know? My neck has been *killing* me. Dad says it's 'tech neck,' or something, from staring at my phone. Is that a real thing?"

She turns her heavily lined eyes to me, and her fake eyelashes blink in expectation.

"Uh, yeah. It's absolutely a thing. You get headaches?"

"Oh my God. All the time! How did you know?"

I nod. "Give me a call. I'll get that fixed right up for you."

"Thanks, Ryan!" She tops off my (still full) mug of coffee, and swipes the card from Kodi's hand before walking away.

My girlfriend–*fake girlfriend,* I remind myself–finally lets loose her laughter, shaking her head as she stirs some sugar into her mug.

"I think you have a new fan," she teases.

"We'll see." I take a scalding sip. "How'd you get one of my business cards?"

"I stole a stack of them last time I was in your office," she says, cheeks pink. "Figured I might as well do a little covert marketing for you in addition to helping you run your business."

"A little tech help is a far cry from *running* my business."

"Keep telling yourself that, *Ryan.*" Her teasing grin transforms into a look of pure terror as her focus slides behind me. "Mom!"

"*Hello,* sunshine!"

I freeze as I hear the sonorous voice of Linda Gander ring out in the *Easy Swallow,* and my shoulders tense as more wandering eyes across the diner zero in on the family reunion commencing at our booth. I instantly rise, knocking my thighs on the table in my haste to show good manners in front of Kodi's mother.

"Hi, Mrs–uh, Linda. Good morning." I hold out my hand to her for a handshake.

Her eyes shift pointedly from Kodi to me, to my wrinkled outfit that is obviously from the day before. She ignores my hand.

"Brian, hello. Marty tells me you still haven't returned his call."

His call? Fuck.

"Oh, uh…I didn't realize he'd called me…"

"You'd think that a young entrepreneur would check his voicemail more regularly. But I suppose you've been…busy."

Her gaze lowers to my clothes once again. My stomach sinks.

Shit shit shit!

If I thought running into Kodi's mom in town was bad when it was only rumored that we'd slept together, it's a hundred thousand times worse now that her daughter and I have *actually* slept together.

Granted, we haven't gone all the way, exactly, but that line seems a little irrelevant when I know the sounds she makes when she's coming on my fingers.

"What are you doing here, mom?" Kodi asks politely, saving me from responding to her scathing comment. Linda clears her throat.

"Meeting the girls for an overdue brunch. What are *you* doing, dear? Don't you have work?"

"Two Bennies, side of hashbrowns and double bacon on the side," Eve interrupts, depositing two delectable-looking plates onto our table. As if sensing the tension, she scurries away without another word. I glance frantically between my breakfast and my executioner.

"Oh, don't let me keep you two from your breakfast. Eat! Please. You don't have that much time, after all. It's already 8:00."

"Shi–I mean, shoot. Right. Nice seeing you, mom."

"It *is* nice, isn't it? You know what might be even nicer? If you would come to Sunday family dinner, Kodi. Your father and I *miss* you. It would mean the world to us to have some family time to catch up on how things are going with you, and your job, and... well. It's just been *so* long!"

I'm still standing awkwardly in between Linda and Kodi, who's still seated, but has yet to take a bite of her breakfast. Instead, she's shifting uncomfortably under her mother's gaze.

Do they not talk very often?

I want so badly to butt in and save Kodi from her obvious discomfort, but I'm equally nervous about making a bad impression in front of her mom. Especially now, that...

Now that her opinion on our relationship might actually matter.

My heart squeezes at the realization that I've been slowly coming to terms with over the last twenty-four hours. The dawning discovery that my feelings for this woman aren't entirely fake. That, despite everything, I might actually be interested in Kodi Gander for more than just her tech savvy, or her ability to make Zeke jealous; I might actually be developing an honest-to-goodness crush on her.

Which makes everything about this interaction about a zillion times more complicated.

"I have a great idea. Why doesn't Brian come, too? In fact, Marty has a tee time for 7:30 next Sunday morning. Brian, why don't you join him on the green for the day while Kodi and I prepare something for both of you when you come home? It'll be a chance for all of us to get to know you."

The blood drains from Kodi's face as Linda shares her horrible idea with me, coming to her senses quickly enough to shake her head vehemently behind her mother's back as she finishes talking. By the time Linda turns to Kodi for confirmation, she's completely schooled her expression back into a polite smile as she nods at her eagerly.

"Umm, I'd uh, love to, Linda! That sounds...great," I finish lamely, and Linda's thousand-watt Crest White Strips commercial smile flashes at me. Kodi stares at me in disbelief, but I can't communicate with her when Linda's beaming at me.

"Wonderful! Well, there's Jane. I'll leave you two to your breakfast. See you next Sunday, sweetie!" She leans down and kisses Kodi on the cheek, and shoots me one last tight-lipped smile before click-clacking over to the bar where another middle-aged woman with big hair is waiting for her.

I finally sit back down, across from a frozen Kodi. Her fork and knife are clenched in her fists, and she stares me down as I settle behind my now lukewarm eggs Benedict.

"What was I supposed to do?" I hiss at her before she can scold me, trying to cover up the sound of our conversation by cutting into my English muffin. "She had us cornered."

"You're condemning me to an entire day of *cooking* with my *mother,* while you *golf with my dad??"* She grinds her teeth as she talks, silverware quaking in her shaking hands.

"I'm sorry," I mutter, feeling every bit like the biggest piece of shit. "I didn't know what to do."

"Well, get ready there, bright eyes. Because you have no idea what you just signed yourself up for."

CHAPTER 32
KODI

Brian walked me to the clinic after breakfast, but the playful energy we'd had all morning evaporated the second my mom showed up at the diner.

I don't hate my mom. Truly. She's a fine woman, and for the most part was pretty good at raising me. But since my injury, she and my dad both have treated me like I'm fragile. Like one wrong look or comment will cause me to crumble before their very eyes.

I left home as soon as I could afford to, simply so I wouldn't have to see their pitying looks anymore. Every time I came down the stairs, or walked into the kitchen for a snack, or looked through the mail, it was always, "How are you, dear? Are you feeling okay?"

Every. Single. Time.

I couldn't exist in their presence without being reminded of how I'd broken once. And I knew that, as long as I was home, I'd never truly be able to get past it.

When I first moved, mom called every day. So I stopped answering. Then she'd text. First twice a day, then five times a week, until finally she just checked in occasionally and invited me to Sunday dinner.

I don't *never* text her back. I keep her updated. Visit once a month or so. But I have an adult life of my own now. I don't *need* her and dad checking in everyday. I'm doing just fine.

I glance at my phone as I put it away in my bag, and check the ongoing text conversation with mom to see when the last time I responded was. I realize I haven't since before Brian and I announced our relationship to the world with our kiss at the match over two weeks ago.

Guilt pokes at my stomach, mixing with the ham and eggs and hollandaise. *Has it really been that long?*

It feels at once like we've just met and like I've known him forever. Butterflies join the cocktail of emotions in my stomach as visions from last night flash through my head, interspersed with the awkward frustration leftover from our hug when he dropped me off at the office.

"Miss Gander, could you come to my office for a moment, please?" Dr. Cratchet calls from down the hall. I sigh, plopping my phone back into my purse on the hook, and smooth the nonexistent wrinkles from my pants before heading over.

"Yes, sir?"

"I can't help but notice that things are getting rather intimate between you and the spine cracker." He levels a look at me over his steepled fingers and half-moon glasses. "That was him at the door earlier, was it not?"

I'm getting real sick of this.

I hold back a frustrated noise as I meet his eyes, not even sure what he wants me to say or what he's trying to glean from this interaction. It's creepy that he's this obsessed with my social life, right? It isn't just me that would think that?

"Yes." I leave out the "sir" out of spite. He doesn't notice, looking out the window, presumably deep in thought.

"And how much longer do you wager he'll continue to be a thorn in our sides?"

I want to tell him to go fuck himself. Seriously. This weird little game he's been playing has been going on long enough. What is *with* this guy? How is he so threatened by a man who can't even prescribe medicine? Someone who isn't even direct competition?

I wonder if he's so worried because having a competent professional in town to actually *help* people with their chronic pain might make all the Tuft Swallowers realize what a hack this man is.

In that moment, as I bite my tongue in Dr. Cratchet's office, holding back all of these thoughts from tumbling forward, it's like a fog is lifted from my head. Somehow, for the past three years I've worked here, I've given my boss a pass for all his disgusting behavior. His gross ineptitude. His weird, creepy comments and cold, grabby fingers. Now that I'm seeing him for what he is–for what he's always been–I can't take it anymore.

When I was at my absolute lowest, I came to Dr. Cratchet for help, and he gave me nothing but pills. I thought I was doomed to live a life of pain and suffering, until Brian came along and showed me that I might actually have a shot at playing sports again.

And he wants to run Brian out of town?

Over my dead body.

"Honestly, sir?" I begin, just as sweet as honey. "Forever."

"I beg your pardon?"

"I don't think he'll leave. In fact, I hope he doesn't."

The look of absolute shock on my boss's gnarly face fills me with more satisfaction than I'll ever admit. *What a goddamn narcissist.*

He actually believed I'd *spy* on a competitor for him?

I may not be able to convince my mother that I can take care of myself. My cornhole team might think that I'm out of my mind. I may be losing my best friend because she thinks she knows me better than I know myself, but you know what?

They're all wrong. I'm not crazy. I'm not weak. I'm *strong,* dammit, and I've put up with enough. I've settled for years of incompetence from everyone I ever asked for help, and now I've finally found someone who can give me what I need. I'm not about to let the shittiest boss on the planet take that from me because he's an insecure little baby.

"What has gotten into you, Miss Gander?" he sputters, rising from his chair and waving at me threateningly with his liver-spotted hands. His glasses start to steam as his eyes bug out of his head. "We had a plan! A mission! You were to be my man on the inside, to use your injury to spy–"

"That's just it, sir," I interrupt him. "I'm not comfortable *using* my injury to spy on a medical professional. I've never wanted to use my injury as an excuse! I don't want to be some injured little flower anymore, to take pity on or advantage of. I never did, nor *would* I ever, agree to spy for you. You just assumed I had, because you walk all over me. But I'm done, sir. I didn't go to Dr. Gosling to be your *'man on the inside.'* I went to see a competent professional to help me with my chronic pain. And you know what?"

I step forward, tapping my finger on his walnut desk to emphasize every word as I look him dead in his rheumy eyes, knowing that these will be the ones that hurt him the most.

"He's a damn good doctor."

Cratchet's mouth gapes open and closed like a fish, and I realize for the first time that I'm actually taller than him. In my two-inch boots, standing tall across his desk, I practically tower over this pathetic old man.

"In fact, I wish this town had more practicing professionals like him."

Stepping back to the threshold of the hallway, I stop briefly to address him one last time.

"I'm going to go back to the office and do my *real* job. The one that I'm paid *twenty-two dollars an hour* to do. I am going to greet your patients, check them in, file their paperwork, and handle all of the necessary responsibilities to make sure *your* floundering practice doesn't fall apart under your gross ineptitude. And you're going to let me do my job, in peace, because deep down you know that this place would absolutely crumble without me.

And because if you don't, I'll report your little espionage scheme to the Clinic board."

And with that, I turn on my heel, march back to my office, and make myself a goddamn cup of coffee.

THE REST OF THE DAY MIGHT BE THE BEST ONE I'VE EVER WORKED AT the Tuft Swallow Clinic. Dr. Cratchet steers clear of me, avoiding the office like a leper colony, as I run everything like clockwork. At lunchtime, I hear him shuffle past my door, the sleigh bells ringing as he slides through the entryway without saying goodbye, and he slips back in without me even noticing twenty minutes later. We dodge each other all day, the only communication passing between us the patient charts he slides into my mailbox.

At 5:00, I turn off all the lights and lock up, the boss nowhere in sight.

Good, I think to myself. *I don't want to hear his dumb fake transatlantic accent anyway.*

I reach for my phone, which has been sitting comfortably on my desk the entire morning, to text Lily.

I'm still not over her conspiring with Brian to "loosen me up" after our argument at practice. It was a shitty thing to do behind my back, even if it did lead to one of the best nights of my life, and it's hard to feel like I can just let our friendship pick up where it left off.

ME

Hey. We need to talk.

CHAPTER 33
KODI

"Why do we have to talk *here?*"

Lily and Callie unroll their rubber mats on the wooden floor of Wingspan, the new yoga studio in town. I've heard Brian briefly talk about the owner, Caleb Masters, as someone he's been networking with. I spied a pile of his business cards on the desk when we walked in.

"Kodi, this is a space of healing and zen. It's a neutral place without memories for either of you, and should be a good spot for you to approach your issues with a fresh perspective," Callie says, centering herself in a butterfly stretch on her mat.

I grumble a little as I grab one of the community mats in the corner next to an entire tower of plants. The whole wall is windows looking out onto the town square, and the more people arrive for the Saturday Sunrise Salutation class, the stupider I think this plan of Callie's is.

"No offense, Callie, but I don't think this is a great location for *any* conversation," I hiss, not wanting to raise my voice. I'm already used to the *Nosy Pecker* blasting my romantic relationships across the front page; I'm not sure that I want to give them any more ammunition regarding the platonic ones.

"It'll be good for you—us, I mean." Lily takes position in the center of her mat, attempting a lotus pose with both her feet pointing to the ceiling. With her thicker thighs, she ends up fumbling each time she tries to get the second foot in the right position, as it sends her legs sprawling apart whenever she tries to wedge it through the crease of her knee.

"Have you ever even *done* yoga?"

"It's literally stretching, how hard can it be?"

A snort comes from somewhere behind us as Lily's other leg snaps open, and she finally gives up on the pose. She pulls her knees to her chest, and Callie furrows her brow.

"Didn't Brian tell you you should be doing more stretches anyway?"

I roll my eyes. "I stretch every day. PT, remember?"

"And how's that working for you?" Lily whispers.

The room is filling in fast around us. Already, there are over a dozen of us here at the crack of dawn on a Saturday. A few I even recognize from the cornhole team, including Ginger and Geneva.

"It's getting better."

Geneva waves at me eagerly as I scan the room, her attention snapping to Caleb as he walks into the room with a bluetooth boombox. Immediately behind him is Brian.

Fuck.

I didn't think it was possible for my stomach to flutter and sink at the same time, but apparently there are all sorts of things my body's capable of where Brian is concerned. Aside from a few texts, we haven't spoken since running into my mother yesterday.

Are literally all of my relationships imploding this week?

I close my eyes, avoiding making eye contact with anyone as I put the soles of my feet together in a butterfly stretch and take a few deep breaths. As I do, I hear the last few stragglers roll out their mats and the sound of a soft, vamping electric guitar fills the room as Caleb connects his phone to the boombox.

"Namaste," his rich voice calls out into the room.

"Namaste," the class responds in unison. I can pick out Lily and Callie's voices beside me, as well as Brian's husky morning baritone directly behind me. My heart skips a beat as my body remembers the last time I heard that deep voice rumble through me.

I open my eyes. *Is it warm in here?* The sign outside didn't say "Hot Yoga," but I swear the temperature just rose about ten degrees. I glance around, trying to see if there are any heat lamps.

There aren't. I tug at the collar of my t-shirt.

"Thank you all for joining me for our Sunrise Yoga. The purpose of today's class is to ease the transition from sleep into a state of mindfulness for the day ahead. We're just going to start with a series of breaths from a comfortable, seated, cross-legged position. If at any point, you feel the need for a bolster or a pillow to allow yourself to reach a more comfortable or supported stretch, please feel free to help yourself to one from the basket by the windows."

A few of the older members of the class rise to grab a pillow or two. As Caleb waits for them to return to their mats, I feel a hand brush against my shoulder.

Brian leans his head close to my ear. "It's good to see you here."

My neck flushes even hotter. "Ha, yeah. You too," I whisper back.

Lily and Callie share a look, and I glare at them. Lily raises an eyebrow.

Ah, shit. Now she thinks something happened between us.

I mean, she's right, but I don't want to give her that kind of satisfaction before we've had our talk. If she realizes that Brian and I fooled around after she sent him to my apartment to do *just that,* she's not going to feel the least bit sorry about going behind my back.

"Okay, now try to focus on sitting tall as we breathe in. Picture a string at the top of your head pulling all the way to the base of your spine…"

Lily's breath tickles my ear as she leans in and whispers beside me. "I know I *love* to feel a stretch at the base of my spine…"

I close my eyes and purse my lips, ignoring her. Just trying to focus on the breathing. *In…out. In…out.*

"As you breathe in, feel the tension in your body, and then release it on the exhale. In: tension, two, three; out: relaxation, three, four. In…"

In: Lily's smug little face. Out: shoving everyone out of my business.

In—my face, out—of my business.

In…out…

"Hmmm, in and out. Kinda makes you think of something else, you know?"

I grit my teeth at Lily's teasing. Her voice is low enough that only I can hear her, but I do my best to ignore it. I know, in her own way, she's trying to make me laugh and break the tension between us. And another time, another day, with another guy, maybe it would work.

But the fact of the matter is, Brian isn't a joke to me. Fake relationship or not, the help and confidence he's been giving me is real. And that isn't just about sex. It's about so much more than that, with my knee, with my rehab…

With the rest of my body…

In, out.

In, out.

"Now on this next inhale I want you to reach your arms up and over your head, feeling that stretch in your spine and your shoulders…"

I open my eyes, lifting my arms with the rest of the class, then exhale and let them sweep to my side. It actually does feel nice, after sitting at a desk all week, and my back crackles a little as I breathe in and out of the stretch.

Lily's hand brushes mine on the way down, and she giggles.

"Sorry."

Ignore her…

In, out.

In, out.

"Alright, now this time as you breathe out, I want you to

collapse forward and reach to the floor with your fingertips. Inhale, round your back, exhale, walk your fingers out a little more, deepening that stretch in your back.

"Now slowly rise to hands and knees, and we're going to do cat/cow..."

He explains the next pose, in which we round our back on the exhale (cat), and then arch our backs on the inhale (cow), sticking our butts in the air and raising our heads to the ceiling. Which of course, means everytime we breathe in, my ass is directly in Brian's face.

"Enjoying the view there, Brian?"

"Oh my God, shut *up*, Lily!"

I rise to a seated position on my knees, scowling at the woman beside me, totally disrupting the class. Faces turn to me in various states of right-side up and upside-down depending on who's a cat and who's a cow at the moment, and I feel absolutely humiliated at my outburst. I shake my head, muttering "excuse me," as I scramble off my mat and run to the door.

Tears prick my eyes on my way there, and by the time I finally slam it behind me and sit down in one of the wooden chairs lining the entryway, they're fully streaming down my cheeks.

What the hell is Lily's problem? She does realize that her immature comments are *not* helpful, right? We're twenty-four years old, for Pete's sake, *way* too old for that kind of nonsense. Especially in fucking Tuft Swallow, where those sorts of things will be front-page news the next day.

The door clicks, and I look up.

Brian's come out to check on me.

"Hey," he mutters softly, sitting down beside me. "What's wrong?"

"You didn't hear her in there?"

He shakes his head. "I didn't hear Lily say anything."

Well, fuck. I guess she was being more discreet than I realized.

So now *I'm* the one who looks like an asshole.

I rub my face with my hands. *Inhale, exhale.*

I never want to stop rubbing my eyes. "She's being a fucking idiot."

"What did she do?"

"She still hasn't apologized."

"For what?" He tilts his head quizzically. I peek at him between my fingers.

"For sending you to my apartment to fuck my troubles away!"

His eyes widen. "You're still angry about that? After what happened?"

He places a hand on my arm, but I swat him away. "Yes, Brian, of course I'm angry. She literally went behind my back. *You*, at least, told me what the deal was and didn't go along with it. Well," I pause. Realizing that isn't quite true. "I mean, you didn't do it because *she* told you to."

I freeze, terrified, staring at him. "You didn't, right?"

"What? No, Kodi, of course not!" Genuine hurt flashes in his eyes, and I find myself believing him. "Everything that happened that night after I walked in the door had *nothing* to do with Lily."

I let his words sink in. "She asked if you were enjoying the view."

"What? When?"

"Just now. Before I yelled at her. When we were in cow pose."

His face flushes, and he coughs. I swear I see a laugh sparkling in his eyes. "Ah, I see."

I cross my arms, eying him. "You were fucking checking me out, weren't you?"

He shrugs. I smack his shoulder.

"Hey now, can you blame me? I may have advised you to come here as a doctor, but I never said I was a saint–if you're coming to yoga you better believe I'm gonna check out your ass whenever the opportunity presents itself."

I try to glare at him, but I can't quite keep the smirk from my eyes. "Pervert."

"Guilty as charged." He reaches out to rub my shoulder again, and this time I don't push him away. "Wanna go back in there for hip openers?"

"Is that the doctor asking, or the pervert?"

"Both." He grins.

I shake my head at him, then sweep the flyaway hairs out of my face. "I don't want to sit next to Lily again."

"We'll roll out our mats in the back, by the windows. I won't even be behind you this time, I promise." He moves his hand down to my knee, and squeezes slightly. "I *do* think it'll be good for you."

I sigh. "Okay. I'll give it a shot."

"That's my girl."

THE CLASS ENDS WITH ALL OF US IN A POSITION CALLED DEAD BUG, where we're flat on our backs with our limbs curled up in the air, sinking our spine into the floor. When Caleb announces for us to take our time rising to a seated position, I stay on my back for a little longer than most of the group.

In fact, the only people left in the room by the time I roll upright are Lily, Callie, Caleb, and Brian.

"You alright there, Kodi? This was your first time. How did it feel?"

Brian reaches out a hand to steady me as I rise to my feet and take inventory of my body. I really think about Caleb's question before answering, consciously trying to separate how I feel mentally (like shit) versus physically (pretty good, actually).

"Good. I liked it. Especially after spending all week at the desk."

"It's great for that," Brian agrees. Caleb nods to him, and he pats me on the shoulder as he shifts his stance to the instructor. "Hey, Caleb, why don't we talk a little more about that member discount idea I was telling you about…?"

The two of them move to the front of the room, and Lily gets out her wallet.

"This one's on me, girls." She puts the money for the class down by the boombox as the three of us leave. Brian locks eyes with me, and gives me an encouraging half-smile. My heart squeezes.

Everything that happened that night after I walked in that door had nothing *to do with Lily.*

"Thanks for paying, Lil," Callie says, breaking the silence as we all walk aimlessly down Main Street. It's a beautiful day outside, the perfect temperature for a morning stroll, and we end up heading in the direction of *Bun in the Oven* on instinct.

"Yeah, Lily. Thanks."

"Don't mention it."

More silence stretches for about half a block, before Callie finally snaps.

"Ugh! I can't take it anymore! This friend group doesn't work when the two of you are fighting. You need to kiss and make up, okay? Now. Or no lattes."

She freezes on the sidewalk in front of us, tossing her yoga bag to the ground and crossing her arms.

Lily takes a deep breath, and turns to me. "Kodi, I–"

"Stop." I hold up my hand. Unlike Callie, I don't have a bag to carry, so I find myself fidgeting as I talk. "Do you know *why* I'm angry with you?"

"Umm…" Lily blinks at me. "Because I said you were taking your unresolved anger at Coach out on the cornhole team?"

I pause for a moment as I take that in. *Huh.*

That's what she thinks I'm angry about?

"No," I start to say, then shake my head. "Actually, well…a little, but no. That's–wait." I take a deep breath, pinching my nose to refocus. "So you think it's *okay* that you sent Brian to my house to have sex with me to get me to calm down after our fight? Like some kind of prostitute?"

"What??" Callie screams, arms flying down to her sides as she gapes at Lily. "You did *what* now??"

"I didn't do that!!" Lily's eyes bulge out of her head as she frantically tries to backtrack the conversation. "Holy shit, Callie, you were *there*. Brian saw our fight at the park that night, Kodi, and he asked why you were so upset. He could see something was hurting you, and he wanted to help."

"Yeah. So you sent him to my house to seduce me with shrimp lo mein and Doritos. Which is totally unfair, by the way! You should know better than to use my love of lo mein against me."

"I did not!" Lily stomps her foot. "Callie, back me up here. All I said was that this whole season has been really stressful for you, and has brought up a lot of old feelings from high school–which is *true*. And that I was really grateful that you had someone like him to help distract you from all of that, because I'd never seen you be with someone that made you so happy!"

"That is pretty much exactly what she said, Kodi. Along with telling him your favorite foods." Callie's face is gentler now, more one of concern than outrage. I glance between them.

Honestly, of all the things I thought Lily capable of, handling Brian's concern with that much…grace was something I never would have expected.

Have I been seeing Lily all wrong? Am *I* actually the one that's more immature in this relationship?

"What–what did he say to that?"

Lily's eyes shine with a shy grin. "He said that he's never met someone like you before. That he never would have known how much you were struggling if he hadn't heard our fight. And that he wanted to make you feel better."

"So *then* she said that he should take you out on a date to distract you on Friday night so you'd cancel cornhole practice–oof!" Lily elbows Callie in the arm and talks over her.

"You ended up calling off practice anyway, so it didn't matter." She shrugs as Callie rubs her arm. "But what happened? Why did you think that…"

When she trails off, I see the cogs turning in her brain, and my stomach twists. I brace myself the second I see the light bulb go off above her head, the most evil smile spreading across her face.

"OH MY GOD, KODI GANDER. YOU DID IT, DIDN'T YOU?"

Callie gasps, dropping her bag and covering her mouth with her hands as she connects the same dots, a mischievous twinkle sparking to life in her wide eyes.

"Keep your voice down!" I hiss, grabbing Callie's bag and shoving them down the sidewalk to avoid any potential eavesdroppers out for a morning bird watching stroll. "That's *not* what we're talking about."

"It is *now!!*" Lily squeals, grabbing my free hand with both of hers. "Tell. Me. *Everything!* Is he actually as big as you remember? Was it romantic?? Did he know it was your first time, or–"

"Oh my God, wait—how far did you *go?"* Callie seizes her bag from me. "I thought you were just friends and faking the whole dating thing! Are you *actually* dating now??"

"No, guys, we're not actually dating now," I mutter, keeping my voice low and glaring at them to do the same. "And we didn't do it…all the way."

The two women squee. I want to sink into the sidewalk. This is potentially the most embarrassing moment of my life.

"Okay, okay, describe it in softball terms. Which base are we talking here?" Lily is suddenly all business, back straight as she lists the bases off on her fingers. We finally arrive at the cafe, and Callie holds open the door for us as Lily barrels through any of my attempted gestures begging her to quiet down. "You've already blown through first, so that isn't even really an option. Second would be heavy petting, so we're talking under the clothes above the belt or over the clothes below the belt." She stares at me pointedly, she and Callie practically vibrating in anticipation of my response.

"Um…we, uh…we went past that."

"You scored a fucking triple with Doctor Hottie and didn't tell me??"

Thankfully, her voice reaches a high enough register that it comes across more like squeaks than words, and I highly suspect that only dogs within earshot would be able to discern her meaning.

Mortified, I nod.

The two women grab my hands and literally hop up and down with their excitement for me. I can't help but laugh at the ridiculous sight they make.

"Oh come on, you two, it isn't that big a deal."

"That's where you're wrong, girl," Lily says, stepping forward as we inch towards the front of the line. "This is a very, *very* big deal. Now tell us: how was it?"

My face catches fire as I look at anything other than my friends. "Amazing."

As Lily and Callie pepper me for more details, I glance around the cafe at the other patrons. And then my eyes catch the headline of the Saturday edition of the *Nosy Pecker* staring at me from one of the tables.

Tee Time with Daddy Dearest: Gosling and Gander Return to the Nest!

Oh no.

CHAPTER 34
BRIAN

Caleb and I grab lunch after his second morning yoga class to hammer out a customer discount plan for each other. It's going well, and I'm enjoying the fried apple cheddar stuffed French toast at the Easy Swallow until I see the headline of the weekend's *Nosy Pecker* emblazoned across another diner's newspaper.

Tee Time with Daddy Dearest: Gosling and Gander Return to the Nest!

Fuck.

"Brian? You okay? You're white as a ghost all of the sudden." Caleb's concern goes over my head as I gape at the front-page article, wondering how on earth the whole town seems to know more about my social life than I do.

"Uh, I'm fine, just–"

At that moment, my cell rings in my pocket. I hold up a finger for Caleb, and check the caller ID.

Fuck. It's Linda Gander. I'd finally added her number to my phone after Kodi insisted I stop ignoring her mother's calls.

"Hello?"

"Hi Brian, it's Marty Gander, Kodi's father. I see here in *The Nosy Pecker* that you and I are due for a date on the green!"

"Um, the green?" I draw a blank.

"You know, the ol' eighteen!"

A moment passes. I rack my brain trying to parse out his meaning.

"Golf, son. A game of golf."

"Oh!" *Duh.* I really am clueless about most traditional sports. If it's not martial arts or something we learned in gym class, don't assume I know anything about it. "Right, yes, Linda mentioned something about that."

"What do you say you and I meet at the Country Club 'round seven next Sunday? Bright and early? You've got clubs, I assume?"

"Uh, no sir, I've never actually played."

"Ah, no worries. We'll have Jeff bring an extra set. You can meet the whole gang! Pretty important, after all, if you're gonna be family."

Caleb's eyebrows raise at me as I melt into the back of my chair.

"Um, well, I don't know if…" I pinch my nose, then sigh. "Thanks, Marty. I'm uh, looking forward to it."

"See you then, Brian."

The call ends, and Caleb waves his hand in front of my face. "Hello, Earth to Brian? You alright there, man?"

I blink myself back to the present, worry infusing my every bone. "Caleb, how much do you know about golf?"

"HOW IS IT YOU'VE GONE YOUR ENTIRE LIFE, OVER THIRTY YEARS, AND *never* played a game of putt-putt?"

Nick, his girlfriend Tina, Kodi, and I walk up to the rental kiosk at *Two In The Bush,* a campground on the outskirts of town with a bunch of cheesy attractions, including a petting zoo and a mini golf course named *Birdie in the Hole*. Because of course it is.

I hand over my credit card to cover the four of us, and we each pick out a color-coordinated club and ball combo. I clutch my bright red ball and Nick takes the club from my hand, before replacing it with a slightly taller one.

"You're gonna want one that works for your height."

Kodi giggles behind her hand, which is holding a neon green ball. It clashes terribly with her cheery orange tank top and jean skirt, which is not exactly *short*-short, but enough for me to find distracting. I have to wrench my gaze away from her tan, toned thighs, which only serve to remind me of the way I had them wrapped around my head last week. Before I had to worry about meeting her Dad for a game of golf.

Tina's ball is pink, and Nick went with neon yellow for his.

"So, are all golf balls bright colors?"

"No, just in mini golf. Out on the big course they're usually white. Some people use different brands of balls, so you can usually keep track of whose is whose with the brand logos." Nick holds open the rustic wooden gate for us as we round up at the first hole.

"There are multiple brands of golf balls? Like Nike and Adidas?"

"Not those brands in particular, but yeah." Kodi squares up to a little rubber mat with three holes in it, drops her ball onto one of them and practices her swing a couple of times. I follow the ball as it falls, tracing my eyes down her long, lean legs. I correct my gaze to focus instead at the end of the straight fake-grass path, where a little wooden ramp with three tunnels running through it sits in the middle.

"Wait, you have to get the ball through one of those tunnels?"

"Or over the ramp. But the tunnels lead straight to the hole." Kodi takes her swing, sending her green ball zipping down the path, directly into the left-most tunnel, where it disappears before emptying out and stopping about three inches from the depressed plastic cup that serves as the hole.

"Nice putt, Kodi!" Tina cheers, and the two high-five.

I swallow. *She's good.*

Whereas before, I was embarrassed thinking about how unskilled I'd be compared to her dad, now I'm worried about how ridiculous I'm going to look when I can't even keep up with my girlfriend at mini golf. Nick pats me on the back as Tina tees up her ball.

"Relax, Brian. It's gonna be okay. Putting is just one part of the game."

"How big are the ramps and tunnels at the big courses?" The three of them laugh, and I stare at them. "What?"

I thought it was a reasonable question.

"The obstacles at real golf courses are more…natural. Think ponds, sand traps, tall grass, that kind of thing." Tina swings, and her ball rolls up and over the ramp, bouncing off the back brick barrier and thunking against Kodi's ball, sending both flying in opposite directions away from the hole.

"Hey!" Kodi shouts in mock offense. She puts her hands on her hips. Tina winks at her.

"What happens if you land in one of those?" I picture myself wading into a pond in my best pair of slacks and a dress polo, while Kodi's dad looks on in disapproval.

"If you can't find your original ball, then you just add a foul stroke to your score and hit a new one from the general spot you landed in."

I pretend to understand as Nick sidles up to the rubber mat, plonks down his ball, and putts it gently and accurately into the center tunnel. It disappears, then rolls straight out from under the ramp and into the hole. "Woohoo! Hole in one!"

Everyone cheers their approval, except for me. I've been dreading my turn this entire time, feeling the weight of meeting Kodi's parents like a leaden x-ray vest hanging on my shoulders. Then I feel a soft hand on the small of my back.

"Hey. It's going to be okay. Seriously. It's just a game," Kodi says, leaning into my shoulder. She meets my eyes and gives me a soft smile. My chest swells. Nick snorts.

"Is that *Kodi Gander* saying that? Am I dreaming?" Nick laughs, and Tina snorts beside him.

"Oh, fuck off!" Kodi sneers, but I catch a twinkle in her eye as she does. I remember her and Lily's fight, and everything she's working through, and the fact that she's still able to comfort me while dealing with all of her own stress amazes me.

If she can get through an entire season of cornhole, in Tuft Swallow, with all of the weight of a championship on her shoulders, then surely I can make it through one game of golf with her dad.

Right?

I tee up my red ball, and whack it with the putter. It flies into the air, bouncing once on the green turf before smacking into the ramp on the incline and ricocheting off into the bushes beside us.

Nick bursts out laughing, and Kodi stifles her own laugh as I slink off into the shrubbery to locate my ball.

"Maybe go a little gentler this time, there B."

I sigh, dig up my ball, and try again.

AN HOUR LATER, WE'VE ONLY GONE THROUGH NINE HOLES, AND there's a pileup of families and players behind us.

I'm on my seventh putt, and I've skated around or over the hole four times already. When the red ball once again wheels past the white plastic cup, I let out a frustrated sigh.

"Let's just go already, guys. Clearly I'm not meant to be good at this."

"Oh come on. You're just figuring out how to aim. Don't worry about them."

Kodi gestures over her shoulder where a family of five skips the hole we're on and moves straight to eleven. The youngest child, a little girl of about four, lines up her ball and putts it directly through the little chute next to the decorative windmill and cheers when she gets it in the hole on the first try.

I growl in frustration. "How the hell am I supposed to aim, then?"

"Here," Kodi says, wrapping her arms behind me and placing her hands on either side of my wrists.

My pulse speeds up as I feel her slight body press against mine from behind, her breath passing over my shoulder blades in warm little puffs. The soft flesh of her breasts makes contact with my back through the fabric of our shirts, and suddenly I forget all about mini golf, focusing entirely on the sensation of her warm body and every point of contact it has with mine.

What's gotten into me? I haven't felt this worked up around a woman since I first started dating in high school. She leans her head around my shoulder, placing her hands on my forearms and moving her arms from side to side, swinging my putter inside my grip.

I swallow, staring at her strong hands clenching around me, as she whispers into my ear.

"First of all, you gotta be more gentle. It's a tap, not a whack. You're only sending the ball seven inches to the right."

The words scrape their way out of my throat. "Seven inches. Gentle."

"Right." Her arms press into mine, and God help me, I revel in the pressure. "So just practice behind the ball for now, picture the line of the movement. Like you would for pool or croquet or anything like that, right? It's motion transfer. From your arms, to your putter, to…"

She pushes my arms out ever so slightly, leaning in even closer against my back, and this time the swing connects, gently tapping the ball in a perfect line directly into the hole. Nick and Tina throw their hands up in victory.

Kodi keeps her arms wrapped around me, sliding them up and in around my ribcage before giving me a squeeze around my middle. My stomach does a little flip.

She kisses my shoulder. "See? Just like that."

"Maybe you should come with me on Sunday," I mutter,

turning to face her and pulling her back in before she slips away. "Be my good luck charm. My little golf pro."

I want nothing more than to abandon our clubs and balls and focus on sinking into an entirely different kind of hole with her, back in the privacy of my home. The heat in my stomach that smoldered to life when I first saw her in that denim mini skirt rises up into my chest as I tighten my arm around her back.

She scrunches her nose and shakes her head. But I don't miss the flush of pink that colors her cheeks at the movement of my arm. "I wish. But I have to help mom *cook* for us."

Nick plucks the ball out of the hole and calls out to us, breaking up the little bubble we'd lost ourselves in. "Come on, you two lovebirds. There are people waiting."

Kodi slips her hand into mine as we head to the next hole with Nick and Tina.

HOLE EIGHTEEN IS A PAR FIVE, WHICH NICK INFORMS ME MEANS IT'S the hardest hole on the course. I've learned quite a bit about the *language* of golf in the past two hours, even if my skill still leaves something to be desired. Despite Kodi's coaching, my score is falling somewhere in the triple digits when we approach the final leg of the game.

"Okay, so this one is the water slide," Kodi begins.

"The *water slide?*"

"Yes." She smiles at me. "It's actually super cool. So it's kinda half Rube-Goldberg machine, half obstacle course. It starts with getting your ball to bounce through the bumpers of the first straightaway, then it sinks through a Plinko ramp and into the water wheel, where depending on when it enters, will spit you out onto one of three circles.

"The first circle is actually a bowl-shaped fountain that will just send you right to the final hole like a toilet flush. The second one is a spinning platform that you need to tilt with a crank to get it into a *different* water slide to the hole, and then the third one is actually a popper: you press on the big plastic bubble until your ball bounces into the the center, which is guarded by a bunch of bumpers, and leads to a *third* water slide which pours directly back into the check in kiosk."

"Each press counts as a stroke."

"Same with the crank on platform two–each full crank is a stroke."

I gawk at the ridiculous maze of engineering before me. "This is insane."

"Yep!" Tina grins. "Some mini golf courses have a pirate theme, some are glow-in-the-dark, but I've never seen another one with a game show-themed water slide."

Tuft Swallow strikes again.

Just as they have with the other seventeen holes, Kodi, Tina, and Nick all go before me. As if they planned it, each of them end up on a different platform, so I get to see how they all work before I wind up at the tee.

It seems like the hardest part to get through is the first straightaway with all the bumpers. There's no clear straight path to the other side, so you need a bit of luck to make it through, bouncing in the correct direction in one or two strokes.

For once, though, fortune seems to be on my side as I send up a Hail Mary swing and fly right over the rubber bumpers and directly into the Plinko ramp. Kodi's face splits into a giant grin as she watches the arc of the ball, and I swear everything becomes technicolor in the glow of her smile. She sprints down the sidewalk to see my ball as it crashes into the Plinko board, and I follow her.

But just as my ball bounces and clunks its way to the entrance of the waterfall bowl, Kodi's foot catches on the brick barrier at the edge of the green, and she tumbles forward into the giant plastic bubble popper.

I watch in slow motion as her full weight clicks the dome down. My eyes widen as the spring-loaded obstacle pops back up violently, shooting her body up into the air a few inches. She's caught completely off guard, and when the dismount sends the toe of her foot directly into the same uneven bit of path that caused her to trip in the first place, her knee buckles. I watch in horror, hearing the hiss of her breath, as she collapses into the concrete of the sidewalk, smacking her knee directly into the unforgiving surface.

"Gah!"

"Kodi!"

I run to her, ball forgotten, and sink to my knees beside her. "Are you okay?"

My heart breaks as I see moisture gather in the corners of her eyes involuntarily. Fuck. I know what it's like to get struck so bad that you can't even hold back your body's tears. She's in serious pain.

Nick and Tina rush over and instantly start trying to help.

"Does she need an ice pack?"

"Here, let's help get her up."

"Did anything twist or sprain?"

"Guys, guys, I'm fine. Calm down," Kodi grunts, attempting to shift back up onto her feet. But as she twists to put her bad leg onto the ground, she winces.

"No no, baby girl, I don't think so." Gently, I shift one arm around Kodi's back and the other under her legs and scoop her into my chest, being mindful of her injury. "Let's get you back to the car."

Nick and Tina return the putters while I carry her to Tina's SUV, which she left unlocked in the parking lot. Kodi curls into me as I do my best not to jostle her too much on the dirt trail out to the car.

"I'm sorry."

Her voice is so small and muffled against my shirt, I don't understand her at first. It's only after I get her to the door of the car that I realize what she said.

"What? What the hell do you have to apologize for?" I set her onto the seat with her legs facing me, and she grimaces while I survey the damage.

"For fucking up my recovery. *Again.* For being so broken."

Her face is red and splotchy from the tears that she couldn't hold back, and as I take in her watery, brown eyes, the dappled sunlight reflecting off the droplets clinging to her eyelashes, I feel my insides squeeze. I release her leg from my grip and lift my hand to her face, where I wipe away the tear tracks with my thumb.

"Baby girl, you are *not* broken."

She snorts, and I reach around to the nape of her neck with my other hand, tilting her face up until we lock eyes. She hiccups on a gasp, and I lean down until my forehead is touching hers.

With her face so close, I can practically taste the salt of her tears. I breathe in the scent of the sun in her hair. I hear her breath rattle as she takes a shaky inhale through her tears.

"Getting hurt by accident doesn't make you weak," I say slowly, emphasizing every word, willing them from my lips into her brain. I cradle her head in my hands, feeling the heat of her breath and the wetness of her cheeks as I hold her to me. "You are so strong. And I l–"

My throat catches, and I take in a breath. *Fuck.*

I was about to say that I love her.

But that's not right. We barely know each other. We just met a few weeks ago. And sure, it's been a crazy couple of weeks, and we've fooled around and kissed and had some pretty deep conversations, and yeah, I've been checking her out this entire day, but there's more to love than that.

I should know.

Zeke and I hadn't said the L-word to each other for almost nine months of dating. I pined after him, waffling for weeks before I finally said it. It was the longest I'd ever waited. Even so, after I said it to him, he still shied away from the word except in very rare circumstances, usually during sex: at the very height of passion between us.

This moment couldn't be any less sexy. We just wrapped up the most pathetic game I've ever played in my life, where I embarrassed myself in front of half of the children of Tuft Swallow with my miserable lack of putting skills. Kodi's face is streaming with tears and snot after she just pitched herself on the eighteenth hole. She's in an extreme amount of pain. And this, *this* is the moment where I almost let slip the L-word?

What the hell is wrong with me? This isn't a moment of romance or passion. Neither of us is sexy right now.

Except...that's absolute bullshit. Because even with puffy eyes and blotchy, tear-stained cheeks, Kodi is the most beautiful woman I've ever seen. All I want is to wrap her perfect body in my arms, press her gorgeous face into the hollow of my throat and hold her and stroke her hair until her pain goes away. This amazingly strong woman, who's been doing everything in her power to get past this injury of hers, only to get beaten down again and again by years of unresolved trauma and just some of the worst luck.

"You what?" She whispers.

"I–"

"We got you some ice," Tina huffs, popping up beside me and handing Kodi a cold, wet bundle wrapped in a towel. She sounds like she ran here. "Sorry, they had to dig it out of the snack bar freezer, but this should keep you until we can get you to Brian's place, yeah?"

"That's probably the best plan. You can get her back on her feet, right, B? Miracle worker?"

Kodi and I pull away from each other, both of our faces red now from getting caught in the middle of a moment by our friends.

Not that we should be embarrassed. As far as they know, we've been dating for almost a month.

"Yeah, that's a good idea." I lift Kodi's thighs a bit and turn her gingerly so she's facing the front of the car, attempting to ignore the way her skirt rides up a few inches in the process. I tug the fabric back down carefully, then I take the makeshift ice pack and prop it under her knee. "Keep it there for a few minutes, and then let it rest. Just cycle it on and off until we get back into town."

"Okay."

I buckle her in and shut the door, turning to Nick and Tina before walking around to the passenger side.

"Never a dull moment with you two, is there?" Nick says, punching me in the shoulder.

"She's lucky to have you around," Tina says. "Never been one to take it easy, that Kodi."

As we make it back into town, I hold Kodi's hand in the middle of the backseat, slowly running my thumb over her knuckles, mulling over Tina's words.

If it weren't for me panicking about golf with her dad, she never would have tripped in the first place. Thanks to this stupid fake boyfriend business, she's constantly needing to watch what she says around town, and is dealing with pressure from her friends and family about me. Meanwhile, I'm forgetting why we got into this arrangement in the first place. Instead of focusing on my business, or figuring out my personal life, I'm seducing her in her apartment. Getting caught up in the act and almost letting the L-word slip in a parking lot while she cries in pain. She needs me to be her *doctor,* not her fake boyfriend.

I was supposed to be doing her a favor. Not causing her more stress.

So how, exactly, am I lucky for her?

CHAPTER 35
KODI

Brian clicks his tongue as he rotates my knee back and forth. I try to keep my own voice from squeaking out of my throat at the pain, but I'm not quite convincing enough. A relieved moan gets past my lips when he finally lowers my leg back onto the table.

"It's not looking good, Kodi."

It's all I can do to keep the tears from falling again. I'm so sick of this knee failing me.

"I thought everything we were doing was supposed to help me get *better.* Why is it getting worse?"

Brian leans into the table beside me and grabs hold of my hand. It's warm, and I can't tell if it's the doctor talking or the man who held me in the parking lot when he answers.

"The frustrating thing is, you *were* getting better. Honestly, it was because you were favoring your leg less and walking more evenly that you were taken so off guard by the sudden trip at the golf course. For years, you've been protecting your knee from any little twist or jerk, but today you were walking normally. Which, in any other circumstance, would have been a good thing."

"But this time, because I wasn't guarding against injury, I got injured again." I snort. The air scrapes through my tear-congested nose with a mucusy pop. "Figures."

"It's a speed bump. You'll get past it."

I turn my head away from him, unable to bear the pity in his eyes. I pull my hand away.

I hate how cold it feels in his absence.

"Face down."

"Maybe I should just give up. Maybe I'm not meant to get better."

I turn as I talk, lowering my head into the face rest, and just as I relax into the table—

Smack!

Brian's hand slaps against my ass. Hard.

"Ow!" I rear up, arching my back as I whip my head around to scowl at him. "What the fuck was that for?"

"Say stupid shit like that, and you get a spanking." Brian's arms are crossed across his chest, and he's meeting me glare-for-glare. The fire in his eyes sends my heart into my throat. I raise my eyebrows.

"Excuse me?"

"Do you honestly think you can't get better from an *ACL tear?*" He snorts. "People get over those every day. You're telling me that Kodi Fucking Gander, Tuft Swallow Superstar, can't handle a little setback?"

"I've been trying–"

Smack!

The strike comes down fast, stinging through the denim of my cutoff skirt and making blood rush to the skin. I can feel pins and needles and heat there as my body reacts, and I gasp at the impact.

I also feel heat begin to accumulate elsewhere in my body, and I quickly hide my face back down in the table so he can't see my blush.

Why do I want him to keep going?

"Brian, stop it." It's everything I can do to keep my voice

steady. My pulse is racing so hard, I'm half-scared Brian can see my ribcage bounce with every beat.

"Are *you* going to stop trying to get better?"

I can feel his eyes on my back, and I clench my legs together as fire continues to spread through my body.

"No."

"You sure?"

And then I feel his fingers press into the outside of my calf. It's a pressure point, I know: one of those angry muscle bunches he's worked on before. But in the past, his hands have felt neutral whenever he's touched me like that. Unemotional.

This time, his hands feel hot, intimate even, and the pain explodes beneath his fingers as my tendons protest. His other hand grips my ankle as he holds pressure, and I tense beneath him.

"Don't fight me. Relax the muscle."

My heart is racing. I try to relax, but then his hand moves again, and my stomach clenches. I feel the muscles at the apex of my thighs, miles away from his grasp below my knee, twitch as his fingers trail higher against the bare skin of my leg.

"Relax."

"Are you going to spank me again?"

His hand freezes. I hold my breath, waiting for his response.

With my eyes staring at the floor through the hole in the table for my face, I don't see him move. I only feel his hand lift from my leg and the warmth of his body radiate against my back as he leans his mouth mere inches from my ear.

"Do you want me to?"

My body tenses again, and his hand returns, this time brushing lightly against the small of my back. "Relax. Tensing isn't good for you right now."

"How am I supposed to relax with you standing over me like that?"

My voice is muffled by the facerest. Brian removes his hand

from my back, and even though my body relaxes, my heart clenches at the same time.

"Am I making you uncomfortable?" Brian's voice breaks on the last word, revealing a vulnerability I've never heard from him before. More tears spring to my eyes when I hear it, making the crinkly paper on the table stick to my cheeks. "What do you want me to do?"

What do I want?

How do I even begin to answer that?

I want my knee to get better. I want to go back to being the town champion, and I want the cornhole team to actually respect me instead of just tolerating my presence at practice. I want to feel like I can actually trust my friends and family instead of feeling like they all want something from me that I can't deliver. I want this stupid paper to stop sticking to my face so I can take a full breath, and I want…

I want Brian to spank me again.

I want to feel his hands grip my thighs like they did when he came to my apartment last week, and he buried his face into my most intimate parts.

I want to return the favor, to *do* something, to watch *him* writhe for once, under *my* touch, and to make him moan and grunt and scream my name like I did his.

I want, for five minutes, to forget that this is all some act we're playing for the town of Tuft Swallow, for his stupid fucking ex, and for his business, and instead just be two people who could maybe, *maybe*, have real, actual feelings for each other.

Slowly, I lift my face and torso off the table, and Brian is there, waiting for me with a firm hand to help me into a seated position. I grasp my fingers around his firm forearm, and once I'm fully seated with my legs dangling off the edge of the table, my head is level with his chest. I reach my other hand and spread my fingers against his t-shirt, before fisting the fabric and pulling him close, so my forehead is leaning against the strong muscles of his abdomen.

I take a sniffling, pathetic sounding inhale that could be a sob or a gasp and somehow, his amazingly warm and comforting scent–like sunshine and baking bread–fills my senses. I feel his muscles flex under me and slowly, his strong hands weave their way around us until they're rubbing down my back.

"Kodi–"

"Don't call me that," I whisper, shaking my head against him, squeezing my eyes closed tight. Dear God, it's like every muscle in my face clenches shut, trying to keep out the feelings that are becoming increasingly clear in my mind. I *know* what I want.

"What should I call you?"

It's then I finally look up, my tear-stained cheeks dragging across the bunched fabric clutched in my hands as I lock my eyes onto Brian's. The sometimes-green, sometimes-blue irises are dark, oceanic outlines of his blown-out pupils in the dimly lit office, and they lock onto me. I see his Adam's apple bob with a strained swallow.

I don't want to say it. If I tell him what I want, it'll be real. He'll know how I feel, how much his words mean to me. He'll want to call this entire deal off, and I'll be lost again, without any chance of recovery.

But worse than that, I'll be alone.

And I can't…I can't handle that right now. Not when everything else is crumbling around me.

"Baby girl…"

My eyes close as his fingers rise from my back and twist in my hair. The words drop from his lips in a barely audible wisp of air. I shiver and pull him closer, squeezing the bunches of his shirt in my hands tighter and tighter until the fabric stretches taught across his torso. He follows my hands, leaning closer into me and pressing my head into the firmness of his chest.

And then I feel another firmness rise and press into my chest.

"Is that what you want?"

"Yes," I breathe, and slowly unclench my fingers. His arms stay firmly latched around me, with one hand twisting into the loose strands of hair that have fallen from my messy ponytail and the other pressing gently against my back. I slide my hands down inch by inch, feeling him grow bigger with every creep closer to his waistband.

"You don't have to–"

"I want to," I interrupt him.

He spoke when I undid his button, but I need him to know that this is exactly what I need right now.

I'm tired of feeling like nothing is in my control. I don't–I *can't–* feel weak anymore. For once, I want to know that my actions matter, that the things I do can have a real effect and impact on my life. It may be new to me, and I might be setting sail on uncharted waters by taking this next step–especially with Brian–but deep down, I need to know that I can leap and for once, for *just fucking once,* a net will appear.

"Brian, I want *you.* That's what I want. I want you to let me make you feel as good as you made me feel the other night."

"Kodi–"

"Don't."

I freeze, my hands clutching to the waistband of his boxer-briefs, his pants having long been unbuttoned and unzipped and pooling around the middle of his thighs. He takes in a shuddering breath as I tilt my head until I'm staring directly down at the tent straining against the stretchy fabric of his underwear, and I see the bulge twitch when I exhale the word. He adjusts his grip in my hair, the pads of his fingers digging deeper into my scalp.

"Okay, baby girl."

"Okay?" I tug on the elastic the slightest bit.

"Okay."

With his permission, I finally pull the fabric down and over his swollen cock.

I'm not sure how I never realized the appeal of it before; when all the other girls in high school and college would fawn over the size of their boyfriend's dicks, I'd always been so confused. What was the big deal, I thought at the time. It's just a penis.

But staring at the beautiful cock bouncing under my gaze now, bursting forth from a neatly trimmed crop of brown curls, I want nothing more than to wrap my lips around its swollen tip.

I free my right hand from his boxers and circle it around the base of his shaft, and a warm tingling filling my chest as I hear him gasp at the contact.

Yes. This is the kind of cause and effect I need. I *crave*. With my other hand, I cradle his exposed backside, grasping his cheek and digging my fingers in as I slowly begin to pump my other fist up and down his hardening length.

A groan escapes, and I can feel his chest rumble with it above my forehead. My lips stretch in a grin. It feels so good to know that I'm not terrible at this. Part of me had been terrified my inexperience would have him pulling away from me.

But those thoughts are fleeting as instinct takes over, and I just follow the lusty inclinations of my limbs, basking in the joy of exploring him in such intimate detail. I study him for feedback as I do.

With each pull of my hand upward, I fan my fingers over the crown of his cock, letting my thumb graze over the notch that points to the slit at the very tip. He inhales sharply the first time I do that, and so I repeat the motion with every stroke, until his hips buck forward.

"Sorry," he grunts, and I lift my head to look up at him. As our gazes meet, I see that his eyes are glazed over and his mouth is parted slightly. He chuckles, a low and throaty sound, and I pause my hand. "Baby girl, you're killing me."

My heart sinks. "Am I doing it wrong?"

"God no," he hisses. "Feeling you around my cock is fucking everything."

With his praise, it's like a thousand balloons inflate in my stomach, and suddenly I feel light and giddy with it.

"I want to suck you," I admit, not ceasing in my stroking up and down. He bucks again.

"Okay."

"But, um…the angle is…"

"You can't kneel." He nods once, gathering the threads I left dangling. If it were anyone other than him, I'd be humiliated admitting that I feel like I can't even get off the drop table without assistance, but I know I can trust Brian.

In one swiftly smooth movement, Brian shucks off his pants and boxers completely and swings me up off the table and into his arms. One arm below my butt and thighs hoists me against him, and the other secures my back. Instinctually, I wrap my legs around his waist and my arms around his neck, reverse-piggy-back style, and he adjusts his grip until I can feel his fingers sinking into the sensitive flesh between the tops of my thighs and the crease of my ass.

All the while, the top of his cock bobs and brushes against the hem of my skirt, hiked all the way up to the crease of my hips from the way he's carrying me.

"I'm going to take you upstairs." His voice is low and insistent right up against the shell of my ear.

I shiver. *Will his voice always send shockwaves down my spine?* "Okay."

He carries me to the stairs, and I tighten my hold around him. As he starts to climb to the second floor, I feel the tip of him rubbing against the apex of my thighs. I maybe moan a little at the contact.

My heart is beating wildly in my chest, my face flushing with the heat rising from his muscly chest and the closeness of him everywhere. His scent is filling all of my senses, to the point where I swear I can taste him, and then I realize that I *want* to taste him. For *real.*

I turn my head into the crook of his neck and bury my face there, pressing my lips to his shoulder. I breathe him in, becoming intoxicated on the smell of his skin as I hear his labored breath beneath my kisses. I become lost when I let my lips part against him, poking out my tongue and licking a long, indulgent line across the curve of his neck.

In no time at all, he's kicking open the door of his bedroom and throwing me onto his bed. In a hazy, horny blur, I see a glimpse of his neatly organized bedroom before he's hovering over me and crashing his lips down on mine.

Brian's mouth. Fuck me, if I go the rest of my life never kissing another man and am only left with the memory of Brian's masterful lips on mine, I'll die a happy woman. His tongue delves past mine and sweeps into my mouth, tasting me as his lips tease and nip at my own. I lose track of where my next breath is coming from as he devours me, and instead allow my body to return his enthusiastic administrations with my own.

I stroke my arms up and down his giant, strong back, sneaking past his big arms and snaking them down his waist and back around to his naked lower half.

When my fingers grasp his hard cock again, his lips break apart from mine on a strangled cry.

"*Fuck,* baby girl, you're gonna kill me!"

"Get back here," I hiss, craning my neck up to capture his dirty mouth once more. He melts back into the kiss, pressing into my hand while curling his own around either side of my head as we sink into the fluff of his comfortable bed.

"I thought you wanted to suck me off." He breaks away again, panting, a smirk gleaming in his eyes.

I waggle my eyebrows at him. "Feed it to me."

His eyes go wide. "What?"

I spread my arms, gesturing to my easy perch with my head against the pillows and the headboard. "We've established that I really shouldn't kneel right now. So you're gonna have to kneel for me."

"You want me to…over–?"

"Get up here and give me your cock, dammit!" I laugh, grabbing hold of his amazing ass and pulling him up my body.

Of course, I'm not strong enough to lift him with just my arms when I'm prone on the bed like this, but Brian follows my lead.

CHAPTER 36
BRIAN

My gaze scrapes up Kodi's body one last time before I follow her instructions.

Her toned, muscular legs, including her swollen knee, tangled in my duvet. That fucking denim miniskirt wrinkled up to the crease of her hips; the slight peek of magenta panties barely visible underneath it. Her fluorescent tank top, hem pushed up to her ribcage and rising and falling swiftly with each of her hurried breaths.

My eyes trace the curved line of her gorgeous tits up to the flushed skin of her chest, the delicate outline of her collarbone, her slender neck, all the way up to her perfect, pouting lips that have just begged me to shove my cock between them.

Never has another human turned me on to this degree. Made me feel so strong and manly while being so *weak* to their desire. I just carried this woman up the stairs, tackled her on my bed, and yet *she's* the one giving me orders to straddle her and fuck her mouth. Because *she wants it.*

Just the thought has my balls twitching with the urge to paint her with my cum.

Fuck, I've never even *thought* something like that before.

But the challenge in her eyes, that goddamn teasing sparkle

I've gotten so used to from her, and those perfect, kiss-swollen lips...

Just as I think that, her tongue darts out and licks the plush heaven of her lower lip, and I lose it. My arms fall to the top of the headboard behind her, and I hover with my hips just in front of her face. Her head tilts up to meet my gaze, and I hold back a groan as her breath ghosts over my twitching cock.

"Is this what you want, baby girl?"

I never called a woman that in my life before her. Those words had never even crossed my mind until I saw that goddamn hot pink vibrator in her bathroom.

"Give it to me."

And with my eyes still glued to hers, I pump my hips forward. The second I feel her lips part around the crown of my head, my eyelids drift closed. I let out a strangled cry.

"*Fuck,* Kodi—"

And then I feel her teeth. My eyes snap open, and she's staring daggers at me. She can't speak with my dick filling her mouth, but her expression carries a warning.

Don't call me that.

"Baby girl," I correct, and her eyes flare. "That mouth of yours..."

She hums in approval, vibrating around me, and her tongue and cheeks replace the threat of her bite. I shudder, pure electricity sparking at every point of contact between her hot, wet mouth and my rock-hard cock, traveling up my entire body and filling my chest with heat. Any plans to go easy, to hold back in an attempt to protect her, fly out the window.

She's not my patient anymore.

She's just *mine.*

I thrust again and again and again into her face, and with every jerk of my hips I hear her sloppy breathing around me. Her lips smack open with an audible pop each time, and the sound alone is so ridiculously erotic and lewd it makes my legs tighten from holding back a premature release.

Then her arms wrap around me, and her fingernails dig into the cheeks of my ass. I groan, nestling my cock inside the heat of her perfect mouth, feeling her hollow her cheeks against me as she pulls her hands apart.

Where the fuck did she learn that?

My arms go weak, and I bow forward over her. I'm twitching, so close to losing it that if I don't pull out soon she's going to choke on my cum. I gasp out a breath.

"Baby girl–let me, I'm gonna–"

"Mmm-hmm," she hums her assent, nodding her head a little and waggling her tongue along the bottom ridge of my shaft.

"Ugh–*fuck!*" I grunt, the tugging in my stomach finally snapping, the stars behind my eyes bursting as waves of ecstasy ripple through me, and my release explodes into her hungry mouth.

I hear the note of surprise in her moan at the thick jets shooting with each jerk of my hips, and the sexy little minx fucking *sucks harder.*

"Jesus, baby girl! You've got my–cock in a–*death grip!"* I choke out the words with every thrust, losing all control as she wraps her tongue around me, lapping up every last drop I give her.

Finally, I sag against the headboard, my muscles unclenching, and the first thing I feel is her fingers kneading the flesh of my ass. I cough out a laugh at her gentle massage, but then my breath hitches in sweet agony as her lips nip up and down my softening cock.

She finally opens her mouth, inhaling deeply, and I slump further down her body as she releases me. She opens her legs, and I thread myself between them, lying prone over her stunning body.

I prop myself on my elbows, resting my forehead on her shoulder, catching my breath.

"Where the fuck did that come from?"

"I wanted you to come," she says simply, running her nails gently up and down my sides. "You've given me so much. I wanted to–no, I *needed*–to give you something back."

I rear up at that, meeting her eyes and frowning at her. "What?"

"What we have…the scales were out of balance. I owed you."

I scoot back, unentangling myself from her and rolling to my side so I can face her more easily. "Kodi—you don't owe me anything."

"That's not our deal," she argues, attempting to get up off the bed, but I grab her wrist to stop her. She pauses, looks at her leg, and settles for simply turning on her side as well, her injured knee resting atop the other one. When I release her arm, she continues. "I'm supposed to be helping you with your software and getting customers, but you've hardly needed me for that the past couple weeks. And you've been without Zeke for almost a month now, so I'm sure…"

My frown has only been deepening the entire time she's been explaining her reasoning. The high of the moment we just had fading with every word.

Was that–was *this*–all to pay me back for her adjustments? Is that what she's trying to say? That us being together like this had more to do with her paying me back for treatment than her actually wanting to be together?

"This," I gesture in between us with my hand, "is *payment* to you?"

"What? No!" Kodi blushes furiously, waving her hands at my question. And for a moment, I breathe a sigh of relief. "Of course not. I didn't mean that. I only meant that…you've been giving me a lot lately. Between my knee, and last week when you–well, when you spent the night–"

My hackles rise again. "I *wanted* to spend the night."

"I know, I know. It had been ages since we'd been seen together and it looked good for the whole image we're going for, but I still felt like I got the better end of that deal."

I blink at her.

I have to be misunderstanding her. Granted, my mind isn't always the clearest immediately post-orgasm, but it sounds like

Kodi's trying to imply that I only went down on her last week in an attempt to keep up appearances.

Appearances that, since I first realized I was genuinely attracted to her, I couldn't care less about.

"Wait a minute, here. I want to make sure I'm hearing this right." I reach for her hand and weave my fingers through hers, then stare into her eyes. She blinks, and I can tell she's uncomfortable keeping eye contact, but I hold her gaze all the same. "You think last week was about me trying to convince a couple of Tit Peepers that we were dating? Honey, unless you called the fucking press, I don't see how me making you come in the privacy of your own apartment does anything to convince anyone of our relationship status."

Her eyes fall to the pillow, and she pulls her hand away. "Oh come on, Brian, you spent the night and we had breakfast the next day. We were all over the *Pecker* the next morning."

"And *I* had nothing to do with that!"

I sit up straight, shaking my head as my heart sinks into my stomach. What is going on here? Why is she pulling away from me right now?

Did I read this whole thing wrong? *Again?*

"Whether you did or not, now you're deep in the middle of all my family drama. You're golfing with my dad in a week!"

"So what? Do you not want that?" I rub my face with my hands, waiting for her to explain.

And just like that, it's like a window shade closes over her eyes. The want, the need, the hurt, the vulnerability that she showed me not twenty minutes ago downstairs in my office disappears, and her walls are back up. She opens her mouth to speak, but I clamp my hand over her perfect lips.

"Don't do this, baby girl. Don't convince yourself that there isn't something here. Don't do that to yourself. Don't do it to me."

Her eyes widen, and I use my leverage to roll us so I'm once again on top of her. I stare down at her, pleading with everything in me that she hears–*really hears*–what I've been too nervous to say until now.

I know it's risky to throw this out on the line. For me, her *doctor,* to tell her that I have feelings for her, completely separate from our ploy to trick Tuft Swallow into accepting me. This isn't about winning over the townspeople, or expanding my business, or winning back my ex.

Who, honestly, never deserved me in the first place.

And I never would have realized that if it weren't for the woman in my arms.

This woman here, in my bed? *She* is what this is all about. It's about helping her learn to trust in her body again. It's about seeing her journey, watching her recover, and most importantly, seeing her open up and share her true self and dreams. With me.

It may have started out as some kind of scheme or ploy, but somewhere along the line I got to know the real Kodi Gander. The one she hides behind her competitive attitude and disaffected politeness around town. The Tuft Swallow Ice Queen, who somehow managed to thaw in my arms, until all that remained was this beautiful, intelligent, and funny woman.

"This isn't just an act to me anymore, baby girl. It may have started out that way, but somewhere along the line, I started believing it. I'm not *pretending* to want you. I'm not spending the night at your place or kissing those perfect, goddamn lips of yours to keep up appearances. I'm doing it because I want to. Because I want *you.*"

Tears start to gather and collect along the dark eyelashes sweeping against her cheeks, and I wipe them away with my thumbs. But she doesn't look away. Her beautiful brown eyes are locked onto mine, and I want nothing more than to sink into them. To see them crinkle with a smile when I tease her, or swell with pride when she's finally able to run again.

"And if I have to embarrass the hell out of myself on the golf course with your dad to prove to you that I mean this, then so be it."

A smile stretches her wet cheeks and she chuckles, and I swear the sound gives my heart wings.

"You are *really* bad at golf," she admits.

"I might be the worst ever."

"Like, it's almost impressive. I mean, how can someone who's so good at so many things, just *suck so hard* at–"

I don't hear whatever else she wants to say, because I'm kissing her. My lips are nipping and tugging and exploring her open mouth, my tongue darting in and out of her, catching the salty tears that escaped down to the corner of her mouth and kissing away each and every one.

And then she's kissing me back, rolling her neck to allow me to delve deeper, our mouths tangling faster and harder until she pulls away with a gasp.

"What about Zeke?" She huffs.

"Fuck Zeke."

Her eyes blow wide. She starts to speak, but I press a finger to her lips.

"He hurt me, yes. And there was a time where I thought I loved him. But *you*…" I drift off, my gaze searching her fiery amber eyes for the words I'm trying to say. "I've been guilty in the past of jumping into things too soon with my relationships. I'll admit it. But I've never–*never*–felt the kind of things with any of them that I do with you."

Her lids flutter half-closed, and the result is such a sultry look that it makes me want to stop talking altogether. I stroke my fingers from her lips to her cheeks to her scalp, threading them into the tangled mass of her sex hair. And then I sink to that delectable hollow of her collarbone, and press more kisses against her freckles.

"It's not nothing to me either," she gasps. "This. What's between us. I don't know when it happened, but—"

"I know."

"It's different."

I nod into her shoulder. "It is."

Her body, which I hadn't realized until that moment had been tense as it held onto mine like a koala, relaxes at her confession, and she sinks further into the bed.

I kiss her nose lightly, smiling when I feel it wrinkle in response.

She admitted it. It's not just an act. She feels the same way I do.

"Alright, alright, we're getting a little cheesy now." She tries to push me off of her, but I squeeze her tighter. Then I get off of the bed, pointing back at her with a strong finger.

"Stay right there," I say. "Don't you dare move."

CHAPTER 37
KODI

For the next five minutes, I just lay in Brian's bed, unmoving, like he told me to.

It's different.

As I lay there, I tilt my head from side to side, checking out the innocuous bedspread and gray-and-navy color scheme that feels like the most generic section of the "home and kitchen" department at Kohl's. *Who is this man?*

I'm suddenly desperate to know the *real* Brian Gosling. Not the hot chiropractor I was pretending to date to get revenge on his toxic ex. But the sweet, brilliant man who can treat my injuries and make me laugh and come and experience all sorts of new and fascinating sensations.

There are some knick-knacks and personal items that lend some personality to the space: a few framed photos of him with his sensei at a martial arts tournament, an abbreviated rainbow of belts along the wall, a small pride flag hanging over a bookshelf lined with old college textbooks.

There's no TV in his bedroom, but there is a lamp on his nightstand along with a nonfiction paperback novel, the place inside marked not with a bookmark, but a Kindle. Which I find funny.

Reading multiple books at once?

The longer I lay there, the more tired I realize I am. And thirsty. My need for a drink becomes more urgent with the salty tang of Brian's cum still lingering at the back of my tongue.

That's something they don't tell you in sex ed.

My knee throbs a little, and I decide to snoop a bit and see what he's reading. When I open the paperback to the e-reader inside, I see the screensaver is the cover for a science-fictiony, fantasy-looking type of book. It's got big, blocky text and a picture of a muscly guy, a creepy spider lady, and a cat with a crown on it. I don't recognize the author. Curious, I go to press the on button–

"Bored already?" Brian pops into the room, dressed only in his boxers, carrying a TV-tray of food and a bottle of water. I jump.

"I'm sorry!" I blurt out, slamming the book back around the Kindle. He snickers.

"It's okay, baby girl. I don't mind you looking through my book collection. Although you shouldn't start that series with book six: you'll be totally confused."

"What kind of book is it?"

"Lit RPG."

"What's that?"

The only books I really pay attention to are the ones I see at the kiosks at the library. I tend to stick to YA or the occasional romance (if Lily can't shut up about it), and have only ever read physical books. But Lily swears by her e-reader.

"It's a genre that reads like playing a video game. Characters level up, fight monsters. Usually there's a bunch of weird mechanics and equipment and stuff in there, too. It's fun, reminds me of playing games on my old Nintendo growing up.

"After I…left home, I didn't really have time to game anymore. I've thought about PC gaming but, as you know, I'm not very good at computers." He shrugs, and sets the tray down onto my lap. It's got legs on the bottom so it can rest on top of my lap without me having to hold it up. His laptop is on it, along with a turkey sandwich and a bowl of cheese puffs. Then he climbs onto the bed beside me and pops one of the puffs into his mouth. "Reading books that feel like video games scratches the itch."

Another piece of the Brian puzzle. I've never played a video game in my life, but I don't tell him that. "Is it any good?"

"It's great. I read a lot. Nonfiction to keep up on new science and stuff like that, research in my field, but then I've got a ton of ebooks on the Kindle for when I need a break from that."

I unscrew the cap of the water bottle that he hands me and take a long, grateful swig. Weirdly, I love listening to him talk about his hobbies like this. It makes him seem so much more… human. Less like the miracle worker who's helping me walk again, and more like Brian, the guy who I have a crush on.

Crush.

I look down at the sandwich he made me, cut twice diagonally into little triangles, and blush. *He says he has feelings for me, too.* It's a lot to take in. And maybe that's weird, considering I just had his dick in my mouth and we've now both given each other orgasms, but something about that doesn't seem nearly as intimate as me lying here in his bed, talking about what kinds of books he likes to read after he just made me a sandwich.

"What do you like to read?" he asks.

"Oh, I don't know. I like John Green, so stuff like that is good. I've read a couple romance books that Lily couldn't stop talking about that were okay. Although the hockey romances she gets into are absolutely ridiculous."

"Hockey romances?"

"Yeah." I sit up and grab a quarter of the sandwich. "First of all, there's hardly *any* hockey in them. Instead, it's all about how muscly the guys are and how possessive they are over the main girl."

"And you don't like possessive, muscly guys, huh?"

He smirks at me. I roll my eyes.

"That's not what romance *is!*" My voice comes out much louder than I intend it to, and I blush, realizing that I wouldn't mind at all reading about Brian being all muscly and possessive.

I cover up my embarrassment with a cough and a sip of water. "Besides, I mean, I like *sports*. If you call something a hockey romance, I feel like it should at least be half hockey and half romance."

"And what ratio does Lily prefer?"

I roll my eyes. "Who even knows! But I feel like she doesn't care about the hockey part at all!"

I take a bite of the sandwich, which is actually quite delicious, and another sip of the water. Brian looks down the bed towards my knee.

"I have some bad news, Kodi."

"Oh *no*," I say around the second quarter of sandwich. The way my stomach drops has nothing to do with the food, and everything to do with the strained look on Brian's face as he examines my leg. "How long am I going to be down for?"

He shifts beside me, stroking his fingers through my hair as he answers. "Without putting weight on it? I'd say at least two weeks."

"Two *weeks*??" I groan. "That's all the way to the playoffs!"

"And even after that, you should honestly take it easy for at least another month." I open my mouth to protest. *That's basically all the way to the championship!* He puts his finger against my lips. "I know it's most of the season. I get it. And frankly, cornhole is not exactly a contact sport: you could probably get away with playing a game or two. But you can't be treating it like the Olympics anymore. If you want to have a leg that works come fall, you're going to need to start treating the cornhole league like the chill, easygoing backyard beer league it is, instead of the NHL."

I snort. "Well, if Lily's books are to be believed, the NHL is more about flirting and foreplay than it is about training."

"Well, if that's the case..." He leans into me, tracing his hand up and down my bare arm. Goosebumps rise in its wake. "Maybe the NHL *isn't* the worst comparison in the world."

And then his face is so close to mine I can feel his breath on my cheek. I swallow and shift down the TV tray. "So, even with the knee, I can still participate in some...extracurricular activities?"

I rub my hand along his thigh, which is only partially covered by his boxer-briefs. I see the tell-tale ridge of his shaft shift slightly as our bodies inch closer together.

"Well, I was going to suggest we snuggle for the rest of the afternoon and watch more *Bridgerton* while you rest, but if you have other ideas..."

"I might have a few, yeah." I try to give him a flirty wink, but I'm betrayed by a yawn that elbows its way up my throat. He laughs when I can't hold it back, weaving his fingers through mine and moving my hand down between our bodies.

"Tell you what," he says, adjusting the TV tray so it's over his legs instead of mine. "Why don't you save those ideas for later, when you can actually climb on top of me without hurting yourself, and for now we can stick with my original plan?"

One part of me thinks that that sounds like a great idea. But the other part, the Kodi-never-quits-a-challenge part, is dying to see if I can make him fall apart again.

But then another yawn works through me, and I realize that maybe it's best to take it easy for now.

As he queues up the series on Netflix and I snuggle into his warm torso, it dawns on me that, without him trying to win Zeke back or me obsessing over the playoffs, it means that there doesn't have to be an expiration date on our relationship. It's not fake anymore. We have all the time in the world to get to know each other, watch TV, read books, and give each other mind-blowing orgasms.

And as I drift off into a nap in his arms, Rege Jean Page's seductive voice playing in the background, I begin to accept that that might actually be a pretty wonderful thing.

CHAPTER 38
BRIAN

I've never been one to want to play hooky, but Monday morning I want nothing more than to sleep in next to Kodi and spend all day exploring her one glorious moment at a time.

But her phone alarm blares at 6:00 am, startling us both out of our cozy slumber.

"I've got to get back to my place and get some work clothes," she grumbles. Her eyes are squinted shut against the couple of rays of sunshine peeking their way through the gap in my blackout curtains. I pull her in closer to my body, luxuriating in the softness of her naked breasts against my chest.

"Or you could *not* put on any clothes," I mumble into her hair. "Just stay here with me all day. Call in sick."

"It doesn't work like that. I'm the only admin at the clinic. If I call in sick, all the appointments have to get rescheduled. Which just makes more work for me."

I rub my arms up and down her back, and her body relaxes into mine. She hums, weaving her hands around to my back and scratching lightly at my spine.

"That's hardly fair."

"Yep."

"Well how about this?" I kiss her forehead and start to disentangle us, but she keeps her arms tight around me. I chuckle. "You stay here, rest, and shower, while *I* go to your place and pick up some clothes for you and some breakfast for us. I'll be back before you're out of the shower."

"How long do you think it takes for me to shower?" She eyes me, her pride glowing from under her scrunched eyebrows.

"I'll be quick. And you can take your time. You do have an injured knee, after all."

Her face falls, and her arms loosen. She flops onto her back and covers her eyes with her hands.

"Fuck. That's right. What do I need to do about that?"

"Do you still have a pair of crutches?"

She nods at me behind her hands.

"Where are they? I can grab them when I get your clothes."

Twenty minutes later, Kodi's made a list of all of the items I'm supposed to gather from her place and given me detailed instructions on where everything is. I scrounge around her purse for her keys once I get downstairs, giving her free reign of my apartment after instructing her on the particulars of the shower faucet and setting out a pair of towels for her.

It's a beautiful morning in Tuft Swallow, with the refreshing morning air warming my skin on the short walk to Kodi's place. I can't help the smile that creeps across my face as I nod to the neighbors walking their dogs in the central square. Even the Tit Peepers with their obnoxious turquoise windbreakers and knowing smirks can't bring down my mood.

For the first time since moving here, I feel like I belong just as much as any of the other townspeople. I'm not sure if it's the fact that I recognize the faces I pass, or if it's the leftover high from waking up to the face of a beautiful woman who cares about me.

Who might even love me.

My chest squeezes at the thought. Last night, Kodi and I actually connected. She was at the lowest I'd ever seen her, but she didn't shut me out. I broke through the wall that had been keeping me from seeing the real Kodi this whole time.

Is this what love should feel like?

As I cross the street to the rowhouse apartments on Walnut and fly up the six stone steps to Kodi's floor, I feel invincible. Like I'm walking on air and floating over the threshold instead of consciously moving one foot in front of the other.

The tidy open living room/kitchenette greets me, light pouring through the sheer curtains at the front of the apartment. I glide back to her bedroom, the clean scent of Kodi's laundry detergent and the lingering smell of whatever she made herself for dinner Saturday night mingling in my nose and bringing me back to the last time I was here. I rifle through her dresser drawers, fighting the urge to linger and explore to see if I can find the rest of her toy collection, but pause when I open her underwear drawer.

She does need a bra and panties for today…

But she didn't say what kind of panties. Which means I get to choose.

Kodi strikes me as the type of woman to consider herself too practical for matching sets of lingerie, but I'm surprised when I pull out the drawer and an array of brightly-colored lace and cotton greets me. While half of the space seems dominated by sports bras–*makes sense*–there are several colorful padded and unlined underwire bras folded neatly across from them, along with a whole rainbow of panties in every style from ones that resemble boxers to…

And then I see them. Wedged all the way in the bottom as if they're never worn, three neon cotton thongs trimmed with lace and little bows on the front.

Bingo.

I snatch two: one hot-pink with the brand name stamped in tiny font across the fabric, and an unpatterned pair the same color as the bright orange tank top she was wearing yesterday at the golf course.

That pair I shove into my pocket. The other I place into the backpack I brought with me, along with a matching black-and-pink satiny, lacy, strappy thing from the bra pile that looks architecturally bewildering, but also like the sight of it on Kodi will drive me crazy for weeks.

Because I know she's likely to give me shit for it, I also grab a sports bra and shove it into the bag just in case. Then I close the drawer and pick out a pair of black slacks and a silky-looking pastel blouse from the closet.

Eyeing the shoe rack, I come across the most difficult part of my assignment: getting the right pair of shoes. Like most women's options for footwear, few of the choices are comfortable or supportive, aside from the athletic shoes that would look awful with her work clothes.

I settle on a pair of black leather flats, which will at least ensure she doesn't have to navigate a heel with her uneven gait. Once all the clothing is packed, I gather the other essentials she put on the list for me to get for her (deodorant, hairbrush, toothbrush, and her makeup bag) and toss them in with the rest.

Finally, I dig into the back of her closet where she stashed her crutches from when she first tore her ACL.

Just as she told me, they're buried under a whole pile of boxes and bags from her "old life," as she calls it. Her graduation cap and gown are bundled in one trash bag that I toss behind me. There's a crate of old binders and books, including one full of yearbooks that I'm itching to look through, but refrain in the interest of time. I glance at my watch, and realize it's already been close to half an hour since I left Kodi back at my place.

I finally spot the rubber-capped foot of one of the crutches sticking out from under yet another box of memories. This one is older, however, and as I shift it aside, the disintegrating cardboard gives up its hold at the bottom corner, spilling out the contents in a fan of papers and composition notebooks. The one at the top is covered in highlighter and gel-pen writing, and I can't help but glimpse at the cover as I move the pile to the side.

Kodi and Lily BFF Dream Diary: KEEP OUT!

A little lock and a heart-shaped skeleton key is drawn on the front in silver and pink paint pen, as well as a skull and crossbones beneath the warning.

This has got to be from middle or elementary school. The handwriting is bubbly and cutesy–far different from anything I've seen in the college notebooks Kodi brought me from her course on medical records-keeping. As I look it over, more drawings along the cover stand out: high heels and a lipstick tube in red marker, a baseball bat and a softball in brown pen, a sticker of a wedding dress with yellow highlighter impact marks all around it as if it were a superhero from a comic book.

I glance at my watch again. I don't have the time to look through it… but the idea of little-kid Kodi and Lily scribbling their childhood dreams into a notebook while amped up on root-beer floats and pizza at a slumber party is just too adorable to toss away.

So I zip it into the laptop pocket of my backpack, unearth the crutches, and make my way back to my girl.

I HAVE FAR TOO MUCH ENERGY AFTER I KISS KODI GOODBYE IN THE morning. She refuses to let me walk her to work, claiming her boss would have an absolute conniption if I showed up at the door. So I watch her hobble away on her crutches from the corner of Main Street, her dirty blonde hair dark and damp and swept up into a bun. Her silky blouse and straight-leg black trousers I picked out for her hide the sexy panties and bra beneath. I grin.

She gave me so much shit for that when she came out of the shower. But I noticed she didn't don the sports bra.

Once she turns the corner of the block and can no longer distract me, I race home, strip out of my joggers and t-shirt and hop into the shower myself. My chest fills with warmth as I breathe in the steam of the shower and see her shampoo and bodywash leaned against mine in the wire caddy hanging from the shower head. It feels good, feels *right,* to see her stuff here in my place.

My place. I freeze under the spray and open my eyes in surprise, realizing that this is the first time I've actually felt at home here.

I don't belong in the city anymore. I'm happy not working for my old boss, trudging into the soulless clinic, treating an endless parade of hurt people whom I can't possibly give enough help in the fifteen minutes they have allotted on the schedule.

I belong *here,* at my own practice, helping my neighbors and gym mates and friends, giving them the full extent of my care and helping them truly heal and live a better, healthier life. Here, with a partner who actually enjoys my company. Who may gripe and tease me when I bring her the sexy underthings at the bottom of her drawer when I'm assigned with the task of picking her outfit for the day, but through it all, actually enjoys my company. Values me. Wants me.

I remember her in her towel, hobbling out of the shower and seeing the clothing I laid out for her on the bed. Snorting when she saw the thong and matching lacy bra. Then slowly letting the towel drop to the floor and pool around her feet as she started a slow, sexy, reverse strip tease in front of me.

My dick twitches just *thinking* about it.

I take my time replaying the scene in my head and stroking myself, knowing that this shower is going to be a little bit longer than usual, but reveling in the knowledge that I'm self-employed and don't have any early morning appointments I need to run off to.

I grunt out my release ten minutes later, but even as I do, I realize that thinking of Kodi going about her work tasks with those sexy underthings on that I picked out for her is going to make this a long, *long* day.

Should I text her?

I get dressed in my gym clothes and get my bag together to head to Put Up Your Ducks for my morning workout. I'm hoping I might be able to get in a round or two with some of the other guys so I can burn off all this extra energy. I'm so well-rested after a full night of her snuggled against me…

I should text her. I whip out my phone and glance down at the screen, and pause.

This is the kind of thing that got me in trouble with Zeke.

My hand freezes over the screen as I hover over the text icon, warring with myself.

This is what I do. Everytime I get myself in a new relationship, I get super excited and clingy and end up suffocating the person I love.

I don't want to suffocate Kodi. I want her to actually stick around.

So I tuck my phone back in my pocket and head to the gym.

"TAP! *TAP!*"

Brad's voice knocks me out of my brain fog and I quickly let him out of my chokehold. He scoots away from me on the jiu jitsu mats in the back left corner of Put Up Your Ducks, under the ridiculous mural with duck versions of all the local townspeople. He rubs the spot just under his larynx, which I notice is flushed from the pressure I was putting on him.

"Oh, fuck, Brad, I'm sorry."

"Never let your mind go blank during a roll, man. You're better than that." Nick bends to help Brad off the mat, and then holds a hand out to me. I take it.

"Right. Sorry. Lots on my mind lately…"

Nick's light scolding is nothing compared to the guilt I'm forcing on myself for potentially hurting my sparring partner. *You are better than that, dammit.*

"Hey, no worries, man. So long as you're not trying to drum

up business." Brad chuckles at his own joke, and my shoulders relax a little.

I smile at him. "Your next appointment's on me, man. I'll keep my head in the game."

"Or don't! Choke me next, man, I could use a free crack or two!" D'Shawn punches me in the shoulder before pretending to try to take me down. I drop my right side into his ribs and buck him off playfully, laughing out the last little bit of stress.

It feels good to laugh like this.

It's been years since I've had a group of guys I could joke around and train with at the same time. I'd had friends in Scouts back in the day, but had realized too late that it was hard to be my real self in that kind of environment. Tae Kwon Do was better, but we were all more interested in competing for clout than establishing camaraderie during practices. Classes were a single-minded, serious affair.

And when I was in chiropractic school, my schedule was so all over the place I could rarely hang out with people, or make it to the gym during open training hours with the other MMA folks.

But here in Tuft Swallow, especially during the summer, there's always a good mix of teachers, cops, students, and various other business owners training at the gym. Nick has made it a welcoming place for beginners and veterans of different styles of fighting, and he's well-versed enough in each one of them to supervise just about everybody.

"Man, you're spacing out again! What's on your mind there, Doc?" D'Shawn punches my arm again and I give myself a shake.

"Sorry, sorry. It's nothing." I walk over to my cubby by the wall and grab a hand towel out of my bag, then wipe the sweat from my neck and forehead.

"Doesn't look like nothing," Brad preens. I eye him warily. His tone is one I'm not used to hearing in a room full of straight guys.

At least, not ones I consider my friends.

"What do you mean?"

He smirks at me, tilting his head, and I try to keep my face neutral. I've dealt with more than enough bullies and assholes at the gym who try to give me shit for being bi. Since that *Pecker* article back when I first moved here, my sexuality hasn't been a secret. Instinctively, my hackles raise, and I can feel the tension in my back and arms begin to coil in preparation.

"This wouldn't happen to have anything to do with cornhole practice being canceled last week, would it?" Brad raises his eyebrows.

That is not at all where I was expecting the conversation to go. "Huh?"

"Oh shit! You're onto something!" D'Shawn pipes in. "You *dawg*. Someone's been thawing out the ice queen!"

A few more heads around the gym turn in our direction, and Brad, Nick, and D'Shawn all take me in with big, goofy grins on their faces.

"Uh...huh?" I repeat dumbly.

Now Nick punches me in the arm. "Ow," I mutter, jerking out of reach before I get a bruise from all the male bonding going on.

"You're distracting the captain! Giving her somewhere else to focus all that ang–uh, energy," the fighter finishes lamely.

Still not quite getting it, and still unsure whether or not the guys are teasing me, I feel my face twitch in confusion. "What are you talking about?"

"You're sleeping with *Kodi,*" Nick mutters with a raise of his eyebrows.

And then I feel a sweat come on that has nothing to do with my workout.

"You've gotten under the steely skin of the Champion!" Brad's voice practically quivers with glee. "I thought it couldn't be done!"

"Hey now, Kodi's not–"

"You didn't go to school with her," he interrupts me. "That girl has only ever had one mode, and that's *hardcore*. I don't think I've ever even seen her smile at a guy unless they scored a point."

"Y'all talking about *Oh Captain, My Captain?*" Logan, one of my least favorite guys at the gym, slithers over to our group. Despite being around the same age as Brad, he seems so much younger than all the other fighters. I suspect it has something to do with his attitude problem–like that of a spoiled teenager. "I didn't think she was into guys."

"Watch it, Gilgax." Nick shoots him a look.

But Logan only shrugs. "Hey man, I just call it like I see it. She never even gave a dude the time of day until Gosling here rolled into town."

Really?

I stifle the little spark of pride that flickers to life at his words, even with the crude intentions behind them. I *hope* that I might actually be as special to Kodi as she is to me.

But letting that spark ignite into something more would be dangerous. Feeding those kinds of feelings only makes me commit too hard, too soon, and ends up with me looking like an idiot. *Like I did with Zeke.*

Sure, Kodi likes me. And I like her. We're dating, having fun. Just because we both admit it's real now doesn't mean I have to make it into something bigger than it is.

"Regardless, it's clear that whatever Brian's doing is mellowing her out." Brad gives me an appraising look. "So. How good *is* it?"

"Is what?"

Logan rolls his eyes. "Come *on,* is she like a dominatrix or what? You know with her best fucking friend being Slutty McRedhead she's obviously into some crazy shit. You're the only one to ever get her in the sack, so..." he gestures with his hands, as we all stare at him open-mouthed. "Oh please. None of you have ever wondered what she's like in bed?"

D'Shawn shakes his head in disbelief, and Nick narrows his eyes as more heads turn in our direction at Logan's outburst.

My hand is fisted in Logan's *Eagle View Track and Field* t-shirt before I even realize I've risen to my feet and crossed the empty floor between us. And then my face is inches from his, his suddenly labored breath stinking up the air between us.

"Maybe the reason she hasn't ever given guys the time of day is because they're all perverted fuckheads like *you*," I hiss.

I feel a large hand on my shoulder, and Nick's voice mutters next to me, "stand down, Doc. This is my gym. I'll handle it."

With way more effort than it should take, I unclench my fingers. Logan teeters on his feet when I release him, and I realize as I take in his wide eyes and red face that I actually lifted him onto his toes a little bit when I grabbed him. He stumbles back, smoothing the deep wrinkles I put into his t-shirt. I clear my throat, suddenly aware of the dead quiet surrounding the group of us, completely absent of the thumps and hums of sparring partners or the metallic clinking of the free weights being lifted and lowered.

All eyes are on me, Nick, and Logan as the ex-MMA fighter levels him with a withering stare.

"I think your workout's done for the day, kid. You should pack up and go home."

"I'll walk you out, man," Brad adds in his cop voice, patting Logan on the back and knocking him out of his frozen fear.

I glance down at my hands, which are shaking and clenched into fists.

Where did that *come from?*

Just as quickly as it started, the altercation is over, with everyone starting back up with their jogging or stretches. Even the elderly couple by the resistance bands is back to their calisthenics in the corner. Nick follows Brad and Logan to the front door, making more easy-going conversation with the officer while the idiot changes his shoes. D'Shawn gets my attention with a nudge, and points a thumb over to the bench in the universal sign for *spot me?*

I nod, and we resume our workout.

As he's pushing out a seventh rep, he picks back up the

conversation with a grunt. "Whatever you're doing, man, keep it up."

"Keep what up?"

Clunk. He ducks under the bar and sits up, and we switch spots. I wedge myself underneath the bar and press upwards.

"Whatever you're doing with Kodi."

"I'm just," *three,* "being," *four,* "me."

I wuss out after rep five, and the bar clatters against the stand. D'Shawn's a lot bigger than I am. I can't do too many sets at his weight.

"In that case, it seems like you two are a good fit for each other." He takes a swig from his water bottle. "She's been different since she started seeing you. The captain I knew at the beginning of the season never would have canceled practice just because we won a game. Maybe you're showing her that there's more to life than winning."

The same little spark in my heart from earlier flickers as his words sink in. I don't say much more as D'Shawn finishes his set, except for a *good work* at the end of it.

Instead, I find myself zoning out again, remembering the way Kodi looked this morning when I handed her her crutches. Not hopeless, like she had at the golf course, and not frantic or fired up, like she did whenever she talked about the cornhole league, but simply…determined.

Like she knew what she had to do, and she could get through it.

I'm still chewing on that when I say goodbye to Nick and the rest of the guys, and even still when I rinse off and change into my work clothes for the day. At my desk, after preparing everything for my afternoon appointments, I get out my phone and pull up my messages with Kodi.

The last message is from yesterday morning, before we met up with Nick and Tina at the golf course. Asking if we were planning on getting dinner afterwards. Of course, we didn't end up going anywhere with them after–she came right back here, where we…

Flashes of our night and morning together playback in my mind, and that tell-tale flicker is back. I remember the thong and matching bra, and the embers glow into a small flame that warms my chest and belly, and even lower.

BRIAN

How's your day going?

I know she likely can't text back at work. I know that *some* people would find my texting during the middle of the day, after we'd just spent practically the whole weekend together, clingy or needy. I know that to most guys, like the ones I've dated before, like Zeke or even just normal, immature straight guys like Logan; the way I feel about Kodi after such a short time together would seem pathetic. Sentimental. Weak.

And then, three little dots appear under my message.

And I dare to allow that little flame to burn on.

CHAPTER 39
KODI

Okay, I never thought I'd be caught dead thinking this, but thongs are *comfortable.*

When I first flossed the damn panties that Brian brought for me this morning up my legs and over the clunky brace he'd lent me for my knee, I thought for sure that I'd be picking wedgies all day. But unlike some of the other fancy, lacy underwear Lily had forced me to buy whenever we'd go shopping together, the pair Brian picked out doesn't even feel like I have anything on. I can't even remember getting these, honestly, and I guess they've been buried at the bottom of the drawer for a while.

I blush while I'm typing up patient intake information, realizing that not only did Brian *pick out undergarments* for me this morning, but he was digging around long enough to pick out a pair that had to have been underneath or behind literally *every other* piece of lingerie I own. The very thought makes my nipples poke into the silky, unlined fabric of the strappy, matching bra he picked out to go with them, and I send up a prayer that no one can see the outlines of them poking through the thin fabric of my blouse.

Fuck. All day, it's been like this. Every little thing makes me think of him, his kindness towards me yesterday, the way his voice was all low and hoarse when we first woke up in the morning, and, of course, the taste of his cock as it slid past my tongue and into the back of my throat when I made him straddle me yesterday.

How do other women do it??

I mean, sure, I guess I've had a small crush or two before. Back in middle school, Lily and I would have sleepovers and gush over some guy or another—but it was almost always her doing most of the gushing. I was far more interested in player stats and scoreboards than boys, and unless our classmates were sponsored by Nike, I couldn't really care less about what they were wearing when they walked into homeroom.

I find myself reflecting on something akin to respect for Lily when I think about how distracted she must constantly be with her endless dating apps and hookups she has going on. All that, and she still managed to get her associates and an esthetician's license?

Impressive.

"Miss Gander!"

I jump, despite the fact that I'm not doing anything wrong, at the sound of Dr. Cratchet's voice ringing through the office. Other than a terse nod or a grunt, this is actually the first he's spoken to me since my outburst last week.

"Yes, sir?"

"When you get a moment, look through these resumes, would you? I need to have the top three most qualified candidates on my desk by the end of the day."

He slaps a pile of papers onto my keyboard, spamming the *g*, *h*, and *j* buttons in the process. I quickly straighten them and set them on the span of perfectly empty space to the left of my computer.

"Resumes, sir?"

He leans against the island counter behind me, and I spin

around in my chair to face him. He folds his hands over his rounded belly and adopts a pensive expression.

"Yes, quite. I pondered what you said over the weekend and concluded that, despite your absolute lack of proper conduct in your *presentation,*" he narrows his eyes at me over the rims of his glasses, then takes a breath. "You *did* have a point. We are woefully understaffed. And while your degree may qualify you for the rather generous salary I pay you for menial office work, it's rather insufficient for delivering the level of patient care for which I've come to be respected and admired for providing."

I blink, taking a second to parse out the meaning behind his flowery language. "You're replacing me, sir?"

He sighs. "Not replacing, no. The board is hiring a nurse practitioner to assist with case load and prior authorizations."

"Oh!" A smile stretches across my face before I can help it. "That's a wonderful idea, sir!"

"Of course it is. Granted, it's one you should have thought to suggest ages ago if you were feeling so overwhelmed with managing your responsibilities. But alas, communication is one of the many skills lacking in your generation…"

He continues to espouse the many shortcomings of anyone under the age of forty while he pours himself a cup of the coffee I made earlier. I ignore him as I start leafing through the pile. At least he's talking to me again, and the first words out of his mouth weren't giving me a pink slip.

I'm going to have a co-worker!

And not just any co-worker. An actual qualified nurse practitioner: someone who can handle all of the insurance paperwork and extra responsibilities that I truthfully shouldn't be taking on the liability for. I should stand up for myself more often!

Maybe I can find someone who our patients would feel more comfortable with, too. Someone more like—

I shake my head before I once again let my thoughts wander to Brian. Now that I have actual important work to do today, I can't be letting myself get more distracted.

A buzzing sound comes from my purse hanging on the hook by the records closet, and it briefly distracts Dr. Cratchet from his monologue. He glances once at my purse, then me, and we lock eyes.

"Sorry, sir. I keep it on vibrate in case there's an emergency."

"You're not getting it out during the work day, are you, Miss Gander?"

"No, sir." *Tight ass.*

"Good. Keep it that way." He nods his head, then heads back to his office, mumbling something about kids and their electronic devices.

Once he closes the door, I check the schedule for his next appointment. "Mrs. Woodcock," I call into the waiting room. "The doctor can see you now."

The elderly woman, who's something of a town matriarch, smiles at me from the waiting room, tucking a copy of today's *Nosy Pecker* in between the seat cushion and the armrest before approaching the door to the hall with all the exam rooms. I grab my crutches and meet her at the threshold, and drop her off at the first room, pushing the call button on my way out. It takes a little longer than usual for me to get back to the office with me hobbling along, and by the time I get back to the island I can hear Dr. Cratchet greeting her.

When the exam room door clicks closed behind him, I snatch my phone from my purse to check my messages.

BRIAN

How's your day going?

Butterflies.

Pathetic. I've got goddamn butterflies from a morning-after text.

What do I even tell him? Do I let him know that we're looking for a nurse practitioner to expand the clinic? I snort at the irony. Dr. Cratchet originally wanted me to spy on Brian for *him,* and now I'm thinking about spilling all the clinic's gossip to my boyfriend.

Boyfriend.

My fingers hover over the screen, waffling back and forth over just how much I want to share about my day. How much he'd be interested in. Normally, I'm the one listening to my friends about *their* days, about their drama. Now that the tables are turned, I'm not sure what he actually wants to know. Whether he's just checking in about my knee, or my mental state, or even just to get a naughty picture of me from the employee bathroom.

Heat rises to my cheeks. Now *that* would be a new experience for me.

I settle for something non-committal.

ME

Pretty good, actually! I'm not fired, at least. How about you?

The three little dots appear next to his name almost immediately.

Why would you be fired?

Shit. I realize that I never told Brian about my outburst on Friday, because it would mean I'd have to fill him in on the context of my boss wanting me to spy on the "competition." And even though that isn't at all the reason I went to Brian for my first appointment–the butterflies soar all over again when I remember him rushing to catch me after I collapsed when we first met–I can't deny that it would totally seem suspicious if he knew why I was able to get off work so often to go to his office.

Eh, you've met the Doc. I'm always on my toes.

Guiltily, I push my phone back into my purse, ignoring the

buzzing that continues through the afternoon while I refocus on the stack of resumes in front of me.

By the end of the day, I have three great-looking candidates, all of whom I believe would help fill a serious gap in our town's limited health care options, particularly for women. Of the three candidates, we have two experienced women and one recent non-binary grad from U Mass, all of whom have great references from reputable medical programs in the state and OB-GYN experience.

All-in-all, I'm feeling pretty confident in the three resumes I put on Cratchet's desk at 5:30. But that feeling fades quickly as I have to navigate my crutches and hobble from his office, back to my desk to shut down my computer, then to the hook to get my purse, all before turning off all the lights and heading out the front door.

By the time I lock up the office, maneuvering outside and realizing I need to get myself down four steps from the landing to the sidewalk, I'm exhausted.

"Hey, baby girl."

My body reacts instantly to his voice. Low and smooth, calming, and sending a shockwave of warmth throughout my body that makes my nipples peak and remind me of how much less fabric there is covering my intimate parts than usual.

I look up and meet his eyes. He's on the top step, holding out a hand for me, gentleman-style, with a bright smile on his face.

"I thought you might want to lean on me instead of those crutches on your walk home."

Okay, maybe it's all the *Bridgerton* we've been watching together, but those old-school manners vibes he's dishing out are making my heart beat double-time in my chest. I hardly trust my voice as my cheeks stretch in what I'm sure is a super embarrassingly cheesy grin.

"Yeah, okay." *How eloquent, Kodi.* "But, it's girl's night, so I'll actually be walking to the Crowbar."

"Ah, of course." His eyes sparkle, even as a slight look of

disappointment crosses his face, and it's like my stomach twists into a helium balloon. "Mondays, right?"

"Yeah," I say breathlessly. Partly because of how amazed I am that he remembers those little details about my life and schedule, and partly because maneuvering the stairs outside the clinic with these crutches is a pain in the ass.

But he offers his hand for me, and the other for one of my crutches, and I accept gratefully, letting his strong presence take away the pain of my injured knee.

LILY'S ALREADY GOT OUR USUAL TABLE CLAIMED, AND THREE PRISTINE Cosmos in martini glasses waiting for us. Well, two of them are pristine. The other is half-drained and tipping precariously in one of her hands as she texts furiously with the other.

"Hey Lily," I greet her, leaning my crutches against the table and hoisting myself on the high-top stool. Brian kissed me goodbye outside the main entrance, asking me to text him if I needed someone to walk me home.

Ugh. He's so frickin' perfect.

I'd be lying if I said I didn't love it.

Lily gawks at me as I claim my Cosmo and take a sip. "Oh my *gosh,* what happened??"

"It's not a big deal."

"Kodi. You're on *crutches.* It is *very much* a big deal! Is this the real reason you canceled practice on Friday?? Why didn't you tell me?"

"No." My face squints at the sweet-and-sour drink. I'm definitely going to need to go back to my usual gin and tonic after this. "I canceled practice because we deserved a break. We won our last game, and we had a bye weekend. It made sense."

"Okay, who are you and what have you done with Kodi?" She crosses her arms. "Don't get me wrong, I love this new version, but I just need to know what we're getting into. If there's a catch."

"A catch to what?" Callie huffs over, pulls out her stool, and drowns her Cosmo in one, long drink, before sitting down and exhaling loudly.

We stare at her.

"What's up with you?"

"I just almost got run over on the street. Winston was in the middle of the road, so of course I needed to get my daily squeeze, and some lunatic almost crashed into us!"

This kind of thing is more common than you'd think in this town. That goat is constantly getting people into trouble.

"Charlene, we're gonna need another round over here!" Lily shouts to the passing waitress.

"Make mine a gin and tonic," I add on.

"Extra lime?" The woman shouts it over her shoulder as she swings her hips past three full tables.

"Yes, please!" I lean into the middle of the table, eyeing my friends. "Do we come here too much?"

"No," Callie and Lily respond in unison.

Then we all burst into laughter. As Callie reaches up to fix her disheveled ponytail, her elbow hits my crutches. "What the–oh no! Is one of you hurt??"

She ducks under the table to hunt for injuries.

"It's me."

"It's Kodi."

Lily and I answer at the same time.

"What happened?" Callie's eyes go wide, and her elementary school-teacher voice comes out, the care and sympathy radiating from her sincere face. Lily eyes me with more judgemental expectation.

"It's embarrassing."

"It's *girl's night,"* Lily argues, grabbing her Cosmo from a passing Charlene before she can set it on the table and taking a big swig. "So, spill."

I thank Charlene for my G&T (she made me a double, the saint) and sigh as I stab the lime wedges with my straw. "I fell at Birdie in the Hole."

My two besties stare at me for a long moment before, once again, bursting into laughter. This time, I don't join them.

"What??" I demand. "Stop it! It sucks, okay? Jeez, I was *just* starting to feel better, and now…"

A sour turn overtakes my stomach and suddenly I don't want my drink anymore. I push it away from me, closing my eyes and fighting the overwhelming sob creeping its way up my throat.

No. No. Stop this. I was fine. I was—

I wasn't fine. I was distracted. First by Brian, and our sexy adventures last night after I lost it on the treatment table, and then with his totally sweet and flirty aftercare throughout the day today. Then I had resumes to focus on at work, and because I was sitting down the whole time I was able to push my grief aside.

I should have known that this would only come up to bite me in the ass later. I'm an idiot. And I'm broken. And—

I'm surrounded by a squishy hug and my face is buried in a mass of red curls.

"It's going to be okay. You're not broken. You're a work in progress. This is just one step back, on a long journey forward."

I feel another set of arms close in around my shoulders, and with Lily and Callie holding me together, I let a couple tears fall. Just enough to release the pressure.

Lily's arm snakes down to my lap, finds my hand, and squeezes it. I squeeze back, finding the strength to sniffle back up the dam that's holding my sadness inside and locking it away for another couple hours.

And then Lily tilts her forehead against mine and murmurs, "Was it that frickin' clown head laughing that startled you? I swear that thing scares the absolute bejesus out of me every time."

My sob turns into a chuckle, and the dam breaks again. The sniggers and coughs shake loose the tears into more manageable streams, and I even smile a little.

"Holy shit, with me it's windmills. I haven't been to the golf course here yet, but it doesn't even matter because every mini golf course has one. And there's never *anywhere* I can stand that's safe from that damn thing. I've been smacked on the back of the head *five times* on a single trip before. Five times!"

My shoulders shake as more tears and snot and coughs of laughter dribble out of me like a fountain.

"It was the bubble popper," I grab a napkin and blow my nose. "I tripped into it with my butt and it popped me up into the air and right onto my bad knee."

Lily pulls back from me, meeting my eyes with a look of horror on her face.

"That. Fucking. *Sucks.*"

I let out a little wail as another sob/laugh overtakes me. "It *does!!*"

The two of them let me drink and cry and snot all over them as I tell the rest of the story, from Tina charging the snack bar for an ice pack while Brian literally carried me back to the car. How he wouldn't let me out of his sight all night, and how he walked me to work this morning and even here to the bar tonight.

They listen and nod, sipping on their Cosmos and rubbing my shoulder as I recount the pain of Brian's adjustment, how I felt–*feel*–so helpless about my recovery, which seems to me to be a goalpost that's constantly moving away from me. I complain about needing to take four weeks off from cornhole, and how I worry I'm going to be an even worse coach and captain to the team now that I can't even demonstrate at practice anymore. At that, Lily and Callie glance at each other, and Lily places a light hand on my uninjured knee.

"You know, Kodi, that might not be the worst thing in the world." My watery eyes snap to hers. I'm bracing for an admonishment, but instead of the usual frustration regarding the team, she's looking at me with understanding and kindness. "You need to take it easy. And the team has been dying to have a little less drilling, and a little more fun, at practice. Maybe this is a sign. A sign to slow down, lean back, and *enjoy* a game for once in your life."

"You always take the game so seriously. You know it's okay to let yourself have fun, right?" Callie smiles at me.

I blink at them, tears slowing now that I've gotten out some of my angst. "But, the championship–"

"It's something we've won *every year since 1969*. Kodi, at that point, it's not a challenge, okay? It's in our fucking blood. We're pretty good, you know? We're good at cornhole. We don't need to *drill*. We hardly even need to practice! We just get together twice a week to play because it's a town beer league. It's where single townies go to flirt with each other and teachers go to blow off steam with other adults instead of being stuck in a room with a bunch of children."

"And where Ginger goes to show off her ass cheeks to all the eligible men in town," Callie adds, and I snort. "It's an excuse to get the whole town together to drink, sell hamburgers, and dress up Winston in the local colors at the matches."

"It's where we can get away with throwing bean bags at all the MMA fighter's tight butt cheeks and call it an accident!"

Each item they list gets more and more ridiculous, until Lily squeals, "It's two nights a week where we can shotgun hard seltzers and ciders in the public park without getting arrested!"

Finally, I join in.

"It's the only place I can embarrass Logan for being a dipshit without having to face any consequences!"

They both cheer at that, and we clink glasses. A few townies at the tables around us look on curiously, and we settle back down, leaning our heads together over the hightop.

"It's where you and Brian first kissed," Callie whispers.

My heart squeezes. She's right. If it weren't for our match against Spitz Hollow and me needing to save Brian from his obnoxious ex, would we even have had a chance to try…whatever this thing is that we have?

This beautiful, wonderful thing?

Lily bolts upright. "Oh my gosh. *Oh my GOSH.*"

"What?" Callie and I both sober and straighten at her change in tone.

"You said Brian walked you to work this morning."

"Yeah..."

Lily stares at me. I stare at her. Callie's eyes dart back and forth between us like she's watching some kind of cerebral tennis match.

"You spent the night at his place!"

My face grows so hot, I can feel the remnants of the tears on my cheeks sizzle dry. Callie's mouth forms a perfect *o* and there's a brief moment of total silence, before...

"Eeeeeeeeeeee!!!" The shrill sound of my excited besties rings out into the din of the bar. I shush them, until they settle for bouncing on the tips of their toes around me.

"Ohmygosh, tell us *everything!"*

"How was it? How was he? Did you finally get to feel his man meat?"

"Is your v-card punched now? Are you officially a woman?"

"Was he super sweet afterwards? Oh my gosh, did he carry you to his bed? Was it like a fairytale??"

"Stop, stop it—*guys!"* I finally shout at them, their questions firing at me like baseballs at the batting cages. "No, I haven't officially punched any cards, and yes, I did spend the night, and... yeshedidcarrymetohisbed," I mumble, burying my face in the bottom of my glass.

Callie squeals again. Lily beams.

"Okay, storytime has officially begun. *Tell. Us. Everything."*

"Spill the tea, girl," Callie agrees. "Seeing as you're the only one getting any."

"What? Really?" I look between them, and Lily rolls her eyes.

"Yeah, it's been a bit of a drought for me with the move. I'm still weighing my options." Callie sips her drink, and her eyes flash. "But it'll pass. Especially if you whet our whistles with a little of your long drink of tall, dark, and well-endowed. Start from the beginning. So, he takes you home from mini golf..."

And I regale them with the tale of Kodi Gander's first blow job.

CHAPTER 40
KODI

Brian looks over the center console of my Subaru, gripping the steering wheel as if preparing himself to make a break for it. For us.

"You sure you're ready?"

"I have to be."

"You totally don't. You could have Nick lead practice."

"Nick?" I snort. "Have you *seen* him play cornhole?"

This is about the twelve-millionth time we've had this conversation today. It started last night after girls' night, when he picked me up as promised and walked me back to his place, where I spent the night. I totally would have jumped his bones, crutches and all, if I hadn't just so happened to start my period literally an hour before. *Ugh.*

While I'm practically positive Brian isn't the type of guy to be squeamish about "woman issues," I really didn't want to lose my virginity on my period. It just feels gross to me. And to his credit, Brian was absolutely fine with simply snuggling all night. He hasn't pressured me to do anything I'm not ready for.

Which only makes him sexier, of course. *Ugh.*

Brian shrugs. "Leading practice isn't about how good you are at cornhole. It's just about overseeing and managing the time clock."

I tap my thumb on the seat belt release, considering. Then glance in the back, where the six practice boards are stacked along with my crutches over the folded-down bench seat.

"No. I have to do this."

"Okay." He turns off the ignition. "Let me get the boards. You just sit here until I can get your crutches, okay?"

I open my mouth to argue, but he shoots me a stern look. So I take a breath instead. "Fine, yeah. Okay."

I feel like the biggest failure as I sit in the passenger's seat of my own car waiting for Brian to unload all the practice equipment. Even moreso, when Lily, Callie, Nick, and D'Shawn rush over to help him with the boards and start greeting each other. Joking around. Without me.

The little bubble of me and Brian, that magical space I'd been living in for the past 24 hours, pops. And I'm back in the reality of sports and injuries.

I sink into the weird, slippery-but-not-slippery fabric of the bucket seat, squinting my eyes shut like some kind of toddler playing hide and seek, convinced that if I can't see the team members looking at me with pity and disappointment in their eyes, then maybe they can't see me for the trainwreck that I am. Then Brian's opening the door, my crutches leaned up against the side of the car.

"Let's go, baby girl."

His eyes are smiling and expectant, completely void of the judgment I've been expecting from everyone, and I dare a glance over his shoulder to see nothing but the relaxed grins of my teammates behind him. *Maybe they don't all hate me after all.*

I take a deep breath, grab his hand, and lean on him as I step out into the world.

• • •

Once again I sit, helpless, on a metal bench on the sidelines as Mr. Landon misses his *fourth* shot by several yards from the cornhole board.

Brian squeezes my hand. "How ya holding up?"

"He's not even looking at the board."

"Who?"

"Mr. Landon. That's his fourth miss of the night."

"Did you notice that D'Shawn and Callie have been neck and neck knocking each other's bags off for the past twenty minutes?"

His comment tears me away from my laser-focus on Mr. Landon's pathetic display, and I turn to Callie and D'Shawn.

He's right. My eyebrows shoot up as I see them go bag-for-bag, each one-pointer being scooched or sunk with every other toss. It's hypnotizing.

Delilah and Jonah have both stopped throwing their own bags, and started cheering them on. Callie makes a particularly impressive throw, pushing off Lily's blue bag and sinking in a hanging red and the airborne bag in one serendipitous arc.

"Fuck yeah, Callie!" I shout, grasping my crutch and flinging myself to standing. I raise my other hand in the air in triumph. "*That's* what I'm talking about!"

Brad and Jonah turn to me with wide eyes, as well as Geneva and Ginger, who's eyes had been focused on their own games. Now everyone's looking at D'Shawn, the pressure mounting.

He tosses, and the blue bag sails across the field of play, lands on the board, and slides until it's clinging to the wood by a corner over the hole. He lets out a disappointed moan. Then Callie steps up to the throw line for game point.

She breathes, she shoots, and she scores.

Everyone erupts into cheers, including Brian, who's clutching my screaming ass in a side-hug and half-carrying me over to my besties.

"Callie, that was so good!!"

"I did it! I fucking *did it*!" Tears spring to her eyes as my friend literally bounces with joy, and the whole team gives her big pats on the back and Brian starts handing out drinks.

When I step back to give the other players room to congratulate my friend, I'm able to zoom out and actually look at everyone on the field at once. The smiles on everyone's faces, the relaxed shoulders and easy laughs as they grab a hard seltzer and knock back a sip.

Have I *ever* seen everyone at practice having fun?

Realization dawns on me as I remember that I have—but not since I took over the position as team captain. Did I ruin it? Am I ruining it still?

"Kodi, can up!" I hear, looking up and seeing a hard cider hurtling towards me. I panic, freezing with one hand lifted lamely from my crutch, when a strong, tan arm appears out of nowhere in front of me and snatches the can.

Brian pops it open with a hiss and hands it to me. "Can up, coach." He winks. "Now would be a great time for a little speech or something."

I swallow, accepting the can and looking out over the field at the smiling faces surrounding me. My heart is beating about a thousand miles a minute. I don't know how to give a pep-talk that isn't related to skill or strategy or *get-out-there-and-make-the-other-guys-pay*. All I've ever known to do is focus on everyone's weaknesses, or celebrate wins: real wins, against rivals.

How do I tell my team that watching Callie and D'Shawn play, or really, watching everyone hang out and cheer them on while I sat on the sidelines, jumbled up everything I thought I knew about captaining a beer league?

"Well, you guys, as you can see, I–" my throat catches. I look down at my knee in its brace, my crutches jammed up into my armpits and my work shirt wrinkling and stained with sweat from the hot, humid, Tuft Swallow summer evening. "I think that the rest of this season is going to look a little different than I thought it would."

The faces around me react to what I'm saying. A few crinkle in confusion, some nod understandingly, and yet others still retain the glow from their earlier cheers. I take a big swig from my can, and look over at Lily, whose stare is intense and supportive.

"I've been a bit of a hardass," I admit. A couple chuckles radiate through the group, and the honesty lightens the weight in my chest. "Okay, okay, a *lot* of a hardass. You all know that my past experience with championships is a little...wrought."

"Oooo, an SAT word," D'Shawn jokes.

More laughter. But despite it being at my expense, I find myself feeling even lighter. I grin. "Yeah, and here you thought I was just a one-trick pony! Turns out, it helps to have a backup when your sports scholarship falls through."

Brian's shoulder leans gently into mine, and I feel his hand reach gently to hold the small of my back. I look up into his kind eyes and take a breath.

"The fact is, I'm not gonna be able to play the next few weeks. Definitely not the rest of the regular season, and probably not even most of the playoffs. Which means," I raise my voice over the little gasps and sympathetic noises that pick up from the group, "I'm gonna need you guys to pick up the slack. And if I see more displays like the kind of relaxed, easy, and quite honestly," I watch as everyone's faces fall as one as I let my voice take on the tight-ass coaching timbre I usually use at practice, before pausing for dramatic effect and scorching them all with a blazing smile, "*best damn cornholing I've ever witnessed* that you all displayed today, well then. I think we'll be in pretty great shape!"

Tears burst from Lily's eyes as she coughs out a laugh, and everybody else joins in as the tension breaks like a party popper. Brian squeezes the arm around my waist, and I feel the warmth of his grin as he stares down at me.

But I only have eyes for my team. The Mighty Swallows, once again looking like the returning champions I hadn't realized they already were.

"To the reigning champs!" I scream, thrusting my cider into the air. A chorus of cans rises to the sky, and we all drink to a new era: for the team, for our practices, and, hopefully, for me.

CHAPTER 41
BRIAN

Gander Grounded for Today's Tussle in Big Tech Territory

The second big rivals match of the regular season is here, sports fans! But is there trouble brewing for the Reigning Champions of the Hawkthorne County Cornhole League?

Kodi Gander, clinic administrator and Captain for the Mighty Swallows, has been benched for the remainder of the season. While her boyfriend may have been helping her keep it hush-hush, the entire flock of pesky pigeons that's taken up residence around our town square this summer witnessed the young captain limping to work everyday this week: the unfortunate result of an unlucky encounter with the popper at Birdie in the Hole last weekend. Our eyewitness source (who has requested to remain anonymous) had this to say:

*"That g****mn golf course is a menace to our little town! I've never thought it was safe, wasn't I just saying that the other day, Francis? And don't get me started on the waste of our precious water and resources in keeping that eighteenth hole running! I saw our dear Kodi trip right into that g**forsaken bubble and get flung clear off her ankles and land right on her injured knee, bless her heart. Wasn't it just awful, Francis? He saw it, too, he was right there beside me watching it happen. She even*

started crying. Poor thing. Never deserved what happened to her in that state championship…"

Rumor has it the incident was followed by an overnight stay for the two lovebirds at Gosling's office/residence on Elm Street. Perhaps a different kind of "sport" is taking priority over cornhole in this budding romance…

Will the Swallows prevail over their rivals without their star tosser? Or will we all be forced to tuck our heads in shame?

Today's match will be hosted by Spitz Hollow at the new Spitz-Shein Sports Complex on County Route 46. If anyone is in need of a ride, the Dirty Hookers are arranging a carpool.

Kodi's face is so red, I'm surprised she isn't going supernova as she clutches the *Pecker* in her trembling hands. I try to calm her down, but her eyes are glazed over in horror, and I don't think she's actually seeing the interior of the diner where we're getting our protein-heavy pre-game breakfast in.

A small whine starts to escape her throat. I tap her on the shoulder.

"Hey. Baby girl. Talk to me." She holds up the paper dumbly, and I shove it flat onto the table between us. "That doesn't matter, okay? It's a gossip column."

"They know."

"They know what, Kodi?"

"Everything." She finally moves of her own accord, sinking her face into her hands and letting out a despairing breath.

I lean forward, reaching for her and trying to figure out what's going on. "What do you mean, babe? What's everything?"

"I *am* letting it take priority."

"Letting what take priority?"

"This!" She flaps her hands in between us, and her voice rises in pitch. I wince, and she mirrors my posture until our heads are almost touching over the table. "This thing between us. Spending the night at your house. Golf with dad. Dinner with mom. I've been panicking about it and I *have* been letting it overshadow the team."

"Baby girl, you haven't even been able to practice this week. Your knee–"

"That's what I mean! I've never let a little sprain distract me from practice! I've always kept my head in the game, even from the sidelines. I mean, sure, the team might be happy that I've been going easy on them, but the town expects–"

"Order up for the Captain!" Eve, the waitress, chirps. She sets down our plates, and snaps her gum in her cheek. "You two are just the cutest. Mind if I Snap a pic? Of the pregame?"

"Can you give us a little privacy, actually, please?" I stick my hand up in front of the phone camera that she's waving in front of us. "And I could use a little more coffee when you get a sec."

She narrows her eyes at me, but gets her phone out of my face before twitching away. "Fine."

"Captain..." Kodi mutters under her breath. I squeeze her hands.

"Hey. *Hey.*" I try to get her attention, but she's spiraling. And I don't know where it's coming from. Sure, the article was a little on-the-nose, but if she was okay with the team and with us she wouldn't be freaking out like this.

Would she?

"Kodi, I need you with me. Zeke's gonna be there today."

"Zeke?" Her eyes finally flash up to meet mine, and I see the gears begin to turn again behind the amber. "Right. Spitz Hollow."

"Yes. And I'm going to be on the bench with you. The whole game." I give her hand another squeeze. "I need to know you're there with me, too."

I haven't seen Zeke since that weirdly charged moment in Most Buy three weeks ago. To be honest, I hadn't really been thinking about him at all since things with Kodi started heating up. But she's not wrong about this being a stressful week: between preparations for golf and dinner with her parents tomorrow and game day today, and of course, her injury, there have been a lot of stressors weighing on both of us.

Being reminded that today's match is versus Spitz Hollow and Zeke, brings up those still painful feelings I buried under the novelty of whatever Kodi and I have. How much he hurt me. How much he *blindsided* me. How could I have thought what we had was serious, when he was so quick to toss it aside? Was I too sentimental, too clingy? Am I still?

I look at the woman across the table from me, still visibly uncomfortable, her eyes still bouncing back and forth across the page of the paper. Finally, I grab it off the table and crumple it up, shoving it into the vinyl seat beside me.

I need her to be present. I need her coherent. I need her with me.

I need *her*.

This weekend especially, we need to present a united front. Especially now since we've basically admitted that we're in a real relationship, if only to each other.

But just because it's real, doesn't mean she's in this as much as I am…

"Are you with me?"

That question is loaded with so much more than just those four words would imply.

She nods. "I'm with you." She picks up her fork and starts shoveling omelet into her mouth. "Let's eat and get moving. Food's getting cold."

WHEN WE ARRIVE AT THE SPITZ-SHEIN SPORTS COMPLEX IN SPITZ Hollow, I'm a little taken aback at the grandiose nature of it. The building towers six stories high in the middle of an office park, just across the street from Spitz-Shein Inc., a glassy, modern-looking behemoth that seems pretty out of place for the rest of the small suburban New England county.

The complex is completely enclosed. A wide, shiny revolving door makes maneuvering our team's cornhole boards inside a little difficult, but luckily the rest of the team helps us carry the items from the parking lot to the lobby of the complex, which overlooks a giant, open, recycled rubber floor beyond.

"Woah," Kodi breathes. "This is...uh..."

"Indulgent," D'Shawn mumbles.

"Huge," Callie and Lily chorus together.

"Unnecessary?" Nick raises an eyebrow at me, and I shrug.

"Certainly for anything I'm interested in when I go to the gym." I give Nick what I hope is a reassuring smile. Tuft Swallow is too small to have any big facilities or gyms like this aside from the high school or the community college, and it would be easy for a small business owner like Nick with his cozy MMA gym on Birch Street to feel a little intimidated at a glitzy workout center like this.

"Oh my God. They have one of those walls with rock thingies for climbing!" Geneva squeals, darting past us and pointing to one side of the massive complex, which does indeed have a permanent climbing structure rising up the entire six story wall like a cliff face. "What are those called?"

"A climbing wall?" One of the other team members follows her over. "That's kind of awesome."

"Alright, guys, focus. Let's find wherever the match is supposed to be and–"

"Oh look! Miss Muffin's Tufties are here to be crushed at last."

That accent. I'd know it anywhere. As soon as the voice drifts lazily about the echoey corridor of the lobby, I look up and see Zeke strutting towards us, with three other Spitz Hollow cronies backing him up. "We were beginning to think you got lost."

"We're half an hour early," Lily snarls. "So stop with the high-and-mighty act."

"Sorry, sorry, I tend to lose track of time while I'm *lifting*." He flexes and tilts his chin at me, and I don't miss the sweat glistening off his toned arms.

He's just trying to bait you, Brian. Keep it together.

"Good to see you, B." He winks at me.

Fuck. I wish I could stop the little twist that happens in my stomach when he does that. Winks have always been a weakness of mine. Especially when a confident, well-built man sends one my way, singling me out in a crowd? God. It's always been one of the hottest things in the world a man could do to win me over.

Kodi looks over her shoulder at me, and her brow furrows. I meet her eyes and give her a grin, but even I can feel that it doesn't come across as easy or carefree as I want it to.

It's not that I want to get back together with him. This man hurt me. Stung me. Cast me aside like I was nothing. I'm not the least bit interested in being with him anymore.

But even with all of that, there's still a part of me that wonders what about me wasn't good enough for him. Despite how much I've taken a liking to Kodi, how being with her makes me feel…

"I'm with you."

Kodi's words from this morning ring through my head, and it's like something warm spreads through my chest, forming a kind of internal armor against Zeke's snarky tone. *That's right,* I remind myself. *You have someone who actually cares about you now.* I straighten my back and lift my chin, meeting his carefree, flirtatious gaze with a more serious one of my own.

He doesn't get to play with my heart. It doesn't belong to him anymore.

Then Zeke finally looks at Kodi, sees her crutches, and scrunches his face in the fakest look of concern I've ever seen. "Gander! What happened to your leg? Do you not know any good chiropractors? You know, I used to sleep with one whom I could recomme–"

"So are you just going to stand there, or are you gonna show us where we can set up our boards?"

I'm amazed that my voice sounds so confident, sure, as it

booms across the lobby to their little clique of muscly fuckboys. Even Zeke's brows raise in surprise when I don't flinch at his insinuated dig. The one that almost gave away to the whole team that *he* is the "mystery ex-boyfriend" that the *Pecker* wrote about all those weeks ago.

"We've already got it all set up. Unlike some of the piffling teams in this league, we can afford enough equipment for everybody when *we* host."

"Woulda been nice if you'd have told us that before we carried everything in," Lily mutters.

The rest of the team mumbles in agreement.

"Here, babe. Why don't you and a few others take the boards back to the car, and I'll go check out the field." Kodi tosses me the keys, and blows me a kiss. I snatch them out of the air, and then pat my cheek with them, as if I caught her kiss, too.

And then *I* wink. Only I don't do it to get back at the asshole standing in front of us.

I aim it at my girl. And the red that blossoms on her cheeks in response sends a whole new sensation into my stomach.

"With you," she mouths at me.

"You too," I mouth back. And without even a parting glance at my ex, I lead the guys back to the car to put away the boards.

Kodi can handle this.

CHAPTER 42
KODI

F*uck. FuckfuckfuckfuckFUCK.*

As Zeke and his cronies guide me through the crisp, immaculate hallways still smelling of fresh paint, down to the indoor rubber track and the indoor turf football field beyond, all I can think about is how fucking *nice* this goddamn sports complex is.

Curiosity beats out animosity in my mind, and I can't help but ask. "When did Spitz Hollow build this?"

"Oh, Spitz Hollow didn't. Spitz-Shein did," The beefiest of the cronies says over his shoulder. He's easily 6'5", with a short, brown buzz-cut and a doughy face that's wider on the bottom than it is on top. In fact, his head just sort of becomes his neck–not in a fat way, but in a way that reminds me of those old *Cartoon Network* animated shows from the 90's. If he had a blonde pompadour, he would look like Johnny Bravo.

I squint at him. "Spitz-Shein?" *Where have I heard that name before?*

"Where we all work, across the street."

Then I remember. Spitz-Shein is that start-up that Dr. Cratchet invests in. The one that seems to be kinda having a moment right now.

They make enough money to build a place like this?

Zeke opens his pouty mouth. "With the kinds of moves we're making, we need facilities that can attract the best talent to our campus. It's not like the bars around this shite town are going to get Google-caliber employees to move out here."

"*You* moved out here," I argue. "It's nice around here."

"*Nice* is a bit of a strong word. Quaint, maybe."

"Twee," another crone chimes in.

"Claustrophobic," Johnny mutters.

I feel my hackles rise.

It's one thing for *me* to feel claustrophobic in and around Tuft Swallow. I grew up here, got stuck here, was condemned to my fate here. It's another thing entirely for some fancy-pants outsiders to come in, steal our jobs, erect a giant chode of a building, and then call our county *twee.*

My armpits ache from hobbling the mile and a half it feels like it takes to finally reach the visitor's sideline. As I wait for the rest of our team to get back, I eye the shiny new boards and equipment scattered throughout the expensive space.

Shouts ring through the giant complex, and I look over towards the nearest entrance, where a small scuffle is taking place.

It seems that the Dirty Hookers, the local knitting and craft circle, brought along Winston for the game. Normally, it wouldn't be a problem, as the county cornhole matches have always been outdoors. No other town can afford some kind of indoor arena to host games in. The closest thing we have to compare it to is the community ice skating rink in Robin Springs.

But in the new, sparkling Spitz-Shein Sports Complex, the appearance of a dirty goat in an orange-and-turquoise afghan is causing a kerfuffle.

"He's our mascot!" Mrs. Dougherty shouts at two employees who currently bar the entrance.

"Ma'am, only service animals are allowed–"

"He's my service animal," a low growl rumbles from the open doorway. "Here's his vest."

It's a good thing the rest of the team is still out taking care of the cornhole boards, because I'm pretty sure Lily might have a heart attack if she were to see Winston's Hot Daddy making puppy eyes while holding up a (likely never worn) service vest for our town mayor.

The giant man pushes past the gaping faces of the complex employees to affix the vest on Winston, tucking it underneath the various crocheted accoutrements. The rest of the Hookers follow him in single-file with arms full of turquoise scarves and orange blankets to hang from the bleachers.

Some of the other Tuft Swallowers begin to arrive, and they tote with them just about everything you can think of in the town colors. Flags, seat cushions, jackets, shirts, banners–you name it. They spread out like a stain over the sterile, pristine space, and it warms my heart to see it.

A minute later, Lily and Brian lead the rest of the team over to the bench where I've been resting. About half the players oooh and aaah like tourists gazing up at the Empire State Building for the first time as they take in the facility around them. Geneva points at Winston and waves at her parents in the stands. The other half have their game faces on.

"Alright, everyone, huddle up!"

They gather around my crippled ass on the bench, and I take in a deep breath to center myself. When I open my eyes, Brian is right across from me in the huddle, carrying the extra drinks cooler with Nick.

He gives me that heart-stopping smile of his, his color-changing eyes reflecting the turquoise of all the banners behind me, and his confidence gives me strength.

"These Spitzers are a bunch of soft-handed, tech-bro pansies!" I shout out, and the group all hoots and hollers in agreement. "They had to build this fancy-ass complex because they're too pampered at their cushy jobs to step outside into the fresh air!"

"They don't even carry their own boards!" Lily adds.

"Yeah, and their colors are boring!"

I hold up my hand, trying to suppress my grin at the interruptions, but failing. If there's one thing that can get us Tuft Swallowers fired up, it's making fun of Spitz Hollow.

I can tell that the team is blindsided by the new building, and the clear influx of money into our rival's town. Even I'm shaken. Adding that stress to the already raging imposter syndrome I feel with my injury, and it's just about everything I can do to muster up the fire for this pep talk. If Brian wasn't here, I'm not sure I could.

"But you know what we have that they don't?"

The team chimes in answers.

"Heart!"

"Winston!"

"More afghans and ponchos than you can shake a feather at!"

I laugh. "Yes, haha, all of that–but we also got one other thing."

They look at me with anticipation, and Brian nods.

"The fucking BEST CORNHOLE TEAM IN THE GODDAMN LEAGUE!"

Everyone erupts at that, and I pick up steam. "Think of all the cornhole legends that have walked past our founder's statue in the town square on their way to victory. Peter Harrelson. Harry "Chugs" Lebowitz. Genie "Hip Bump" Bouchard. And of course, my predecessor, 54-year reigning team captain John "The Toss" Bosco."

"May he rest in peace," the team chants.

"These are our mentors," I say, gaining momentum, feeling the spirit of all of our past champions flowing through my veins. "*These* are the legends we carry on, for ourselves, for our progeny, for TUFT SWALLOW!"

"For Tuft Swallow!"

"WHO ARE WE?"

"The Mighty Swallows!"

"WHO? ARE? WE??"

"THE MIGHTY SWALLOWS!!"

At the swell of pride from the team, the Tuftettes, our rag-tag cheering squad comprised of young girls and boys and their dance moms, start chanting to psyche up the crowd. The giant gymnasium fills with the sound of a bunch of toddlers and what feels like the whole town spelling out "aggressive" as the little girls wave their sparkly pom-poms and their moms take dozens of pictures with their iPhones.

The noise and the adrenaline fill my chest, and Brian drops the cooler of drinks and thrusts his hand into the circle. My stomach clenches.

"Mighty Swallows on three!" He shouts.

Everyone throws their hands on top of his and we all join our voices as one.

"One, two, three–*Mighty Swallows!*"

"Let's go out there and fucking *corn some holes!*"

I collapse back onto the cold metal bench. Somehow, I'd risen to my feet during my little speech. The players scatter with their partners to their starting lineup: Lily and Callie on board one, D'Shawn and Geneva on board two, and Tammy and Cooper on board three. Piper, Mr. Landon, Ginger, and the others are on deck for the second round.

Our little county cornhole league is not huge. We only have a handful of teams: The Spring Chickens, Robin Springs (The Fightin' Robin's), The Eagle's Peak Dolphins (don't ask me why they insist on being called the Dolphins—apparently, some shithead in their town stuffed the ballot box on mascot day and was never caught), us, and of course, Spitz Hollow. We make sure every team gets to play every other team at least twice to fill out the summer schedule, before starting our playoff bracket in August.

While the early season games are smaller because most towns are still filling up their rosters for the season, these mid-season games have three rounds of three so everyone gets a chance to play. In the beginning of the season, we actually had more players than we do now, so almost all of our tossers are going to have to play twice, especially now that I'm on the bench.

Brian sits beside me, and Nick next to him as the players tee off against the red shirts. The loudest, most obnoxious buzzer I've ever heard in my life rips out of the giant speakers in the ceiling, and it's off to the races.

Thankfully Rowenna, the leader of the Tuftettes, brought a boombox along to play music for the pom squad to dance to, so it's not completely silent as the first round begins.

The brand-new, freshly painted boards across the field reflect the fluorescent lights directly into my eyes, practically blinding me from actually observing the game. I begin to wonder if it's sabotage. The boards are painted the SH colors of red and white: the red ones on our side facing the home team, and the white ones on their side facing us. It's immediately clear how much they're affecting the players, as players from both teams that are situated on the home side are playing better than the ones in front of us.

The other thing I notice is the colors of the bags. Spitz Hollow's bags are black, which stand out from both of the boards easily, making it easy to gauge and aim, but the bags they gave our team are this shitty red-and-white gingham that read horribly on both boards. Add that to the fact that half of our players are blinded by the reflections, and even our best players have their bags slipping off the boards half of the time.

While we started out pumped, morale quickly dips once it becomes clear that we're behind in the first round. D'Shawn and Geneva are in the lead with their match, but the others are floundering. To my despair, Lily and Callie are the first to lose their match; a giant, glaring red "1" appears on the scoreboard next to HOME and five minutes later, the score sits at 2:1, Spitz Hollow.

Brian rubs my back and I bite my lip as the players gather round the bench before the second period. Nick passes out Gatorades. Pharrel's *Happy* blares annoyingly from Rowenna's boombox as the Tuftettes do their prepared half-time dance beside us. On the other side of the field, the older, more promiscuous cheer squad for Spitz Hollow start doing a suggestive pom routine to *Cherry Pie* that seems equally inappropriate for the current mood of the match, albeit for different reasons.

"I can't see a damn thing out there! And those plastic boards they have are super slippery. Who can play with those?" Lily kicks her foot into the turf as if she's attempting to fold it up like carpet.

D'Shawn nods. "Seriously. We haven't practiced on plastic boards before. All of our sliding moves are useless."

"You seemed to adjust well, though," I point out. "Got any tips?"

He nods. "You gotta arc the bags high. If they don't land almost perpendicularly to the board, they're gonna sail right off."

"I threw all mine like *this.*" Geneva demonstrates a clumsy underhand throw. I clap my hands together.

"Alright then, that's the strategy. We've practiced this, you guys: high arcs like the ones to sink hanging chads. Only do low tosses if you need to knock one off. Sound good?"

Nods all around. Not nearly as enthusiastic as they were twenty minutes ago.

"Okay. Ginger? Mr. Landon? You're on board one. Jonah and Delilah, you're on board two. Now go out there and show the world how unbeatable the Mighty Swallows really are!"

The buzzer sounds again, and the second string drifts off to their places. Brian leans into my ear.

"Do you think all this new equipment and stuff was on purpose?"

"Oh I absolutely do," I whisper back. "They're playing dirty."

"It seems a little silly for something like cornhole."

I stare at him, eyes wide. "Dude, this is like, the most important thing in Hawkthorne County. Teams try to cheat all the time."

"Try?" He smirks. "What do you mean, try?"

"Well, there aren't many ways to cheat at cornhole. People almost always get caught. We've got an intra-team Board of Standards that checks out the specs of every play field and all the equipment before each match, too."

"Wait—seriously?"

His jaw drops. I bob my head emphatically. "Oh yeah. Honestly, I'm surprised they allowed these new boards in the first place. I mean, I guess they're the same for all players, so it isn't technically cheating, but the fact that only Spitz Hollow can afford new equipment and they're the only ones who've practiced on plastic boards is kinda bogus. I wonder if we could find a few online to practice on..."

My mind is already racing with ideas for how we can better prepare for the next match. I zone out for a second, thinking of places that might sell plastic cornhole boards (I mean, seriously. Who plays on plastic boards??) when a kiss to my temple interrupts my thoughts.

"You're pretty amazing, you know that?"

"Huh?"

I look up, and Brian's eyes are doing that color-shifting thing again as he meets my gaze. "You're already thinking of how the team can train to be better, aren't you?"

"Well, yeah," I say. "That's my job."

He pulls me in close next to him, and puts his finger under my chin, tipping my head so his lips aren't even a breath away from mine. "The way you asked D'Shawn what he did to win, and engaged everyone in their own moves to improve...that was good work. Good captain-ing." My heart beats in overtime as his compliment makes my chest glow. "You're a champion, baby girl."

Heat rushes up to my cheeks as he claims my lips with his, right there on the bench, in front of the whole town. If I were a Looney Tunes cartoon, little wings would have sprouted on my feet and wrists and I'd have floated into the air. With just the slant of his pillowy lips gently nipping onto mine, my insides melt away, and my heart feels a million times lighter as my head fills with helium.

"Wow," I whisper as he pulls away. He grips my shoulder and squeezes me in close.

"Yeah. My words exactly."

The buzzer stabs through our bubble, and with a jump I turn my head to the scoreboard.

Shit. 5-1.

The Spitz Hollow asshats all break out in gross growls and jeers of celebration as my players trudge back to our sideline. The Tuftettes break out into a pre-school rendition of "Single Ladies," their tight spiral-curled ponytails bouncing in the fluorescent light. The crowd behind us starts murmuring and muttering amongst themselves behind me, and I can feel their worry and worse—their judgment—aimed at the huddle forming around the bench.

"I can't see a goddamn thing out there," Ginger sneers. "Seriously, who's idea was it to make the boards Vanta White?"

"I don't think Vanta White is a thing." Mr. Landon sneezes then, making Ginger jump back in disgust. "Just Vantablack."

"Whatever you want to call it, it's obnoxious, and between that and the gross warehouse lighting in this dump, I'm feeling super off my game."

Brian squeezes my hand, and I take a deep breath. *Don't yell at her. Try to be encouraging. Don't be so hard on everybody.* "Ginger, nobody's blaming you. It was totally a dick move on their part."

"Yeah, Kodi, I know no one's blaming me. Why would they? I'm fucking great."

I hold back an eye roll, and glance back up at the field. It's then that I notice that half of the Spitzers that were playing in the last round have sunglasses on. At first, I assume it's just because they're the type of assholes that wear sunglasses inside, but then it clicks, and a growl builds in my throat.

Those fucking bastards.

"Were they wearing sunglasses when they played last round?"

Mr. Landon looks over his shoulder at the players, and nods. "Yeah. I thought that was odd…"

"Quick, who has sunglasses with them?"

Ginger, Geneva, Lily, Nick, and D'Shawn raise their hands. I rub my hands together, forming a plan.

"Okay, this round we're five teams against five, which means we still have a chance to beat them or get them down to a tiebreaker. Nick, give your glasses to Jonah. We're going to have the five of you with sunglasses face the white boards next round, which should at least help with you not having to squint so much. As for the slippery boards…I can't do anything about that, but if we follow the original plan of high underhand throws we might be able to at least get back on the board."

Single Ladies ends, and a lukewarm round of applause scatters through the indoor arena. The buzzer blares once again.

I try to fill my voice with as much motivation as I can muster. "Alright, y'all, get out there and show everyone that the Mighty Swallows don't give up!"

Ginger mutters about my use of the word "y'all," and the rest of the team scurries away in higher spirits than they huddled with. They're still pretty subdued, though.

Meanwhile, the home crowd has started chanting on the other side. Only, instead of cheering on their own players, they've come up with a couple rhymes to specifically call out and insult *our* players. None are particularly clever. But when they break out into "Gander's on the bench / Her team can't bear the stench," I feel my hackles rise.

Brian narrows his eyes at them. Ginger, however, laughs, and I remind myself to punch her in the face later. My pocket vibrates, and when I pull out my phone I can see that Lily texted me.

LILY

dont let them get2u

When I look up, I can see she's holding her phone behind her back and typing it one-handed, to avoid getting caught by the refs with her phone out. For some reason, the board decided that texting on the field was cheating a few years ago. I'm torn between shouting at Lily to put her phone away, and thanking her for the encouragement.

That thought evaporates, however, when the red-and-white fans change gears and focus their less-than-stellar poetry skills on *her.*

"Coo-ley's such a ditz / Her only asset is her tits!"

"Fowl!" I call out to the refs. But I'm too late. Lily stomps across the field, heading for the head cheerleader with the megaphone.

"This is a family sport!"

But as I'm shouting, my best friend reaches the squad and grabs one of the scantily-clad dancers by the ponytail, and all hell breaks loose. Whistles erupt through the space and both crowds start booing—or in the case of a group of teenage Spitz Hollow boys sneaking beer behind the bleachers, hollering inappropriate words of encouragement.

By the time the refs separate the two women, the cheerleader's limping away with a torn skort and Lily's got a massive shiner blooming an angry red around her left eye. As she's escorted back to our side of the arena, I notice a tuft of blonde hair hanging limply in her clenched fist.

The ref approaches me. "You know the rules, Gander. If a team throws punches, they forfeit the match."

"What?" I thrust my hand out, gesturing to Lily. "Look at that black eye and tell me that *she's* the one who threw hands."

He shakes his head. "Not how it works, missy. Cooley's a player. Fans are off-limits. That's the rules."

"Didn't you hear their chant?? They were egging her on! Unsportsmanlike conduct!"

Tears are springing to my eyes, and I try to blink them back. I grab my crutches and force myself to stand right in the ref's face.

These guys aren't playing fair!

Lily hangs her head. The rest of the team circles around to get an understanding of what's going on. I keep arguing with the ref, until Brian comes up behind me and puts his hand on my shoulder.

I shrug him off. *No, dammit.* It's one thing to lose. It's another thing to fucking *forfeit* on a *technicality.*

I wasn't taught to play like this. This isn't how Kodi Gander runs a team.

Suddenly, the other ref is standing in the center of the turf field, and his voice crackles over the intercom. "Mighty Swallows forfeit by foul play. Victory goes to Spitz Hollow."

My mouth goes dry, all the extra water going straight to my tear ducts. No amount of blinking can keep the hot, angry rivers from rushing down my face. Brian reaches out again to calm me down, but I wave my crutch at him.

"This isn't over, dammit!" I scream at the centerfield ref. "I'm appealing this call to the board!"

"Kodi, no," Lily mumbles beside me. "It was my fault, okay? I'm sorry."

"It wasn't your fault! It was fucking–"

"Easy there, Gander. You might take flight if you keep waving those crutches like that."

My shoulders tense, and I slowly turn at the smug, irritating British drawl behind me. "Go fuck yourself, Zeke."

"You mean like you fucked my ex?"

All the air whooshes from my lungs as the circle around us goes eerily quiet. I feel Brian stiffen behind me, and it's like Zeke's words are a suckerpunch to both of us at once.

As quickly as the post-game chatter disappeared, a swell of whispers rise to fill its absence, mine and Brian's names audible within them. I shake my head at Zeke, furious not just at him, but at myself, because my gut reaction is to shout *"We haven't even done it yet!"*

But that would only make Zeke *more* smug, wouldn't it? It would only widen that cocky smirk across his face, deepening that infuriating dimple in his cheek, and worst of all, convince him that Brian and I aren't actually as serious as everyone thinks we are.

I want so badly to look back at Brian, to see what he's thinking in reaction to all of this, but he's still a foot away from me since I shrugged him off earlier. His comfort, that I threw in his face mere seconds ago, is now the only thing I need to get through this unbearably awkward moment.

His comfort? No, that's not right. He told me earlier that *he* needed *me* when it came to Zeke. I'm supposed to be comforting *him.*

"Did I hit a nerve, Gander?"

"Fuck off, asshole." This time, it's Nick that speaks up, and while Zeke appeared confident when facing off against just me and Brian, he shrinks back a little when the former MMA fighter steps forward and rolls up his sleeve. "Seems like you're a little confused. This cornhole is a family-friendly event. The kind you're talking about doesn't have a place here."

Great. I can't even come up with my own comeback for this asshole.

The Spitz Hollow captain smirks at him. "All is fair in love and war, Duckie."

I want to speak up, talk back, but the anger swirling in my chest is choking any words from coming out. The refs are stalking toward us, the fans are all listening in, and I feel cornered.

Anything I say is just going to get twisted somehow. I can't get myself out of this.

My gut lurches.

I can't get Brian out of it, either.

"Well in case you haven't noticed, this isn't either of those," D'Shawn rumbles. The refs are only feet away from us now.

Just before they break us up, Zeke opens his fuckboi mouth, and his words pierce right through my ribcage.

"I think your *Captain* would disagree."

CHAPTER 43
BRIAN

The loss hits Kodi *hard*. The whole ride home, she's quiet, but not in a *comfortable silence* kind of way. More in a *my entire world just came crashing down around me and no matter what I try I'm always going to fail* kind of way.

Thank God for Nick. If he hadn't been there to help drag the two of us away from Zeke there at the end, I think Kodi would have actually snapped. As for me, I was just...*tired.*

Zeke is exhausting. Has he always been so petty? So manipulative?

I shake my head. Out of the corner of my eye, I steal a glance at Kodi in the passenger seat of her Subaru. Silent tears are streaming down her cheeks in skinny little trails, and I want nothing more than to swipe them away.

But this is more than just losing a game to her. This was her first game on the bench, and it ended in one of the worst possible ways it could: disqualification.

"If I'd have been playing, I'd have been able to hold Lily back."

"You don't know that."

"I do, though. She wouldn't have gotten caught off guard like that if she hadn't been texting and trying to fill my shoes on the field. Her brain was in too many places, and she was stressed out, and then when they insulted her like that, she just–"

"Hey," I interrupt her, "Lily is an adult. She's her own person. Everyone on the team is. None of this is your fault."

"Yeah, tell that to the Nosy Pecker. Tell that to my parents."

Her face goes white as a sheet then and I almost pull over, thinking she's about to be sick. "Kodi??"

"*Fuck.* My *parents.*" She sinks her face into her hands. "We have dinner with them tomorrow. I have to *cook* dinner with Mom all day while you're out golfing with Dad. She's going to talk about this the whole time."

"We can cancel," I suggest. She snorts.

"Yeah, no–that's not an option. You've met my mother."

I swallow a lump in my throat. Sadly, she was right. Still, I tried to lighten the mood. "Aw, come on. The whole time?"

"Yeah." Kodi stares sullenly out the window. "Trust me."

I force out a laugh, but it scrapes my throat on the way out. I know first hand how mad parents can be. Kodi glances at me, concerned.

"So, change the subject."

"After she's been hearing about it all morning from all the Tit Peepers at Church?"

I let out a sigh. "Sounds like you're determined to see this in the worst possible light."

Her jaw drops. I brake at a stoplight as she stutters at me, and I turn to face her. "Seriously, Kodi. The team lost one game. It's not the championship. It's just one silly game, and the other team was basically cheating the whole time. Why would you assume everyone is going to say it's your fault?"

"Because this town *lives* for gossip!" The light turns green, and I force myself to break eye contact. "Are you forgetting how the Pecker pounced on your breakup with Zeke like, the *day* it happened?"

My hands flex on the steering wheel. Truth be told, since the gossip in the paper had shifted to the stories we'd *meant* to end up there–the mostly positive opinions of Kodi and me getting together–I had kinda forgotten about the early stories of them basically outing me to the whole town.

I guess, since it didn't end up affecting my business or the friendships I was forming, I assumed it wasn't a big deal anymore.

They couldn't have overheard Zeke after the game, could they?

"Look," she says after taking in a big breath and letting it out in a *whoosh*, "I want to believe that this town is full of kind, understanding people. But the truth is, everybody's down for some *schadenfreude*. And for some reason, I'm always the one that everybody loves to see suffer. And now I'm dragging you down with me."

"Baby girl–"

"Don't," her voice cracks, and I look over to see her wiping a tear from her eye. "I don't want your pity. It's even worse than theirs."

We spend the rest of the drive to Tuft Swallow in silence.

THE NEXT MORNING, MY ALARM BLARES TO LIFE AT 5:30. THE FIRST thing I do after I silence my phone is check to see if Kodi's texted me.

But there's nothing. I haven't heard a single thing from her since I dropped her off at her place yesterday afternoon.

The bed feels cold in her absence, even with the sunny July morning dawning bright and humid outside my bedroom window. I'd gotten used to her lithe, athletic body curled next to mine in the mornings. To the sound of her cheesy xylophone alarm ringtone waking us at the crack of dawn so she can get to the clinic. Returning to bed after making her coffee and breakfast, just to breathe in her scent for a few more moments before getting myself ready for work.

Then getting so worked up thinking about her that I end up jerking off to the thought of her sucking my cock while I can still smell her in my sheets…

Since that amazing moment between us after she hurt her knee last weekend, we haven't done anything more sexual than kissing and cuddling. She's been focused on her recovery, on work, and the team, and I've tried to be understanding of that. I bought condoms to have on hand, but the last thing I want is to push her. Taking the next step would mean a lot more to her than it would to me, seeing as I would be her first, so I've been letting her set the timeline.

But now she's pulling away completely. I know the loss is hitting her hard. I know the injury is, too, even with me helping her out with daily stretches and PT and adjustments whenever she needs.

My feet hang off the side of the bed, and I fist the sheets beneath me. *I can't help her if she isn't here!*

I throw the blankets off and head to the shower. Her shampoo, body wash, and razor are still lined up along the shelf. I wonder if she has extra at home, or if I should drop them off on my way to the country club.

Country Club. Ugh—just the thought of it makes me cringe. I've never been one for the hoity-toity hob-knobbing that goes on in those kinds of wealthy circles. From the way Kodi talks about her family, I know they're not *rich*-rich, but they certainly seem interested in managing their appearances with a "keeping up with the Joneses" sort of flair. They aren't rich enough to send their daughter off to an out-of-state college without a scholarship, but don't want to seem so poor that they let their membership at the local golf course lapse.

I shake my head. I know those are two different things, with two different price tags. But after seeing how hard Kodi works, and how much she's been let down, it can't help but feel hypocritical to me. Parents are supposed to support their kids, dammit.

Not that mine ever supported me.

I lean against the shower wall, letting the water pummel my neck and shoulders. Suds circle down the drain, and I will the memories of my own broken home life to float away with them.

I haven't even thought about my parents in years. In general, I tried not to think about *parents* at all. I figured if I ignored the idea of golf and dinner with Kodi's parents for long enough, maybe I wouldn't have to worry about it. She hardly talks about them. Maybe she wouldn't really care about the whole "meet the family" thing.

That's bullshit. This is why you've always gone for the emotionally distant ones, Brian. Sure, you might long to be close to someone, and you might pretend to be serious. But really crossing that line? It brings up too many memories.

Clenching my fist, I bang the side of it against the white tile. The slippery *thud* isn't nearly as cathartic as I was hoping for, but the answering throb in my wrist is enough to convince me that I let at least some of that anger out.

Hopefully it'll be enough to release the pressure before I climb into a golf cart with Mr. Gander.

"Brian! Meet the guys!"

Here we go.

Three older men stand around a large golf cart to greet me when I arrive at *Swallow Springs Country Club*. In the middle is the man who just spoke, a well-built older gentleman with pale skin peeking beneath the halo of thinning hair atop his scalp, who I assume to be Kodi's dad. He's about five inches shorter than me, dressed in a salmon-colored polo shirt and khaki shorts, with tall socks pulled over the swell of his calves.

"Nice to meet you, Mr. Gander."

"Please, call me Marty," he answers as I shake his hand. Then he gestures to an elderly man leaning against one of his clubs next to the backseat of the golf cart in an easy stance. "This is Harold Woodcock. His son is Jonah, the police chief! Good man to know!"

I nod my hello to the familiar man and shake his hand. I remember him from the first cornhole game I attended right after I'd moved to town. Though he's older, his clear eyes sparkle in his strong-jawed face. He pushes his arm out from his broad shoulders to give mine a shake, and I notice he's got a surprisingly firm grip for someone his age. "Pleasure, Doc."

Then I turn to the last man, who looks about the same age as Marty, but isn't wearing it nearly as well. His hair has long since receded to an awkward ring of long straggly grays that border the base of his skull, which he hides with a ratty-billed cap that reads *Eagle View Heavy Hitters,* and bears a logo with a baseball and a bat. His polo stretches over his beer belly, and the waistband of his shorts is hidden below the swell. But by far his most disturbing feature is his watery gray eyes, which focus in on me like a wriggling piranha. When he shakes my hand, he squeezes the blood from my fingers as if he's trying to prove a point.

"Lyle Blevins," he barks out. "But most people 'round here call me coach."

"Coach?" I slip my hand from his, leaving the question dangling.

"He used to run the softball team at the high school!" Marty beams. "Lyle and I were on the team together back when we were in school—he loved it so much, he never left!"

The two men laugh, but I sense a little hesitance in "Coach"'s wheeze. My spine tingles in warning.

This is Kodi's old coach?

"So, Brian, Marty tells me you don't have your own clubs," Mr. Woodcock breaks in. "I brought my old set for ya. The woods are a little beat-up, but they still whack a ball just fine."

I smile at him, pretending I understood a word of what he just said. "Oh, great! Thank you."

"Yeah, well, you and I are a bit taller than these two. Chiropractor or not, wouldn't want to wreck your back swingin' with Marty's clubs!"

The three of them laugh, and I grit my teeth in what I hope looks like a grin.

It's one day. For Kodi, I remind myself.

And then I'll never have to play this godforsaken game again.

I'M PREPARING TO TEE UP FOR THE FIRST HOLE WHEN I START regretting my decision. As I pull a random club out of Mr. Woodcock's bag, he eyes me with surprise.

"A six-iron, huh? On the first hole? That's quite the choice!"

"Uh..." A lump forms in my throat. I play off my lack of knowledge. "You know, I'm not familiar with this brand of clubs...what would you recommend?"

"Ah, well this here's a long par three. I'd go for the 3-wood myself."

Marty nods in agreement as he picks out his own club: a big-looking monstrosity that I imagine can pack a wallop.

I observe Kodi's dad walk up to a central spot on the lawn by a white stake and put down a skinny wooden stick with a flared end. Upon that, he places his ball, straightens just behind it, tilts himself back to the left, then twists forward to swing his club (and the ball) off into the far distance.

Woah! What the hell is he launching it for? I screw my jaw tight until I can feel my molars begin to strain with the pressure. As my only experience is mini-golf, I'm a little slow to realize that this game is even more difficult than I imagined. *Nick didn't prepare me for this...*

Sure, he and the girls mentioned that the holes in real golf were bigger than mini golf, but I assumed they meant, like, 100 feet bigger. But this guy just swung that tiny ball so far away I can hardly see the white dot sink into the manicured runway across the course.

"Not bad, there, Marty," Coach hollers. "Remember not to favor your left, though–it's kicking you to the side. You could have made it another twenty yards down the fairway if you weren't fighting that ankle."

Marty lifts the side of his mouth in a practiced tic that could be a smile or a grimace, but it passes before I can suss it out for sure. "Ah, right, right. Why don't you show me how it's done?"

"My pleasure," the watery-eyed man drawls. He selects a slightly smaller club before making a show of selecting a spot near a blue stake on the lawn, about 10 yards behind from where Marty took his swing. He places his tee and ball, takes a good couple of minutes to practice swinging the club back and forth in front of the ball, before backing up half a step, taking in a loud breath, and grunting as he swings for the hills.

Or perhaps I should say trees. As soon as it's clear the trajectory of his ball is heading straight into the wooded borders of the hole beyond the cart track, he lets out a howl.

"Gahhh–that sun! Got right in my eyes as I looked up. Didn't realize the glare from back here!"

Marty nods sympathetically as Harold marches up with his club and ball to the white stake and calls over to me. "Brian, my boy, would you place my tee for me? These knees aren't what they used to be."

"Sure." I jog over, a little surprised at his request. From the way he was walking, he didn't look particularly stiff or uncomfortable.

"The place we're standing is the white zone– gives us a little handicap on the distance. The red zone up ahead is for women golfers or first timers," he hisses at me as I kneel before him, leaning on his club. "When you swing, keep your legs straight and your eyes down until you hit the ball, got it? Don't look where you're swingin', it'll make you go cock-eyed every time. Watch me."

I straighten, step back, and nod when he locks eyes with me to make sure I understand.

"Thank ya, my boy!"

He slowly adjusts himself to the tee as if his knee is acting up, but now I realize he's moving slow so I can index his movements and copy them when it's my turn. His technique is much more relaxed than the other two men in the group: his elbows hanging more naturally and his legs bend only slightly to keep his knees from locking. When he winds back, he keeps his head pointed down, trusting his arm to land where he aims, until–

THWACK!

The wood slams against the little white ball and sends it sailing in a beautiful arc right down the center of the fairway. In fact, it lands just a few yards ahead of Marty's ball, but in a location that looks to be a little easier of a shot to get to the flag marking the hole.

Then again, none of the shots are easy to someone like me. My brain replays the scene of me on my eleventh putt on one of the holes at mini golf, as a little girl whined to her mom about not being able to get ice cream after because the tall man in front of them was taking too long.

I decide to stay in the white zone for my first swing, so as not to draw out the judgment of Coach Blevins right away, taking my borrowed ball and tee out of my pocket and piercing it into the soft dirt in front of my feet. I try to mimic Harold's stance, relaxing my legs and shoulders, practicing swinging a few times until I get used to the weight of the club.

I look out into the course, zeroing in on the orange flag of the first hole, squaring my shoulders and feet so that they're perpendicular to where I'm aiming.

Alright. Keep your head down, and...

THWACK!

As I hit the ball, I flinch–worry consuming me at the last minute that I'd somehow scoop the golf ball directly up into my face at fifty miles an hour. The head of the club kicks to the right, sending my ball even further afield than Coach's, sailing up, up, and away until it sinks beyond the treeline and into oblivion.

I blink, and the four of us stare for a second. Then Coach cackles behind me.

"Well, Harry, I guess you're not getting *that* ball back!"

I sure do hope Kodi's having a better morning than I am.

CHAPTER 44
KODI

It's 11:30am on a Sunday, and instead of getting diner food Doordashed to me in my pajamas, I'm dolled up in a *dress* and strappy blue sandals that Lily had to let me borrow for cooking Sunday dinner with my mother.

Linda Gander doesn't believe in lazing about in pj's. She doesn't believe in wearing anything less formal than a sundress and wedges on the Lord's Day: even if you've just re-injured a chronic knee strain.

I guess I don't look awful. It's not that I hate dressing up, I just hate *being forced* to dress up. In my universe, I want to be ready to tag into a game of flag football at a moment's notice, and skirts don't typically play nice with my active lifestyle. I remember the first time I learned that.

Mom had gotten me a brand new white-and-pink gingham party dress with a flared skirt and a big, pink organza bow that tied around the waist, and shining white patent leather Mary Janes for a Church potluck. She spent over an hour that morning taming my unruly, blonde hair into pigtails and curling them into tight ringlets, hairsprayed so stiff that the ends of the tails whipped around and stabbed my cheeks. She insisted the stylist at the salon cut bangs into my hair the week before, so I had to squint in order for my eyebrows to show.

As soon as Sunday School let out, the boys sprinted out into the open lawn outside the fellowship hall and broke out into a game of kickball. Of course, I ran out to follow them.

It had rained the night before. By the time the final notes of the postlude were ringing through the lobby and the adults spilled out of the sanctuary, all of us kids were covered head-to-toe in mud. The straps of my shoes had ripped beyond repair when the third baseman tripped me halfway through my home run, but I'd managed to slide the rest of the way home in the rain-slicked soil, unraveling my organza ribbon to shreds in my wake.

Mom was furious. I smile at the memory.

She let me wear pants to Church after that.

I have to maneuver the crutches a little to get the doorbell, but it's only a few seconds before Mom throws open the front door and greets me in her immaculate tea-length skirt, cap-sleeved blouse and apron.

"Kodi, honey, there you are! So sorry to hear about the news."

I flinch. "Yeah, the loss is hitting all of us pretty hard."

"Oh, I didn't mean that. I meant…" She trails off, her cheeks going slightly pink as she looks me up and down. "Didn't you see?"

"See what?"

"Today's…" Mom hesitates, and I know that can only mean one thing.

She's an avid follower of all of the town gossip, but she absolutely hates the name of *The Nosy Pecker.* She used to call it "the paper," until Dad got angry with her one day for confusing it with the *actual* newspaper that we got delivered each morning.

I can feel my shoulders tensing, even as I edge my way back into the kitchen/dining room, where I'm certain there will be a fresh copy waiting for me.

Past Lover Revealed: Ex Flexes Past Sex at Big Tech's Sports Complex!

Since Dr. Gosling first arrived here in our storied town, his romantic exploits has been a topic of interest among our eligible men and women. This Pecker was the first to break the news of the Gosling's break from his former nestmate, and the one to break his blossoming romance with our own Kodi Gander of the Tuft Swallow Mighty Swallows. But this is the first we've heard of the good doctor having a kink for Captains...

This little birdie overheard trash talk between Captain Gander and our chief rival Spitz Hollow's team captain Zeke Chopra, that revealed that the new chiropractor's ex is none other than Chopra himself! The sower of our discontent, and the mastermind behind Tuft Swallow's devastating loss yesterday at the new Spitz Hollow Sports Complex!

Perhaps someone should inform our *Captain of his fraternization with the enemy before it is too late, and it distracts her from yet another championship.*

TEARS SPRING TO MY EYES. MOM, OF COURSE, MISREADING ME LIKE she always does, puts an arm around my shoulder.

"Oh honey, I'm so sorry you had to find out like this."

I shrug off her patronizing touch. "That's not what I'm upset about, mom." My hands are shaking as they clutch the incriminating document, forming wrinkles in its thin paper. Of course they'd make a big deal out of this. And of course they'd make it seem like I'm so helpless, so *distracted,* that I wouldn't even be able to figure out the meaning of Zeke's taunts.

Not only am I still the town failure in their eyes, but I'm dragging everyone else down with me. The team. Our record. And worst of all, Brian.

The person I was trying to save from all of this.

"Did you know? About his...*past*?" She hisses the last word, implying a whole host of assumptions and connotations that make my stomach twist. Of course, she'd be appalled and upset by my dating someone outside of typical conventions. She was always the one to bat away any questions of my own sexuality back in high school. Telling anyone at church who gave me the side eye that I was just a late bloomer, that my love of sports was a phase, that one day I'd grow into the lovely woman she knew I was deep inside and settle down with a nice, Christian boy…

"You mean his *present* bisexuality? Yes, Mom. I have known the whole time. Everyone has known. This is not *news*."

She presses her hand to her chest and purses her lips, as if not really accepting any of those words as having meaning. "I meant about his *ex*."

I fidget a little. *Yes,* hovers on the tip of my tongue, wanting to thrust it forward like a dagger out of my mouth. *That was the whole reason we started pretending to date in the first place.*

And in that moment, the true weight of us lying to the town about our relationship presses down on my shoulders like lead. The image of the foundation of *us,* of Brian and me, that I have in my head starts to teeter.

Do I really want to tell my parents how we started dating? The story of how we met? With me convincing him to date me so he didn't instantly get ostracized by the town, so I could use him to heal from my injury?

I'm so embarrassed by it now. Especially because it makes it all feel so *cheap.*

I like Brian, more than I've ever liked anyone, and yet we started this whole relationship as an act. A farce.

And what's more, the initial terms of our agreement–keeping Brian safe from the town gossip mill–were something I couldn't even stick to as a *real* girlfriend. He held up his end of the bargain, but I…

The crutches dig into my armpits, which are still flexing uncomfortably as the paper condenses into a smaller ball in my hands. The frustration and shame must radiate off my body in waves, because Mom tries to console me with a hug.

"Oh, Kodi…"

"Ugh, *stop it!*" I shriek, pushing her and her pity away from me. "Yes, I knew. That's not why I'm upset. I could never be upset with Brian about something like that."

The hurt on Mom's face twists into confusion. "Then what are you crying about?"

"Crying?" I mutter. I swipe at my face, surprised to see that the tears that threatened earlier are now spilling down my cheeks. More anger knocks at the dam inside. "This is too much. I can't do this today."

"Honey, stop–" Mom starts, but I'm already swinging myself out the door.

Right now, I need to be far away from Tuft Swallow.

CHAPTER 45
BRIAN

The poor bird twitches helplessly on the edge of the fairway.

"It's a Black-bellied Plover," Harold notes sadly. "They're hardly ever seen this far inland. What a shame, he's a beautiful bird."

"I'm so sorry." My head hangs in shame.

If I thought this game couldn't be going any worse, I know now not to tempt fate. We've been on the course *five hours* now: cart after cart of golfers have overtaken us as we limp along at my soul-crushingly slow pace. I've had to accept a double-par on every hole just to keep us moving forward, and even that is a more forgiving score than I deserve.

Even worse, Marty and I have hardly spoken the entire time. Whenever I try to ask him about his interests or bring up Kodi, "Coach" Lyle Blevins cuts in with some critique of my form, or launching into an old glory days story about when he led this team or that one to States. He makes more than a few comments about how he can't imagine Kodi falling for someone who is so *"clearly uncoordinated,"* and it's all I can do to keep from snapping Mr. Woodcock's nine iron in half.

The avian casualty is the result of my third attempt at landing a swing in-bounds on the ninth hole, but in my focus on freeing the ball from the woods, I missed the small gray bird nesting twelve feet above us at the edge of the trees. Using the angled wedge-shaped club that Coach Blevins "helpfully" suggested, I pitched the ball high into the branches, and plowed the plover perfectly in the pecs.

Its feathers spill out in a ruffly impact wound that only partially hide the blood spilling onto the edge of the fairway.

Harold removes his hat. "Shall we say a few words?"

"Oh come off it, Woodcock," Coach gruffs. "This is simply natural selection at work." Harold's jaw drops in horror. "You got power, Gosling, but your aim is shit. I can offer you lessons, if you like, to get your swing in better shape—"

Just as he launches into his pitch, a giant hawk dives from the sky and snatches up the plover in its claws. We all jump back. Harold gasps, whipping out his phone to snap a picture of the scavenger, muttering "how majestic!" as Coach jumps back in horror of his "natural selection" at work. I sneak a glance to Marty, who I see with a shudder is drowning himself in his upturned flask.

Great. Just great. So much for making a good impression on the parents.

He lets out a sharp sigh as the alcohol disappears down his throat. "Well, men, whaddya say we call today at nine holes? I don't know if I have another six hours in me."

"It's all in the position of your arms, you see..." Coach continues to prattle on about technique the entire cart ride back to the clubhouse. His arm is twined around my shoulder in a far too familiar gesture, and his lukewarm breath fans across my face in labored puffs between words. He smells chronically dehydrated. Both Harold and Marty are engaged in their own conversation in the front seat, which leaves me hostage to the fetid conversation.

The last thing I want is this hack coaching me on my least

favorite game of all time. Seriously. Who invented golf? What kind of miserable twat would come up with this idea and want to *share* it with others? Were they a sadist?

Marty interrupts Coach's monologue and my internal pity party when we park the cart back at the clubhouse lot. "Well, let's hope Linda and Kodi have at least been cooking up something nice for Sunday dinner, eh, Brian?"

His words remind me of the reason I'm putting up with all of this: *Kodi.*

"Oh, yeah, tell me Marty," Coach leans forward, unfortunately pulling me with him since his arm is still gripped around my shoulder. "How is Kodi doing these days?"

"Oh, You know how she gets after a loss. I haven't spoken to her, but I'm sure she's hittin' the books hard today to see where the game went south."

The tips of my fingers go cold, my heart rate slowing at their conversation. *What does he mean, hitting the books?*

"She's probably not working the team enough. Maybe you oughta talk to her, see if she's running the drills like I—"

"Excuse me." I really don't give a shit if they excuse me or not. "Are you blaming *Kodi* for yesterday's loss?"

"Well, a team is only as good as its star player," Coach huffs. I finally wedge myself free of his sweaty arm. "If she's not pushing them–"

Pressure starts to build in my chest as I get pulled into defending her. "First of all, she's not playing right now. She's injured. And second, no one needs to *push harder*. It's cornhole!"

"Doesn't matter what it is, it's the *game!*" Coach bellows, chuckling a bit. "Son, lemme tell you a thing about–"

"Don't call me son."

My voice is low, and barely above a whisper, but the cart goes deadly quiet. Coach's eyes narrow, and he tilts his head in a gesture that either insinuates he isn't used to being challenged, or he doesn't like to be.

Or both.

When he responds, his voice is toxic. "I think I'd be a little more careful about whose toes you start stepping on when you can't even swing a golf club, boy."

I square my shoulders and swing my leg out of the parked cart. "I think I don't care enough about your opinion to worry about stepping on your toes." I can't even see his reaction to my words, because my view is turning red. Since moving to Tuft Swallow, I've never been so angry at someone, except maybe Logan—but he's practically still a kid. I can understand why *he's* such an idiot.

But this guy? How on earth did a man get to his age and never grow out of that peacock posturing? Never realize how many people he's hurt with it?

It doesn't matter how many people he's hurt. It only matters that he hurt one person.

Kodi.

And he's still trying to hurt her, through his connection to her dad and his misguided opinions.

Marty rises from the driver's seat reluctantly, and Harold follows suit. Neither of them have said a word since I first challenged Coach, and I wonder if maybe I went a step too far. I'm angry, sure, and I'm not going to stand by as someone talks trash about Kodi—but I'm also supposed to be making a good impression on her dad. Is he insulted by what I said?

Harold leans into me as he's getting up, almost as if he needs to borrow my arm for support, and I hear his voice low in my ear.

"'Bout time someone take him down a peg."

He winks at me, before leaning back and stretching his lower back. "Same time next week, Marty? Maybe we can pair up with Jonah and Finn."

I silently thank him for not including me in the foursome, but pay close attention to Marty's response.

"Yeah, yeah, sounds good, Harry," Marty says. He avoids my eyes, instead turning his head right past me. "Coach, let's do lunch at the clubhouse this week?"

"Sure, sure." Coach hasn't taken his hazy eyes off of me. He pins me with his watery glare even as he responds to the man beside him. "It'll be nice to have some time away from the *kids.*"

My fingers curl into fists at my side. *Don't let him get to you. Don't let him get to you.*

As I walk back to my car to follow Marty to the Gander house, anger swirling in my gut, no amount of self-talk can force me away from the truth.

Coach Blevins absolutely got to me.

And even worse, he got to the woman I love. And even with all my skills and education, I don't know if I'll be able to undo all the damage he left behind.

CHAPTER 46
BRIAN

When I pull into the driveway behind Marty's SUV, I don't see Kodi's Subaru anywhere. I was hoping we'd get a chance to clear the air before we get in the house, but I've barely even switched off the ignition when all hell breaks loose.

"Marty! Marty! Kodi's gone!" Linda Gander is frantic as she bursts out of the front door. She keeps blathering a mile a minute as Marty climbs out of the car. "I wanted to go after her but I'd just put the roast in the oven, now she won't pick up her phone and she ran out of here so fast I didn't have time to—"

"What happened?" I'm at her side before I even realize my feet hit the ground. "Where'd she go?"

"I don't know! She got upset after..." As if her brain finally caught up with her mouth, her words trail off as she looks me up and down. She purses her lips, as if unsure if she should say anything more.

"Uhh, Mrs. Gander? If you have any information, I might be able to figure out where she went."

Her eyes narrow slightly, but Marty puts a hand on her shoulder. "We can trust him, Linda."

The few seconds that follow feel like they're happening underwater. My brain moves slowly as I try to parse out why on Earth this man is defending me after everything that went down at golf this morning.

"A moment, Marty?" Linda hisses, sending a brief fake smile my way before turning the two of them and speaking low in her husband's ear. I can't make out all of what she says, but I hear "article" and "trust" in there, along with a word that sounds suspiciously like *gay.*

That's when I start to sink. The slow, painful pressure of trying to impress these people weighs heavier and heavier with every quirk of Linda's eyebrows as she whispers. *This is it,* it all seems to say. *You never actually belonged here, Brian. No one wants you: not your exes, your parents, this town, or your girlfriend.*

"No."

That one word snaps me out of my underwater world and my head breaks through the surface. Marty is shaking his head at Linda and stepping away.

"I don't care what that old gossip rag says, Linda. And you shouldn't either. In fact…" The man takes a deep breath and looks over his shoulder at me, before finally turning his whole body to face the two of them back in my direction. "I wouldn't be surprised if that's what made Kodi run out of here in the first place."

"What? What do you mean?" Linda's hand flies to her chest. "I had to let her know what people were–"

"That's enough, honey."

Marty looks tired. Truly bone-weary, and a flash of guilt shoots through me, remembering how exhausted he seemed out on the golf course.

"I haven't spent a lot of time with you, Brian, but I'll say this. Until today, I've only ever seen one other person stick up for my daughter the way you did, and that's her friend, Lily."

Both Linda and I raise our eyebrows. Of all the things that might have come out of Marty's mouth, that was the last one I expected.

He shakes his head and continues. "When Kodi got back from the hospital, back when she first tore her ACL, that girl wouldn't leave us alone. Knocking on our door as soon as school let out to bring Kodi her homework, locking the two of them in her room to study, and then showing up every weekend once she was off bedrest to get her back out into the world. I don't think even Kodi realizes how much that girl worries about her. And until today, I didn't think she'd ever open up enough to let anyone else care that much about her."

I'm absolutely speechless. Apparently, Linda isn't.

"She's hardly been a good influence on her."

Marty gives her a disbelieving look. "It might be hard for you to understand this, honey, but not all friendships are about keeping up appearances." He takes a pause, and I wonder if there's more to Marty's apparent friendship with Coach than meets the eye. "Brian, it sounds like Kodi left after reading the *Nosy Pecker* article about the loss yesterday. Do you know where she might have run off to?"

I don't. I wrack my brain for any clue as to where she might have gone, but I realize with a horrible jolt as I do that Kodi and I don't know each other nearly as well as I wish we did. We may have opened up about some things with each other, but the normal things that couples learn about each other when they start dating: favorite movies, hang out spots, where they feel safe…I don't know any of that.

But after listening to what Marty just said, I realize I might not have to.

"No, but I know someone who might."

CHAPTER 47
LILY

I roll out of the side of the unfortunately familiar bed, squinting at the bright afternoon light blazing through the broken spot in the blinds. Hating myself for overindulging the night before at the Crowbar, I sit up as quietly as I can and hunt around for my underwear and clothes.

Dressed, I sneak out of the bedroom and grab my purse on the floor by the door, dodging the maid as I do. *Fucking nepo-baby and his gorgeous apartment with his cleaning crew.*

I let my hair fall to cover my face as I run on tiptoes down the brownstone steps, not that it does any good. Not by blocking the sun from my over-sensitive, hungover eyes, or from keeping my identity secret on my walk of shame. Anyone in Tuft Swallow could pick my bright red hair out of a lineup in a second: especially when it's roughed up after a night of casual sex. Lord knows I've slept with enough of the men in this town that they'd recognize my sex hair when they see it.

But it's Sunday afternoon, and most folks are either inside their homes or already invested in some activity that isn't walking around the residential blocks of town. Not to mention, the whole team is probably still nursing hangovers after we all drank away our sorrows last night. No one is interested in showing their face today. Especially me.

I can't believe I slept with him again.

I really need to start picking better coping mechanisms.

As I reach the front steps of the outside of my dingy apartment complex, my phone rings. Which is weird. I always prefer to text, so getting a phone call is super random.

Did he wake up and see I was gone?

Pft. As if.

Then I recognize the number. *Brian?*

"Hello?"

"Hey, Lily—sorry to call on a Sunday."

"That's okay. What's up?"

I hear him inhale sharply, and my shoulders tense. This is weird. Something is wrong.

"Kodi's disappeared."

My heart stops. "What do you mean, *disappeared?*"

"We were going to have dinner with her parents today, and she apparently walked out on her mom a few hours ago. She was upset. Do you know where she could have gone?"

Fuck. Fuck fuck *fuck.*

I knew something like this could happen. She's been getting better about practices, but this recent bout with her injury has been hard on her. And with yesterday's loss…

But why would she run away?

That's dumb. You know why.

I'll be honest: I'm not the biggest fan of Kodi's mom. In fact, for most of high school, I rarely came over to my best friend's house because her mom is such a control freak. She's obsessed with appearances, and never appreciated Kodi's physical talents or love of sports, claiming it made her an "unapproachable tomboy."

Because Kodi was almost always pulling extra hours at school for practices and training, she didn't spend a ton of time at home.

Linda Gander was something of a jailor to Kodi on evenings and weekends, forcing her to study or help her with chores in her limited free time.

When I finally got my driver's license, I would drive over to Kodi's place once or twice a week just to bust her out of there. I knew if I called and asked if she could come to the mall or a movie with me, Mrs. Gander would say no. But if I showed up at her house out of the blue, Mrs. Always-Be-Polite-And-Proper wouldn't turn me away. If she did, the neighbors would talk, and she couldn't have that.

Despite my prodding for Kodi and I to *actually* go to the mall or a movie whenever I'd kidnap her, we rarely did. Neither of us had a ton of pocket money (between sports and classes, neither of us had time for part-time jobs), so we'd usually just go for a drive. Our favorite place to go was the state park on the edge of Hawk-thorne County: far enough from town that people rarely ventured out there except for the ornithological reserve near the welcome center.

There's a hiking trail that borders a creek there, and a path that leads to a secluded lake that we loved to hang out and skip rocks at. We spent hours there the summer before senior year, talking about our future: her accepting a softball scholarship and going to college out of state, and me meeting my future husband at community college and starting a family.

As we got older, we had less and less in common. I knew that she was so ready to leave me behind, go off to school and never see me again. We'd been growing apart for years. But that summer? That summer, we had the lake.

And for a time, that was enough.

After she got injured, I had to hang out with her at her house. I refused to let Mrs. Gander stifle her with visions of sugarplums and debutante balls or whatever the hell kind of plans she envi-sioned for her temporarily-crippled daughter. It might have been *her* dream come true to see her daughter give up softball, but I knew that Kodi was absolutely crushed. She needed a friend then more than ever, and she needed a safe place to mourn the plans she'd had for the future.

By the time she was back in a walking brace, the first place we went was the lake. The trails weren't easy, but her physical trainer told her uneven ground was good for her, so Kodi insisted. For a while, it was part of her rehab.

But then we were in different programs at community college, and she got an office job, and I…

No. I don't need to think about that.

"Lily?" Brian's voice cuts through the memories swirling through my head, and I snap out of the past. "Do you have any idea? Where she might have gone?"

"Yeah," I croak. "I'll drive."

Brian and I meet at the Gander's. Kodi's mom is beside herself, tears streaking her typically immaculate mascara down her cheeks as Mr. Gander wraps a comforting arm around her shoulders. She keeps crying about Kodi's escape being "all her fault," and I can't help a flare of satisfaction in my gut that ignites at her words.

About time you fucking realized it.

But before I can pile on her pity-party, Brian runs up to me. His face is splotchy and red in a way I've never seen before.

Has he been crying?

"You know where she might be?" His voice breaks halfway through his sentence.

I nod hesitantly. "I have an idea."

Let's just hope I know her as well as I think I do. With Kodi, I can never be quite sure.

My insecurity is nibbling at the edges of my brain as Brian and I climb into my Bug. He has to duck a little to climb into it, and his knees are folded up to his chest when he buckles in, which would paint a far funnier picture if we weren't both worried about our girl.

If Kodi would only talk to me like an actual best friend, instead of holding everything in, I wouldn't need to worry that this whole chase is in vain. No matter how hard I try to get her to open up, it's always like pulling teeth to know anything that's in that girl's head.

And I've tried *everything*. Weekly hangouts, boring her to death with endless stories of my dating life, endless text messages...all just to get her to open up. I've tried asking her, pestering her, *boring* her—nothing works.

Or at least, nothing did. Until Brian came to town. And that brick wall she erected around herself slowly began to crumble.

I glance over at him in the passenger's seat as I look both ways at a stop sign, before pulling onto County Route 16. He's tapping his fingers on his knees, leaned forward and half-hugging himself awkwardly in the tight space.

"You know you can lean the seat back, right? Or move the whole seat; the release is underneath."

"Oh." He adjusts it until he almost resembles a normal-sized human. "Thanks."

"Don't mention it. You're taller than my usual passengers."

He quirks an eyebrow at that, but doesn't say anything. "So where are we going?"

I take a deep breath. "Cardinal Lake. Or, at least, the state park welcome center where the trail head is. We've got a bit of a hike to get to the actual lake itself. Not sure how far Kodi would have gotten with her crutches."

"She's gone to a hiking trail? With *her* injuries?" Brian asks, dumfounded.

I shrug. "She's always been one to power through. Does it surprise you?"

"I guess not." He bites his lip. "But I would've hoped she'd learn better by now."

That makes two of us.

A few silent minutes pass, and I turn on the radio to give my fingers a beat to twitch to. It's about a 25-minute drive out to the edge of the county, and Brian and I aren't exactly besties. But I can't help but wonder how he's so oblivious to what's going on with his girlfriend. I've never seen Kodi listen to anyone the way she does with Brian. For once, her hard-headedness seems to have found its match. Or maybe he's impressed her enough with his various *skills* to actually warrant her attention?

Either way, she's actually listening to a doctor's advice for the first time since her post-surgery PT didn't go as well as she'd hoped. She went through the normal six-week recovery routine after she tore her ACL, but got frustrated with the fact that she couldn't run or train the way she used to.

When her doctors told her that might just be her lot in life now, she refused to accept it; she tried every diet and exercise program she could find to bring her full range of motion back, but with the lack of actual direction she started to flounder.

It didn't help that, at the time, she was still living at home, and her dad would come back from golf with some new idea Coach Blevins had come up with to get her back to "tip-top shape" again.

What a hack. I think it was after he'd suggested taking cold, hour-long baths everyday to *"re-invigorate her brown tissue to promote healing"* in her leg that I finally convinced her it was time to move out of her parent's house. It wasn't enough that he had to push her to her breaking point back in high school, but now that she'd graduated, he had to control her through her dad?

Being away from all of that is good for her.

"Hey, I have a question for you," Brian asks, turning down the radio.

"Yeah?"

"Your old softball coach. Was that Lyle Blevins?"

I almost stop the car. *Was he reading my fucking mind?* "Uh, yeah. Why?"

"He was at golf." He makes a face.

I look over at him, and we meet eyes. "Fuck that guy," I say, and Brian's eyes widen for a second, before he lets out a relieved laugh.

"Seriously. My thoughts exactly."

The tension in the car snaps a little bit, and suddenly it feels like I can actually breathe again. I didn't even realize how heavy the air had been until he started laughing. "What the hell is that guy's problem?"

"He likes to convince everyone he knows better than them. And preying on high school kids makes that *real* easy for him." The steering wheel squeaks under my hands, and I realize my knuckles are white from gripping it so hard. I consciously remind myself to relax.

"He's the one that pushed Kodi to the breaking point?" Brian asks.

I nod, not trusting my voice when it comes to that asshole.

"Coach, my shoulder's not feeling great."

Kodi's voice was hesitant in the dugout. We just wrapped up the sixth inning, and we were only up by one. For the first time in twelve years, Eagle View made it to the State Championship, and it was almost entirely on Kodi's shoulders as our star pitcher. No wonder they were sore.

"Maybe you should take a break, Kodi. Have Lindsey sub in for you for the last inning. Kayla and I can totally get a few runs in–"

"Are you outta your damn mind, Cooper?" Coach's grubby, gray eyes were practically bugging out of his head as he snapped at me. I shrank back, and Kodi glared at me for speaking up. But I'd been watching her rolling her shoulder after every pitch for almost a week. I knew she'd been icing it after practices, too, even the extra ones Coach had been forcing her to do three or four times a week since we won County. "You sit out this inning. Drink some water or something. Gander, we need you out there. Forget your shoulder. You throw with your whole damn body, *you hear me? I wanna see you pitch from the tips of your toes!"*

"Yes, sir!" Kodi shouted, letting go of her arm and thrusting it into the middle of the huddle. "We can do this, guys! Let's show 'em!"

I didn't realize at the time how stupid his advice was, if you can even call it advice. Kodi's form got worse and worse throughout the inning, and between every pitch she was shaking out her arm.

How was no one noticing how uncomfortable she was?

She'd been training nonstop for months. She was clearly overworked, tired, and needed a break. But Coach kept shouting at her.

"Come on, Gander! Power through the pain! You're not gonna feel it once we win this thing!"

From the bench, I could see it when she started to compensate for how tired her shoulder was. She started twisting at the waist more first—that got two batters on bases. Then she started to twist at her hips.

"Harder, Gander! What the hell is wrong with you? Speed, Kodi, we've talked about this!"

"Shut up, you fucking slavedriver," I muttered. "She's tired. Give her a break."

But Kodi didn't stop. She shot a pained grin over her shoulder at the dugout, signaled the batter, and then made the most desperate attempt yet.

I watched as she wound up with her whole body, lifting her knee up to her chest for a full second before launching her torso forward and slamming her ankle down into the ground, twisting from her knees to her shoulder as she launched the ball from her hand.

I saw her face scrunch up in a wince when she unwound, favoring her knee as if she strained it, which she obviously did. She threw the next three pitches the same way. And then she ran the whole rest of the inning on it.

But it wasn't until she was up to bat with two outs and no one on the bases that she really fucked it up. She'd practically limped up to home base to swing, Coach still refusing to let me bat for her. As if she still had to prove herself to him. As if she hadn't done enough.

She was so tired. When she swung, it connected—but it didn't go nearly as far into the outfield as she needed. She threw herself into a sprint, rounding second when she should have stayed put, only to miscalculate as the shortstop ran towards her with the ball.

She twisted one more time into a slide, dropping all of her weight onto her strained knee, only for the catcher to ram into her from the side.

"Gaaaaaughghh!!!"

"Out!"

I can still hear the scream.

"He's the one."

Brian shakes his head. Even though Coach is the last person in the world I'd ever want to talk about, I'm relieved to see that Brian can tell just how terrible he is. *And he gathered that from one golf game.*

I wish the rest of the town had been better at seeing through his act. Before he'd ruined Kodi's life. *Although*...I look at Brian a little more closely in my periphery.

Maybe her life isn't ruined after all. Maybe he can help her fix it.

I pull into the Welcome Center parking lot, and Brian and I both get out of the car. Sure enough, Kodi's Subaru is parked in the far corner of the lot by the trail head. My whole body sinks into a sigh of relief.

"She's here!"

Clouds have rolled in while we were driving, and I feel the wind picking up as it licks its cold tendrils across my exposed arms when we jog across the lot. Brian follows my lead as I head down the left-most fork toward the lake trail.

"It's gonna storm," he shouts over the increasing wind. "The ground is going to get slippery, we need to find her!"

"It's just another half mile or so. We'll make it!" Even as I say the words, another gust whips them out of my mouth before I'm sure they can carry back to Brian.

Summer thunderstorms are worse out this way, as elevation changes are more severe. That summer, when this was our place, Kodi and I got caught in a few big storms. We'd hole up in the picnic shelter and play M.A.S.H. or write ridiculous stories in whatever composition notebook we'd thrown in our backpacks while munching on squashed granola bars.

It's there that we find her, right as the storm breaks, rocking back and forth and shivering with her arms wrapped around her good knee on top of one of the picnic tables.

CHAPTER 48
KODI

"You're actually here."

It's the last voice I'm expecting to hear, but I'd know it anywhere. And when I look up, my heart leaps in my chest.

Lily.

And Brian.

I didn't think I wanted anyone around me right now, but if my body's reaction is any indication, I was dead wrong.

"Guys," I sniffle. "It's you. How'd you find me?"

Brian looks at Lily, but she's staring right into my soul. "Dummy. This is where we'd always go to escape your mom." She walks over to the picnic table and parks herself next to me, wrapping one arm around my shoulder. "Luckily, Brian knew to come get me when no one knew where to find you."

I look up at him then, and realize his eyes are glassy and wide. He's taking in me and Lily, standing off to the side as if he doesn't know what to do with himself.

"You can come over," I say, patting the table beside me.

But he shakes his head. "No, that's okay. Lily's the one who found you. You probably need—"

"Ugh!! How are you guys *so bad* at this??"

I jump back a little as Lily shouts out of nowhere. When I give her a look, she rolls her eyes and crosses her arms over her buxom chest. "Seriously, you two. What is actually going on here? First, you kiss out of nowhere at the cornhole game. Then you claim it's all an act. Then *you,*" she points at Brian, "rock this girl's fucking world after I send you to her house to convince her to chill out about cornhole, and now y'all are…what? Still pretending that you don't actually care about each other? Trying to trick Kodi's parents into thinking you're dating when you're not dating but you actually *are* but neither of you want to admit it yet?"

I'm in shock. I don't even realize my mouth is open until I look over at Brian and realize his jaw has dropped, too.

"That's not—" he begins.

"Bull. *Shit.*" Lily stands up on the bench of the picnic table, until she towers over both of us. "Her, I understand. She's never dated before, so I get why *she's* a little confused about the whole thing. But *you?* You're like, in your thirties. We all know *you* have a dating history; the whole fucking town can't stop talking about it!"

My cheeks flush with heat. "I'm so sorry, Brian."

"What? Why?" They both say in unison, and their bewildered expression when they look at each other is almost enough to choke the sob that escapes my throat.

"It's all my fault. You, getting rolled into the small town gossip machine. I thought I was helping you, but in the end, I just dragged you down with me."

"Dragged m–Kodi, what the hell are you talking about?"

"The fucking *Pecker* article!" I can't hold onto the angry energy anymore, and I burst from my seat, forgetting about my knee until I fall back onto the table with a *thud.* I let out a muffled scream of frustration. "I couldn't stop Zeke from opening his big fucking mouth, and someone overheard, and now the whole town knows who your ex was. I couldn't protect you. And after all you've done for me, I…"

My throat closes up, and I can't choke out anymore. But that should be enough. He should understand now.

I broke our deal. The whole reason we started this relationship, whether it's fake or real or whatever it's become, was so I could keep the town from gossiping about him and Zeke. And, I guess, to help him with his business, but now that that's taken off, what good am I to him?

He doesn't need me for his business. I can't protect him from the *Nosy Pecker*. I can't even prevent the gossip from stinging as much by leading the team in a revenge victory against his ex.

I'm a bad girlfriend. I'm worthless.

My head sinks until my forehead rests against my knee, and my shoulders shake as tears finally overtake me. The thunder rolls overhead, indicating that the center of the storm is about to engulf the park.

Mom's probably furious with me. Dad, too, since he usually follows mom's lead. Is there anyone in town left on my good side?

A warm hand covers my back, rubbing gently back and forth, in that perfectly soothing way so lacking in expectation that I know it can only be one person. And in this moment, I hate him for it.

How can he comfort me? Again? After all my failures?

"Huh. Maybe you got this after all."

Lily's the one that breaks the silence as Brian's warmth suffuses into my shoulders. I raise my head to tell her not to leave, but the grin she gives me is so full of hope and sadness, that the words evaporate on my tongue.

"You don't always have to be the one to save everybody, you know. Sometimes, you can let someone else carry you for a bit, girl." She says.

She directs the next few words above my shoulder. "Don't fuck it up, alright? Or else you'll have me to deal with."

"I'll try."

She points with two fingers at her eyes, then points at Brian in a threatening gesture, followed by a wink in my direction. "I assume you can find your own way home."

She turns to leave, but I call out before she's out from under the roof of the shelter. "Thank you, Lily. I–I'm sorry you had to come find me."

She shakes her head, then smiles that same, sad hopeful smile again. "I'm just glad you still need me for something."

CHAPTER 49
BRIAN

Lily's words sink in, and it starts to make sense why Kodi's pulling away from me. *She's always been the one everyone counted on.*

From her coach, to her team, to her boss… Kodi thrives on being capable. On being the best: the star player, the knowledgeable captain, the perfect office manager. But when it comes to leaning on others, or when she just *can't* do something, it kills her.

"She's gonna get drenched," she sniffs, watching her friend jog off towards the parking lot.

"We are too, when we go back." Another peal of thunder rumbles in the distance, and the wind picks up. Kodi's bare shoulders shiver, and I take in her form again.

She's so beautiful.

Today, she's in an adorable little sundress that shows off her freckled, golden skin. I've got a great view of the hint of cleavage that peeks beneath her neckline as I wrap my arms around her from behind and dip my chin to lean against her shoulder. Her lean legs stretch out in front of her, a black brace cutting off the long curve of thigh into calf, and I swallow the lump that rises in my throat as my gaze tracks back up her feminine form.

The mental image of that dress soaking wet, transparent and

plastered to her waist and hips, is enough to make me want to carry her back to the car right now.

But instead, I wrap my arms around her from behind, encouraging her to lean her weight back into me. She's still shaking with sobs, and all I want to do is take all that weight and pressure from her. Like Lily, I want her to need me. To lean on me.

Well, maybe not quite like Lily…

I don't know what today's paper said about me, but I can make an educated guess. Zeke made it obvious enough with his comments yesterday that he and I had dated; of course the town gossips would jump on that.

But surprisingly, I find that I don't care. None of my friends did. Nick, Caleb, and all of the other teammates let that information totally wash over them, as if it didn't even matter.

Because it doesn't, I realize. *They've met the real me. We work together, train together. No friend is going to hold something like that over my head. Just like they don't treat me any different because I'm bi.*

Even Mr. Woodcock didn't treat me poorly at golf this morning, which is surprising, considering he's one of the Tit Peepers. The only people who *did* were the ones who would have been jerks anyway, like Coach.

It's weird how I hadn't even realized how much that meant to me until this moment, how it didn't sink in until I saw how much the article affected Kodi. And then her words from yesterday ring in my head.

"I want to believe that this town is full of kind, understanding people. But the truth is, everybody's down for some schadenfreude. And for some reason, I'm always the one that everybody loves to see suffer."

"Why do you care so much what they think?" I mutter into her skin. She freezes.

"Huh?"

"Lily doesn't care about whether or not you win the championship. Callie, Nick, me—none of us care about that. Why does it matter what anyone else thinks?"

She shrinks even smaller within my hold, and I squeeze her

tighter. She's not going to escape from me this time; I won't let her.

"You don't understand. In this town—"

"You've got plenty of people who appreciate you for exactly how you are," I finish for her. "Whether or not you win some silly championship. You've got patients who trust you to get them in and out of their appointments. You have friends who show up to girls' night every Monday because they want to hang out with you. You've got a boyfriend who thinks you're the strongest woman–" my tongue gets thick in my mouth, and I clear my throat. "It's just…I can't believe how strong you are, baby girl." Her fingers grip my forearms and squeeze. "Why does anyone else matter?"

I feel her mouth open, but no sound comes out. She stays like that for a moment, as the sky darkens and rain begins to pound in earnest against the roof of our little shelter. When she does finally speak, I almost can't hear her over the roar of the storm.

"I don't know." She turns in my hold, catching my gaze with hers, brown eyes glistening with leftover tears. "You really think I'm strong?"

I adjust our position until we're facing each other, and she's in my lap with her legs wrapped around my waist. "I think you're extraordinary."

Her brow furrows.

"And strong," I add. Just to make sure there isn't any confusion about that. "And you know what else?"

"What?"

Her blotchy cheeks radiate heat as I bend my forehead to rest against hers. I let my hands wander the smooth skin of her upper back, walking my fingers down the back laces of her dress until they can cup the glorious curve of her ass in my lap. "I think I'm falling for you."

"Now?" She hiccups.

"Mm-hmm."

"But this is like, my lowest moment!" She tries to pull out of my embrace, but I squeeze her tighter. She struggles for about half a second before she goes limp, then finally rests her arms on my shoulders and sinks into my hold. "I'm pathetic and weak and can't even stand up against your ex for you."

"None of that is even the littlest bit true."

"It *is,*" she argues.

I slap her ass cheek, and she grunts in surprise. "Will you stop lying about the woman I lo-like already?"

We both instantly tense. *Fuck.*

I tried to save it, but the hardness of her body proves she heard me almost say it. The L-word.

You did it again, Brian.

Just call me Mr. Overcommits. It's one thing to say I'm falling for someone–that's sweet and innocent, that's the thing it's *okay* to say after only dating a couple months.

We haven't even been really *dating for most of that.*

"Do you really feel that way about me?"

I sigh. Here it comes. She's going to push me away, like everyone always does whenever they realize I'm a crazy person that falls way too hard, way too fast. I grip her tighter, trying to hold on for just a few more seconds until she breaks away, staring at me.

I didn't even get to be a real partner to her.

And now it's going to be all over.

"Yes, Kodi. I can't help it. I love you. I'm sorry."

She tilts her head until her lips graze across the sensitive skin where my neck meets my shoulder. I hold back a shiver. "Why are you sorry?"

"Cause now you know the truth. *You're* not the weak one here, Kodi, I am. I always fall in love too fast, and it scares everyone away."

An agonizing moment stretches between us as I try to soak up the last bit of heat from her body while she's letting me. She's going to pull away any second. In three, two, one…

"I'm not scared."

Lightning flashes bright enough to illuminate the whole forest around us, and the clap of thunder that follows explodes so loudly we jolt apart, staring into each other's eyes. The wind blows a stream of cold rain into the shelter, spraying us with its fury. Goosebumps erupt over both of our exposed flesh, and I watch the hair on her arms rise as she reaches towards me.

"I've never loved someone before," she admits. "Is it–does it actually feel like butterflies in your stomach whenever you see the person? Or when they hold you, is it like—like you could just melt into their arms and the world wouldn't matter?"

All the air leaves my lungs. "Y-yeah, sometimes."

"And when their fingers brush against your skin…" she lifts my wrist and returns it to the back of her waist, where the strings criss-cross over the hint of bare spine just above the skirt of her dress. My nails graze the exposed sin, and she shudders in a way that has nothing to do with the wind. "Does it make your stomach, and your insides, *pull* almost?"

The familiar tug she's describing throbs below my belt, and I nod. "Technically, that can just be lust, I suppose…" Now I'm just word vomiting nervously, as her fingers start to play across my ribcage the way mine are tickling at her back.

She shakes her head. "It's different. I know what horny is. I don't feel that *here.*" She splays her hand across my lower stomach, so fucking close to my growing erection I feel heat spread through me like wildfire. "Or here," she adds, pushing her other hand onto my sternum until I fall backwards, dragging her with me until she's straddling me on the picnic table.

"I have condoms now," I blurt out *like an idiot.*

"You know I'm on the pill."

"I know, but you'd said you weren't ready, and I was waiting for you to broach the topic, and—"

"I'm ready now."

"What's that?" My voice comes out half-strangled, as my dick is now pushing so hard against my zipper I feel like I'm about to explode. Kodi Gander is sitting on my torso, her injured leg stretched above me to the side of my head, her arms rubbing up and down my chest like she's kneading dough. I can feel her ass teasing at the head of my straining cock.

Her eyes sparkle, all traces of tears gone. "I want you. *All* of you. I'm ready now."

I squeeze my eyes shut. "Baby girl, I don't want you to do this just so I don't feel bad about saying I lo–"

Her lips crash into mine, and she's pushing my mouth open with her tongue. Claiming me, devouring my mouth in a way I've never felt before. *Oof—and there's the lust.* The tugging in my khakis becomes almost unbearable as she sweeps the inside of my mouth, tangling me in her hungry kiss like a woman starved.

Another gust of wind coats us in a sheen of rain, and she redoubles her efforts, pressing her entire body against mine and grinding down onto my lap like no virgin I've ever been with before. Even with one leg injured, she swivels her hips like a pro, and I break away from her lips on a groan.

"I'm not doing this because I pity you," she pants. "I don't pity you. I would never do that to you."

We're both breathing heavy. "Then why–"

"I want to know what it feels like to have the *man I love* inside me."

CHAPTER 50
KODI

His mouth drops open, and before he can stop me, I thrust my tongue back down his throat.

God he's delicious. I can't stop tasting him.

Heat has been building in my core ever since he wrapped his arms around me. At first, I tried to ignore it. I was so mad at my mom, at the town, at myself—I just wanted to run away from all of it. And at first, I thought Brian comforting me wouldn't be any different from the rest of them. The hollow sympathy I'd become all too familiar with, only to read what people really thought in the *Nosy Pecker* or hear it from mom and her friends at Church.

But then he showed up here, with Lily, and something inside me snapped.

Lily. I've been so awful to her. She's a better friend to me than I ever realized, remembering and understanding things about me that I've never given her credit for. She led Brian here, knowing I needed him even before I did. A chuckle rises in my throat as I think about her yelling at us, and how bad we are at admitting we like each other.

Ha, well look at me now, Lily.

Well, not *now,* I guess. That can wait. Especially since I'm about to rip off my clothes and let this man fuck me senseless.

Later, I'll tell her all about it.

I won't even try to get out of it this time.

"What's so funny?" Brian gasps under me when we pull apart for air.

"Just thinking about how happy Lily is going to be when I tell her all about how I lost my virginity."

His face blushes scarlet. "You're going to tell her everything?"

I straighten, and start to untie the strings at my back. "Yeah. Tomorrow is girls' night, after all."

I squeak as Brian pushes himself up underneath me, flipping us so I'm laid out on my back on the picnic table. The wind picks up, sending a cold spray of water and air against my flushed skin. I shiver beneath him.

And then he stands and turns to the center of the shelter.

"Where are you going?"

"Well, if you're going to tell all your friends about this, I need to make sure I do it right." He walks across the cozy space to the giant stone mantle against the enclosed wall of the shelter, and he starts bending like he's gathering supplies.

"What are you…?" I prop myself up on my elbows to get a better look, and see that he's taking inventory of a stack of firewood next to the open grate nestled inside the stone.

"Ah, here we go," he mutters, finding a box of matches in a wooden chest beside the fireplace.

I observe in awe as he sweeps the burned concrete floor in front of it, then stacks some abandoned logs and kindling in the firebox and gets it to catch. Within minutes, a happy fire is crackling in the shelter, and he's pulling the grate closed to protect it from the rain blowing in the open sides.

"Were you a boy scout or something?"

He smiles. "Would've gotten Eagle Scout, if–" his face darkens briefly, and he shakes his head. "Yeah. I was."

He crosses the room and pulls my ass to the edge of the table, situating himself between my legs. He starts in to kiss me, but I put my hands on his chest, holding him off.

"If what?" He tries to brush off the question, but I shake my head at him. "Nope. None of that. We're in this now. I want us to be honest with each other."

He sighs, but I hold firm until he relents.

"If they hadn't kicked me out of Scouts."

"What?" I pull away in shock. "You got kicked out?"

"It's not as bad as it sounds. I was eighteen, so really the only thing left was my Eagle project..." he trails off. "It doesn't matter. I ended up getting kicked out because they found out I had a crush on one of the other guys. He and I were in Tae Kwon Do together, and I was out to some of my friends there. After I confessed to him, he told the Scouts. At the time, the organization didn't allow queer people."

"Are you fucking kidding me?" I can't believe it. "When was this? The eighties?"

"Kodi, I'm thirty-three. This was only fifteen years ago."

"Boy Scouts didn't allow gay people until *2010??*"

He shrugs. "Shit, my parents didn't even allow gay people."

I blink at him. "Hold up. Your parents kicked you out, too?"

He nods, a shadow passing over his face. My mouth drops open.

"I mean, I turned out okay," he says.

"Brian, that's awful!"

"Yeah, but like. I'm good. I mean..." He shakes his head then, and blinks at me. "Weren't we going to have sex?"

"Yeah, but like, are you okay? I don't want–" This time, he's the one that cuts me off as he wraps me up in his arms and dips his head, taking the words right out of my mouth. I sink into his perfect lips, letting him work my head into a beautiful, spinning kaleidoscope of butterflies and tingly sensations.

He breaks off, pulling me in closer to his warm body and enveloping me in his strong embrace. "I don't want to waste my breath on anyone who doesn't accept or love me for who I am anymore. Haven't we both spent too much time doing that already?"

I hug him back, letting the sentiment of his words sink into my whole being.

Obviously, we're going to talk more about this later. Someday.

Now that we're done pretending we don't like each other, we have all the time in the world to learn all about each other's pasts.

But for now, he's right. This moment doesn't have anything to do with the people who've hurt us. This moment is about two people who love and accept each other for who they are, scars and all.

And it might be too soon to say it, but the feeling's been welling in my chest for the past week. I've just been too afraid of my own shortcomings to admit it. But we both just laid bare so much of our inner worlds to each other, and we're still here.

So I take a deep breath in, inhaling the scent of his warm, baking spice smell and lingering woodsmoke, and I finally say the words.

"I love you, Brian."

His eyes glow turquoise, and he doesn't even hesitate. "I love you too, baby girl."

This time when his lips brush against mine, they're soft and gentle. Almost feather-like, as they caress first my top and then my bottom lip, nipping lightly as I open my mouth to him. He moves in with his whole body, wrapping me up until I feel like I'm a love letter in the envelope of his strong arms. He scoops me up, cradling my body and laying it down in front of the warm smooth floor in front of the fireplace, protected from the storm still raging outside.

He kneels between my legs, peeling off his shirt and revealing his gorgeous chest. The subtle indentations of his musculature flicker in the firelight, only to be lit in stark contrast as a matrix of lightning flashes across the sky beyond us.

His voice rumbles low beneath the thunder as he leans in and whispers, "I'm going to make you even wetter than the storm."

Heat pools between my legs, and I worry that my panties

might already be soaked just from his words. That, and the closeness of his body.

He curls his fingers into the hem of my dress and creeps it up my thighs, and I revel in the stark contrast between the damp coolness of the fabric and the warm air radiating from the fire.

This is going to make one helluva "how I lost my virginity" story...

But any and all thoughts of storytelling completely leave my head when Brian sinks his head between my thighs. He's disappeared under my skirt, and I can only imagine how delicious he looks right now as I *feel* his scruff brush against the sensitive skin of my lower stomach. My eyes flutter closed and my head tilts back as he catches the waistband of my lacey panties between his teeth, and I feel my lower lips slicken with arousal.

Oh God, that was a promise, wasn't it?

The drag of his facial hair through my folds, down the apex of my thighs, crawling all the way to my knees, calves, ankles, before he finally unhooks the thin fabric from my feet and rises to face me leaves me writhing. I clench my thighs together, rubbing the surprisingly slick skin between my legs, as I watch him slowly lift his hand, crinkle my panties in his fist, raise them to his nose, and inhale deeply.

Fuuuu-uck.

His other hand returns to my thighs, tracing the smooth skin up and pushing my skirt the rest of the way above my hips. Despite the glow of the fire, my core is so hot right now the comparative cool of the smooth floor sends a shiver up my spine when it makes contact with my bare ass.

He grins.

Shucking his pants down his trim waist and over his hips, he steps out of them, before rubbing his growing erection with my underwear.

"You see this, baby girl?" He croons, and I swear another spurt of wetness dribbles between my thighs. "This is how I play with myself when I'm thinking of you."

"With my panties?" I tease, knowing damn well I've never left my clothes at his house. But the answering glint in his eyes makes my stomach flutter. "Wait. You don't—"

"I stole a pair," he grunts, moving his free hand up and around my hips, then sinking a finger into my soaking wet heat. I gasp. "When I picked out your outfit last week. I stole your panties. And I've been using them to stroke my cock every day since then."

His deft fingers roll back and forth through my folds, working me up into a tizzy. I can barely form words it feels so good, but he isn't making sense. "B-but, I've been spending the night. You haven't...*ah*..."

"I haven't jerked off in front of you, no. But in the mornings, when I can still smell you on my sheets..." He moans, pumping inside his hand as his thumb finds my clit. A zip of pleasure makes my hips jerk forward, and he spreads his other fingers wide under me to grip my ass as he continues to work my pleasure with one hand, his other clutched around his cock and my panties.

I don't want to admit how fucking hot that is. He's been wanting to fuck me this whole week while I've been staying with him? So much, that he's had to jerk off every morning after I left?

His two middle fingers wander forward and find the entrance of my pussy, slick and pulsing. I whimper as his thumb moves in faster, lighter circles across my clit, pulling sounds from me involuntarily. Pleasure pulses in my core with every move of his hand, and it begins to build deep in my belly.

"What do you imagine?" I breathe, staring him down as he fists himself. "Doing to me? With my panties around your cock?"

His whole body shudders, and I watch him clench his jaw so tight I swear I can hear his molars crack. He lets go of his cock as if it's burned him, my panties flying out of his hand and landing somewhere in the mess of my hair above my head. His crystal eyes flash molten as they bore into mine, and his fingers finally sink into my channel.

Deep, deeper than I thought physically possible. My back

arches, which makes the outstanding pressure feel like it's pressing even further into my center, until a tightness in my stomach coils and clenches so deliciously that I squeak from the pleasure. He curls his fingers, and the noises coming out of my throat settle into a hoarse groan. I arch further, my arms seeking, reaching forward to grab onto him, needing something to anchor me before I snap and soar off into oblivion.

"You can't say things like that to me, baby girl. Not before I've had my fill of you. You're not allowed to make me cum until you've screamed my name."

"Bri–*aaahh*!"

"Doesn't count." He smirks at my delicious torment. "How many times do you think I can make you say it before you're begging for my cock? Will you be able to form words at all?"

He curls his fingers again, rubbing that spot inside me while his thumb still circles my clit, and my vision goes blurry.

"I want your–"

He covers my body with his, devouring my lips to keep me from finishing my plea. His fingers move faster, harder, and I moan and scream into his mouth, shaking and jerking and begging without words. My core is wound tighter than a mouse trap, and I just know if I had his cock inside me my body would explode.

I want it.

I *want* it.

I need it.

"Fuck!" I scream, breaking off his unyielding kiss as my head tosses back in ecstasy, the tension finally cresting as wave after wave of pleasure erupt from his fingers, through my core, and up and down my whole body. "Brian! I'm coming!"

"That's one." He kisses me again, then sinks to his knees and hikes my ass up until it's practically sitting on his chest. "Now I want to taste you."

"Brian!" I don't even recognize my voice, and I thank God that

the pounding rain outside the shelter is drowning out my cries of pleasure as the man digs into my soaking pussy.

He tosses my legs over his shoulders, burying his face between my thighs with my ass beneath his chin. I'm feeling so good that I completely forget about my injury until I see him cradle my knee brace gently behind his neck before lowering his hands to support my lower back.

Then he's like an animal. Any signs of the gentle, sweet man disappear as he dips his tongue between my folds and shakes his head greedily, working his face and chin between my thighs until his cheeks are soaked with my juices. I'm still shaking from my first orgasm, and here he is licking and sucking and panting me into another.

My clit is on fire as his tongue swirls around it, drawing more and more sounds from me I didn't know I was capable of making. My dress is falling further up my body with every jerk of my spine, until the fabric pools across my throat and my entire body is spread out before him. I'm sure I shout his name at least a dozen times, but I lose track as my head spins higher and higher, heady with the pressure building once again in my body. Only now, my walls are clenching around nothing, and it makes it feel like a tease.

An incredible, earth-shaking tease, that rattles my very soul as it finally breaks. He moves one hand to reach up and paw at my breasts, and something inside me erupts. Pleasure zings from my nipple to my clit to my toes, sending electricity up my spine and making me shiver all over again. I hear Brian hum excitedly as I feel wetness gush down my thighs, coating my over-sensitive places. He continues to lick and suck before finally pressing soft kisses to my inner thighs and the outer edges of my mound as I slowly come down, my thighs tensing and relaxing on top of his shoulders.

Tremors still zip through my body, both warm and cold as the fire ebbs a bit. I have no idea how long he was devouring me, it could have been minutes or hours. It's still daylight outside despite the darkness of the storm. But the wind isn't as extreme as it was before and the intensity of the rain has lessened slightly; only a soft, steady drum patters against the roof.

My throat is raw. I flutter my eyes open, vision blurry and head fuzzy from the relentless orgasms. I manage to lift my arms, which feel like they weigh about a thousand pounds, up to the amazing man who just made me come harder than I ever have.

He sinks into my arms, leaning on his elbows above me and weaving his fingers into my loose hair. He massages my scalp, and I moan again in pleasure.

"How many times did I say your name?" I croak.

He chuckles. "Thirty eight."

I'm amazed he actually counted them all. "And did I beg?"

"Oh yeah." He leans in and presses his lips to mine, and I can taste myself on him. Salty and tangy. The sweetness of his kiss rounds out the flavor cocktail until it soothes the rawness of my throat, and I sigh into his mouth.

"Give it to me, Brian."

"Baby girl…" he hesitates, and I weave one of my hands in between us, until I'm stroking his still-firm cock. His breath catches, and even though I've already come twice, that sound stirs the lust in my belly all over again.

Now *I'm* the animal. With his hard length in my hand, and his labored breath fanning my face, I know he wants me as much as I want him. It makes me feel sexy, bold. I lift my mouth to his ear.

"Don't you want to know how my tight, virgin pussy feels squeezing around this cock?" I feel it twitch inside my grasp as the dirty words leave my mouth, and he groans. And then I go in for the kill. "Because I want to know how it feels to have you fill me up, Brian. I need you."

And I do. I can admit it now.

I need him. In my life, in my bed—right here, in front of the fireplace. Because I love him.

He curls his hand around my face, and presses a kiss to my forehead, then my nose, and then my lips again.

"That's all I need to hear, baby girl."

CHAPTER 51
BRIAN

It almost feels too good to be true, that the person I find so incredible: so driven and desirable and *amazing,* wants me back. Wants me inside her.

I shudder at the anticipation of feeling those soaking wet walls that taste like musk and honey clenching around my cock. I've wanted her for weeks. But I've been waiting for her to be ready. I've been known to jump in headfirst into new relationships, and sex can always make things seem like they're moving faster than they are. I don't think I've ever waited until *after* saying I love you before doing the deed.

I *do* tend to say it right after. Or during. It can just kind of... come out prematurely. No pun intended.

But this time, I don't have to be afraid of that. I love this woman. And she knows it.

So we both have family issues. We have past hurts and traumas that we need to work through. All of that can happen with therapy and time. But right now?

Right now, I have a strong, smart, beautiful woman in front of me who wants me inside of her, and I would be an idiot not to oblige.

I've been lying beside her, leaning on an elbow as I look across at her perfect form in the firelight. If I could make my brain a camera, and capture this still: the bronze tan of her arms and legs transitioning to the pale, creamy skin of her torso and breasts. Freckles dot her shoulders and decolletage, and a few dip below her collarbones.

I trace the melanin constellations, letting my fingers graze from her wrists, to her triceps, up and around until my fingertips press into the forgiving flesh of her glorious chest.

The human form is so beautiful. I've always admired athletes and their musculature. Not even in a sexual way necessarily, but professionally, getting to work on someone whose body is a textbook of anatomy is alway an exciting prospect. I've dated many fit men, and a few women, but looking at Kodi's body is something else entirely.

She's strong from years of training. Her arms in particular are beautifully defined, and I can't help but admire the way the light shifts across her triceps as goosebumps erupt across them at my touch. I follow the lines of her body as biceps give way to deltoids, rippling below pecs, and down to...

Her nipples pebble under my gaze, and as I circle one with my thumb she mewls in pleasure. I feel an answering tug deep in my stomach, and feel the tension in my cock reach a fever pitch. Before I'm even inside her.

Fuck. Am I even going to last?

I've already almost lost it once tonight. I can't help it. She's a work of art.

Reluctantly, I leave the kneading of her breasts and reach for the condom in my wallet. Once I shove my wrinkled pants away and slide back to her, my hands glide to the dip of her waist and up the slender curve of her hips. This part of her feels familiar, as this is where I've been digging my fingers for the past hour. She parts her thighs in answer.

"Please, Brian," she moans. And I nod. I rip open the foil packet and slowly roll the condom down my straining shaft. Her eyes flash as she watches me.

Before I settle into position, I post above her and capture her lips with mine. She's still hungry, sucking on my tongue as if she can pull me inside her with the force of her lips alone. We break apart, and I'm already breathing heavy again.

"You're so beautiful, baby girl." I know she loves it when I call her that, and the blush that blooms across her cheeks confirms it.

I sink between her legs and stroke the flushed head of my cock up and down her dripping folds.

"Yes," she moans. *"God,* give it to me. I have to know–I want–"

As slowly as I can bear to, I slide home.

I expect resistance, but after two orgasms she is slick and ready for me. She lets out a low groan that rises in pitch and breathiness as I sheath myself fully, and the sound is positively *sinful.*

"Yes!" She shouts when I bottom out inside her, following the tight path my fingers and tongue mapped for me earlier.

She feels incredible. My balls instantly tighten, and I have to freeze to catch my breath for a moment as we accommodate to each other. Her arms snake their way around my waist and she hooks her good leg behind my hips, pulling me closer.

"Easy, baby girl. You feel too good," I grit out. *Fuck,* it's been years since I've been with a woman like this, and the pressure and sensation of Kodi's pussy is so different from what I'm used to. She's squeezing me from base to head, and I swear I can feel every flutter of her velvet walls like a heavenly vise.

"I need more, Brian," she breathes in my ear. "Please. Fuck me. *Please."*

Her begging only makes me twitch harder inside her. But my baby girl needs me to move, needs me to give her everything.

So I slowly pull out, dragging my cock against those hot, slick walls, until only the very tip of me is still inside her. As I do, I look deep into her amber eyes, seeing the desperate plea glowing within them. Her plush lips, red and shiny from all our kisses, open tantalizingly on a moan, and I pause for the slightest second just to take in the perfect picture she makes as she gets lost in her own pleasure.

And then I slam back in.

"Fuck!" She cries out, and I'm right there with her. I piston my hips out and in again and again, cherishing the way her core splits open around me every time.

My blood is pounding in my ears, so much so that I can hardly hear her fevered cries as I pound into her. It's *so* good, so *perfect,* and I feel myself edging closer and closer to ecstasy with every stroke.

Her body tenses, and my whole body shudders as she squeezes around me. She's meeting me now, pushing her hips up to crash into mine, driving me even deeper inside her precious heat. *Fuck,* it's incredible. I shift above her, cushioning the back of her head with my hand as both of our movements become more and more erratic. Her hair tangles in my fingers, her neck slender and perfect in the palm of my hand as I bury my face into that sweet, soft curve above her collarbone.

I feel her approaching her release when the movements of her hips start to lose their rhythm. My core tenses like a rubber band as her inner walls flutter over my cock, and I struggle to keep hold of myself.

I'm going to lose it. It's too good. I can't let myself come until—

"Brian!" she gasps in my ear, and somehow it breaks through the sounds of blood rushing and rain falling and the lewd smacks of our bodies against each other. "I'm gonna–"

"Me too, baby girl," I groan, and that's when I pull back and see her eyelashes flutter over her flushed cheeks, her eyes rolling back into her head. Then I *feel* her.

That all-encompassing squeeze that had driven me crazy with lust when it had clenched down around my fingers, now grips my cock in a chokehold. I buck my hips forward once, twice, until the pressure building inside finally breaks in a euphoric burst of pleasure, and I spill myself inside her.

"Fuck, baby girl," I grunt out with my release. "You're so. *Perfect.* So. *Fucking. Good."*

Words have left her. Her full lips part on a soundless scream, and I collapse on top of her, holding myself up just enough to allow her breathing room. The rest of me wraps around her, my head sinking to the crook of her sweaty neck, my cock softening slowly inside her perfect pussy, still twitching in tandem with the aftershocks skittering through her body.

We lay like that in a timeless haze, until I finally extricate myself enough to lean on my side next to her and pull the condom off. With great effort, she turns to face me, landing a slender hand on my hip and scooching closer until our legs touch.

"Thank you," she whispers.

"For what?" I chuckle, looking at her with disbelieving eyes. "You know that was just as amazing for me, right? As I hope it was for you?"

"Oh my God, it was incredible." A tired smile lights up her face, and a softer warmth and tingles bloom in my stomach at the sight. She was already beautiful, but with joy lighting her eyes...

She's radiant.

I drape my arm over her and press her pliant body flush against mine. "You're so beautiful." I murmur the words into her hair, which smells like strawberries and woodsmoke. "I love you."

I've trained myself to be content when, after sex, I spill out my soul and my feelings only to be met with silence. I'm used to these moments being quiet. Just comfortable. With me bearing all my emotional vulnerability and my partner simply snuggling in response.

So when Kodi presses a kiss to the hollow of my chest and whispers back, I'm not prepared for the swell of happiness and pride that fills me to my core.

"I love you too."

CHAPTER 52
KODI

"We're not going back to your parents'. You have twigs in your hair."

I reach up into the rat's nest of tangles that I somehow managed to coral into an elastic after Brian and I rinsed off our post-coital sweat in the rain. One nice thing about the torrential summer thunderstorm was that we had the whole state park to ourselves. It didn't matter that we were naked.

We'd attempted to air dry ourselves by the fire, but the meager logs that had been left by the last set of campers who'd passed through had long since burnt to ash by the time we'd gotten ourselves clean and gathered up our shirts, dresses, and pants from every corner of the picnic shelter. So we'd still been damp when we'd covered back up with all of our clothes.

Except for my underwear. Brian claimed it had fallen into the fireplace and burned away. But the mischievous gleam in his eyes as he said it had me suspecting he'd once again stolen them from me. A shiver passes through me that has little to do with the cool evening breeze that drifts across the trail on our slow walk back to the car.

I hardly want to admit it, but Lily was right. Sex really *is* all it's cracked up to be.

"You said that mom and dad were worried about me. We should check in."

"So *call,*" he argues. "It's getting late, we both need a real shower, and I'm not quite ready to give up having you all to myself." He lightly touches his hand to the base of my spine, careful to make space for my crutches.

"Mom always keeps me on the phone for *hours.*" I whine, but my heart isn't in it. He's right. I'm pretty pooped from the impromptu afternoon hike, the abundance of orgasms, and losing my virginity. Dinner with my parents after all of that would require physical and emotional energy I just don't have, especially after this roller coaster of a day.

"I'll keep you on task. If you want to end the conversation early, hand the phone to me. I'm pretty sure your mom won't want to keep talking *then.*"

Is his voice a little bitter when he says that? It's hard to tell if his humor is genuine after learning about his own fraught past with his parents.

Sure, my relationship with my mom isn't perfect. I moved out as soon as I could afford it just to get out from under her thumb. But there's a big difference between *choosing* to move out of your childhood home and not being allowed to return.

I must be making a face, because Brian chuckles. "Meaning, I don't think I'm her favorite person at the moment. But don't worry. Your dad and I seemed to part on good enough terms."

"Oh shit!" I stop, slamming my palm to my forehead. "I totally forgot. How was golf?"

He grimaces. "We don't need to talk about that."

I eye him curiously. I know he's bad at golf, but it sounds like there's more to that story than he's letting on. "But you said you and Dad got along?"

"Eventually."

Nebulous. I decide not to pry and take the win. After all, we have all the time in the world to get to know each other better.

And the last thing I want is to ruin what little goodwill he has with my parents by overanalyzing it with him now.

As we reach the stone steps at the edge of the trail, I pause on my crutches. "Hey."

He turns around, reaching out a hand to support me. Without me even having to ask. I normally would shy away from someone offering me a hand walking up the stairs, but this time it's different. Firstly, because it's Brian, and he's already seen me at my most vulnerable, so refusing help at this point would be futile. I don't need to prove anything to him. He's seen me broken, and still thinks I'm strong.

I almost even believe him.

"I hope, someday, you *do* get along with my parents. That even with all you've been through, you might be able to feel like you have a family here. Well, not *here,* here..." I start to ramble. "I mean, like, in Tuft Swallow. With your business and friends and–"

I'm cut off with a *whoosh* as Brian grabs my crutches and scoops me up into his arms in one quick movement. *How–?* And then he's kissing me right on the lips, and I melt without asking any more questions.

"Oh, baby girl. I already do. More than I ever have before."

My heart glows as he carries me all the way to my car.

CHAPTER 53
KODI

The next few weeks fly by in a blur of physical therapy, work, cornhole, and amazing sex. I may have been a late bloomer when it comes to the horizontal hokey-pokey, but Brian's helping me catch up on everything I've missed. With the schedule we're keeping, it's amazing we have time to fit in anything else.

My knee is getting stronger again, barely; its recovery is too slow for my liking. He says I'm doing great, though, always reminding me that 'harder or faster isn't better—*better* is better.'

Luckily for me, I've got the best guy I possibly could on my recovery team.

I'm reminded of how great he is when I wake up to his arms wrapped around me, fingers massaging my breast and plucking at the hardening nipples. I let out a little hum of pleasure and sink my little spoon ass into his thickening big-spoon groin.

He moans. I smirk. *Still got it.*

Part of me is terrified that I'm going to wake up one morning and it will all have been a dream. I mean, I'm Kodi Gander: sexless–*well, not anymore*–Ice Queen of Tuft Swallow, and he's...the sweetest, smartest, sexiest, most amazing guy on the planet.

And he's my *boyfriend.* For real this time.

"I need to get ready for *work,*" I whine, but my heart's not really in it. He seems to pick up on my insincerity, as he only grinds himself temptingly against the cleft of my ass.

"This is working pretty well for me."

I smack his hand (playfully) and throw the sheets off our bodies. As I move to stand, he bolts upright. "Careful! Make sure you're getting up evenly on both feet, balancing–"

"My weight evenly across my hips and my ankles, I *know.*" I roll my eyes. "I got it Dr. Handsy, okay? We've been working on my rehab for four weeks now. I even survived the last match against Robin Springs without so much as a tweak."

Which had been a hell of a victory. The last three weekends had been win after win for us, and now that I'm back on the field I'm ready for revenge against Spitz Hollow in the championship game.

"Doesn't mean you're going to be jumping into action anytime soon. You're doing great. Don't ruin it."

"The only thing that would ruin it is seeing Zeke's smug face if Spitz Hollow beats us this weekend."

His hand reaches out and his fingers curl into the curve of my hip. "Don't even think about that man. Trust me. He isn't worth you getting hurt over."

"Speaking from experience?" I look over my shoulder at him. The briefest bit of sadness flits across his face before he meets my eyes.

He scoots closer and presses a kiss to my shoulder. "I got off easy, getting over my broken heart. You, on the other hand, have a history of repeat injuries. Don't let your competitive spirit get the better of you."

"Yes, Mom." I *carefully* stand and throw back the blackout curtains, letting in the late August sunshine. Brian flinches from the light, but I bask in it.

Waking up on the second floor means I can stand naked in front of the window at six am without fear of the morning joggers seeing me. I could get used to this being my new everyday.

Brian kisses me goodbye an hour later, and I walk to work with just my brace and no more horrid crutches, optimistic for once about the week ahead. Today, Dr. Cratchet is interviewing candidates for our new nurse position, and I'm secretly hoping he recommends the Nurse Practitioner I selected to the board for hire. While he doesn't have final say on whoever we bring on, what with the Clinic being a non-profit entity, the board will likely go with his number one pick. They've always done whatever he says in the past: hence why it's taken this long for me to get any actual help in the office.

Just as I gather my things to clock out and meet Brian at the Easy Swallow for lunch, the sleigh bells above the front door jingle a new arrival.

"Hello?" A tall woman with wavy, brown hair and a round face comes through the door. She's dressed professionally, in gray slacks and a mint green button-down that highlights the light green sparkle in her eyes.

"Can I help you?"

"Yes, I'm Maureen Bailey. I'm supposed to have an interview with Dr. Cratchet?"

"Oh! Yes! Right this way." I smile at my favorite candidate. "I'm so excited you're here. I was really happy to see your experience at the women's health clinic in Boston on your resume. We could really use someone like you around here!" I grab my purse and walk around to the door beside the check-in counter to let her in the back, and direct her to Dr. Cratchet's office. "Sir? Maureen Bailey's here for her interview."

"Lovely, lovely…" he says, scrolling on his computer, clearly not paying attention. I walk around to the side of his desk, glimpsing that he has his stock portfolio up on the screen again.

Only this time, the number's even *higher*.

I avert my eyes, trying not to pry, even though he doesn't even notice that I've gotten closer. "Dr. Cratchet?"

"What?" He looks up, and his eyes finally focus on me from

behind his glasses. "Oh! Miss Gander. Why are you here and not at lunch?"

"Because your interview is here."

"Ah, Ms. Bailey. Thank you for coming in. Let's talk about…"

He gets right into the interview, so I nod goodbye and make my escape. When I meet Brian on the sidewalk outside the diner, his appraising look up and down my body is a mixture of pride and hunger that sends shivers down my spine.

"Well you look happy," he says, holding out his elbow for me to grasp.

I do. "Yep. Maureen came in for her interview just as I was leaving. She's perfect for the job. I really hope she gets it."

"It would certainly make your life easier. Maybe she can even take over for the Doc!"

"Wouldn't *that* be something?" I'm almost afraid to hope. No matter how detestable he is, Dr. Cratchet seems to be the only qualified physician that the clinic board has been able to keep around this tiny town. "He's been our town doctor for as long as I can remember. It would be nice to change it up."

"It seems like a lot of new people have been coming to town lately, myself included." We're seated at a booth by the window, and Brian takes a look at the laminated menu. My leg bounces in the seat, and Brian raises his gaze to me. "What's got you so excited?"

"I'm thinking about practice tomorrow. How I'm going to tackle it."

"What do you mean?"

"It's time to get serious. The championship is this weekend. And it's going to be at the Spitz-Shein complex again, which means plastic boards and glaring lights." The hostess drops off tall, red plastic cups full of water for the two of us, and I take a big sip. "We have to come in with a plan."

"You know, I was thinking about practice too, actually."

"You were?" I feel a happy flame warm my chest.

Brian's been accompanying me to practices ever since I hurt

my knee again, and having him there cheering me on has been a reminder for me to stay calm. To take it easy, and actually have fun. The team has noticed too, because everybody seems to relax when they see Brian helping me carry the equipment into the park.

Plus, he watches to make sure I don't re-injure myself. While the first few practices without my crutches were frustrating as he helped me navigate how I should and shouldn't move while I recover, it's become almost second nature to incorporate healthier movements now since we've been doing PT everyday.

"Yeah," he says. "I don't think you need me watching you at practices anymore."

His words throw cold water all over my happy flame.

"What? But...I thought you were starting to get into it!"

"Get into cornhole?" He snorts, and the sound is like a dagger in my heart. He's so derisive about it. Like being invested in the game is beneath him. "Sorry, Kodi. I'm into *you,* and your health, and I'm happy to support you and the rest of the folks on the team, but I mean...the whole 'small town backyard sports tournament' really isn't my thing."

He reaches across the formica tabletop and grabs hold of my fingers. I start to pull away, but then the waitress comes to take our orders, so I leave my hands where they are. But my frustration builds with every swipe of his thumb against the back of my hand.

I thought Brian wanted to *help* me. Be there for me. I thought he *liked* supporting me and my goals.

All I am is sports. That's my whole life. That's all I've ever been. If I'm the subject of a conversation in town, you better believe my name is accompanied by words like *former star pitcher* or *almost state champion.*

But now, the one person who's supposed to be the most important–my *boyfriend*–doesn't even want to watch me play? Doesn't want anything to do with the *'whole small town backyard sports tournament'* thing?

The waitress walks away, and he lets go of one of my hands to take a sip of water from the big red plastic cup she just sat down beside him. I tug my other hand out of his grasp.

"I didn't realize you hated small towns so much," I mutter.

He coughs, choking a bit on his water. "What? What makes you say that?"

"You just seem so embarrassed by us and our hobbies."

"Kodi." He levels a look across the table. "I didn't say that. I'm not embarrassed by cornhole. I just…" he takes a deep breath. "I think we should both have things we can do outside of each other. For both of our sakes. I don't want to be the kind of boyfriend that suffocates you."

Suffocates, he says.

I know how it feels to be suffocated. Feeling like you're meant for something bigger, something greater, only to have it thrown in your face and dangled out of your reach. Ending up right back where you started.

I clench the cup in my hand, the condensation squeezing out from between the plastic and my fingers and beading up in rivulets around the outline of my grip.

"You don't *suffocate* me."

"That's good." He chuckles, sounding relieved.

"Do I suffocate you?"

His eyes widen, and he pushes back into the vinyl of his seat. "What? Why would you think that?"

"It just feels like you're pulling away right now. Like, I was trying to tell you that I really care about practice tomorrow and wanted to bounce ideas off of you and now you're saying that you don't want to be there and have never even *liked* going to practices or matches–"

"I didn't say that," he interrupts me, and anger spikes again. I realize I feel really hot, and my voice has gotten louder. Embarrassment flares in my stomach, and suddenly I'm no longer hungry. I want to yell at him, but a couple of curious faces are peering at us over their plastic menus, and I'm hyper-aware of their *suffocating* glances. "I just mean that we've been spending a ton of time together lately—and I love it, don't get me wrong. We wake up together, we have lunch together, we go to practice together..."

He drifts off, and I lose my patience waiting for him to spit out his point.

"And you're what? Getting tired of me?"

"No!" Now his voice is too loud, and the listening eyes around us multiply. He glances around nervously, then leans forward, whispering. "Kodi, I don't think I could ever get tired of you."

I cross my arms. "Then why don't you want to come to practice anymore?"

He sighs. "Do you really want me there?"

"Yes!"

We stare at each other (okay, maybe in my case it's more of a glare), and I study the hesitation in his face. But his eyes take me in, and apparently he sees what he needs to, because he leans back and takes another deep breath, letting it out on a *whoosh*.

"Okay then. I'll be there, baby girl." He smiles at me, and that little flame inside me that gets going whenever I hear him say those words sparks into a flicker.

"Promise?"

"Promise."

Our food arrives, and I dive back into the details of how I want to approach Spitz Hollow's defeat. He nods along, seeming on the outside to be engaged and like he's enjoying himself, but in the back of my mind, one word keeps playing on repeat.

Suffocating.

CHAPTER 54
BRIAN

Deep breath, Brian. This doesn't have to be scary.

Except it's terrifying. This is something I've kept myself from doing because I'm not prepared for the consequences should it go horribly wrong. Which, knowing me and my history with dating, it's almost certain to.

Except...it feels different this time.

As I stare at the empty dresser drawer in front of me, my phone buzzes. Leonard Landon, wanting to come in for a follow-up adjustment. He tweaked his shoulder at the library last week, and apparently I helped him feel so much better he wants to come in regularly. I've been getting more and more calls and texts from the people of Tuft Swallow: word's getting around that I'm the guy to help with injury recovery and chronic pain. Even with the *Nosy Pecker* gossiping about my love life.

I worried after moving here that a small town wouldn't have enough clients for me to eke out a living by myself. When I'd first bought this place on Elm Street, I'd assumed that I'd only be alone here for a few months before Zeke might move in with me.

I shake my head. *I sure misread that.*

That's why I'm trying to make sure I take things more slowly with Kodi. We may have moved a bit fast at first, kind of stumbling into our attraction before we intended to–*or even without intending to*–but that doesn't mean we have to start picking out wallpaper.

In the past, I dove head-first into fantasies about forever with someone before knowing their real interests or where they come from. Moving in together after only a couple months, only to end up being completely incompatible and getting on each other's nerves. This time, I want to do things right: starting small.

My gaze flicks back to the piles of my own clothes that I emptied from the middle drawer of my dresser to make room for Kodi's things. One drawer, one shelf–just enough to let her know she's got a safe space here, without making her think she needs to spend the night every day of the week. Now that she's back on her feet, I want her to know I trust her to handle the rest of her recovery without my constant supervision.

I walk over to the laundry basket, where the three pairs of underwear I've sequestered away since we started dating are freshly laundered and folded. I place them and some pajamas I bought for her in the drawer. Then I put the card I found for her at *The Plot Chickens,* the local bookstore, along with a book that the couple who run the shop recommended to me when I told them my girlfriend liked John Green novels.

I want to learn more about you, I want the gifts to say. *I want to support your hobbies.*

Especially after that misunderstanding in the diner earlier today, I feel like I need to clarify that I'm okay with her doing things that aren't my cup of tea. Whether that's the books she reads or the sports she plays. I even cleared out some space on one of my bookshelves where she can keep some of her things if she wants to.

I push the drawer closed, excited for her to come home from Girls' Night so I can show her. As I'm folding the rest of the laundry and putting it away, I come across something hidden behind Kodi's crutches on the top shelf of the closet.

Kodi and Lily's BFF Diary: KEEP OUT!

I chuckle, wedging the composition notebook out of its hiding place. I'd forgotten that I stole this the morning after our first sleepover. At the time, I thought it would be a funny thing to hold over her head when she was in one of her hyper-competitive, show-no-weakness moments.

But since Lily helped me find Kodi after she ran away from dinner with her parents, I feel differently about their history and friendship. There's a lot more to the flighty redhead than meets the eye, and she knows more about Kodi's past than I've learned from her in the short time we've been together. In fact, their friendship is something I want to be particularly supportive of: not just for the health of our relationship, but for Lily too, who seems to need her friend far more than she lets on.

As I'm trying to parse out what to do with the journal, whether I should sneak it back into Kodi's closet where I found it or come clean about having stolen it in the first place, I hear the old floors creak as footsteps approach from the hall.

"Hey honey," she calls from the doorway. I quickly shove the journal back into the closet.

"Hey!" I lean in the doorway, trying to look like I *wasn't* just sneaking her childhood diary under her crutches. "How was girls' night?"

She eyes me curiously. "Good. Why are you in the closet?"

"I was putting away laundry." I leave the half truth. "I have a surprise for you."

The suspicion fades from her expression and she tilts her head, her bottom lip pouting temptingly. "Oh?"

"Mmhmm." I can't leave her alone with her looking like that, so I cross the few feet between us and wrap my arms around her waist. I give her a real greeting, nipping at her pouty lips until her mouth opens to me. I can taste the discount margarita on her lips, along with something spicy that makes me think she might have had tacos for dinner. But as she relaxes into my hold and the kiss deepens, those surface flavors fade and make way for the more familiar sweetness that is simply *her*.

I sweep my hands up her sculpted back and shoulders and lift her to tiptoes before stepping back. "I wanted to give you something."

"What?"

Her eyes sparkle, a smirk lifting the corners of her mouth, and I nod my head to the dresser. "Open it."

Her slender fingers skim across the wood of the handle, and she looks to me once more for confirmation before sliding it open.

"My underwear!" Her expression shifts from curiosity to surprise to pure heat in less than a second. She grabs the silky blue pair from our first time and waves it at my face, narrowing her eyes at me. "I *knew* they didn't burn up in the fire!"

"Guilty," I tease. "There's more."

"How many of these did you fucking stea–" her breath catches as she spots the book. She abandons the panties and runs her fingers over the gold-colored cover. "What's–?"

"The Longspurs suggested it. You said you like stuff like John Green, and they said this author is similar, but with more adult themes. Plus, the main character plays tennis, so I thought there might be more sports in this one. Since that was a complaint you had about hockey romances…"

I'm one-hundred percent rambling now, nervous that she might absolutely hate this gift. I mean, have I ever even seen her reading? But I'm also trying to telegraph reassurance into every word: *I care about your interests. I want to enjoy them with you, even if I don't fully participate.*

Once I pictured what that might look like: my beautiful girlfriend curling up on the couch reading one of her books while I sit beside her reading on my kindle, talking about them over dinner and then snuggling to watch something on TV together before bed…the vision was so appealing I couldn't help but want to stuff my shelves with books she'd enjoy. Fill the house with excuses for her to stay by my side forever.

But then I remembered that I'm starting small.

I let my words trail off, and she opens the card. Moisture gathers in her eyes as she scans over how proud I am of her and her recovery, and my explanation that this is *her* drawer now, so she never has to worry about whether or not she can spend the night. She mouths the last few lines:

The journey of you getting stronger the past two months is my new favorite story. I can't wait to be by your side as you write the next chapters. Maybe even here, at my place.

But I don't want to move too fast. So how do you feel about starting one drawer at a time?

I zero in on the back and forth movements of her eyes, holding my breath until they land on my signature at the bottom, where I'd signed *Love, Brian.*

Her hand rises to her mouth, and she glances back at the drawer.

"I cleared off a shelf for you too."

The tears clumping her eyelashes catch the light as she turns to me. "You want me to move in with you?"

"Not right away!" I assure her. "I know I tend to move too fast, and it's bitten me in the ass before. But I just want you to know that I'm serious about us, and I want you to feel comfortable–"

Wet cheeks brush mine as she throws her arms around me and tackles me on the bed.

"Stop talking," she mutters into the comforter beside my head. Then she kisses me on the cheek. "This is the sweetest gift anyone's ever given me. I love it."

"Even the book?"

She laughs. "Yes, even the book. In fact, I need to decompress. Maybe I'll start reading it tonight."

"Oh? Was Girls' Night not good?"

She shrugs. "I'm just nervous about the championship and it's getting to me. I appealed to the league about the plastic boards last week and the complaint got thrown out. And Lily thought I was making too much of it, but–" she stops herself, glancing at me, and lets out a deep breath. "I'm just stressed about it all."

"Wanna talk about it?"

She bites her lip, then shakes her head. "No, no, that's okay. I just want to curl up with you and go to bed."

She kisses me, squeezing her legs around my waist where she has me pinned beneath her, and I feel the tell-tale thickening below my belt.

I gasp for air. "I might not be ready for bed just yet…"

"Oh?" She grinds her hips, understanding lighting her amber eyes. "What do you have in mind?"

I kiss her again, and since my mouth is occupied, I decide to *show* her what I have in mind instead.

CHAPTER 55
KODI

"Again!"

Groans echo across the falling twilight of the park. Everyone's exhausted, but we aren't done yet. As things stand now, we'll never beat Spitz Hollow.

Brian taps my shoulder.

"What?" I mutter.

"Don't you think it's been enough? It's almost nine o'clock. You have work in the morning."

"Not until everybody sinks at least one bag."

"Kodi, don't let me hold everybody back. Seriously. It isn't worth it." Nick's chin falls to his chest, and his shoulders sink. "I'm probably not even going to play on Saturday unless we're way ahead, so what does it even matter?"

"That's not our motto anymore, Nick. We need everybody to work together. This isn't just one person's team. It's all of our team."

"That doesn't mean everybody has to be as good as you, Kodi. It means that you accept people where they're at," Lily says.

"Yeah, even if they're fucking horse shit."

"Ginger!" I glare at her. "Not helping!"

I take a deep breath, and look out at all the shadowy faces, backlit by the sidewalk's bright street lamps that flickered to life almost an hour ago. "Look, everybody. The championship game is going to be back at the Spitz-Shein Sports Complex, which means we'll be using those Godforsaken plastic boards again. We're not used to them, so we're going to have to sink as many bags without counting on sliding or knocking them in as we can. I know last time we lost on a technicality, but–"

"Technicality? You mean we lost because of Lily's giant tits!"

"You fucking bitch!"

Lily and Ginger start throwing hands, Nick and Jonah both crowding in to pull them apart from each other.

"Guys, if you get hurt before the game this weekend we'll stand even less of a chance!" Geneva whines. Ginger snaps another comment about Lily throwing her own back out with the weight of her boobs, and then Callie has to help Nick restrain the red-faced redhead.

"Stop it! You're acting as bad as them!" I shout, but they're way beyond listening to me. "Seriously, guys, stop–"

Then Ginger yanks her elbow out of the police chief's grasp, and the momentum sends her careening forward. She trips over Mr. Landon's feet, which causes him to topple into Delilah. Jonah, seeing this, immediately jumps to grab her before she falls onto her ankle, trampling D'Shawn's toes in the process.

The history teacher's howl catches everyone's attention. Unfortunately, it also distracts Nick and Callie enough that Lily springs free of their hold, and then she and Ginger are grappling on the ground.

I start to run to pull them apart, but Brian holds me back.

"Are you crazy? You'll hurt your knee again."

"I need to stop it!"

"Not by putting yourself in danger–"

"That's enough!"

Everyone freezes as Police Chief Jonah Woodcock's commanding voice pierces through the night. His deep blue eyes look black in the limited light, and he's all the more menacing for it as his muscular chest inflates with authority.

Even Brian sucks in a breath at the sight of him. I, meanwhile, feel miniscule under his cop's glare.

"Kodi Gander, if this is the way practices are going to go for the cornhole league, then Delilah and I are out. I can't endorse this kind of behavior."

Delilah nods, fingers wrapped securely around the Chief's biceps. I swallow.

"Sir, I–"

"I'm out, too. You bimbos can't even take a joke," Ginger snaps, flipping her mussed hair and baring the bottom of her ass cheeks as she bends and snaps up from the ground like she's impersonating Elle Woods. Geneva averts her gaze, but some of the other members of the team nod along with Ginger's statement. "Good luck on Saturday without me. *Not.*"

She twitches away, and about half the remaining players follow her and the Woodcocks out to the sidewalk, leaving only Lily, Callie, Nick, Mr. Landon, Geneva, Brian, and me standing in the middle of the grassy field.

"Fuck," Lily mutters. "She took half the team."

My jaw drops. "What the hell, Lily? This is partially your fault!"

"My fault?"

"Yeah! You and your temper!" I let out a growl of frustration. "Why can't you just ignore it when people say shit about your boobs? You've had them for over a decade now! Ginger's always picking fights. You don't see me trying to punch her in the face over it!"

"Oh, way to deflect the blame!" Lily shouts back. "*You're* the one who pushed us all past our limits! After we all told you to chill the fuck out!"

Her words are like a slap in the face. I stumble back into Brian, who holds his hands out to steady me. "You, of all people, know how important this is to me!"

"Yeah, and it's high time you fucking *let it go!*" Steam practically rises out of Lily's ears as she shakes with fury. The remaining players back away from her slowly, giving her space. "How many more people have to suffer because of that softball game, Kodi? Huh? How many? It's bad enough that Coach got *you* hurt. Why are you still letting it control you?

"You don't have to be like him! You don't have to hurt *us!* So *why? Why* do you insist on training us as hard as he trained you?"

Tears spring to her eyes as she screams at me, the words scraping out of her throat like claws. Tearing into me and exposing parts of my past I thought I'd gotten over.

"I'm not hurt anymore," I say, realizing as I do that I'm also crying. It makes the words sound bubbly and weak. "I'm better now. I'm stronger now!"

"You're not stronger *because of him,* Kodi. You're stronger *in spite of* him. You're better now because of all of the work that Callie and Brian and m-me—"

A big sob wretches its way into her words, and my view of everyone else blurs as I blink repeatedly at Lily. Her shoulders shake up and down with her uncontrollable breathing and Callie steps forward and wraps an arm around her shoulder. I see her tense, like she's going to shrug it off, but then she sinks into our friend's embrace.

Then, all their shapes get fuzzy. My tears well up, until all I can make out is how separate Brian and I are from the rest of the team.

Or what's left of it.

"Go home," I mutter finally, wiping my eyes. "Practice is over."

"But what about the match?" Geneva asks.

She sounds so concerned. So oblivious.

So young.

"We'll figure it out Friday." I let out a shaky sigh. "If we even have enough players."

"We don't," Lily says, stronger-voiced than I would have expected. "Because I quit."

"What?"

"I can't watch you go through that again, Kodi. I quit."

She and I meet eyes. For a long moment, the only sounds are the chirping of the evening crickets as we stare each other down. And then, Mr. Landon breaks the silence.

"Well, then, I'll uh…see the rest of you on Friday."

That breaks the spell. People drift away until only the four of us, Callie and Lily, Brian and I, are left.

"Lily…"

"What?" She wipes her nose, but her gaze doesn't leave mine. "*What?*"

But I don't know what to say. What can I say? I can't beg her. She's made her position perfectly clear. She's been telling me to let go of my 'trauma' from high school for months now, but what she doesn't understand is I've never been trying to *relive* my glory days. I've been doing everything I can not to repeat them.

But nothing's worked. I'm *still* the town's biggest failure. I'm the reason everyone's quit the team. I'm the one that the *Nosy Pecker*'s going to blame for our loss. And worst of all…

"Everyone's going to hate me again."

There. The truth. She might think she's helping me, she might think she's proving a point, but really, the only thing she's doing is condemning me to repeat the worst parts of my past. The whole town is counting on me. And now I can't bring home the gold.

Again.

She looks away, squeezing her eyes shut as if she's in pain. Fresh tears trail down her cheeks, and she shakes her head.

"*Everyone* didn't hate you then, Kodi. I wish you understood that. Maybe then, everyone wouldn't be leaving you now." She gives Callie a look over her shoulder, and she nods. "I'll see you around."

As she walks away, the finality of her tone sinks into my chest, and I realize that even though she's crushing me right now, I still don't want to lose her. She's my best friend. She helped me open up when no one else could. If it weren't for her, I never would have admitted my feelings to Brian. I would be truly alone.

So I cling to the one thing we've always made a priority, ever since we moved out of our parents' houses and needed something just for us. The thing that's always endured, between all the spats and boyfriends and job changes and injuries. "Girls' Night?"

I sound pathetic. Small. Pitiable. It's like everything I hate about myself bares itself to the world in those two words.

She shrugs. "Maybe."

And then she walks away, and my world narrows down to two.

BRIAN DRIVES MY SUBARU BACK TO HIS PLACE, AND AS SOON AS HE parks I burst out of the door and start pacing. I bounce my foot as he unlocks the door, and once I'm inside I'm storming up and down his living room in a tight circle.

"Baby girl, calm down."

"I can't right now. I don't want to stand still, okay?"

If I stop moving, then I lose momentum. And I need momentum to keep moving forward. If I stop, then all the consequences of tonight are going to catch up to me, and I'll be well and truly fucked.

"Baby g–"

"Shut up!" I yell at him. "I don't want to be sexy right now, okay? This isn't something you can just seduce away this time."

Hurt flashes across his face, and I wince. *Fuck.* Now I'm pushing away the only person I have left.

He pauses for a moment, and I hear him inhale a deep breath as I turn away, wearing a path into his old wooden floors. He exhales, and I can feel my shoulders inch towards my ears to protect myself from the yelling I'm sure is about to start. How could it not? I deserve it.

"Kodi, you need to talk to Lily."

My feet stop dead in their tracks. "Huh?"

He walks forward and puts a hand on my shoulder, rubbing up and down my arm. I'm torn between whether to lean into the comfort or get back to moving, but my brain is fuzzy from his random response.

"She doesn't want to talk to me," I say slowly. Maybe he didn't understand what he just saw. That wasn't a normal Kodi-and-Lily fight. Honestly? We hardly ever fight. This summer, we've been at odds more than we ever have.

In the past, I've just listened to whatever vapid topic she's monologuing about, then she pesters me until I finally get something off my chest that I didn't even realize was bothering me. And then we go back to talking about her latest sexual conquest and at the end of the night, we both feel better.

But we don't usually go deeper than that. Or at least, we haven't in a while. That night with the ice cream was one of the only times like that I can remember since…high school? Maybe even earlier.

It may have been a bit shallow and repetitive, but that's how childhood friendships age, isn't it? People grow apart, life gets monotonous. That's just what happens. And it would have been fine, if not for…

Brian and I lock eyes, and I can't stand still anymore. I pull away from his arm, and he shakes his head.

"Running isn't gonna help."

"I'm not running. I'm pacing."

"You're trying to pace around the problem."

"No, I'm trying to come up with a *solution* to the problem. We don't have enough people to play this weekend. We need six, and without Lily, we only have…" I tally the members on my fingers as I list them. "Callie, Geneva, Mr. Landon, Nick, me, and…"

My eyes widen and I look at Brian. "You could–"

"No," he cuts me off. "I'm not the answer to this problem, Kodi."

"Why not? Don't you love me? Why won't you play for me?" My voice has gotten whiny, and those fucking tears are back, stinging the backs of my eyes as I try desperately to blink them away. "Why don't you want to help me now?"

"I *do* want to help you. With the *actual* problem."

"This is my problem!" I throw my hands in the air to keep them from bunching into fists. "Fuck, why aren't you *listening* to me? Why does everyone think they know what my problems are better than me??"

He runs his fingers through his hair and sits on the couch, watching me as I cross from one corner of the living room to the other. He leans his elbows on his knees as he leans forward. "Okay. What *is* your problem?"

"My *problem* is—is…" My throat catches on my brain, and suddenly all I've got in my head is static. Static and rage. "Like—the fact that, you know, everyone is…*ugh!* You don't understand, okay?"

"What don't I understand?"

"You don't get what I went through when I lost us the championship before, okay? How awful it was."

"Explain it to me," he says simply. As if it's the rules of baseball or how to microwave a Hot Pocket, and not the single worst thing to ever happen in my life.

I scoff. "Oh, like you've explained all your trauma to me? What happened with your parents, huh? What if you were in my shoes, and you had to face all of that rejection–" I cut myself off as I watch Brian's face twist in a mix of grief and pain and something else I can't place.

He hangs his head over his lap for a moment, and then rubs his hands together.

"Okay." He inhales a big breath and lets it out slowly, adjusts his posture. "Let's start there then. But you have to sit down."

He pats the couch beside him. I cross my arms and tap my foot, refusing, but he just stares at me expectantly.

I stare back. Then I sit.

"Thank you," he breathes again. "Yes, my parents kicked me out. I was eighteen, and luckily I was able to stay with a friend, a classmate of mine who was also queer. He ended up being my first boyfriend, actually."

I tilt my head. "What does this have to do–"

He holds up a hand. "Let me get through this, okay? I've been thinking about it a lot lately." I nod. He continues, "I was desperate for people who'd accept me for who I really was back then. I'd just lost my scout troop and my family, and life was moving fast—like it does for everyone at that age. I was about to leave for college, which also meant I was abandoning what little support system I had left. So when Jeremy and I hooked up that summer before college, I clung to him. When we went our separate ways, I called him every night. Until he finally stopped picking up, and I was abandoned again.

"Then it became a string of relationships, one after another. Men and women. Some better than others. I stayed safe, explored my sexuality, learned a lot about sex, relationships, and, I thought, love.

"I was always the first to say 'I love you.' Until a few partners in a row told me that I was coming off as too clingy, and I stopped talking about my feelings so openly. I started fantasizing about my partners instead, building futures in my head that weren't there. I did that all throughout chiropractic school too, until my long-term boyfriend moved away after graduation and broke up with me. Then it was Grindr and Tinder dating for a while, where I found Zeke."

"That makes sense," I cut in.

He chuckles. "Yeah. He's definitely the Tinder type. But I'm not. I didn't do too well with the apps. I wanted something serious, something more than a hookup, so that's what I gave to Zeke. Whereas he...well, you've met him. He wasn't interested in anything serious. So when I moved to start my own practice, specifically looking for properties closer to him, I didn't tell him what I was doing. I thought I'd surprise him with some grand gesture, and then, finally, I'd prove to him that I was worth being serious about."

Sadness for the man beside me starts to saturate my other emotions. I'm angry at Zeke, too, for being such a shitty person to someone so amazing. I put a hand on his knee, and he quickly covers it with his own, holding it there. "Brian, you weren't the problem. He was!"

He shakes his head. "Not entirely, no."

I start to interrupt, but Brian holds up his hand. "I was part of the problem, too. I can admit that now. I wasn't being a good partner by putting all of my unrealistic expectations on him. By making him the emotional support I needed in my head, I was just as guilty of ignoring his needs as he was of ignoring mine. Did it hurt when he dropped me so callously? Of course. But I wasn't good for him, and he was never going to be what I needed. Truthfully, no one ever could be.

"I'm still processing how much my family fucked me up. But in order to do that, I had to see how *healthy* families, friends, and communities are supposed to be. School, martial arts, work... they're all very structured. There's a hierarchy to them. I couldn't get my bearings as a single person in a community there. Not when I didn't have any good examples to look to.

"And then I moved here."

I stare at him, mouth open. I clarify, "here? Tuft Swallow?" He nods, his eyes crinkling at the corners a bit as he grins at me. "You think this town is *healthy?*" I snort.

He's lost his fucking mind.

He laughs, a true belly laugh, and some of my concern ebbs. "Oh, it's got its issues, don't get me wrong. That gossip paper in particular is something else."

"You can say that again," I mutter.

"But the people support each other. The whole fucking town turns out for *cornhole games.*"

"Yeah, but that makes sense."

I'm not sure I'm understanding the point he's trying to make. That's just what all communities do for each other; we turn out for our teams.

He blinks at me. Then shakes his head. "Okay, you've lived here your whole life, so I'm not going to burst your bubble. The point is, people here actually care about each other. That's not the case in other cities, where people just hope they can pair up with someone to get through life with. Here, it's not just one person being someone else's everything. It's a whole network of folks looking out for each other.

"Look at my business." He spreads his arms around the downstairs living room, which doubles as a foyer and waiting room for his practice. "I've got patients here every week because people refer them to me. I have a network with Nick, and Caleb, and friends of patients who come in because people *want them to feel better.* It's hard to build a business like this in a big city, because everyone wants to know what they're getting out of it when they help someone out. But here, I had one or two people have a good experience, and suddenly everybody knows about it. People talk to each other, people share. That's a pretty amazing thing."

"I guess…" I think about that for a second, wondering if that's really so special. Then realize we've gotten off track. "But what does that have to do with your trauma?"

He squeezes my hand. "I cling to people, to partners, because of my trauma. Too hard, too fast. Probably because I don't want to be abandoned again, or something like that. I'm still working on it, and honestly I should get therapy—I'm sure there's a lot more messed up about me under the hood that I'm missing.

"But *you,*" he lifts my hand then, shaking it between us. "You pull *away* from people because of your trauma. You try to fix everything yourself, when you don't need to. You live in a supportive environment. You can ask for help. In fact, I'd argue you *need* to."

"Yeah," I scoff. "Because everyone's been so willing to help me in the past. Like it wasn't all down to me in the end anyway."

"See? That's *your* trauma. You were part of a *team,* but your fuckwad coach made you think it was all up to you. It wasn't. Your injury was not your fault, or the team's failure. Your coach's insistence on winning at all costs was the problem."

"But I was the one everyone blamed," I argue.

"Hence the trauma." He gives me a knowing grin, but I don't share it.

"So you're saying I couldn't have done anything to prevent it?" This is ridiculous. Obviously, I could have worked harder or done something better–

"Exactly."

I stare at him as his words sink in. *What?*

He continues, "You trusted the adults in your life to set you on a positive path, and they failed you. Some part of you recognizes that, otherwise, you wouldn't try to do everything on your own. You'd have more faith in Lily, in me, in the people around you."

For a solid minute, I don't say anything.

Is that *right?* Do I actually think, deep down, that I was betrayed by Coach or my parents, and that it's fucked me up somehow? That now, I'm incapable of asking for help because I couldn't depend on them when I needed someone the most?

It's a lot to process.

He squeezes my hand again, which I'd forgotten he was holding. "I'll be right back," he says, before letting go and running up the stairs.

When he comes back down, a notebook in his hands, I'm still chewing on his explanation. Trying to parse out my own feelings around it. Do his words ring true? Have I actually pulled myself away from trusting people because I felt betrayed after my injury?

I think about my job with Dr. Cratchet. How for the most part, I just keep my head down and let him be the absolute worst, most insecure boss and doctor in the world, treating me like crap, even sending me to *spy* on his competition. How that kind of manipulation and bullshit didn't even phase me until I cared too much about Brian to keep up the ruse. When I finally put my foot down.

I think about moving out of my parents' house, as soon as I was physically able to. Not because they were outwardly hurtful or abusive to me, but because I felt like I wasn't truly welcome in my own home. I wonder if maybe I've actually resented *them*, for not standing up for me when the whole town whispered about me behind my back.

And reluctantly, I think about Coach: everything Lily's been saying about him this whole time. How even now, after I've been out of high school for almost six years, I still don't go back to visit my teachers or attend softball games for fear that I might run into him. How I don't even let myself *think* about him. How I've been convinced this whole time that I pushed myself to the nth degree because *I* wanted it, and how that had to mean that it was *my* fault that I failed everyone.

Is this what Lily's been trying to say?

And has it all been holding me back? Not just from enjoying cornhole or recovering from my injury, but from enjoying my life to the fullest?

When Brian sits back down beside me, I look over to the book he's holding in his lap, and am shocked to see something I haven't seen in *years*.

"Where did you get this?" I whisper, reaching for the highlighter-colored composition notebook.

"I promise I didn't read any of it. I found it in your closet back when I got your crutches. At the time, I thought it was funny, but the longer I sat on it, the more I realized it might be kind of important."

"I haven't even *thought* about this since middle school."

The cardstock cover crackles as I open it, groaning at the movement after so many years frozen in time. On the first page, there's a game of M.A.S.H. for both Lily and I, circling our eventual futures in red sparkly gel pen. She was going to live in an apartment with her husband Chief Woodcock and drive a 2005

Ford Mustang to her job as a marine biologist. Whereas I was going to marry our classmate Rowenna Swan's older brother Cooper, live in a shack, and drive a toilet-on-wheels to my job as a veterinarian.

Oh, man. I remember wanting to be a veterinarian. That was my dream back when I was like, nine years old. Mom wouldn't let me get a dog, but I was convinced that I would love nothing more than to raise a puppy.

"It'll destroy our couch, Dakota! Absolutely not."

In the margin, I saw Lily's loopy purple scribble spelling out, "Suck it, Mrs. Gander!"

A giggle bubbles out of my throat, along with more waterworks. I wipe at my eyes, turning the page to see some sketches of our future wedding parties. Lily's bridesmaids' dresses are hot pink, of course, with sweetheart necklines and poofy mini skirts. Mine are a more tasteful powder blue sheath style, with spaghetti straps.

I remember Lily fighting me on that. She *hates* spaghetti straps. Says they accentuate her armpit pouches, whatever that means.

A pain shoots through my heart so intense, I almost crumble right there on the couch. Wet spots bloom on the lined paper as tears fall freely from my eyes, staining the page.

I shove the book away, not wanting to ruin it, and Brian wraps his arms around me, cradling me to him. I snot all over his t-shirt, but he doesn't pull away. Just rubs his hands up and down my trembling back and shoulders until the sobbing calms.

"I wish I'd had a friend back in high school who cared *half* as much about me as Lily cares about you."

"You mean *cared,"* I cry. "She's done with me."

"No she isn't," he mumbles into my hair, cradling me closer. "Not if you let her know you still need her."

"How do I do that?"

I lean back, searching his face for the answer. Her loss writhes in my stomach like a living, dying thing. I need to fix this. Need my friend back.

To help me remember who I am outside of competition.

He wipes my cheeks with his thumb, presses the sweetest, softest kiss to my lips, and then touches his forehead to mine before answering.

"Why don't you start with admitting you need her help to win this championship?"

CHAPTER 56
LILY

Despite it being 85 degrees outside, Callie makes me a cup of tea in my tiny-ass galley kitchen. She hisses as she pulls the mug out of the microwave, and I hear her leafing through the plastic tub of individually-wrapped tea bags that I keep in the cabinet.

"Blueberry green tea or peach black tea?"

"I want vodka," I mutter.

"That's a terrible idea. You work the opening shift at the salon tomorrow."

I grunt. She's right. Doesn't mean I'm happy about it. "Peach."

"You got it." I sit on my futon and stare at the blank wall of my small studio apartment, barely more than enough space for a bed and a TV, as Callie finishes preparing my tea and places it on the nightstand for me. She plops down beside me, then tugs on the foot of the pink canary Squishmallow I'm hugging to my chest. I hand it to her.

"This thing is so fucking cute." She squeezes it. "I need more pillows like this for my place."

"I don't have room for any more." I don't say it like I'm upset about it. Normally, I don't care that much about how small my apartment is. It's the thing I can afford with my job at the salon, and I don't even end up spending half my nights here most of the time. I prefer to live my life *outside,* with people, spending my money on experiences and activities. I don't need to worry about homemaking until I find someone I can actually share a home with.

I pick up the scalding cup of tea and sigh. If only I could get that part of my life in order, none of the rest of it would matter. Even Miss Never-ever-going-to-get-a-boyfriend herself was able to find somebody. So what's *my* problem?

"So. You wanna talk about it?" Callie tilts her head at me, pink highlighted hair falling across her face.

I stall, taking a sip of my tea, still wishing it was alcohol. The steam wafts into my face, making my already sweaty brow start to drip down my temples. "Not really."

"Lily. You know I'm here if you need to get anything off your chest, right?"

"Like what?" She gives me a look. I sigh again. "Yeah, I know."

"Just like you know you can't actually quit the team the week of the championship."

I almost spit out my tea. Instead, I just end up swallowing it too fast and it burns a column of scalding flesh down my throat. "Argh! What?? No I don't!"

A little wrinkle forms between her eyebrows, and her lips turn down in a frown. "Kodi needs you."

"No she doesn't. She has *Brian* now." I let the warmth of the mug seep into my hands. She rubs a hand in circles along my back. It feels nice. I take another painful sip of tea. "She's just ignoring her problems, you know."

"A lot of people ignore their problems. It's kinda part of life."

"Well, it's dumb," I grumble.

Callie chuckles, shaking her head. "Yeah, I suppose it is. But that doesn't mean you just abandon them altogether."

"What am I supposed to do if she doesn't let me in? Every

time she's in a crisis, it's like pulling teeth to get her to even talk to me. She doesn't even want my help!"

"That's not true. She asked you for it tonight."

"No, she just yelled at me tonight. And then didn't say anything."

"I think she said plenty. You just weren't listening the right way. She needs you. You *both* know she needs you."

I down the rest of my tea in one excruciating chug. Then I steal back my Squishmallow. "I don't know shit."

Knock knock knock.

"I'll get it," Callie says, rising from the bed and going on tiptoe to peer out the peephole. "Oh!" She undoes the lock, and reveals Kodi behind the door.

She's still in her cornhole clothes, and she has a notebook clutched to her chest. I look up, stunned. *What is she doing here?*

"Lily, you're right. I've been an absolute idiot, and I need my best friend. Will you forgive me?"

CHAPTER 57
KODI

"I'm so, so sorry."

I'm standing in the doorway of Lily's crappy studio apartment, feeling like the shittiest friend of all time. I haven't been here since I helped her move in almost a year ago, and I had to scour our text messages on my phone to find the apartment number. Looking around, I can see why she always wants to hang out at the bar or the park or literally anywhere other than here. Not that she doesn't take care of it–but the hissing fluorescent lighting that is at once too bright and insufficient coupled with the stained ceilings and peeling wallpaper would be difficult for anyone to brighten up.

It's a straight line from the front door to her bed. Callie invites me in, and Lily just stares at me, clutching a pink pillow animal to her chest.

"You're just saying that because you need me for the team."

Oof. I deserve that. But it still stings to hear her, in her own words, admit that she doesn't think I care about her.

I squeeze the friendship journal tighter, and say the next words slowly, trying not to deny how much I've hurt her. "I *do* need you on the team, yes. But if I had to choose between you coming to the game on Saturday, or you coming to Girls' Night on Monday, it would be Girls' Night every week of the year."

She snorts, the sound coming out squelchy and wet from the tears that have started flowing down her cheeks. "Yeah right."

"Listen to her, Lily."

Callie nods at me, and I hold out the notebook. "I want to remember who I was before I lost the championship. Before all I cared about was sports and winning. I don't want to give them up entirely–because it's still a part of me–but I've got too much," I suck in a breath, "*trauma* around all of that for it to be my whole identity anymore."

Lily's eyes widen, darting from me to the notebook in my hands.

"You kept this? All these years?"

I nod, gesturing for her to take it.

She does, flipping through the pages and shaking her head. "I didn't think you even cared about stuff like this anymore."

"I'm not going to pretend that it's been hanging on my wall or anything. It was under my crutches in the closet," I admit. "But I never would have thrown it away. Ever. And I don't think finding it again now was a coincidence."

It wasn't, of course, because Brian found it and gave it to me on purpose. But that doesn't change the fact that both he and Lily were totally right: I need my friends. And needing someone to remind me of that doesn't diminish the realization.

It *proves* it.

"I'm sorry that I don't talk about my problems. That it takes so much poking and prodding to get me to tell you anything. I just–ever since I had to change gears after that game, when my whole life just imploded, it felt like I couldn't lean on anybody. And I was too broken to realize how much you helped me through all of that.

"It was so hard for me to see the joy in life, to see anything other than what I'd had as worth fighting for, you know? I was terrified to think that I might find something better, only to have it all taken away again.

"Maybe I was even pushing you away. Assuming you'd find what you actually wanted and move on, too, leaving me alone again. I *felt* alone, like no one understood, so I ended up forcing that belief on the only people who did. Like you."

"Jeez, Kodi, did you like, go to therapy or something?"

I laugh, and it feels so good I want to cry all over again. "No, although I probably should. But now that I've been healing physically, *finally*, I think that's starting to loosen up all of the emotional crap that's been locked up in my injury all this time. You know?"

"I know that you have a sexy, mature chiropractor who's been pushing your buttons," she smirks.

"And it sounds like he also maybe helped talk you through some of this just now," Callie adds.

I feel the blush bloom on my cheeks, and I shuffle my toes on the ratty carpet. "Well, yeah, maybe. I mean, this is why I need people in my life, okay? You guys to help me know *when* I'm being an asshole, and Brian to help me know *why* I'm being an asshole."

Lily gets up and wraps her arms around me. I squeeze her back, and we stay like that for a moment.

Still holding me, she says, "you know what? That sounds like an alright arrangement."

"So you forgive me?" My words come out muffled as my face squishes into her hair.

"Yeah, girl. I forgive you."

"Thank *God*," Callie sighs, throwing her arms around us and squeezing until Lily's boobs start to push the air from my lungs. "Now, what are we going to do about the match on Saturday?"

"You mean, you still want to play?" I blink at them, and Lily rolls her eyes.

"Uh, *duh*, bitch, we're not going to let you lose *another* championship."

"Especially one as important as this."

I look back and forth between my oldest friend and my newest one, and for the first time feel like it isn't all up to me. "That's amazing. Because I could really use your help."

Spitz-Shein Soars Whilst Swallow Squad Splinters

Good news for folks with local investments: Hawkthorne County employer Spitz-Shein Inc.'s stock prices soared yesterday, bringing some outside enthusiasm close to the roost. Apparently, talks of acquisition of the Spitz Hollow start-up by tech giants in San Francisco and Seattle are the cause of the bump. Morale was high in the neighboring township yesterday which caused some rowdy crowds; calls to Tuft Swallow PD kept Chief Woodcock and his team busy writing tickets for public indecency and vandalism near the town line.

Although rumor has it the Spitters had a second reason to celebrate: The Mighty Swallows may not have the number of players they need to qualify for the Championship match-up this weekend. For the first time in League history, we've seen a mass exodus of players from the team. The culprit?

Our anonymous sources point to none other than former star pitcher Kodi Gander who, as you all know, is kicking off her tenure as cornhole team captain with some questionable decisions. Romantic entanglements with the new town chiropractor, Dr. Gosling, may be the cause for her shifting mood throughout the season. Although no one can deny that the recovery from her mid-season injury has been impressive—benefit to getting handsy with a healer, one might say!

Jury's still out on whether or not Gander will be able to win over enough skilled players to defend our unbroken championship record. But for the sake of all of us Nosy Peckers, we can only hope she and her few remaining teammates can pull off a miracle.

I CRUMPLE UP THE PAPER AND TOSS IT IN THE DESERTED WAITING ROOM trash. I don't need to worry about what anybody is saying about me in the *Pecker*. I'm doing everything I can to right this sinking ship—with a little help from my friends. And if, at the end of the day, we've done everything we can and it still isn't good enough?

Well, I guess we'll have to forfeit.

And…that's okay.

Really.

I can live with that.

"Miss Gander!" I jump as Dr. Cratchet bursts into the entrance to the clinic, sleigh bells crashing in a cacophonous alarm above his head. "Do you have a copy of that insufferable gossip rag?"

"I just threw it away, sir."

"Well retrieve it at once!"

His eyes practically pop through the lenses of his fogged glasses as he rushes to my side, pushing my shoulder back down into the trash can.

"Sir–stop–"

"Quickly, quickly, this is of utmost importance!"

My fingers snatch the crumpled ball from the rest of the garbage and I toss it to him. He flinches.

"Oh, my that simply won't do," he mutters, throwing it back onto the floor and scuffling off to my chair in the office where he pulls up the browser on my computer. "I'll need to snare a copy from the deli on my way to lunch. I'm rich, I'm rich!"

By the time I clean up his mess and follow hurricane Cratchet into the office, he's pointing at some numbers on a screen and clapping his hands together in glee. The wisps of white hair bounce around his crown as he does a little wiggle in the wheely chair.

"It's a good thing I was proactive in hiring you assistance, Miss Gander. It looks as though you'll be needing it!"

"Sir, what are you talking about?"

He points at the screen, and I peer over his shoulder.

And my jaw drops.

"Is that…*seven* zeros after that number?"

"Oh dear, I *did* advise you to invest your paycheck wisely,

Miss Gander. To think where you might be if only you had listened to your elders!"

He pops up from the chair, giving me a patronizing pat on the head as he does, before grabbing his man purse from the island and darting back into the waiting room.

"Cancel all my appointments from now 'til forevermore! Ms. Bailey will be here on Monday to start her new position as head practitioner of the Tuft Swallow Clinic. *She* can deal with the lot of you ungrateful scallywags. I, delightfully and wealthfully, *resign!"*

I follow him, pausing in the middle of the floor as he once again swings open the door and sets the sleigh bells into song. "Sir, don't you want to close out of your account before–?"

"You've been a perfectly satisfactory employee all these years, Miss Gander. I thank you for your mediocrity. Now I'm off to catch a cruise to the Dominican–don't try to reach me! I won't be caught dead wasting any of my hard-earned fortune on Royal Caribbean's superfluous wiffy."

I blink. "You mean wifi, sir?"

He places a hand on my shoulder and sighs. "This is the kind of millennial knowledge that will serve you well as you flounder in the absence of my tutelage, Dakota. May God bless you for the rest of your pitiable working-class existence."

"Um. Sure. Thank you, sir."

With that, he skips down to the sidewalk, and the door jangles closed.

I guess this means I can text at work now.

After canceling all of Dr. Cratchet's appointments for the next week, starting with calling all of today's patients, I print out a sign for the front door of the clinic that reads **Closed for Change of Management**. Then it's phone calls with different members of the board for the next hour. The chairwoman assures me that my job is still secure, but tells me I can take the rest of the day off while they figure out the plan moving forward.

Which gives me almost twenty-four hours to prepare for tomorrow.

• • •

ME

So it looks like I have the rest of the day off? You'll never guess why. Want me to bring you lunch at the salon and we can brainstorm my grand gesture of apology to the team?

LILY

Ooh, yes. I'm craving wings.

Hope you're also craving tea...

CHAPTER 58
KODI

By the time I arrive at *Tease Me* salon, Callie's already there, getting her pink highlights refreshed at Lily's station. I pull up a chair in between Callie and the tower of products in spray bottles in front of the wall of mirrors. Lily paints strips of her fading lavender hair with some blue goo and wraps them in tin foil as we talk.

"So what gives? Crotchetty never gives you Fridays off."

"He quit."

"What??" The two of them squeal in unison. I set our takeout down on the floor beside us, recounting the story of his stocks taking off and his impromptu cruise to the Caribbean. Their eyebrows climb higher and higher as I weave the tale, pausing only to make room for the scoffs and derisive noises at my reenactment of the Doc's not-so-subtle insults to my intelligence. When I get to the part about his skipping off to catch a ship, Lily sighs.

"Ugh, I'd love to go on a cruise."

"Really?" Callie shudders. "Have you *seen* the shit that washes up on shores after typhoons? Or the creepy monster creatures that David Attenborough talks about on *Blue Planet*? I'll get my thrills on land, thank you very much."

"All I know is, the more ocean separating me from Dr. Cratchet, the better. I've spent too long letting toxic old men ruin my life."

"That's my girl," Lily says. I meet her eyes in the mirror, and she winks at me. She wraps the final strip of Callie's hair in foil and pats her head. "That's gotta cure for a few minutes, hun."

I pass out silverware, then hand her the styrofoam container of mango habanero boneless wings. Callie's face is thoughtful as she accepts her napkin.

"I'm happy for you, Kodi. It sounds like you've made some important realizations lately."

I see an embarrassing blush creep up my cheeks in the mirror before I look away. I fiddle with the takeout container in my lap.

"I don't know about that. But between all this cornhole drama and Brian helping me with my knee, I've definitely had to take a hard look at my life." I take a bite out of a honey barbeque wing, and offer the container to Callie. She spears one with her fork. "When it comes down to it, I can't force anyone to see things my way. And even if I could, why would I want to? What if I'm wrong about something?"

"Like with Coach, you mean?" Lily asks around a mouthful.

"Coach, Dr. Cratchet…for years I've let people's perception of me shape me. Even over the voices of people who actually *cared,* like you. They made me feel helpless, and it turned me into someone who gave up altogether. I don't want to do that anymore."

My eyes bounce from Lily to Callie in the mirror in front of us, and they both meet my gaze with heartfelt grins.

"Don't get me wrong, I still need to own up for my own mistakes. I was wrong to ignore you all those years. And I still have to apologize to the team. But I'm not going to get stubborn about things I can't control anymore. Maybe it's a good thing that Dr. Cratchet is leaving, and maybe it's a good thing that I give up on the championship once and for all. Change doesn't have to be bad. Sometimes, change can mean something better than you ever imagined."

"You're not talking about cornhole anymore, are you?"

Callie's perceptive gaze locks on me, and I don't even have to look in the mirror to know that my cheeks are bright red.

"If it weren't for Brian making me question my recovery plan, and everything else–"

"Everything else, meaning?"

"Her chronic sexlessness, of course," Lily giggles, and her face turns thoughtful. "I oughta write that guy a thank-you note. Most boyfriends steal girls away from their friends. But yours brought you back to me. Through the power of his *healy hands.*" She wiggles her fingers.

I bury my face in my hands. "I swear to God, I never should have told you that's what he calls them."

"Oh no, I *love* it! Please, tell me again what *miracles* Dr. Hottie can work with his fingers–"

"Uh, Lily?" Callie points a saucy finger to her scalp. "It's burning."

"Oh, fuck, gimme a sec to wash my hands."

For the rest of Callie's hair appointment, we prepare my pep talk for the night. My friends agree to reach out to a few of the people who've quit to see if they'll reconsider, even though I'm not particularly hopeful.

But even if the worst does come to pass and we lose to Spitz Hollow, I meant what I said earlier. I'm not going to throw away my own well-being for a championship. That was something the old Kodi would have done.

After Callie pays and leaves, Lily goes back to her station to clean up. I watch as she plucks the combs and brushes from the sanitizing solution and starts gathering the little bowls of dye and bleach, contemplating.

"That was my last appointment of the day. Wanna get a drink or something?"

"Actually," I eye the hair supplies. "What do you think about doing something a little crazy?"

Her eyes sparkle. "What do you have in mind?"

I tug the elastic from around my ponytail, letting my dirty-blonde hair fall around my shoulders. "I'm thinking this new me calls for a new 'do. What do you think?"

Her squeal of pleasure is the only answer I get before she shoves me into the chair and gets down to work.

CHAPTER 59
BRIAN

"I haven't stood this straight since my wedding day!" Harold Woodcock announces as he rises from the table. "You're a miracle worker!"

I shake my head, but smile at the compliment.

"You weren't in that bad of shape to begin with, Mr. Woodcock. Seems like you stay pretty active!"

"Oh, you're just being nice."

I wasn't, but I don't bother correcting him as I walk him out to the porch. "Just take it easy the next couple of days—everything might feel a little loose for a while."

"That's what I'm counting on! Wait 'til the wife sees how *loose* these hips can be!"

Heat rises to my cheeks as I watch him walk back to his two-story Colonial down Elm Street, doing everything in my power *not* to imagine his words.

I check my phone. *Six pm.* Just about time to help Kodi get all the equipment ready for cornhole practice. But just then, a text from her comes in to let me know that Lily and Callie are taking care of it, and that she'll see me when she gets home.

No way I'm going to let *that* happen.

I was wrong to try to pull away from attending practice with her. And now that I realize asking for help is something she struggles with, I'm not about to ignore her when she said she wanted my support with this in the past.

I change into shorts and a t-shirt and walk on over to the park to see what the girls have up their sleeves.

As I approach the field where they usually warm up, I inventory the number of players gathered round in a circle. There are only six of them there: Callie, Lily, Nick, Geneva, Mr. Landon, and some lady with blue hair with her back to me.

Kodi's nowhere in sight.

I run to catch up, thinking something bad must have happened if Kodi Gander is skipping practice, but then I make out the woman's words echoing across the field.

"I wish I had realized it a lot sooner, but the truth is, I got caught up in all the pressure. Nick, I shouldn't have pushed you to play when you're uncomfortable with it. You give a lot to this team as our resident water-boy, and it was wrong of me to diminish that.

"Geneva, Mr. Landon, you both are some of our most dedicated players, and I would never want you to think I don't value you. I value *all* of you, truly, and I'm sorry I took you for granted. I'm sorry I made you do shuttle-runs and stay past sunset and put so much pressure on you to–"

"Kodi??"

I don't mean to, but my shout is out of my mouth before I can stop it.

What the fuck did she do to her beautiful hair?

Standing at the head of the pack is my girlfriend–my beautiful, *blue-haired girlfriend*–giving an apology speech that I realize I just interrupted. Lily and Callie snicker behind their hands as I gape like a fish at her head of turquoise strands, blown-out and styled like she's about to go to some kind of mermaid photo shoot.

"Brian! I told you I'd see you after practice!"

The rest of the team looks at me, and I feel my face heat.

"Sorry to interrupt, but…" I flounder for words, still trying to reconcile the fact that *that's* my girlfriend. Not that she's ugly, by any means, but it's just a big surprise. "You're *blue."*

"Neptune, technically. It's the closest thing we had to the team colors," Lily says.

"Yeah, especially since she didn't want to look like Carrot Top."

Callie and Lily smile at me, and the rest of the team nods in agreement, making me feel like an idiot.

"Do you…not like it?"

Kodi looks at me with wide eyes. Nick coughs.

"I did it to show my solidarity for the team," she adds.

My shoulders slump, and I chuckle. *Of course she did.*

"It looks great, baby girl."

AN HOUR LATER, WE WALK HOME HAND-IN-HAND, HAVING JUST completed a successful practice in which the small team just played some cornhole. It was a relaxed affair, with Nick and I handing out ciders and beers and shooting the shit while the rest of the players had fun for a change.

At the end of it, Kodi pulled everyone into a circle and gave what might have been her last pep-talk of the season.

"No matter who shows up tomorrow, I just want to say thank you for giving it your all this season. Even if, in the end, we show up and get disqualified for not having enough players, we're not losers. I mean that," she said.

It was enough to make my chest swell with pride.

"You know?" I say, breaking the easy silence between us as we walk down Oak Street in the beautiful summer evening, "it's growing on me."

"My hair?"

"Yeah. It suits you."

"It suits me?" I nod. She smirks. "What about it *suits* me?"

"It's a risk. And you're a risk-taker."

She snorts. "Am not. I've never been a risk-taker."

"Maybe in the past, no," I concede. "But that was the old Kodi. The *new* Kodi? My sexy little mermaid girlfriend? *She* takes risks. She challenges old beliefs. And I'm proud of you."

"Proud of your sexy little mermaid, huh?"

"Yeah. I am."

"You tellin' me you have some kind of tentacle fantasy or something?" She raises her eyebrows. I laugh.

"Oh, baby girl," I shake my head. "You aren't ready to know the fantasies I have involving you."

"Maybe *old* Kodi wasn't. But I'm new Kodi now. I'm a *risk-taker*." She stops on the first step leading up to my porch and spins around so she's eye-level with me, shooting me a lusty grin. "Why don't you try me?"

I lean in close to her, breathing in the scent of the fancy salon shampoo and the heat of her freckled skin, and whisper into her ear. "I recall the old Kodi being a little hesitant about butt stuff."

I feel her suck in a breath.

"Perhaps *New Kodi* might be willing to explore?"

I pull back to take in her expression, and her eyes sparkle, even as they widen with apprehension. "*My* butt? Or…"

She leaves the insinuation dangling. I wink at her. A tentative smile stretches across her face.

"New Kodi could be down to…*experiment*."

I lean in, wrap my arms around her and lift her off the step as I crash my lips to hers.

"Well then it's a good thing I snuck a new toy into your drawer this afternoon…"

CHAPTER 60
KODI

I wake up with a healthy helping of nerves coursing through my veins on the morning of the championship. Brian stirs beside me as I sit up, reaching up a hand to stroke my turquoise hair as it tumbles across my shoulders.

"How's my mermaid feeling?"

My stomach flares with heat at his new nickname for me. It takes me back to last night, when we tried some things in this bed that were firsts for *both* of us.

And I have to admit. It makes me pretty excited to see what other fantasies Brian has in mind for New Kodi moving forward.

But now is not the time for sexy distractions. Now, it's time to face the music.

"Nervous."

He sits up and presses a kiss to my shoulder. "No matter what happens, I'm still proud of you."

"Thanks," I say. And I mean it. It's nice to know that even if I fail, I'm not alone. "Let's get to it."

MR. LANDON, GENEVA, AND I ARE WARMING UP AT THE SPITZ-SHEIN Sports Complex at quarter-til showtime. Brian and Nick are manning the water station and chatting up any Tuft Swallowers that come up to the sidelines to wish us luck or ask where the rest of the team is.

Lily texted me twenty minutes ago to let me know she was running a little late, but she and Callie would be there soon. I believe her, but that doesn't stop my heart rate from increasing ten bpm for every minute she still isn't here.

Come on, Lily.

Across the turf, Zeke smirks at me with his dark, beady eyes. He eyes the countdown clock on the scoreboard pointedly, then taps his wrist. *Time's running out,* he mouths at me.

I almost chuck a bean bag right down his handsome throat.

For his part, Brian's been ignoring his ex completely. I overheard a few nosy Tit Peepers make inquiries about him by the water cooler, which he fielded with grace.

"We dated a while back, but then I found out how much of a jerk he really is."

I couldn't help but smile when he said that. We locked eyes, and I felt the words he left unspoken.

"I've got someone better now."

I aim a few more bags at the plastic boards on the sidelines, getting a feel for the slippery surface. It's not ideal, but it isn't as bad as I assumed it was based on how badly we did last time. I weigh a beanbag in my hand, trying to tell if it feels light or heavy.

Something feels like it isn't adding up.

At five minutes to showtime, one of the refs approaches me. I suck in a breath. Lily and Callie still haven't appeared, and with only three of us playing, there's no way they're going to let us compete.

My shoulders sag. *It's too late.* Even if Lily and Callie weren't running late, we still don't have the seven minimum players to qualify.

The glare from Zeke's fluorescent teeth travels all the way

across the field as he grins wide, following the ref's path with his eyes.

Don't let him get to you, Gander. You're a new woman. You're not a failure. You're–

"We're here, we're here!"

Callie's voice rings out into the busy arena, and she waves her arms frantically as she bursts in through the side entrance.

The complex goes quiet as both sides of the stands turn to face her. And then the doors open, and Lily walks inside.

Behind her is the last person I *ever* thought I'd see.

"Logan?"

The blonde asshole struts into the building, tossing a beanbag casually into the air, flanked by Brad and D'Shawn on either side. "Miss me, Captain?"

Oh jeez.

I didn't. But at this moment, faced with a slack-jawed ref and a whole team of assholes on the other end of the field who were champing at the bit to see my downfall, even Logan's smug mug is a welcome sight.

"Get over here, Gilgax."

I grab him by the shoulder and shove his head down into a noogie as I ruffle his hair.

"Hey!"

"It's good to see ya, kid." I let him go, and he narrows his eyes at me.

"Helluva way to show your gratitude!" He smooths his hair with his hands, and I laugh.

"Well, you missed my big apology last night, so that'll have to do."

"I don't think so, Kodi," D'Shawn pipes up. "Lily said you have something to say to us?"

I lift my head to face the other two guys that came in with Logan and Lily, and my chest clenches. Because it isn't just the three of them.

The *whole team* stretches before me. All of them. Even the ones who quit early in the season. They're all here, looking at me expectantly.

Tears spring to my eyes, and I hear a cough.

"Jeez, Kodi, I think I've seen you cry more this summer than I ever thought I would in my life."

I wipe my eyes. "Sorry, Ginger. I'll try not to make a habit of it."

"You better not."

I glance at Lily, expecting to see her roll her eyes. But instead, she returns the big, goofy grin that I can feel stretching all the way across my face.

Thank you, I mouth to her.

You're welcome, she mouths back. Then makes a *go on* motion with her hands.

I turn back towards the waiting team, and take a deep breath.

"I'm sorry I've been such a menace all season."

Looks and noises of surprise spread through the small crowd, and I let out a laugh. "Yeah, yeah, I know. Never thought I'd say it either, but I've been a real hard-ass this summer. Y'all didn't deserve it. As a wise woman once said, this is supposed to be *fun.* And for the past two months, I've sucked just about every bean of fun out of this game.

"But today? Today, I want to make up for all of that. Nick?"

The muscly man jogs up with a cooler full of expensive craft beer, ciders, and canned cocktails that I spent a whole week's paycheck on this morning at the Plume N'Zoom. He opens the lid, and a few of the players mumble their appreciation.

"Everyone grab a drink! I want to make a toast." Nick hands me a canned gin and tonic, and everyone else picks their can or bottle of choice. Once the whole team has got their alcohol (and Geneva, her Gatorade), I raise my can to the ceiling. *"To the love of the game!"*

"To the love of the game!"

"To beating the Spitters!" Lily shouts.

"To heartfelt apologies!" Callie adds.

"To *holy shit,* this is good beer!"

I laugh, and chug another crisp, refreshing sip myself. "Who are we?"

"The Mighty Swallows!"

"And what do we say?"

"Spitters are quitters!"

And for the first time in…well, forever, I charge the field with the whole team behind me.

AT THE END OF THE SECOND ROUND, WE'RE BEHIND.

The score sits 4-2, and it's up to me to decide who gets to play the final round. There's no tie-breaker to decide the end game this time; it's down to the final three teams, and we all have to win to secure the championship.

I've been saving Callie and Lily as my aces in the hole. Cooper and Tammy are also shoe-ins, as they're probably our best players after them. I also have yet to play, and it's between Mr. Landon and Logan as to who my partner is going to be.

He'd be my last choice in any other circumstance, but I can't deny that Logan's a better shot than Mr. Landon is. I call the seven of us into a huddle.

On the other side of the field, Zeke huddles with five of the Spitz Hollow guys, and I see they've also pulled a few boards over to practice their shots in the last remaining minutes before the round. As if that will help.

I kick myself for not thinking of that.

"Okay, guys. This is it. The final round."

"We know how it works, Kodi."

Lily elbows Logan in the stomach. His *oof* is very satisfying.

"Cooper, Tammy, you guys are always good in a pinch. I know you got this."

Tammy holds up her sunglasses, and I grin. The whole team brought them today, and they've been a game changer in helping out with the glare. I find myself, once again, so grateful that I leaned on Callie and Lily to help me fix my mistake. I look toward them next.

"Lily, I want you to team up with–"

"I'll play with Logan."

My jaw drops. "Really?"

He smirks at me. "Not *everybody* thinks I'm that bad, Captain."

"Oh no, you're that bad," Lily counters. "I just know that you and Kodi would be a terrible match. So I'm taking one for the team."

He rolls his eyes at her, but I shoot her a grateful smile. "Thank you, Lily. Then that leaves me and Callie for the last pair." I frown at the seventh player in the huddle. "Mr. Landon, I'm sorry, but–"

"No, no, that's alright," he says, waving me off. "I wanted to get some fries from the concession stand, anyway."

We share an understanding smile, and he walks off to the other side of the field to get in line for food. I turn to the rest of the team. "Alright then. This is it. No matter what happens out there, I want you all to know that–"

"Aaarrrgh!"

We all jerk up as a man's strangled cry echoes across the sports complex. Confusion spreads across the crowd as everyone on the field and off try to locate the source of the noise.

A solid five seconds go by before I spot the screamer. Mr. Landon lay prone on the opposite sideline, and Brian's rushing over there to check to see if he needs medical attention. As he gets close, he slides a little on the turf, and catches himself by dropping to a knee to the man's side.

That's weird.

I look back to the huddle and hold up a hand, letting them know I'll be right back. Then I jog over to the other side of the field to see if Mr. Landon's okay.

In the same spot that Brian slipped, I slow down, noticing that the patch of plastic grass around them is slightly shinier than the rest of the turf. It's a little slippery, too.

"Is he okay?" I ask Brian.

He nods, slowly tilting the man's wrist back and forth. "He caught himself. Might be a sprain, but it could just be a little sore from the impact."

"Do you two hear that?"

"Hear what?"

Mr. Landon cups his uninjured hand to his ear as he sits up. "It sounds like something's hissing..."

Brian and I tilt our heads as we try to listen in, but over the sound of the crowd gearing up for the final round and the Tuftettes dancing across the field, I can't hear anything like he's describing.

"What–"

"Shh! Listen!"

And then I hear it. Super faint, like air letting out of a bicycle tire, or someone using a can of spray paint.

I look around to see if maybe the teenage boys from the last game are vandalizing the walls behind the bleachers, when Brian points to the Spitz Hollow huddle behind us. "There!"

I follow his finger, to see that Zeke and his two meathead cronies are huddled over the boards they stole from the field. Zeke's kneeling over one, and in his hand is a can of...

Is that *cooking spray??*

"Cheating! *Cheating!!"* I shout, jumping to my feet so fast I kick Mr. Landon in the shin. He groans under me, and I shoot an apology over my shoulder as I run for a ref. "Sorry, Mr. Landon! Hey! *Hey!* Spitz Hollow is *cheating!"*

Zeke and his cronies spin around, and I watch as he slips the cooking spray into a gym bag at his feet. I flag down the ref's attention, pointing angrily at him.

"Ref! *Ref!* Number 17 is oiling the boards!"

"What? That's preposterous," he drawls in his pompous accent, shoving the gym bag under the team's bench with his foot. The ref comes over to me, and I rush over to Zeke to reveal our discovery.

"What's all this about?" The ref asks. I point to the gym bag under the bench, which Zeke immediately steps in front of.

"Zeke's spraying the boards with cooking oil!"

The ref eyes him up and down. Zeke shakes his head, then looks at me with pity in his eyes.

"Oh, Kodi. You poor, sweet summer child. Letting your jealousy get the better of you, eh?"

Fire ignites in my chest.

Nobody looks at me like that anymore.

"What the hell are you talking about, Zeke?"

"You just can't handle that your boyfriend and I used to date, can you?"

My mouth opens wordlessly, and the ref's eyes bounce between us like he's watching a tennis match. I shake my head. "Ref! The can is in his gym bag. If you look–"

"Gary, I'm so sorry about her. You might remember, she's the one who couldn't hold back the redhead that started the fight at the last match versus Tuft Swallow. You see, her boyfriend and I have a history, and–"

"That's got nothing to *do* with this!" I shout, wincing at the way my words come out all shrill and screechy. "You're *cheating,* and if you'll just look–"

"Now, Miss Gander. You've already been disqualified once this season for disorderly conduct. I suggest you calm down." The ref nods at me, hands on his hips.

"Calm–calm down??" I sputter, and Zeke's cheeks crinkle in that shit-eating grin of his over the ref's shoulder. "He's *cheating–*"

"Excuse me," a calm, deep voice cuts in beside me. Brian steps into the confrontation, and I freeze as he places a hand on Zeke's shoulder.

Zeke jumps, and his dark eyes trace a line up my boyfriend's muscled chest and to his face. Time seems to slow down as I watch Brian give him his most heart-melting smile, the one where his sometimes blue-sometimes green eyes go all sparkly and send my head into a tailspin. The look seems to work on

Zeke, too, because his eyes widen and his lips part just the slightest bit as Brian's healy hands make contact with his deltoid.

"B…"

Brian keeps eye contact as Zeke stutters on his name, and then he slowly kneels beside him.

Zeke and I are both speechless as we watch his head lower, down to his chest, then his abdomen, until…

He reaches behind Zeke's foot into the gym bag, and pulls out the can of cooking spray.

"Here you go, ref. He was spraying it on the boards."

He straightens, tossing the can to the referee and walking to my side without giving Zeke a backwards glance.

The ref's eyes widen, and he blows the whistle. The sound is shrill and piercing and super close to my ear, but it doesn't even phase me. Because Brian's looking straight into my eyes, and I'm melting in the teal ocean of his gaze.

"Spitz Hollow is disqualified—unauthorized ingredients on the field! Automatic forfeit to Tuft Swallow. Mighty Swallows win the Championship!"

I know the words are important, but they all kinda blur into the background as I look into my partner's eyes. He stood up for me. He saved the day.

We both did.

A smile tilts his lips, stretching his scruffy cheeks in a truly delectable expression. As the complex erupts into a swell of jeers and jubilation, he sweeps me into his arms and nods to the scoreboard.

"Looks like you're a champion," he says.

I kiss him.

In the swirl of my periphery, I hear the team all circle around us, cheering and hollering and drinking and carrying on like we're bringing home the Stanley Cup instead of just defending a title we've had for the past fifty-four years. *Or fifty-five now, I suppose.* Hands clap my back, voices scream my name, Lily and

Callie cry tears of joy and Winston the Goat *baaaaahs* in triumph as he accepts the gold medal as our town mayor.

And through it all, I kiss Brian. Again and again, over and over, until I get tired of it. And then I kiss him some more.

Because I never get tired of it. And deep down, I don't think I ever will.

EPILOGUE

KODI

I brew the strongest pot of coffee and down three ibuprofen on Monday morning as soon as I get into the office to nurse my hangover from the long weekend of celebrating. Charlene and Ginger insisted on free shots all weekend for the entire Championship Team, so of course we got hammered. Brian didn't complain once as he carried me to his place, as I sang "We Are The Champions" at the top of my lungs all the way down Birch Street.

He packed me a bacon sandwich to eat for breakfast once I stop feeling nauseous, and as I settle down into my wheely chair for the day, I thank my lucky stars that he's mine.

Now I just need to help Callie and Lily find guys as great as him.

I flinch when the mail drop clatters with the arrival of today's bills and news, and I refill my mug on the way to collect them. I'm about to drop them on the island and get back to my computer, when the *Nosy Pecker* headline catches my eye.

Acquisition Falls Through, Spitz Hollow Cheats Their Way to the Loser's Circle

Karma has never tasted sweeter than it has today, as the rumors surrounding Spitz-Shein Inc.'s acquisition were revealed on Sunday to be unfounded. In response to inquiries sent by Yours Truly, both Alphabet and Meta replied to questions of their interest in tech start-up Spitz-Shein with, "Who?"

Wall Street also seems to have sniffed out the truth, as pre-market trading has shares for Spitz-Shein Inc. down just under 800% of their peak estimation last week. Let's hope no one was banking their early retirement on that *stock!*

But of course, the real story of the weekend concerns our own Kodi Gander's nail-biting comeback, as she led the entirety of the Tuft Swallow Mighty Swallows to victory against the dirty rotten cheating scumbags from Spitz Hollow. Congratulations, Swallows! Each and every one of you are Champions in our eyes.

WELL, I'LL BE. NEVER THOUGHT I'D SEE THE DAY.

"Kodi?"

I glance up from the paper to see none other than Maureen Bailey peeking her head around the office threshold.

"Dr. Bailey!" I set down the mail and walk over to shake her hand. "It's so nice to see you. Thank you for starting on such short notice. I know the board and I are super happy to have you."

"Sounds like you all have had quite the upset. Dr. Cratchet just up and left?"

My mind wanders to the pathetic man, adrift at sea while his fortune evaporates into thin air without his knowledge. "Sure did."

"What an ass."

I raise my eyebrows, and she covers her mouth with her hand. "I'm so sorry, that was rude of me."

"Not at all!" I assure her. "He *is* an ass. Would you like some coffee?"

"Only if it's strong. Going through his paperwork and rescheduling all of his appointments…it's going to be a long day."

I pour her a cup. "I have a feeling you and I are going to get along great."

"Any chance you know the Chiropractor in town? I've heard he's amazing. It might be a good idea to reach out to him to see if we could refer patients to him for chronic pain."

My lips pull up in a grin. "As a matter of fact, I can attest first hand to his skills. He's my–"

The sleighbells clang as the front door slams open, and I groan as the sound pierces into my skull.

"Dr. Cratchet! Dr. Cratchet!" A tall, dark-haired man bursts into the lobby, three-piece suit askew. "Where is he?"

Maureen and I stare at him through the check-in window.

"He quit," we say in unison. She grins at me.

"I can't get a hold of him, and I need to discuss his investments pronto!"

He tugs at his tie, which already hangs off-kilter. Once he stops running long enough for me to take him in, I recognize him as Milton MacGuire, Lily's landlord. I lean onto the counter.

"Sorry. He left for the Carribean last week. Something about how he was rich and could retire early…?"

The man pales. "The C-Carribean?"

"Yep. I remember he expressly requested that no one attempt to contact him, that he was going off-grid for the whole trip."

"Off-grid."

"Well, he actually said that he wasn't going to pay for wifi–"

"I don't need the details!" Mr. MacGuire crashes onto one of the loveseats. "Oh God…what do I do? Do I sell? Hold? Hope this all might turn around?"

"Is this about Spitz-Shein Inc., Mr. MacGuire?" I ask.

He sinks his head into his hands. "I told him it was a sure thing…he sank his entire portfolio…"

Dr. Bailey hands him her cup of coffee. "I think you need this more than I do. What do you say we come on back to my office for a quick psych evaluation, Mr. MacGuire? In moments like this, bouts of depression can be quite common…"

Out of habit, I wait until the two of them are safely behind the closed door of Maureen's office before I get my phone out to text Brian the daily gossip.

I'll tell Lily all about it at Girl's Night. It's Monday, after all, and I would never leave my best friend hanging.

BRIAN

A LITTLE LESS THAN A YEAR LATER

"You sure you want to do this?"

I eye Kodi over the stack of boxes lining the bedroom of her apartment. She's folding up the last load of laundry and piling it neatly in the hamper, along with a few other items that didn't pack up so neatly in cardboard.

She matches the last pair of socks together and tosses them on top of her pajamas. "100%."

My chest warms.

Tina drags a handcart into the bedroom and wedges it under a stack of boxes. "Nick's here with the U-Tow. Ready to get out of here?"

Kodi flashes her a thousand-watt smile. "So ready."

Outside, Nick's blocking out the parking space behind the moving van with some orange traffic cones. As I climb down the steps of the five-story brownstone that houses Kodi's apartment, he waves.

"Hey man! Any news yet?"

I pat my pocket for my phone and check the notifications.

"Nothing yet. But Finn checked in an hour ago to say it shouldn't be long. He and Callie are on their way."

As if the very words summoned him, he pulls up and parks behind the cones just as I put my phone back. But the passenger's seat is noticeably empty.

"Where's Callie?"

"She got waylaid with your housewarming present."

"Present?" Kodi appears, box in hand, Tina rolling behind. "Y'all better not have gotten us dishes or anything— we've already had to donate so much stuff."

Combining households proved to be a pretty involved process. After ten years assembling my stuff, I wasn't keen on Kodi keeping all of her budget dishes and cookware that she picked up at the thrift store after college. And then we both had to get rid of some furniture to make room for stuff that suited the both of us. Like our new queen size bed that I'm very excited to break in tonight.

Considering the fact that Kodi's basically been living with me for the past couple months, we've done a pretty good job changing up my upstairs apartment by transforming the guest room into our room, and repurposing my room into a hangout space for us: it's got shelves for all of our books, my old loveseat, and Kodi even found an old RGB TV at The Cuckoo's Nest that she said would work for the Super Nintendo she got me for our anniversary last week. I was just about floored when she gave it to me.

No doubt about it: I've found the perfect woman.

I can't imagine we'd need anything else to make it feel like home.

"She wanted it to be a surprise. Lily helped her come up with the idea."

Kodi looks at Finn dubiously.

"Any news yet?" Tina huffs as Nick takes the handcart from her and wheels it up the ramp and into the van.

"Still waiting."

Kodi glances at me, and I give her a reassuring smile. She's been so stressed out for Lily this whole week, and I know she wishes she could be at her best friend's side right now. But the lease ends tomorrow, so we really couldn't wait any longer. And it's good to know she isn't alone. Dr. Bailey has also been sending Kodi updates whenever she can.

By the time we have the van all packed up and ready to go, Kodi shoves the hamper and a few houseplants into the back of her Subaru.

"Go on ahead, honey. I'll meet you after I do my last walk-through and turn in the key."

Her half-dirty blonde, half-bleached flyaways frame her face around her messy bun. She's considering dying it again for corn-hole season, but I've got my fingers crossed that she'll let her natural hair grow out. I mean, putting up with her multi-colored hairs in the drain is worth it if it means I get to wake up next to her every morning, but there's nothing like seeing those amber eyes peeking out at me behind those bronze locks.

I push a few strands back from her forehead when she closes the car door and pull her close. Then I cup my fingers around the soft skin of her cheeks, and tilt her chin until our lips are only a breath away.

"I'll be waiting, baby girl."

The heat travels from her neck, to her cheeks, right up to the fire in her eyes as she meets my gaze. She gives me the slightest, sweetest brush of her lips against mine–a promise for more to come later–then winks at me before climbing back up the steps to her building.

"Make sure Nick doesn't drop my Kitchenaid," she calls out, and I chuckle before walking the two blocks to my–*our*–place.

A couple hours later, we're almost done getting the boxes out of the U-Haul and ready to call in our pizza order to Tina's place when Callie pulls up behind the caravan of cars outside my place.

But nothing prepares me for the bundle she carries in her arms.

"That's not Fettucine," Finn comments, as the light brown blob begins to squirm.

"Uh, Callie..." I start, when Kodi pops out from the front door, wiping her hands on her jean shorts.

At her appearance, Callie adjusts the bundle of fur in her arms and holds out a tiny, panting bulldog puppy. "Surprise! Happy Housewarming!"

"And house training," Finn adds under his breath, sending me a wink.

I feel the blood drain from my face, but the answering glow in Kodi's is enough to keep my mouth shut. She positively beams as she runs down the wooden steps of the porch, signs of any past knee injury gloriously absent, and scoops up the little thing in her arms. Her mouth drops open slightly in a pout as she takes in the smooshed, wrinkly face of the adorable puppy. The little thing's ears are twitching frantically from flopping up and down to tucking back behind it's head as it sniffs its new holder with unabashed curiosity.

Kodi laughs as its tiny tongue darts out to blep her jaw, then up to her ear, as it scrambles up her torso. Her wide eyes sparkle as she tries to keep hold of the thing, before Callie clips a leash to it's red paisley collar and hands the handle to her.

She gratefully accepts it, and lets the puppy down into the grass to sniff and explore and relieve itself.

"Where did you get a puppy?" She squeals, eyes still trained on the little thing, which is now bounding playfully as it tests the extent of its leash, tangling in between her athletic legs.

"Piper's cousin's half-brother's uncle's stepdaughter has a pet rescue in Robin Springs!" Callie says in a rush. "The second she told me about the litter of little pitbull puppies they found in an abandoned house down south, I knew I had to help her find homes for them. This little guy," she crouches down, and the pup in question bounds into her arms and starts wagging his tail so quickly it blurs, "was the last one! His brother and sister got adopted earlier this week. Poor boy is pretty underweight, but

I've got some food and supplies in the car for you to get started."

"Does he have a name?" I hedge, stepping closer for the first time to the group.

The tiny pup, who is small enough to fit in my cupped hands, cowers a bit closer to the girls as I approach. I freeze, and Kodi shoots me a reassuring look.

"Oh my God, don't let her name him," Finn jokes, and Callie gasps.

"Ex-cuse you! I am a fucking brilliant pet-namer, thank you very much!"

I lean into Kodi, confessing into her ear, "I have no idea how to raise a dog."

That spark in her eyes glows brighter as she watches the puppy get distracted by a butterfly fluttering by. "You're a smart man. You can learn. We both will."

She nudges me with her hip, and I put an arm around her as Callie continues the conversation.

"At the shelter, they gave the whole litter "D" names. So there was Domino, Daisy, and this one was Declan."

"Declan, huh?" My heart squeezes as I watch the woman I love more than anything in the world untangle herself from the leash around her legs and crouch down beside the pup, who pads over to sniff at her lap. She holds out her fingers and gives him little high-fives, tilting her head at him. "Whaddya think, little guy? Are you a Declan?"

Immediately, his ears perk up, and he tilts his head at her.

"Declan?" she asks again, and he tilts his head the other way.

"Deeeeeeeec-laaaaaaaaan" she sings, and he goes fucking crazy, pumping his little front paws in bicycle circles on her thighs and leaving little puppy scratches around her recently healed knee.

She bursts into giggles, scooping him back up into her arms and nuzzling him close to the crook of her neck. "Oh yeah, that's his name alright. Hey Declan! Do you know who that is?"

She points at me, and the little guy scrambles with his paws until he turns his tiny body to face me. My stomach twists as his pale eyes meet mine.

Aw, fuck.

He's adorable.

"That's your new Daddy."

Another sensation entirely grips my stomach as Kodi introduces me to Declan and plops him into my unsuspecting arms. I curl my fingers around the teeny, tiny ribcage, being careful not to squeeze him too hard as he tries to wriggle his way free. Eventually, though, I curve my left hand under his belly with him straddling my forearm, and pull him against my chest, petting his head with my other hand.

His little heartbeat thumps against my fingers, and my eyes widen. He licks at the buttons on my polo.

I look up to meet Kodi's eyes, and they're shining with an emotion I've never seen in their amber depths.

"Oh fuck, Kodi, you better watch out. A big, strong doctor with a puppy in his arms? You're gonna need to beat off the ladies with a stick."

A nervous laugh bubbles out of my throat, but then Kodi wraps her fingers around my arm, drawing close and sandwiching Declan between us.

"We're a real family now, B."

"Yeah." I choke back a couple tears. "I guess we are, huh?"

She winks at me. "You make a damn fine Doggie Daddy."

At that, Declan whimpers and wiggles out of my grasp, and we barely burst apart in time to lower him so he doesn't splat as he hits the ground on all fours. I just manage to get my fingers through the leash to keep him from racing off after a robin that flits through the front yard.

"Is that a song thrush?" A voice echoes from one of the neighboring houses.

"No, I think it's just an American robin!"

"Its head is too gray to be a robin, are you sure it isn't a rufous-bellied thrush?"

I hold back a smirk, looking down at my girlfriend as she tucks into my side. Our friends shake their heads as the Tit Peepers continue to argue over bird species out the open windows lining the street. "My neighbors are a little nosier than yours. You sure you want to move in, baby girl?"

She smiles: a real wide, toothy grin that stretches from ear-to-ear. "I've never been more sure of anything in my life." Then she lowers her voice. "Daddy."

I groan. "Oh God, please no. This one's gonna be enough for me for a while."

Kodi laughs. "Me too. Although, I've got a feeling it's about to get a lot more rambunctious around here for our little family."

Looking over our home, our friends, and our new puppy, I can't help but agree. And even here, in crazy Tuft Swallow, I have to admit…I'm not upset about it.

THE END

FOWL PLAY READ-ALONG PLAYLIST

You can listen on Spotify! The playlist is public on my author profile :)

9 to 5 - Dolly Parton
Casual - Chappell Roan
Tension - Kylie Minogue
Crush - Jennifer Paige
You Need To Calm Down - Taylor Swift
Work Bitch - Britney Spers
She's Kerosene - The Interrupters
We Could Still Belong Together - Lisa Loeb
Thunderstruck - AC/DC
Kiss - Prince
Something To Talk About - Bonnie Raitt
Last Friday Night (T.G.I.F.) - Katy Perry
Pennies from Heaven - Louis Prima
yes, and? - Ariana Grande
Favorite Liar - The Wrecks
Wannabee - Spice Girls
Fight Night - Migos
Peacock - Katy Perry
Dirty Little Secret - The All-American Rejects

Hands to Myself - Selena Gomez
I Wanna Be Yours - Arctic Monkeys
Lose Control - Teddy Swims
Color - Todrick Hall, Jay Armstrong Johnson
Blow Your Mind (Mwah) - Dua Lipa
You Only Want What You Can't Have - Chronic Tiger
Cold as Ice - Foreigner
Somewhere Only We Know - Keane
Delicate - Taylor Swift
Stronger - Kanye West
Hold My Hand - Jess Glynne
Shout Out to My Ex - Little Mix
Unwritten - Natasha Bedingfield

Want to participate in making the next playlist? Email me to request to join my beta or street team at cassandra@cassandramedcalf.com .

EXTRA GOODNESS

Want more of Brian and Kodi? Get the bonus epilogue and a spicy bonus chapter for free from my website, at
cassandramedcalf.com/freestuff

Want more Tuft Swallow? Be sure to check out the rest of the series from these amazing authors:
That's Cockatoo Much, by Kristin MacQueen
Tit Me With Your Best Shot, by Chantal Roome
Flock and Roll, by Vicki Hilton
Don't Give a Cluck, by Karigan Hale
This is Hawkward, by Joelle Evans
No Egrets, by Susan Renee

And make sure to sign up for the official Cassandra Medcalf newsletter at cassandramedcalf.com/subscribe to hear about upcoming Tuft Swallow adventures, as well as all of her new releases and events.

ACKNOWLEDGMENTS

Wow. Every time I get to this section of a book, it gets longer.

Here's the truth: two years ago when my friend and fellow author Jo Preston told me that she and Kristin MacQueen were building a shared rom com world, I was far from ready to write another book.

I was struggling, at the peak of my struggle with PCOS, endometriosis, and a newly diagnosed eating disorder, along with the anxiety and depression that came with them. I had just finished the Fixer Upper Series: having published over 200,000 words in under a year and feeling completely and utterly spent.

Writing is not a completely thankless endeavor, but when one is starting out, it can be an incredibly difficult one. Talking to Jo about the town of Tuft Swallow and getting swept away for a few minutes as she described the Woodcocks and *The Nosy Pecker* and the cornhole rivalry with Spitz Hollow gave me a few moments respite from my pain and my ongoing battle with insurance and my chronic pain. It was then I realized that I wanted to live in Tuft Swallow for a little while, and get to know this community of unforgettable characters.

Since then, it's been a whirlwind. This is the first book I've completed since starting medication and feeling better, and I quite honestly could not have done it without the following people.

Joelle, Kristin, Chantal, Sam, Susan, Vicki, and Kari: thank you for co-building this world for me to write in. I am so fucking proud of this series and cannot *wait* to dive into round two with Lily's story next year. Whenever I was stuck or blocked, I knew I could hop into the Discord and pick y'all's brains for a minute to get back on track. I am having so much fun reading your books. Thank you for being part of this world.

Writers support other writers. Elle, thank you for being my author bestie and supporting me and venting with me as I tried my hand at writing a *sports* romance of all things. Can you believe it? I'm still planning to do that bowling series, too—don't you worry.

I have an amazing critique group, and Bailey Merlin is our fearless leader. Bailey, Jack, Eren, Michael, Sarah, Thoren, Taylor: thank you for your invaluable feedback and helping me become a better writer. Bi+ Book Gang, you are my buoy in rough waters. Thank you for letting me be myself and read your stories, and inspiring me *so much* with all you do. Wednesday accountability is the highlight of my week!

But who can talk about accountability without mentioning KM and Sara? I mean, sure, writing is my passion, but it's narrating that pays the bills (until this book becomes a New York Times Bestseller—make it happen, BookTok!). Thank you two for cheering me on with all my crazy schemes, and joining me for co-working sessions, and inviting me to have dinner with you those many months ago in NYC. I love you both so much.

And now, my beta readers! Brooke, Kaiidth, Danie, Eren, Bailey, Jack, Sam, Karli: holy shit. Can I ever say enough thank you's to fully express my gratitude? From catching my typos and street names to all of your emoji comments and ZEKE!'s, you all have helped make this book and the accompanying playlist so much better than it was. Thank you!! I feel so blessed to have such a great team of critical and supportive readers.

Which leads me to my Patreon, and the infamous Discord server. You all make me happy to come to work in the morning. Thank you so much for supporting me and keeping me engaged, and enjoying the content that I put out into the world. You have no idea how grateful and humbled I am by your comments and the conversations we have everyday. Special shout-outs to my financial supporters on Patreon:

Danie Sue Who
Danielle
Gennifer
Jess
Kitt3n Br33
Terri
Alorrah (who named Kodi and Brian's puppy, Declan, in the bonus epilogue!)
Sam
Luna
Liv
Sharon
Katelyn
and Kaiidth.

We found each other on TikTok, and since then we've become an amazing group of friends. I love sharing pet photos and dinner recipes with y'all, I love our book club where we read House of Night and ACOTAR together and share memes, and most importantly, I love how supportive we are of each other. You are such wonderful people, and in the entirety of the internet, I'm so glad that you all choose to be part of my community. Thank you.

Last but not least, my wonderful family. Mom, Dad, Kelley, Sue: thank you for your constant support and love. And Andy… ermergerd. You are the inspiration for every book boyfriend I write. I love our life together, herner: I love our puppies, I love our home (as rundown as it may be—we'll afford that new siding someday!), and I love the dreams we make and share together. Thank you for being my rock and my squeeze and making me coffee every morning. I love you and Bonnie and Ogun more than all the words could ever say.

ABOUT THE AUTHOR

Cassandra Medcalf is a writer, narrator, audio engineer, food enthusiast, wine taster, do-it-yourselfer, and an amateur film critic (despite barely having seen any movies). She lives on a future vineyard, in a future dream home in upstate New York with her adorable husband and their even more adorable dog. You can follow her and her family's hare-brained schemes and lofty pursuits on her website, cassandramedcalf.com (or, if you're just here for the smut, on TikTok @CassandraMedcalfVO).

Made in the USA
Middletown, DE
10 July 2024

57091150R00312